Duets™

Two brand-new stories in every volume... twice a month!

Duets Vol. #73

Popular Julie Kistler serves up not one, but *two* hilarious stories this month in a very special Double Duets. Join in the fun as the identical Tompkins twins change places just before a very important wedding—with unexpected results! Julie is the award-winning author of over thirty books for Duets, Temptation and American Romance.

Duets Vol. #74

Put on the coffee, then sit back and enjoy two great tales guaranteed to perk you up—PERK AVENUE and TO CATCH A LATTE! Patricia Knoll is "a must read," according to *Romance & Friends* reviewers. Joining her is talented newcomer Jennifer McKinlay, who drank her share of lattes while writing her first book.

Be sure to pick up both Duets volumes today!

"Entering the Great Chef Showdown?"

"Of course, I'd be crazy not to." With one eyebrow raised, Lainey glanced at Gabe. "And you?"

"I'd be crazy not to," he responded, echoing her.

"I thought you said you weren't a cook."

"No, I said I'm not a great baker, but I am a terrific cook," he explained.

"So, you're thinking of a main dish of some sort?"

"Yes, there's a definite dish on my mind," Gabe replied, with a wide smile reaching across his sexy lips.

Lainey opened her mouth to fire a verbal volley right back at him. But nothing came out. Instead, she stood there returning his smile, wondering two things: first, when had he gotten those sexy lips, and two, would he be averse to planting them on hers?

For more, turn to page 9

To Catch a Latte

"Great. Now some dork will cop a feel when he puts the garter on me."

Annie sighed. This just wasn't her wedding.

"What are you talking about?" Fisher demanded.

"It's a wedding ritual. Whoever catches the garter puts it on whoever catches the bouquet. And since I caught it..." She waggled the bedraggled bouquet.

"Not while I'm here."

Suddenly he looked forceful, determined. Was her tenant going possessive on her?

"Fisher, you don't have to. One quick feel and it's over."

"Wish me luck. I'm catching that garter. If anyone is copping a feel, it's going to be me."

Amazed, Annie watched an unsmiling Fisher angle his way amongst the bachelors. In a move that no government paper-pusher should know, he dived and plucked the garter before it hit the ground.

Triumphant, he strutted toward her. "Now, about that feel..."

For more, turn to page 197

HARLEQUIN DUETS

ISBN 0-373-44140-1

Copyright in the collection:
Copyright © 2002 by Harlequin Books S.A.

The publisher acknowledges the copyright holders of the individual works as follows:

PERK AVENUE
Copyright © 2002 by Patricia Knoll

TO CATCH A LATTE
Copyright © 2002 by Jennifer Orf

This edition published by arrangement with Harlequin Books S.A.

® and TM are trademarks of the publisher. Trademarks indicated with ® are registered in the United States Patent and Trademark Office, the Canadian Trade Marks Office and in other countries.

Visit us at www.eHarlequin.com

Printed in U.S.A.

Park Avenue

Patricia
Knoll

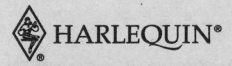

TORONTO • NEW YORK • LONDON
AMSTERDAM • PARIS • SYDNEY • HAMBURG
STOCKHOLM • ATHENS • TOKYO • MILAN • MADRID
PRAGUE • WARSAW • BUDAPEST • AUCKLAND

Dear Reader,

Welcome back to Calamity Falls, Arizona. I had so much fun creating this town and its eccentric inhabitants when I wrote *Calamity Jo* that I decided to pay it another visit to tell the story of Lainey Pangburn and Gabe Camden, who own rival coffee houses.

While they're trying to entice each other's customers away, Gabe's young nephew is falling for Lainey, three sweet bodybuilders appoint themselves as her guardians, the city council is running a competition to discover a "signature food" for the town and there are rumors of long-lost gold to be found. And, oh yes, while all this is going on, Lainey and Gabe discover they have a hard time keeping their hearts from getting involved.

So cruise on past the city limits and enjoy this visit to Calamity Falls!

Happy reading,

Patricia Knoll

Books by Patricia Knoll

HARLEQUIN DUETS
 3—MEANT FOR YOU
21—CALAMITY JO

This book is dedicated
to my mother, Orzola Forsythe,
always good for a corny joke.
I love you, Mama.

Prologue

Arizona Territory, 1879

"IT'S NO BLOODY USE, Shipper," Albert Battlehaven said, collapsing onto one of the rocks they'd dislodged from the landslide that had covered their promising gold strike the day before. They'd spent most of the past twenty-four hours trying to uncover it once again.

Rudolph Shipper kicked at a stone, then whimpered as pain shot up from his toe. He slumped down beside his partner. "All that gold," he moaned, holding his head in his hands. He was bareheaded since he had already removed his hat and stomped on it. "The richest strike I've ever seen. Gone. All gone. I never even saw anything like it when I was panning for gold in California. Who would have thought an earthquake would happen out here?" He glanced around mournfully at the desert landscape, then at the gurgling waterfall that had been created by the stones falling into the creek, which was now pouring down from the Mule Mountains. Shipper had already named it Calamity Falls.

"Well, there's nothing to be done, but to start again," Battlehaven pointed out.

Shipper gave 'Lord' Battlehaven a skeptical look. He didn't like the sound of that. So far, in their partnership, he had done all the heavy work while Battlehaven provided the bankroll. The Englishman was a remittance man, well-paid by his family to stay an ocean away from them. Shipper had already discovered that Battlehaven's idea of work was to direct Shipper while *he* worked.

He hadn't minded at first because he'd believed he'd soon be rich. However, they had traveled out from Minnesota together, endured miserable train trips, stagecoach and mule rides and been under attack by Apaches because, during a stop at an Apache village, Battlehaven had tried to seduce the future bride of some young warrior. Rudolph's scalp still tingled at the memory of how he'd almost been parted from his hair. Hurriedly, he grabbed his squashed hat and clamped it on his head. There, that was better. Not that he was really worried about Apaches—at least not since their first day in Arizona. As long as there were no young maidens around for Battlehaven to flirt with, Shipper thought they would probably be all right.

As far as he was concerned, the only good thing about his partnership with Battlehaven had been the gold they'd found…and now lost to an act of God.

Rudolph wondered what he'd done to make God mad at him.

He stood and looked around morosely at the merry, tumbling waterfall, then began gathering up his equipment and returning it to his pack mule.

"Look at this," he exclaimed in disgust, hefting the equipment so Battlehaven could see the thick gray-blue mud clinging to the shovel he'd been using to pry rocks away from their fabulous gold strike. With a disgusted curse, he scraped it off with the toe of his boot, stowed his things and mounted his mule. "The dang-blamed stuff is everywhere."

When they'd returned from staking their claim at the government office in Tucson, he'd seen several other miners in the area who seemed to be interested in examining the thick, dull mud. "Fools," he snorted. "That stuff's worth nothin'." He couldn't see any good in it and, as far as he was concerned, they could have it.

Battlehaven didn't care one way or another. If it wasn't gold, it didn't matter. But before he could reply, they heard the rapid thunder of hoofbeats. He turned in his saddle and glanced back curiously. A band of Apaches was bearing down on them.

"Aborigines!" he screamed, spurring his mule into action. He was an excellent horseman, but he'd not yet mastered the riding of a mule. Cursing and flailing, he tried to get the animal to go faster—or to go, at all. Rudolph, who had seen the danger at the same moment, did the same.

Shipper reacted to the crisis by kicking at his mule while pulling back on the reins, thoroughly confusing the animal. All the while, he shrieked, "Hurry, Battlehaven. They'll be on us in an instant." His cries startled the mule, who began dancing around in circles, bouncing Shipper up and down in the saddle. He shrieked again each time his bottom hit the hard leather.

They finally got their mules turned in the right direction and spurred them into a dead run.

"Albert," Rudolph yelled worriedly. "You don't think the leader of that pack is the young buck whose girl you..."

"Nah!" Battlehaven yelled back, while trying to

load, shoot and stay in the saddle all at the same time, but he freed a hand to run over the thick pelt of rich brown hair that was his pride. Panicked at the thought of losing it, he kicked his mule even harder. If it was that bloodthirsty young warrior, Albert knew he'd better make his peace with God. He was too busy right now, though.

Their flight was swift and useless. The Apaches overtook them, not killing them as the two men had feared, but taking the pair of hapless miners prisoner and snagging the supplies that were packed on the mules. Shipper and Battlehaven's wrists were tied and they were forced to march along beside their captors' horses while the Apaches passed Battlehaven's favorite porkpie hat from one to another, squabbling as they tried it on.

When they reached the Apaches' camp, they were pressed into slave labor, carrying water and doing the kinds of tasks the women usually did. As they struggled awkwardly at these jobs, the Apache women laughed uproariously and poked at them with sticks.

Shipper was glad to still be alive—even if he was currently at work picking mesquite beans off the desert floor. Battlehaven, his face screwed into the expression of a man wearing a dead fish for a necktie, plucked the dry, white bean pods disdainfully between thumb and forefinger and tossed them into a basket, all the while complaining bitterly that a member of the British aristocracy should be treated in such a manner.

"To think," he all but sobbed. "A son of the Battlehaven family reduced to this. It's shameful. Unthinkable. There is royal blood flowing in these veins." He stopped to pluck a thorn out of his palm. "And for it to be shed in this manner rather than honorably on the field of battle…''

Fed up, Shipper clapped him across the side of the head. "Shut up. We're still alive, aren't we?"

"Barely," Albert blubbered, his once full-fleshed face looking drawn and sunburned from their misadventures. "Look at me. This is a disgrace."

"You do look pretty bad," Rudolph admitted. Albert's hat was gone, along with his pants, both items finally snagged by the warrior leading the band that had captured them. One of the women now wore his favorite tattersall vest and his boots. Another had his coat. His sole garment was his long underwear and socks, but another of the women, a short, heavy-jowled one, who was watching them from the shade of a mesquite, had been eyeing his underwear for two days now. Nervously, he moved to stand behind a low creosote bush, trying to hide from her acquisitive stare.

"I curse this miserable country," he sobbed, wiping his nose on his sleeve in a gesture that would have given his mother the vapors. "I don't know why I ever left the bosom of my loving family to come here."

Rudolph gaped at him, then jogged his memory helpfully. "They kicked you out, remember? It had something to do with a couple of Drury Lane actresses and a naked ride through Regent's Park."

Battlehaven answered with a sour look.

Precisely when Rudolph thought he couldn't stand any more of Battlehaven's complaints, the heat, flies, work and misery, they were miraculously ransomed by the two miners who'd staked a claim near theirs and who had watched their kidnapping from atop the rockfall left by the earthquake.

Rudolph was pathetically grateful to the two men

who had followed them at great risk to their own lives, bringing goods to barter for their release.

Albert, on the other hand, felt differently.

"Forty pounds of sugar," Battlehaven grumbled when he found out what had been paid for them. "A member of the distinguished Battlehaven family ransomed from aborigines for forty pounds of sugar. Unthinkable."

"Shut up and be grateful," Shipper told him as they rode away with their new friends. "At least we're out of there." He looked askance at Albert's sole remaining garment. "And that woman didn't get your drawers away from you."

Battlehaven answered with a stony silence.

The two miners took Shipper and Battlehaven back to Tucson and all four of them checked into one of the town's pitiful little hotels.

"Gentleman," said one of the miners, named Frost, at dinner that night. "Ransoming you two was a mighty big risk for us to take and that forty pounds of sugar cost a pretty penny."

Battlehaven puffed out his chest. He'd managed to procure a pair of baggy pants and some cracked boots to make himself presentable. "My family will be happy to reimburse you."

"No, no," the other miner, Jenkins, said. "We don't want money. We'd like the deed to your claim."

Battlehaven and Shipper looked at the two men and then at each other. They could barely keep from laughing into what was left of their ragged sleeves, but they quickly agreed and went to bed that night chortling over the deal they'd made.

"The fools," Battlehaven said. "I'm worth a great

deal more than that worthless pile of rocks, but so be it.''

Shipper wasn't so sure, but he was glad to be alive, in a real bed, out of harm's way—and still in possession of his hair.

Within a week, they learned that the annoying gray-blue mud on their claim was silver, the most abundant vein anywhere in southeastern Arizona. It ran, deep and wide, straight through what had once been their property.

Battlehaven and Shipper hurried back to Calamity Falls where their rescuers were gleefully digging away.

Battlehaven patted Shipper's back while he cried into a rag torn from the hem of his shirt. ''Cheated,'' he sobbed. ''Earthquaked, kidnapped and cheated. We're two sorry mugs.''

''Without a doubt, the two most lamentable creatures on earth,'' Battlehaven agreed. Frowning, he studied the area around them. The other two miners looked up and waved. ''Do you think there are any diamonds in this place?'' he asked thoughtfully.

1

WHEN THE PORSCHE drove through the plate glass window of Perk Avenue coffeehouse, scattering tables, chairs and coffee-loving patrons in all directions, Lainey Pangburn knew that Saturday in April was going to be a very bad day.

At the first squeal of brakes, she looked up from the iced vanilla latte she was preparing for Jason Sachs. Squinting against the bright morning sunlight, she couldn't locate the source of the noise, but her customer threw his bicycle helmet into the air, screamed, "Run for your lives!" and vaulted over the counter to cower at her feet.

Before she could grab him by his scraggly ponytail and haul him out, a crash shook the windows all along the street. Her head snapped up and she saw an electric blue Porsche careen off a street sign, hitch two wheels onto the curb, then skate down Battlehaven Avenue. Tourists dove headlong into doorways while shopowners dashed outside to see what was happening. An instant later, they, too, were scrambling backward.

Lainey watched the unfolding catastrophe for a full three seconds before she realized the Porsche wasn't going to make the sharp left turn when the avenue did, but was heading straight for her shop. Echoing Jason's sentiments, she yelled to the customers who were gazing out at the action. "Get back, everyone! Get away from the windows."

Hearing her panic, they followed her orders and scurried for cover.

A few seconds later, the Porsche mowed down the parking meter out front, snapping it off like a match stick, then roared over the sidewalk and crashed through the big plate glass window. Shards of glass flew through the air in a dangerous shower while everyone inside cowered behind tables and counters.

The car finally came to rest with its front wheels where Mr. and Mrs. Olmstead had been sitting moments before, enjoying coffee mochas and the morning paper. The Olmsteads were now huddled together beside Lainey and she goggled at them dazedly, wondering how two people in their eighties had managed to cross ten feet of space and scale a four foot counter in five seconds flat. White-faced, the Olmsteads clutched each other and gaped back at her, seeming to be wondering the same thing themselves.

When the glass stopped falling, Lainey stood and blinked at the once-beautiful German sports car which now had its front end smashed in and its windshield cracked.

Pulling her wits together, she made a frantic scan of her shop. "Is...is everyone okay?" she quavered, then cleared her throat and tried again. "Anyone hurt?"

Shaky answers from her customers assured her that everyone was all right, so she made her way to the car. Steeling herself for the gory sight she was sure would meet her eyes, she reminded herself that as assistant fire chief of Calamity Falls, she had to be prepared for whatever might happen. Taking a deep breath, she leaned down and peered in the window of the low-slung vehicle.

The deep-set, dark blue eyes of her nemesis blinked back at her.

"Gabe Camden," she said in a shocked whisper. Irritation followed shock, but, responding to her training, Lainey reached for the handle and opened the door.

"I'd better check you for injuries," she said, gripping his arm, but Gabe waved away her hands.

"I'm all right," he growled, attempting to untangle his long legs from his car and half-falling at her feet.

"That's what you think," she answered. "You can't even stand up."

He gave her an annoyed look and managed to get his size twelve shoes on the ground so he could stagger out of the car. He stood, swaying slightly, all six feet of him, ready to topple over like a giant redwood in a windstorm.

Muttering, "Stubborn fool," under her breath, Lainey shot her arm around his waist to hold him upright, bracing them both. If he fell, they would topple over together.

"If you ask 'Where am I? What happened?' I'll kick you in the shin," she said, just to make sure he understood she harbored no warm feelings for him even if she had dragged him from the wreckage of his car. Rescuing people was part of her training. Nothing personal in it.

"You know, your bedside manner could really use some work," he said dryly. "My brakes failed and unfortunately your store was in a convenient place to stop me." Frowning with concern, he asked, "Is anyone hurt?"

"I don't think so." Lainey gave him a hard look

before releasing him. She didn't like having her arm around him anyway. It was like clutching a...a steel light pole. Straightening away from him, she gave him a severe frown. "No thanks to you."

"Hey, my insurance will cover it."

"It had better," she answered darkly. She turned away, heading for the phone to call the emergency medical team, but before she reached it, she heard sirens in the distance. One of the no doubt dozens of people who had witnessed the accident had called it in. Fighting off the need to sit down, recover herself and stiffen up her knees that wanted to bend like Gumby's, Lainey hurriedly examined her patrons and found they were, indeed, unhurt.

That gave her a moment to consider Gabe: dazed, shaken up—and still too darned attractive. She almost asked the cliched question, "What are you doing here?" but she already knew. He was a recent arrival in Calamity Falls, which was tucked into the foothills of southeastern Arizona's Mule Mountains. The town attracted many fly-by-night businesses which opened to cater to the large numbers of tourists who swelled the usual population of three thousand as they arrived to view the town's eccentrics. Lainey could only hope that Gabe's was one of these short-lived establishments. He had opened a coffee bar just up the street from her, undercut her prices, hired away Delilah Gonzalez, her best baker, and now he had wrecked her shop and terrified her patrons.

There were only six of them thanks to Gabe who charged fifty cents a cup less for coffee, causing some of her patrons on fixed incomes to display their fickleness and abandon her. Her customers picked their way to the front of the store to survey the damage and watch the ambulance as it careened around the corner, taking the same route Gabe had taken, though, Lainey fervently hoped, with brakes.

Seeing that help was on the way, she stopped for a moment to catch her breath. She knew she was in shock, too, and had better sit down, but finding a chair seemed to be more than she could handle so she leaned against the counter instead and examined herself for injuries. She shook a few splinters of glass from her long red hair, the turned-up cuffs of her sunny gold silk shirt and the hem of her full, brightly patterned skirt.

As the glass tinkled to the floor, she thought distractedly that she should find the broom and begin cleaning up. And she would, too, as soon as she stopped shaking.

She heard Gabe Camden speaking to Jason Sachs and looked up to see the two men standing before the car, surveying the damage. Seeing him in the middle of the wreckage he had made somehow put a dose of starch into her shaky knees.

When Gabe had moved to Calamity Falls, she had actually gone up the street and around the corner to see his shop, Coffee & Such, and welcome him to town. It had been a foolish move on her part, but she hadn't known it at the time. In fact, she'd been taken with that killer grin of his, the dimple that winked in and out of his right cheek when he talked, his thick, tobacco brown hair and navy blue eyes.

Secretly, she had admitted that she was simply too susceptible to a man who was good-looking, intelligent and successful—not to mention single—because she'd had little experience with such men. True, there were any number of men in Calamity Falls, mostly retirees,

but few her age. Even they numbered among the eccentrics, however.

Jason Sachs, in spite of his scruffy appearance,
would have been an interesting man to date if not for
his singular interest in the history, manufacturing and
maintenance of bicycles. Maybe she was just picky, but
she wanted to have a conversation that extended beyond two-wheeled vehicles.

For a while, things had brightened when Gabe Camden came to town. After all, he was good-looking, successful and—rare for Calamity Falls—normal, unre-
markable.

Lainey gazed uncertainly at him. She should have
known something strange was going on because as
soon as she had met him she had felt a weird sensation,
a tingling across the backs of her hands. She now realized it had been an ominous premonition.

She glanced down. In fact, she felt a tingling there
now, and it had nothing to do with the small cut above
her knuckle. If this tingling had happened a few
minutes before she would have known to be on the
lookout for Gabe. What good was a premonition, she
thought grumpily, if it didn't come in time?

Her attention was caught by the curious crowd filling
the doorway of Perk Avenue offering help, but she
waved them back as a frightened-looking teenage boy
pushed his way through.

"Lainey?" her new assistant, Cody Jeffers asked as
he stumbled inside. He looked around, his Adam's apple bobbing alarmingly. "Are you okay?" He'd been
making a delivery, so he'd missed the accident. He had
worked for her less than a week, but she'd found him
to be very responsible, and best of all, with his California blond good looks and shy smile, he'd drawn in

a fair number of teenage girls—not that he seemed to notice them, but they noticed him, came in to try to get his attention, spent money, and that's what mattered.

His eyes were wide as he viewed the wreckage. When his gaze fell on the Porsche, he looked as if he was going to faint. Alarmed, Lainey felt adrenaline surge through her and she darted forward, hands outstretched. She'd had no idea he was so sensitive.

"Everyone's okay, Cody," she began, her arms going around him in comfort. He was just a young boy, after all, and had probably never seen anything like this. "Don't worry."

But he wasn't listening to her. On legs that seemed to stumble with every step, he walked right out of her arms and spoke to Gabe. "Uncle Gabe?" he asked in a voice that rose and cracked. "Are you all right?"

"*Uncle* Gabe?" Lainey echoed, looking from the fuzzy-cheeked, blond teenager to the tall, dark thorn in her side. She lifted her hand and pointed from one to the other. "This is your uncle?"

Neither man answered her.

"I'm fine," Gabe said, his quick gaze taking in his nephew's pale face. He reached out, snagged a chair, and whirling it around, scooted it under Cody's rubbery knees. Grabbing the boy, he eased him into it, then bent him forward quickly. "Deep breaths, Cody," he ordered, vigorously rubbing between Cody's shoulder blades. "Just take some deep breaths."

In spite of her surprise, Lainey felt her heart soften as she watched the tenderness Gabe showed his nephew. She could have used a few deep breaths herself.

At the moment she thought this, and felt herself softening toward him, Gabe looked up and cocked a curious eyebrow at her as if to ask what she was looking at. Darned if she knew. Lainey felt heat rushing to her face in a swift flush. Baffled, she turned away, but out of the corner of her eye, she saw Cody straighten and give Gabe a wobbly smile.

"Sorry, Uncle Gabe," he said. "I'm okay." His voice cracked as if to prove him a liar. His expression stiffened with embarrassment and he cleared his throat.

She looked at her new employee once again. The boy was taking big gulps of air as if trying to convince his stomach that it really did want to hang on to his breakfast. She felt a confusing mix of sympathy and annoyance.

"What's going on here?" she asked, her brown eyes narrowed, this time at Gabe Camden. "Isn't it enough that you've stolen away my best baker? My customers?"

"I didn't steal anyone. It's only business." His eyes narrowed. "Exactly like you offering twenty percent off *my* coupons."

His annoyance cheered Lainey considerably. She'd been extremely proud of that tactic, which had come to her as soon as she'd seen the coupons he'd had printed in the Calamity Falls *Ingot*. She couldn't hold back a smile. "You're right. Only business. Exactly like you hiring Delilah away from me...."

"And you hiring my nephew. And don't pretend you didn't know."

She hadn't known, but she smiled again as if she was hiding a secret. "Only business." Then she glanced around at the mess, and her smile collapsed. "However, smashing in the front of my shop is different. I—"

"I certainly didn't do that on purpose."

He didn't have an opportunity to finish because at that moment, the fire truck arrived and her fellow volunteer firefighters tumbled out. In the lead, fully clad in his protective yellow coat, was her grandfather, Julius Pangburn who strode toward her, fireman's helmet under his arm, silvery white hair flowing, eyes snapping like bright beacons.

"Wow." Eyes wide, Cody gaped at the impressive older man, then murmured in awe, "The Avenging Firefighter."

"Lainey," Julius boomed. "What happened here? Are you all right?" He gave her a quick, thorough check, looked into her eyes, held two fingers in front of her, then nodded in satisfaction that she wasn't injured. "Anyone hurt?"

"No one's hurt," Lainey said, giving Gabe a sidelong glance. "Mr. Camden's brakes failed and he drove through my window." Remembering the crash sent shudders through her and she found herself feeling a spurt of sympathy for Gabe who'd been inside the car when it had made its grand entrance.

Julius turned his laser-like eyes on Gabe, who straightened to face him despite his nephew's whispered assurance, "Uncle Gabe, you're toast. Better kiss your butt goodbye."

"Sheriff Watson will have to see this," Julius said severely, letting Gabe know that they took a dim view of such goings-on in Calamity Falls. He turned away to examine the damage to his granddaughter's store.

Behind Julius, in their own bright yellow coats, which were a bit too small, marched Bruiser, Bison and Bull Fina, three newcomers to town.

While researching her family tree, their mother had

discovered that one of the town's founders, Rudolph Shipper, had been her great, great uncle. On a vacation last winter, the Fina brothers had come to see the place where old Uncle Rudy had met so much good and bad luck. They said they'd felt an immediate connection to the place.

Deciding to stay, they had recently opened a gym where they worked on their already massive muscles and trained others to do the same. They were sweet boys, approximately the size of dump trucks, and were close enough in age and looks to appear to be triplets, though they weren't. Lainey just figured their mom and dad hadn't been pulling from a very diverse gene pool when these three had been born. Now that their gym was established, they had decided to spend their spare time searching for the gold their ancestor had found, then lost. Lainey wished them luck. People had been looking for the lost gold of Calamity Falls for more than one hundred twenty years, with no luck at all.

Bruiser, a newly licensed emergency medical technician, shuffled up to her in his protective boots, set down his medical bag, and said, "All right, what's happened here?" in his most authoritative tone. Unfortunately, his voice didn't actually carry much weight because it was tiny, squeaky and somewhat breathy, a little like what Mickey Mouse might sound like with a mouthful of helium, Lainey thought, with a spurt of affection.

Fearing that if she had to explain the obvious one more time, she would scream, Lainey instead reached up and turned his helmet around. "It goes this way, Bruiser," she said gently.

He gave her a surprised and grateful look. "Hey, thanks. I thought it felt funny, but we were in a rush when we left the firehouse—it being our first real emergency and all. Now, who was in that car when it came through the window?''

"I was," Gabe said, and Lainey could hear reluctance dragging at his voice as he eyed Bruiser, then looked at her as if he expected her to rescue him.

Wiggling her fingers at him, she went to join her grandfather. Gabe scowled. She was going to make him pay for this in more ways than one.

"Then you're the one we need to check out," Bruiser said, advancing on Gabe and thrusting a hamlike hand up in front of his face. "How many fingers am I holding up?"

GABE WINCED at his abrupt manner but he answered obediently. After what he'd already done today, it probably wasn't a good idea to be less than cooperative.

What was this anyway? The Keystone firemen? These three guys seemed to fill the entire room. Under Julius's direction, the other two bustled into action, checking on the patrons who'd been in the building, then letting them go home if they chose. The one called Bruiser took his job very seriously, examining Gabe's head and neck by gently prodding with fingers the size of frankfurters. "Does that hurt?" Bruiser asked.

"Only when I laugh," Gabe replied, deadpan.

Bruiser gave him a suspicious look. "Why're you laughing?"

"Never mind," Gabe reminded himself not to try to make jokes with a guy who carried a fire axe, outweighed him by eighty pounds and had no sense of humor.

While that was going on, Gabe gave his nephew a

concerned look. Cody was still pale, which gave Gabe reason to hope. In spite of the differences they'd been having for the past year, Cody seemed genuinely relieved that he wasn't hurt.

He couldn't say the same for The Peppery Ms. Pangburn, as he'd begun to secretly call her. She'd be just as happy if he disappeared altogether. The lady didn't like competition, and she wasn't overly fond of him.

Too bad, he thought, as his gaze took in her long slim figure and the shining red hair that hung past her shoulders and cascaded down her back. If she was less prickly about having competition, the two of them could have been colleagues. Well, maybe that was asking too much, he thought as he rubbed the place on his jaw that had grazed the steering wheel. They wouldn't have had to be enemies, though, if she wasn't so suspicious of his every move. That wasn't his big worry, though. He was mainly concerned with Cody. "Troubled" would be a kind way of describing his relationship with his nephew and he had moved them to Calamity Falls in hopes of making a new start.

He was here to stay, and Ms. Lainey Pangburn might as well reconcile herself to it.

2

A-1 GARAGE SENT a tow truck to pull Gabe's car out of the front of Perk Avenue and haul it away. With it gone, Lainey could get a clearer view of exactly what kind of repairs needed to be done.

"*Extensive* is the only word that comes to mind," she told Julius morosely. With the car gone, most of the onlookers had departed, as well. Only a few people lingered outside the shop, including one of the local eccentrics, Redmond Finn, who was busy scribbling notes about the incident. He collected disasters, had notebooks full of them at home. He was in his element, dancing merrily around the maw of the hole, measuring the hole itself, the skid marks leading up to it, everything except the extent of Lainey's distress.

She stood beside Julius, her shoulders slumped in uncharacteristic defeat. A lump had formed in her throat that she couldn't seem to swallow. Everything was tied up in Perk Avenue; three years' worth of hard work, her hopes and dreams. Everything. She knew the place could be repaired, but she was too fragile and overwhelmed to think about that very clearly right now.

"You should have taken my advice when I told you to have traffic posts inserted in the sidewalk outside the shop," Julius pointed out as soon as the tow truck had left. He had pushed his fireman's hat to the back of his head and his snowy white hair was plastered to his brow in sweaty tufts. "If you had, you wouldn't be standing here surveying a huge, gaping chasm." His tone was stern, but his arm was around her in a comforting embrace.

"I *know,* Grandpa," she said in a low voice, glancing at Gabe out of the corner of her eye. He was busy talking to Cody so he hadn't heard them, which was just as well because she certainly didn't want him to think she was responsible in any way for this fiasco. It was all his fault, she thought, giving a fed-up look to the new fresh-air feature Gabe Camden had created for her with his brakeless car.

"But when I talked to the city council about it, the only ones they would allow were four feet tall, two feet around, and painted bright orange." She shuddered. "Hideous."

Julius raised a shaggy white eyebrow at her and she sighed. "I'll have the posts put in as soon as the repairs are finished."

"Good girl."

She would also ignore any comments from the locals about 'closing the barn door after the horse was out.'

That was one of the few things about Calamity Falls she didn't like—everybody knew everybody else's business and commented on it. Which made it seem all the more impossible that she hadn't known Cody was Gabe's nephew. Except that Cody was very quiet, rarely talked about himself. He didn't have friends yet at the high school. He had something of an air of mystery that seemed to attract girls to Perk Avenue. When he wasn't busy with customers, though, Lainey had noticed he usually found an excuse to be near her. She found his awkward attention flattering and amusing.

Lainey acknowledged that she was truly a pitiful human being if she was flattered by the attentions of a sixteen-year-old. She needed to get out more.

There were days like today when she envied her best friend Jo Quillan Houston who had married and moved to Phoenix where not many people knew or cared about her personal business, and it certainly wasn't food for gossip up and down the main street.

Ordering herself to stop with the self-pity, Lainey turned to see who was left in her store because she needed to get everyone out and decide how she was going to secure the place from the weather and, possibly, intruders. Not to mention how she was going to remain open, attract customers, support herself and pay her help while her shop was undergoing repairs.

She glanced over at Gabe who looked perfectly calm and collected as he spoke to his nephew in a corner of the shop. Nonchalantly, she drifted that way, determined to find out if Gabe was trying to lure Cody from her employ.

After the way Gabe had purloined Delilah away from her, Lainey wouldn't put anything past him. She was determined to stay close and eavesdrop on what they were saying. For camouflage, she pulled a box from beneath a cloth-draped table and began loading bags of coffee beans into it.

"You're shaken up, Cody," Gabe was saying in a low, soothing tone. He had laid a hand on his nephew's shoulder and was talking to him earnestly. "Why don't we go on home? You don't have to stay here."

Cody, who had been stacking chairs on top of tables and sweeping up glass, stopped to look at his uncle. His jaw took on a rock-like set and his knuckles whitened on the broom handle. He cast a sideways glance at Lainey, who placed her filled carton on the counter and pretended to be examining the contents. "I can't do that, Uncle Gabe. Lainey needs me here."

"Oh? She does?"

In spite of his carefully neutral tone, Lainey could feel Gabe's gaze drilling holes into her back. For some reason, that annoying tingling she'd felt the first day she met him started again, this time across the back of her neck and shoulders. She longed to back up against a doorpost and rub that tingle away.

"Exactly what does she need you for?"

Unable to resist, she sneaked him a baleful look. What was that crack supposed to mean? Both men were turned away from her so she couldn't read his expression.

"I work here, Uncle Gabe," Cody insisted in a low voice. "She depends on me."

"You could work for me," Gabe said testily, shooting the tension in the air up several notches.

"Tried that, remember? Couldn't do anything to please you." Pointedly, Cody turned away and noisily stacked some chairs.

Lainey released a breath she'd been unaware of holding. It saddened her to realize that the two of them were at odds with each other.

Gabe looked as though his jaw was going to shatter from the strength he was using to grind his teeth together. His hands fisted at his sides for a moment. The tension in his shoulders was so strong, Lainey figured she could have dropped a brick on one of them and it would disintegrate into dust. As annoyed as she was with him, she wasn't brave enough to try it, though.

Spinning around, he stalked over to Sheriff Terell Watson. "Since I've given my statement and my car has been towed away, may I just go?'' he asked in a staccato voice.

When the sheriff said he could, he whirled and started out, but was brought up short by the sight of Lainey.

His dark eyes gave her a swift once-over look taking in the irritation on her face, the tight twist to her lips. ''I'll take care of these repairs,'' he said.

''No,'' she blurted. ''I'll do it.''

''Insurance will pay for this. You don't have to roll up your sleeves and begin pounding nails and hanging windows. I'll make sure my insurance company pays for these damages as soon as possible.''

''No. I don't want anything from you.''

''Now you're just being stubborn.''

Yes, she was and she knew it, but there was something about him that brought her stubbornness galloping out. She finally lifted one shoulder in a shrug of capitulation and said, ''Okay, fine. I'm sure we can work it out.''

When she didn't continue, he gave her a hard look and said, ''I'm glad to hear that. In the meantime, I'd...''

''You'd what?''

His eyebrows drew together. ''I'd like to know how you managed to entice my nephew into working for you.''

Lainey gaped at him, ''What?''

''What did you offer him that made him decide to snap up this job?''

''What did I *offer* him?'' Slowly, she placed her hands on her hips like a gunslinger getting ready to draw. Her straight red hair swung forward around her face and her eyes narrowed. "Exactly what do you mean by that?" she rapped out.

"I mean he had a perfectly good job at Coffee & Such, so why did he leave?"

Lainey jerked her thumb toward her chest. "It had nothing to do with me. He's sixteen and he's certainly able to make up his mind where he wants to work.

"I'm happy to have him working for me because he never slacks off." Lainey glanced at Cody who happened to be leaning on his broom and gazing at her with a dazed expression on his face.

"Um," she floundered, wondering what was wrong with the boy. "And he only takes authorized breaks." She gave Cody a wide smile. "That's right, Cody, you just catch your breath for a minute."

With a look that asked if she was completely sane, Gabe said, "*I* know he's a good worker. Who do you think trained him?"

She pressed her lips together to keep from admitting that obviously it had been Gabe. To her relief, they were interrupted by a flurry of activity at the front of the shop. Several women rushed in led by Martha Smalley—wrought iron artist with the muscles of a stevedore, surrogate grandmother to Lainey and fiancée of Julius.

"Lainey, we just heard," she exclaimed, rushing to embrace Lainey in a hug that sent vertebrae crackling all along her spine, then holding her away and looking at her to see if she was all right.

Lainey choked and fought to stop the watering in her eyes as she battled for oxygen. Eventually, she recovered her breath enough to make assurances yet again that no one was injured. Really, she thought, pulling air into her deflated lungs, the medicine of chiropractic had lost a potential star when Martha had decided to take up her welding tools and iron to become an artist.

The other women fanned out around the shop, surveying the damage, and treating Gabe to speculative looks, which he returned. A couple of them drifted over to speak to him. Flirt with him, Lainey amended, noticing the slow, easy smile he turned on the two women as they asked him about the accident. Maybe Gabe didn't know about the formidable reputation enjoyed by Martha and her friends. That thought cheered Lainey. What he didn't know might possibly hurt him. She winced, wondering if she was becoming malicious. It was only the shocks of the day, she assured herself.

As much as she loved Martha, Lainey had to admit that she and her group of friends could be very intimidating. It was rumored around Calamity Falls that the women practiced some form of homegrown voodoo. Men who displeased them had been known to develop strange tics and quirks. The husband of one had a gambling problem until his wife met Martha. Now he claimed to have a fiery burning sensation in his palms whenever he even thought about betting on a poker game.

These allegations worried Lainey, but didn't seem to bother Julius who took such statements as a challenge to be good to Martha. Lainey fervently hoped that he would be.

He looked up and smiled adoringly now as Martha approached him and spoke to him in a quiet tone.

They both then glanced at Lainey, who walked over to them. "Something wrong?" she asked.

"Honey," Julius said, his craggy face folding into a

frown. "We hate to bring this up, but we were wondering about the wedding cake."

"The wedding cake?" She shrugged. "There's nothing wrong with my kitchen," she said, nodding toward the back of the shop.

"But…well… We thought you might be too shaken up to make it for us, so we'll find someone in Tucson to do it so you won't even have to worry about it at all." Martha gave her a crooked, self-deprecating smile. "I'm only mentioning the cake at this worst possible moment because it will take me a while to find someone."

Defensively, Lainey lifted her chin. "I'm fine. You know I'll be glad to make the cake for you." She fought the urge to look over her shoulder and make sure Gabe wasn't listening, though she knew he was. Mentally, she added eavesdropping to his list of crimes.

"Yes, sweetheart, but you weren't going to actually make it, remember?" Martha said apologetically. "Delilah was going to do it since she used to own a cake shop, and…"

This time Lainey couldn't resist the urge, and turned casually to sneak a peek over her shoulder. Sure enough, Gabe had stepped away from the two women he'd been charming, and was listening with interest to everything being said. "And Delilah no longer works for me. Even if I couldn't do it—and I certainly *can*," she added for Gabe's benefit. "Stavros could… What?" she asked as her grandfather began shaking his head.

"Stavros has gone to an astrology conference in Sedona. His restaurant is closed until he comes back with signs from the stars on what direction his cuisine should take this fall."

Behind her, she could hear Gabe stifling a guffaw. She gave him a sour look. So what if Stavros consulted astrology charts before beginning his day's meal preparations? He was a master chef with a successful Greek restaurant. Oh, why didn't Gabe just go *away?*

Perversely, Gabe took her glance at him to be one of invitation. He stepped forward and pushed himself into the conversation. "Excuse me. I couldn't help overhearing."

"Yes, you could have," Lainey responded in a frosty tone. "You could have left."

Julius and Martha gaped at her rudeness, but Gabe ignored her. "I'll be glad to make sure Delilah has the cake ready."

"No, you won't," Lainey said angrily. "It's absolutely none of your business."

Martha gave him a quick up-and-down look. "Who are you?"

Dark eyes twinkling and dimple flashing, Gabe said, "Delilah's new boss." His tone was so charming and full of cheer that Martha drew in a startled breath, then laughed unexpectedly.

Lainey felt as if something was slipping through her fingers. She lifted her hand as if to speak, but couldn't think of anything. Gabe's eyes flickered to her and she sensed a spark of empathy, which she resisted.

"Oh, yes," Julius said with a thoughtful nod. "Lainey said that some low-down, no-good rat had hired Delilah away."

"That's me," Gabe admitted, shooting a sidelong glance of self-congratulations toward Lainey.

Annoyed by the mixed signals she was receiving from him, Lainey said, "It certainly is."

Martha gave Lainey a helpless look and said, "Not

that I want to be disloyal to my almost-granddaughter, but Julius and I are getting married in five days and because of today's events, I don't see a wedding cake looming on the horizon.''

Lainey frowned. She was a good baker, but not a terrific one. Her skill level didn't stretch to emulating the fabulous cakes that Delilah could bake. Her grandfather and Martha deserved the best and at the present time, Delilah was the only one in Calamity Falls who could provide it. As much as she hated to deal with Gabe in any way, she couldn't be so petty as to deny them the beautiful cake they wanted.

To show that she could be big about this in spite of all the crimes this man had committed against her, Lainey said, ''Go right ahead and ask Delilah to do the cake, Mr. Camden. She'll do an excellent job for them. In fact, she's a fabulous baker.'' The words ''Much better than you deserve'' hung in the air between them, but the quirk of Gabe's smile told her that he'd caught her unspoken message loud and clear.

''I'll ask her to call you and make the arrangements, and it's on the house, ma'am,'' he said. ''It's the least I can do after the damage I've caused to your almost-granddaughter's shop.''

''Oh no it isn't,'' Lainey muttered, but Martha and Julius were so taken with his generous offer that they didn't hear her. Julius shook his hand and clapped him on the back. Lainey gleefully noticed that her grandfather's hearty thanks nearly sent Gabe onto his knees. Martha flexed her muscles and gave him a hug that turned his face bright red and had his eyes bulging, cartoon-like, from his head.

When she let him go, he staggered slightly and wheezed, ''You're welcome.'' Martha made a move as if to give him another hug and he stumbled backward, feebly lifting his hands to ward her off as he said, "I'd better be going. I've uh, got to see about uh, repairs...." Turning, he gave his nephew a wave and left, listing slightly to one side as he fought to regain his breath.

Now she knew how to get rid of him, Lainey thought with satisfaction. Puzzled, she looked down at the backs of her hands. There was that darned burning sensation again. Was it some kind of rash brought on by proximity to Gabe? She wouldn't be the least bit surprised.

Within the next few minutes, Julius wound up his report and the sheriff finished his investigation. He approached Lainey, tapping the edge of his clipboard against his palm. "From what I can tell right now, this entire incident looks like an unfortunate accident. I'll know more after I inspect Camden's car."

Lainey could only give a dejected nod.

"Hey, cheer up," Julius said. "I'm sure Gabe's insurance will cover everything."

Lainey gave Gabe's retreating back a quick glance. "So I've heard," she answered with a sigh. In the meantime, what was she going to do next?

GABE MADE his way slowly toward Coffee & Such. Climbing the incline of Battlehaven Avenue while fighting for breath and checking himself for broken ribs kept his mind occupied for the first several minutes of his walk. He spoke to the few people he knew in town and assured them he was unhurt, as was everyone in Lainey's shop. At the top of the hill, just before the turn onto Nugget Street, he looked back to see the damage to Perk Avenue, wincing at the huge, gaping hole his car had left.

He felt terrible about the accident and the damage to Lainey Pangburn's store. It only made the situation between them worse. In spite of what she had said, he didn't think she understood that his hiring of Delilah was strictly business on his part. It was the way he always did business—find the best person for the job he needed filled and offer them a salary they couldn't resist. It was what had made his two restaurants in Tucson so successful, and what would make his new venture a moneymaker as well.

What he hadn't counted on was Cody's defection. They hadn't been in Calamity Falls five days before the two of them had had a huge argument over the same things they'd been arguing about for weeks—Cody's involvement with a girl who'd broken his young heart, his despair over their breakup, their move to Calamity Falls because Gabe had thought it would be a good change for the boy and Cody had seemed too apathetic to care if they left Tucson or not.

The apathy was what had frightened Gabe the most. It reminded him too much of Cody's mother. Shelly had been wild during her high school years, lurching from one misadventure with a boy, to another. When these boys had dumped her or disappointed her, she'd been depressed for weeks, snapping out of it only when she met the next unsuitable guy. It had driven Gabe and their parents crazy and seeing what looked like the same pattern repeating itself in Cody, Gabe had made swift changes to keep his nephew from making his mother's mistakes. The boy didn't yet see the benefits of their move, but Gabe was hoping he'd settle down soon and see that Calamity Falls would be the best thing for both of them.

Now, however, Gabe didn't know whether to be elated or dismayed that Cody seemed to have come back to life. In fact, he didn't know much about his nephew anymore. He'd raised the boy since he was two, when Shelly had died without ever saying who Cody's father was. Gabe had known and understood everything about Cody until the past two years and all the problems that had culminated in their move to Calamity Falls.

The goofy little town had seemed like a good place to make a fresh start, for the two of them to work together and mend their relationship, but Cody had changed things by marching into Lainey's shop and asking for a job. Gabe knew he wasn't being entirely fair when he'd accused her of enticing Cody, but his nephew was young and mixed up and running into a woman like Lainey only minutes after a fight with Gabe had probably skewed his judgment.

It would help if she was homely, had skin like a dried apple rather than a fresh peach, hair like dried straw instead of the shiny russet of fall leaves.

But she was beautiful and smart, and the thought of Cody being around her every day had Gabe's palms sweating. He glanced down as he reached for the door of his shop and his hand skidded on the knob. Or maybe his palms were sweating for a different reason. He'd heard stories about Martha Smalley and her friends. Martha herself liked him. Didn't he have the broken ribs to prove it? But Lainey might be a different story. Perhaps she'd put a wet-palm curse on him.

He rubbed his hands on his jeans to dry them, opened the door and went inside. After he called his insurance company, and the lumber yard, he might ask Lainey about a possible curse—if he was feeling particularly brave, that is.

THE SOUND of rhythmic pounding drew Lainey from the back of her shop where she'd been busy storing things away and trying to make room for everything that must now be moved out of the front of the store and secured away from looters. She trusted the people of Calamity Falls, but there were always strangers in town who might not hesitate to make away with some of her merchandise if given the chance. She didn't yet know what she was going to do about closing off the front, but she'd sent Cody to the hardware store to see about materials to do the job.

She didn't know how long the pounding had been going on, but when she left the kitchen and entered the front of her store, she stopped with a cry of dismay.

Gabe Camden had propped a ladder, with a price tag still dangling from one rung, against the outside wall and was attempting to haul a huge sheet of plywood into place.

She dashed outside. "What are you doing?"

Gabe, who had been precariously balancing the plywood and attempting to get his hammer and nails into position, rocked backward, shouting "Whoa!" as he let go of the plywood. He regained his balance, but the wood crashed to the sidewalk, its unwieldy bulk thumping against the wall, and then the ladder, causing Gabe to shout again and throw his weight forward to keep the ladder in place.

"Why did you yell like that?" he demanded, clinging to the ladder.

"Because there's a crazy man on a ladder outside my shop," she shot back.

"I'm trying to fix the hole I made earlier."

Lainey threw her hands in the air. "Don't do me any favors! The way you're going at it, people will think my place is not only damaged, but condemned. Did you bring some spray paint with you so you can graffiti a few obscene messages on the outside, as well?"

Gabe came lightly down the ladder and stood in front of her, his head thrust forward, a vein throbbing in his neck. "I'm only trying to repair what I damaged. I told you that was what I was going to do."

"And I told you not to, that I'd take care of it."

"It's my responsibility."

"Fine." Lainey folded her arms across her chest. "Since you're such a hotshot with your fancy German sportscar and all, you should be able to get some carpenters and a glazier to come out from Tucson and repair this the right way."

He clamped his hands onto his hips. "Oh, don't be—"

"Today."

"What?"

"I said today. You pay for the proper repairs and then your insurance company can reimburse you."

"There's no way that I can get someone out here today."

"Well, you're not going to do this your—"

"Something wrong, Lainey?" a voice interrupted.

She glanced up to see Bruiser, Bison and Bull Fina crossing the street toward her and Gabe. The three massive men lined up alongside her and stood gazing at Gabe who regarded them warily. Lainey noticed that his grip tightened on the hammer, and she understood why. Even without their firemen's gear, the Fina brothers were massive. They had shaved heads, huge shoulders, thick necks, arms and legs like tree trunks and fists the size of five-pound hams. In fact, they had everything one would need in order to be as intimidating as possible.

"Why're you back here?" Bison asked, his fierce gaze on Gabe. "You got something against Lainey?"

Gabe looked outraged. "No, of course not! My brakes failed, and I—"

"'Cause if you got something against Lainey, you need to take it up with us."

"With you?" Gabe asked warily, eyeing Bison's upper arms and wondering why he wasn't named Bicep.

Lainey flapped a hand at Gabe to make him be quiet. "What do you mean?" she asked.

Bull stepped forward, hitched his pants up a little higher, and said, "Julius asked us to keep an eye on things while he and Martha are on their honeymoon."

"What do you mean by *things?*" she asked, her suspicion growing.

"You."

Stunned, Lainey stared at him. "You're kidding." Out of the corner of her eye, she could see Gabe's lips twitch in amusement as the Finas' attention switched from him to her.

"God's truth," Bison said. "We owe him a lot. If it wasn't for him, we'd've never got our loan to open our gym. We'd still be driving garbage trucks."

"Instead of just being constructed like one," Gabe said under his breath.

The Fina brothers looked at him with identical expressions of concentrated suspicion. "Did you insult us?'' Bull asked. His brothers seemed to be puzzling over the same question.

"Oh, no," Gabe answered in a sincere tone as they surged forward. "I was commenting on the good shape you three are in."

The Finas preened. "We gotta look good," Bison said. "Otherwise our customers wouldn't think we know what we're talking about when we tell them how to bulk up so they'll look like us."

Lainey watched Gabe's expression as his gaze swept from their bald heads, over their beefy bodies, to their size fifteen feet. "Do you have a lot of customers wanting to look like you?" His tone was so full of amazement, Lainey had to bite her lip to keep from laughing, then she frowned. Darn it, she didn't want to like anything about this man. Not even his sense of humor.

"Oh, yeah," Bruiser answered. "You'd be surprised. There's lots of people here who want to work out, get into better shape. Mostly old guys, though, like Julius, and Cedric Warrender. He just got married and wants to build up his stamina." Bruiser scratched his shiny pate. "Course I can see why that would be. These old guys don't have much goin' for 'em—in their looks, I mean, so they—"

Lainey stepped forward. "Why did you three say you stopped by just now?"

Bruiser blinked as if he was trying to remember, then looked at his brothers, who appeared to be as blank as he was, but then his frown cleared. "We were on our way over here to see if we could help fix things up, but it looks like old Gabe here's got a start on it." The three of them stood shoulder-to-shoulder and regarded the plywood and ladder. "I'm kinda surprised, though, that you could lift that, you being so puny and all."

Lainey snorted with laughter and Gabe gave her a dark look.

"I wouldn't say I'm puny," he said with a defensive edge to his voice.

"Oh yeah?" Bull grabbed his arm, shoved up the sleeve of his polo-style shirt and forced him to flex his biceps. Lainey thought the muscles that bounced up didn't look too bad at all, but Bull said, "Look at those muscles. Pathetic. Pa-thet-tic. They're just cryin' out for someone to build 'em up, show 'em who's boss." He looked right into Gabe's eyes and said, "Buddy, we could really help you out here. You ain't exactly a babe magnet."

Outraged, Gabe jerked his arm away. "Thanks, I'll keep that in mind," he growled.

Laughter bubbled in Lainey's throat. She'd managed to keep it under control, but it was fighting to escape. "I...uh...I was telling Mr. Camden that he needs to have someone who knows what they're doing come and make these repairs."

"And I was telling Ms. Pangburn that it won't be possible to get anyone out here today, so we need to secure the building."

The Finas looked from one to the other of them, then Bruiser said, "We agree with him. We'll help."

Before she could protest any further, the brothers picked up the plywood and hefted it into place over the window while Gabe scrambled to grab hammer and nails and pound the wood into place.

"Great," Lainey murmured, and went back inside. By the time they had finished the nailing, no light at all came into her shop. She flipped on the lights. "Just great. Now I'm the proprietor of *Dark* Avenue. I'm Lainey, Mistress of the Dark Roast."

3

"STOP FEELING SORRY for yourself," Lainey muttered aloud. She took a deep breath, released it, then went back to the job of cleaning up her shop as she gave herself a mental pep talk.

So it had been a bad day. Well, okay, the worst day of her life, so far, but it was time for her to stop being the queen of self-pity and begin thinking what to do next.

On the positive side, her shop was now secure from the weather and from possible looters, though she couldn't imagine anyone in Calamity Falls actually feeling the need to lift coffee beans or mugs from her shop. They were odd, but not dishonest.

Another positive note was the fact that she didn't think Gabe would delay in getting the damage fixed. Thinking about Gabe made her get that quirky tingling in her palms again. What was causing that, she wondered in annoyance. She put down the box she'd been packing with mugs and wiped her hands on her skirt. Maybe she needed to see a doctor.

"Hey," a voice called from the doorway. "I missed all the excitement."

She glanced up from inspecting her palms to see Starina Simms standing in the doorway. Starina, who always moved as if being pushed by a strong wind, whirled into the room. She was dressed in her usual mechanic's overalls and her short, white hair stood up like a rooster's comb. "This is a mess," she said, looking around with avid fascination. "I'm sorry I didn't get to see it. A person can really learn a lot from these kinds of disasters."

"Yeah," Lainey said dryly. "Like the need to have barriers out front."

"Nah," Starina said, taking a small notebook from her pocket. "I mean about force and motion." She scribbled a few notes.

Lainey shook her head. At least she didn't have to worry about Starina being overly sympathetic about the ruin of Perk Avenue. She saw it in purely scientific terms. An engineer with a degree from MIT, Starina had retired from her job with an aircraft manufacturer and moved to Calamity Falls so she could work on her perpetual motion machine. She claimed to have almost had it a couple of times, but the machine always blew up just as she was about to reach perfection with it. She'd lost her eyebrows and most of her hair in the last explosion several months ago, but it was growing back nicely now.

When she was finished with her notes, Starina scooted out the door again without saying goodbye. That was one thing about the unusual citizens of Calamity Falls. They were so single-minded in their pursuits, they didn't waste much time on sentimentality. Lainey knew she needed to be more like that, but looking around at the ruin of Perk Avenue made her heartsick.

The pounding had stopped outside, so she knew all the plywood was in place. What were they doing out there now? Standing around talking, no doubt. The

Fina boys were probably trying to get Gabe to sign up for membership in their club.

Curious, she set down a handful of chocolate-dipped coffee spoons and drifted over to the front of the shop where she spied a knothole in the plywood that she hadn't noticed before. It was at about waist level, so she bent over to peer out. A deep blue eye stared back at her.

"Oh!" Startled, she stepped back. From the other side of the slab of wood, she heard Gabe's rich chuckle. A few seconds later, he strolled through the open door, followed by Bruiser, Bison and Bull who immediately began moving around the shop, making sure it was secure against bad weather. The front door was intact, but hanging by one hinge. They patched it together.

"Checking to see if we were finished, Lainey?" he asked. "Or were you checking out something else?"

She stared at him for a second before she realized what he meant. A knothole that was waist-level on her hit him below the waist since he was taller. Completely of its own will, her gaze drifted downward.

She lifted her chin. "I don't know what you mean," she said, then winced at the trite phrase.

He laughed again and a surge of warmth rushed through Lainey's system. This time she felt the tingling sensation from head to toe. Obviously, she was breaking out in a rash.

She was glad when Bruiser spoke up. "We're going back to the gym now, Lainey. Had to close it to come over and help you, but we'll lose business if we don't get back."

She smiled at her three friends. "I appreciate your help."

"We promised Julius we'd keep an eye on you," Bull said, puffing out his chest importantly.

She heartily wished Julius would stop being so protective of her.

"Um," she glanced from the three brothers to Gabe, who looked decidedly wary. "Thanks, I guess, but in spite of what my grandfather said, you don't need to watch out for me."

The three brothers shook their heads stubbornly. "We promised."

Uncertainly, Lainey looked from one to the other of them. "What form will this 'watching out for me' take?"

"Making sure nobody bothers you," Bull answered. "Drive you home from work..."

"Drive me home?" She pointed in the direction of the outside staircase, one of many in town that connected the levels of streets cut into the foothills. "I only live two streets away, why would I need someone to drive me?"

"Or walk you, whichever you prefer."

She stared at them in dismay. "That really isn't necessary."

They ignored her feeble protest. "What time are you leaving today?"

"I don't know," she said, looking around helplessly. "I've got a lot to do."

"We'll be back." They turned as one, heading for the door, the floor vibrating with their measured tread. They paused to give Gabe some advice. "You be nice to her, and stop by the gym later. We'll start working on that puny body of yours," Bruiser said.

The three of them stumped out as Lainey caught the

look on Gabe's face, a mixture of outrage and amusement.

He puffed out his chest much as Bruiser had done though the results weren't quite as impressive. "I'm not afraid of those three. Or, at least, that's what I keep telling myself."

A moment of shared amusement flashed between them.

"As I said earlier," Gabe went on. "I'll get someone here to fix this as soon as possible. My insurance company is good about paying off these kinds of claims quickly."

"Had a lot of them, have you?" Lainey asked, tongue in cheek.

Gabe's smile kicked up, pocking his dimple into his cheek. He rocked on his heels. "You know we'd get a lot further if you'd quit sniping at me."

Lainey shrugged. She knew she wasn't being reasonable, but once she started, it was hard to stop. She pressed her lips together and gave him a steady look in what she knew must be the expression her friend Jo called "Lainey's-Scare-Off-Any-Man-Look."

"I'll wait to hear from your insurance agent, then," she said. "Was there anything else?"

"Cody," he said.

"What about him?"

"He's vulnerable, right now," Gabe said bluntly. "I don't want you taking advantage of him."

Amazed, she clapped a hand to her chest. "Me? Taking advantage of him? What are you talking about? I pay him a fair wage."

"That's not what I meant. I mean because you're…" His gaze swept from her russet hair to the hem of her swirling skirt and the hot turquoise that peeked out beneath the hem. "Attractive." It didn't sound like he necessarily thought that was a good thing.

Lainey was so stunned, she could barely speak. "Are you kidding? He's sixteen."

This time, Gabe was the one who looked embarrassed. "He's vulnerable," he repeated stubbornly. "Since he's been through a lot of changes, he's not sure what he wants right now, and you look very...appealing to him."

The annoyance she'd been feeling all morning bubbled over into fury. "What you're suggesting is not only repugnant, it's a felony."

Gabe seemed to realize what he'd said, and began to backpedal. "Well, maybe I didn't mean it quite the way it sounded."

"I should hope not."

Distressed, Gabe ran his hand over his face. Hell, he was making a royal mess of this. She looked ready to spit nails—straight at him—and all he'd been trying to do was give her fair warning, and to watch out for his nephew.

"Do you need me to help you close up here?" he asked finally, trying to make amends.

"No. There's nothing more that can be done except to lock the front door. Thank God, it was spared when you made your grand entrance. It'll probably take weeks to get the place fixed up and open again. In the meantime, what am I going to do for employment? How will I pay...?" She stopped as if realizing who she was talking to and unwilling to say she was worried about how she was going to pay her bills.

He turned away. "As I said, I'm sorry about all this, and—"

"How many employees do you have?" she asked unexpectedly.

He looked over his shoulder. "What?"

"How many employees do you have?"

He didn't like the glint in her eyes at all. "Four, besides myself," he said, turning slowly to face her. "Why?"

"Now you've got five. What time do you want me to start tomorrow?"

"What?" He felt like he was tied to the railroad tracks and a train was bearing down on him.

"It makes perfect sense," she said, turning her hands palm-up and fairly dancing on her toes with excitement. This was the perfect solution. She would call the three people who worked for her and tell them the store would be closed for a while. While she waited for that to happen, she needed to work somewhere herself.

"You're responsible for destroying my store. I need employment until it's fixed. You run a store just like mine." She paused, considering. "Well, certainly not as good, but still, I can work there until the repairs are made here and I can reopen."

Lainey nodded as if to punctuate her decision, but Gabe was shaking his head emphatically from side to side. "No. You're not going to work for me."

"Why not?"

"Because you're the competition."

She flung her arms out to encompass her ruined shop. "Obviously not now, I'm not."

"No." He looked at the stubborn set of her chin and knew he was losing, but he fought on. "It would never work. You're not the kind of employee I would ever—"

Blithely, she waved that argument aside. "Oh, don't

be ridiculous. I'm better qualified than anyone else in this town. I make a coffee mocha that would knock your socks off and my lattes are to die for.''

It wasn't her mochas and lattes he was worried about. It was her ability to distract people. Customers. Well…him.

He grasped at straws. "What about Cody? You made such a point of wanting him to work for you. How will you employ him if you're working for me?''

She paused and he was delighted to see that he had her stumped—but not for long. ''There's still work to be done here, cleaning up to do,'' she finally said. ''I'll pay him to do that out of what I earn working for you. What time do you want me to start tomorrow?''

''You're not starting tomorrow.'' Why did he have this panicked feeling kicking him in the gut?

''I usually open here at six. I'm assuming, since you've copied so many other things from me that you open at the same time.''

''Not six.'' With the wild desperation of a man going down for the third time, he repeated it. ''Don't come at six.''

He looked pained, as if the idea of facing her that early in the morning was too much for him.

''Seven, then.'' With brisk efficiency, she took his arm and marched him to the door. ''I'll see you then.''

''Ah…'' Every word he'd ever learned seemed to dry up in his throat. He found himself standing outside her shop while she gave him a bright little smile as she wrestled the patched-together door shut. ''Ah, hell,'' he muttered, then lifted his voice. ''You're not going to do this,'' he called. The lock clicked. ''I said you're not going to do this,'' he repeated, yelling this time as he saw her disappearing into the shadows.

"That's one of them, Marge," he heard someone whisper behind him. "This town's full of eccentrics, but I didn't realize there was one who yelled at doors."

Annoyed, Gabe turned to see two women, obviously tourists, staring at him avidly. "Do you talk to any other inanimate objects?" one of them asked, scrambling for her camera.

"No," he grumbled as he strode away. "Only bone-headed ones."

THE NEXT MORNING, Lainey arrived at Coffee & Such full of self-congratulatory praise at having thought up such a clever solution to her problem.

She paused at the door, took a deep breath and plunged inside. With a bright smile, she waved to the customers grouped around the small tables and marched behind the counter. Several people who had been her regular customers gave her guilty glances and tried to hide behind their newspapers and coffee mugs, but she blessed them with a forgiving smile. Once her shop was open again, she would soon win them back. After all, it was her ability as a *barista* that had won them in the first place. All she had to do was prove herself here at Coffee & Such and her customers would follow her right back to her own place—as soon as she had learned everything Gabe had been doing to pull her customers away.

She swung around the end of the counter and encountered Gabe, looking somewhat sleepy-eyed, tousled and sexy in spite of his crisp navy blue apron and the strong scent of coffee in the air.

"Good morning, Gabe. I'm ready to start to work. Where do I find an apron?"

He turned to her, his deep-set eyes taking a slow

perusal of her jeans, crisp sunny yellow camp shirt and sturdy shoes. His gaze then came back up to meet hers as a slow smile spread across his face.

Lainey blinked, then stared, mesmerized as he stepped close to her. She should step back, put some distance between them, she thought, say a mile or so, but something had nailed her shoes to the floor.

Gabe's thick black hair looked as if it had been freshly washed and carelessly combed but his jaw was smooth and shiny from his shave. The subtle scent of his soap and aftershave curled its way through her senses. She wanted to close her eyes and take a deep breath.

What was going on here? she wondered. Sure, he was an attractive man. Okay, drop-dead gorgeous and outrageously sexy, but she'd noticed that before. This was something else, something that made her insides melt like a chocolate bar on an August afternoon.

Her eyes met his and when he leaned close to her, Lainey's breath squeezed off completely.

Gabe lowered his voice. In a tone meant for her ears alone, he said, ''You can find an apron down the street and around the corner at Perk Avenue, of course.''

Startled by the gentle puff of his breath on her cheek, Lainey jumped, then recovered herself quickly. She pinched her lips together and wrinkled her nose. ''Grouchy this morning, are we?'' she chirped. ''Do you need a good cup of coffee to wake you up?''

''I'm wide awake, thank you, and if I wasn't that shirt of yours would have blasted me awake.''

Lainey reached up and sassily plucked the shoulder seams away from her shoulders. ''Thank you. I wanted to make a bold statement this morning.''

"Oh, and what would that be? Yield to incoming traffic?"

She crossed her arms at her waist and said, "Yes, as a matter of fact, that's exactly it. I thought if I wore this, maybe the same thing wouldn't happen to your shop that happened to mine yesterday."

Gabe glowered at the reminder, but then jerked his head toward the back of the shop. "In there," he said.

Lainey fetched a clean apron from the storeroom and tied it on. Positioning herself by the espresso machine, she called out, "Anyone need a refill?"

When Cedric Warrender and his new bride, Charlotte Quail, approached the counter, she said, "The usual skinny decaf vanilla latte for you two this morning?"

They exchanged glances as if egging each other on. Though newly married, the retired couple seemed very much in tune, almost always ordering the same things, or sharing one order. Cedric, a retired landscape architect from England, had come to Calamity Falls because he liked the live-and-let-live attitude of the citizens. He'd bought himself a house with a beautiful garden full of wild bushes which he'd trimmed into the shape of characters from *Alice in Wonderland.* He had frequent conversations with them and recorded them in large notebooks. Charlotte, took all this in stride, just as Cedric accepted her avocation of giving risqué daily lectures on the mating habits of the Harris hawk.

"Well, uh, Gabe over there suggested we might like to try something a little more daring this morning. Since we've been on our honeymoon, my garden has gotten way out of hand and I've got to get it trimmed and back into condition."

Lainey nodded, knowing he would eventually get to the point.

"Also, Charlotte has a particularly challenging lecture to give this morning," Cedric said. "And Gabe says something new might give us a little more 'oomph.'"

Lainey slid a glance at Gabe. "Oomph, hmm? And what did he suggest you two might like to drink?"

"A triple shot of espresso in an iced mocha drink." He tapped a display of vitamin supplements she'd been too busy to notice. "And throw in this stuff called, New Youth."

Curious, she picked up the packet and read its ingredients. Her eyes widened. "Are you sure about this, Cedric? It has things in it I've never even heard of, and besides, a triple espresso? Are you sure you want that much caffeine?"

"Excuse us for a second, folks," Gabe said as he stepped up beside her, wrapped his hand around her arm and pulled her gently back. He murmured, "Did you ever hear of the saying 'the customer is always right'?"

She turned and gave him a fierce look. "I can't believe that old saying is referring to a couple of seventy-year-olds who haven't had a caffeinated drink in who knows how long." She waved the packet at him. "Not to mention this…this…"

"Vitamin supplement?" he suggested.

"Sex aid," she blurted, then blushed because she sounded like such a prude. She didn't even know where that idea had sprung from.

Gabe snorted with laughter. Taking her by the shoulders, he turned her to face Cedric and Charlotte who had lost interest in what Gabe and Lainey were saying and were busy gazing into each other's eyes. Cedric had clasped his bride's hands.

"Does it look like they need a sex aid?"

She had to admit that it didn't.

Gabe whispered so close to her ear, she felt the heat of his lips, which for some reason gave her that melting chocolate bar sensation again. "Exactly what is on your mind, Lainey? They're perfectly harmless vitamins and minerals."

She didn't *know* what she'd been thinking. Somehow her mind had been erased as clear as the chalkboard that announced the daily specials. It had all seemed to go together a few minutes ago—Gabe, sex, a kick to the libido.

"It's referring to giving the customer whatever he wants." Gabe said when she didn't answer him. "You insisted on working here. Is your intention to drive my customers away, and back to you when you reopen? If that's so, you're not going to be helping either of us. By the time you reopen, they'll all be drinking herbal tea."

She finally came to her senses, dipped her shoulders and twisted out of his grasp as she said, "I have a concern for *my* customers, even if they are *your* customers temporarily."

"Give them what they want," he ordered.

"Fine. I'll do it, but it'll be decaf."

She snatched the vitamin packet from his hand, then stepping forward, she gave Cedric and Charlotte a smile and began assembling their drinks, finishing them off with a swirl of whipped cream, a dusting of cinnamon and a chocolate-covered coffee bean which she swiped from an unopened bag she spied under the counter. All the while, Gabe watched her as carefully as one of Charlotte's favorite hawks.

"I think you should..." he began at one point, until her stern look made him back off.

"I'm an expert at this," she reminded him.

Charlotte's eyes widened with pleasure as her husband paid for their drinks. "This is beautiful. Lainey, you have an artist's touch."

"Thank you, Charlotte." Lainey rang up the sale as her friends found a table. She gave Gabe a smile. "Don't try to tell an artist how to create."

"You're using *my* ingredients," he pointed out, hotly.

"Yes, I know, but I have to make do with the inferior materials you've provided."

His face darkened and for a minute Lainey thought she'd gone too far. She didn't quite know why she was baiting him like this. The coffee and other ingredients he used weren't inferior at all. And she was still surprised at the way she'd pushed herself in here. Even more surprising was the fact that he'd let her do so. No doubt he was feeling guilty about yesterday's accident.

She didn't think that feeling would last long. As for her... She gave him a sidelong glance as he began making hot chocolate for a couple of teenage girls who'd stopped in on their way to school. She watched as he added even bigger swirls of whipped cream than she'd used on Cedric and Charlotte's mochas. He finished off the girls' drinks with curls of dark chocolate. They paid him and turned away from the counter balancing their cups carefully so that the top-heavy cream and chocolate wouldn't plop onto the floor. Moving as carefully as tightrope walkers fighting a bout of vertigo, they found a table.

He gave her a smile that said, "Top that."

Lainey's eyes lit up and she felt that crazy tingling once again as if the excitement of a challenge had electrified her. "That was adequate," she said as the next person approached. "Watch this."

When the next customer ordered a coffee mocha, she poured it into a clear glass mug, chocolate on the bottom, creamy coffee, a bouffant pouf of whipped cream on top, chocolate curls and a coffee bean. The man walked away looking as if he'd hit the jackpot.

"Acceptable," Gabe said, but there was a gleam in his eyes as he waited on the next patron, who wanted a latte. Gabe made the drink, layered it with foam, laced it with a criss-cross pattern of caramel, dusted it with tiny chocolate chips and sprinkled tiny slivers of pecans over the top.

"Adequate," Lainey said in a disparaging tone, but she couldn't disguise the fire of competition she was feeling.

Word spread up and down the street that something was going on at Coffee & Such. Customers crowded into the store, ordering drinks just to see what kind of fabulous concoction would come their way. Gallons of coffee were consumed, quarts of chocolate syrup were used, pints of whipped cream were mounded on top of everything in sight. By noon, there was barely standing room in the store and both Gabe and Lainey were tired, but showed no signs of letting up.

A couple of people pushed their way to the front at one point to talk to Gabe, but he could barely listen to them because his attention was on Lainey's latest creation, something involving what looked like every enticing thing from the refrigerator and even appeared to have halves of ginger snaps standing at attention on top. He was surprised that so many people were willing to let them take such liberties with their drinks. Most coffee drinkers were very serious about their brew. The only explanation he could come up with was that in Calamity Falls, people expected such things. The out-of-town customers probably thought he and his establishment were as odd as everyone else in town, but the sweet-sounding ring of the cash register took any sting out of that thought.

"Quite a crowd," Julius said, finally snagging Gabe's attention to order two cups of plain coffee. "You two giving away free samples?"

"No," Lainey answered. "Customers are paying full price and they're happy to do it."

Gabe grinned as Martha said, "I'll bet Gabe's happy they're paying full price, too."

He saw the instant that the truth dawned on her. She paused with one hand on the handle of the espresso machine and turned to give Gabe a wide-eyed look.

He winked at her. "Best day of profits I've had since I opened."

Julius chuckled. "Looks like you're aiding the enemy, honey." He took Martha's arm and the two of them squeezed through the crowd and went outside.

Lainey opened and closed her mouth a couple of times, speechless as he'd never before seen her. "That was a sneaky trick," she said with annoyance simmering in her voice.

"I didn't invite you here. This was your idea." He could see that she had no answer to that, but she was too stubborn to admit it. Her brown eyes darkened to the color of the rich brew she was pouring into a cup.

"I was merely attempting to recoup some of my losses," she said haughtily. "I'm sure you realize that you'll have to share some of today's profits with me."

He leaned against the counter and crossed his arms over his chest. He should probably be horsewhipped for the way he was enjoying this. In fact, the morning would have been perfect if not for the way he kept recalling yesterday and the way Cody had gazed at Lainey with puppy love shimmering in his eyes. Gabe wouldn't have been surprised to see a big, red heart beating, cartoon-like, on his nephew's chest.

Thank goodness, Cody was at school and Lainey was right here beneath Gabe's watchful eye. Besides, he was enjoying the heck out of this. He'd never before had such fun baiting a woman, or even felt the need to. There was something about Lainey Pangburn, though, that brought out the devil in him. "Of course," he said, just to watch the anger spark in her. "You'll get minimum wage, just like I pay all new employees."

"I don't think so," she answered in a singsong tone. "If it hadn't been for me, you wouldn't have had all these customers, and…"

"That's not true. They would have come here, anyway, because mine is the only coffee bar open in town."

Lainey tilted her chin down as if she wanted to head-butt him. If she did, he would reach out, wrap his hands into the long, red braid that swung between her shoulder blades and hold her away from him. His gaze took in the bright spots of color on her cheeks, the challenge in her eyes. He wished she wouldn't pinch her lips together like that. It disguised their fullness and made him want to kiss her, just for good measure.

Before she could say whatever blistering words she was preparing to blast him, someone called his name.

"Hey, Mr. Camden. Lainey."

He looked around to see Red Franklin of Franklin's Emporium, a general store that catered to the tourist crowd—just as everyone else did in Calamity Falls. Red was also the newly elected mayor of the town. After years of trying to supplant the longtime mayor and city council, he'd finally succeeded last November and was determined to make changes.

When he saw that he finally had their attention, he gave them a toothy grin. "You two seem to have good teamwork going here."

"Red, don't let appearances fool you," Lainey said, sweeping Gabe with a frosty stare. He winked at her again.

"Uh, yeah, well, we—the council members and I— are going around and letting people know about the little contest we're going to be having."

"Contest?" Gabe and Lainey said the word in unison, then gave him their complete attention.

4

THE MAYOR PREENED. "One of the big changes we're trying to achieve is to put Calamity Falls on the map, make it known for something besides the, uh..." He glanced over his shoulder at Charles Leppert who was approaching the counter carrying a small electronic gadget with which he claimed to be able to measure the earth's magnetic field. It went with him everywhere. "Interesting, uh, citizens. We're having a contest to find a dish that will be the reason people come to Calamity Falls."

"A dish," Gabe said in a flat tone.

"Yes, a food that will be known the world over as originating in Calamity Falls." He nodded firmly, warming to his subject. "Just like people think of Chicago and pizza, of New Orleans and gumbo, of Boston and baked beans, they'll think of Calamity Falls, and..."

"Mixed nuts?" Lainey suggested dryly.

Red looked insulted. "Now that's just the image we're trying to lose. No, this food will be whatever the finest cook in town creates. It could be a main dish, a dessert, we don't care, just so it's unusual and delicious and everyone will want to visit our town to taste it."

Gabe and Lainey looked at each other, the fire of competition once more igniting between them.

"What's in it for the winning cook?" she asked before Gabe could get the words out of his mouth.

"Five thousand dollars and the right to advertise themselves as the creator of the famous dish. The only thing we ask is that everyone who competes actually develops the dish themselves and doesn't try to pass off someone else's creation as their own. The competition will be held in one month, and all entries will be judged by a panel of expert chefs from some of the finest resorts and restaurants in the state. We're calling this the Calamity Falls Great Chefs' Showdown." With his little piece spoken, Red beamed at them, shook hands all around, and left.

"Five thousand dollars," Lainey murmured, mesmerized by the thought. She could really use that money. "The right to advertise..." She reached behind her back and began untying her apron. "Well, Gabe, it's been fun, but I've got to go."

"Are you kidding? After you've pulled in this crowd of customers?"

She gave him a sassy wink like the ones he'd been giving her. "It's nice to hear you admit I'm responsible for this, but I've got things to do."

"Going to enter the competition, are you?"

"Of course. I'd be crazy not to." She gave him a sly glance. "And you?"

"I'd be crazy not to," he responded, echoing her. He tilted his head and narrowed his eyes as he considered her. "What, do you have in mind?"

"You mean for the competition?"

"That's what we're talking about here, isn't it?"

Lainey crossed her arms at her waist and gazed at him. "Now why would I tell you what I've got in mind? That would be exactly like Hannibal signaling the Romans that he was heading across the Alps on elephant-back.''

Gabe frowned. ''I see your point. Or like the Greeks cutting little windows in their wooden horse to wave out at the Trojans.''

''Or Genghis Khan sending three fourths of his army to attack the Persians while he flanked them and took their cities from behind.'' Lainey fought a grin. She was enjoying this, though she couldn't have said exactly why. One-upping him was getting to be a habit. ''A good general doesn't signal the opposition what the next move is going to be.''

''And the opposition would be…?''

''You.''

''I see.'' Gabe considered that for a moment while Lainey waited for what he would say next. Even more than this little barbed talk, she had enjoyed the entire morning.

''You don't think you have to worry about the other restaurant owners in town?'' he asked.

She held up her hand and ticked off her response on her fingertips. ''Stavros Pappas is definitely someone to be worried about, but he'll only prepare what the stars tell him to cook so pinning himself down to one dish that he would have to prepare over and over in order to perfect it…well, that just wouldn't be possible for him.''

Gabe's half smile faded. ''You're kidding.''

''No. I'm deadly serious. May Ling Schultz over at The Lotus Blossom is a fabulous cook, but she's expecting a baby in a couple of months and I doubt she'll feel much like getting into the competition.''

''There are other restaurants, other chefs.''

''Uh-huh, but I'm better.''

"I thought you said you weren't a cook."

"No, I said I'm not a great baker, but I'm not bad, and I'm a terrific cook."

"So, you're thinking of a main dish of some sort?"

"Maybe." Actually, she'd hadn't thought that far yet, but there was no reason for him to know that. "And you?" she asked nonchalantly. "Do you plan on getting Delilah to bake something?"

She knew she hadn't fooled him when his dark eyes grew wary and his brows drew together. "No, we have to create this ourselves, remember?"

"And you think you can do that?"

"Oh, I've got a few culinary tricks I can use."

"Such as?"

He only grinned mysteriously and said, "So, this showdown is probably all going to come down to you and me, right?"

Something about the way he said it had that crazy tingle starting up her right arm, dancing across her shoulders, and then skiing down to her left palm. She forced herself not to shiver. "That's right. I'll be your major competitor."

To her alarm, he grinned, then he threw back his head and laughed. Customers turned and stared, then smiled at the rich sound.

"What's so funny?" Lainey demanded.

"I think I'm really beginning to like this town."

Lainey gave him an uncertain look. She didn't quite know what to make of his answer. Instead of responding, she turned toward the door. "I've got work to do in my own shop. I'll see you at the Showdown."

"Oh, you'll see me before that," he said, his voice still full of humor. "Martha is so happy I'm having

Delilah bake the wedding cake she invited me to the wedding.''

"MEATBALLS," Lainey muttered, flipping through her recipe file. "Nah, not Southwestern enough."

"What about meatballs with chili in them?" Cody asked. "That's pretty Southwestern. After all people grow chili here, cows, too. Put 'em together. Chili meatballs." He beamed at her and Lainey smiled back.

He was a nice kid. It wasn't his fault he had such an annoying family member. He was a hard worker, too. She'd arrived back at Perk Avenue and had immediately begun the recipe search. Cody had arrived after school and cleaned the place up. The last of the items from the front of the store had been moved into the storeroom. It was ready for the repairs to be made—as soon as everything was straightened out with the insurance company and someone was hired to do the job. She wasn't going to worry about that right now, though. She had to come up with an idea for a recipe.

She flipped a few more cards in the index. "How about a salad of some kind?"

"Too ordinary," Cody said.

"It's a possibility," she murmured, "but I think you're right."

She flipped the cards again, trying to think of something wonderful, unique, a surefire winner. Gabe came to mind. Somehow he'd decided she wasn't a great baker. In fact, he was sure of it. Ha! She'd show him. "A dessert?"

"With chocolate. Most people like chocolate." He propped his elbow on the counter and put his chin in his hand as he gazed at her. "I like chocolate."

"You do?" She was only half-listening. A dessert would be a great idea. After all, what did people think of when they thought of cheesecake? They thought of New York. If she came up with something truly fabulous, it might be duplicated all around the world. People would think of Calamity Falls, of Perk Avenue, whenever they ate it.

"Not the gooey stuff, though, like in a box of chocolates. Guys like it in brownies, cookies, stuff like that."

She looked up and blinked. "What?"

"Chocolate," he said earnestly. "It makes people fall in love."

Lainey almost laughed but then she saw how serious he was. "Really?"

"Yeah." His eyes, which she now realized were a great deal like his Uncle Gabe's, took on a dreamy look. "We studied it last year in biology. It sends off sparks in your brain, endorphins that make people fall in love."

She nodded. "So you don't think it would be playing with fire for me to create a chocolate dessert? After all, we could have people falling in love right and left in here."

He brightened. "You think so? I could help you with taste tests and stuff." He paused and she watched, fascinated as a wash of red touched his cheeks. "I'd be your guinea pig."

"That's very sweet of you, Cody," she said, reaching out to give his arm an affectionate squeeze. "I'll take you up on that offer."

The red in his face deepened and with an embarrassed laugh, he lurched to his feet. "I'd better get home. Gabe expects me to get some stuff done around the house before he gets there. See you tomorrow.''

Lainey called goodbye to his retreating back and then chuckled to herself. She recalled her teenage years well enough to remember how painful it had sometimes been to talk to members of the opposite sex. She didn't know if Cody was shy around her because he was always shy or because she was a woman. He would have to get over that someday. Thinking about him, brought her thoughts back to Gabe. She wondered what had taken place in their lives that had caused Cody to be living with his uncle instead of his mother or grandparents. Someday when Cody was less shy around her, she would ask him. In the meantime, she had a fabulous dish to create. She just wished she knew what the heck it was going to be.

THE WEDDING of Martha and Julius took place in the local community center and was as unusual as Lainey had expected it to be. She had looked forward to seeing what the bride and groom would come up with and she wasn't disappointed.

Along with the traditional ceremony performed by a local minister, they also had a rabbi and a leader of a Wiccan group participate in the ceremony. They were all friends of Julius's and he hadn't wanted to hurt anyone's feelings by asking only one of them to officiate. The music had a definite New Age tone to it. After the ceremony, Lainey's grandfather and his new bride had walked down the aisle to zither music and then through an arch of fire axes held aloft by the volunteer fire brigade. As assistant fire chief, she had participated in that. Everyone had then followed, crowding into the large annex of the center for the reception where a five-piece band was playing. The entire evening was shaping up to be an event that would be talked about for years. Even in a town where oddities were an everyday occurrence, a wedding with so many things going on at once was unusual.

Lainey had seen Gabe and Cody in the crowd and felt glad that the two of them had attended together. She wondered if it had been much of a struggle to get Cody into a jacket and tie.

She had made her way through the throngs of people—greeting some, meeting others, managing to pull a beaming Julius and a radiant Martha aside for personal congratulations.

Eventually she found herself at the table where the wedding cake was on display, ready to be cut. The cake turned out to be as beautiful and unique as Lainey knew it would be. Three tiers tall, the cake itself was chocolate and the frosting was caramel, beige as desert sand, decorated with replicas of desert plants. Tiny yellow flowers like those of a palo verde tree were scattered across it, as were frosting representations of many other desert plants. The only thing that didn't seem to fit were the bride and groom on top. They didn't resemble anything Lainey had ever seen before—a grizzled old prospector and his snaggle-toothed wife. Dismayed, she stared at the little figurines, wondering where they'd come from.

"I know," Gabe's voice said from behind her shoulder. "Delilah and I were both stunned when Martha dropped them by the store."

"Where did she get them?" Lainey asked. "A joke store?"

"A gift from the Fina boys."

"Oh, and she and Julius were too polite to not use them."

"Actually, I think she and Julius like them. There's no accounting for taste, is there?" he said.

Even though that was exactly what she'd been thinking, Lainey felt compelled to defend her grandfather and his new bride. She turned to him. "Those figures have a certain rustic charm."

"Like the Finas, themselves," Gabe responded. "Did you know they're planning to do some prospecting around here, looking for the gold their great, great, great uncle Rudolph found and then lost?"

"I know. Good luck to them. People have been looking for that for over one hundred twenty years."

"They say they have an edge because they figure maybe they think like Rudolph did and that will eventually lead them to the treasure."

"I'm not sure that's such a good idea. Everything old Rudolph Shipper tried turned to dust. He was bad luck on the hoof."

"The Fina boys say they don't believe in luck, only hard work."

"You seem to know a lot about the Finas," Lainey said as she gave him a surreptitious inspection. Darn, he looked good in a black suit and a silvery gray tie. His shirt was a bright, crisp white, a striking contrast to the healthy, even bronze of his skin. Inwardly, she sighed, thinking it was a crying shame that such a good-looking man should be so annoying.

"They've been around Coffee & Such lately," Gabe answered, his eyes shifted slightly. "And I joined their gym."

Lainey grinned. "What kind of sales pitch did they use on you? The old arm-twisting routine?"

He winced. "Nah, arm wrestling. I lost." He reached up and rubbed the muscles in his right bicep as if they still hurt. "The bet was that if I won they'd quit bugging me about it. If Bison won, I'd join."

"And Bison won. How did you get suckered into that?"

Gabe shrugged as if sorry he'd ever brought it up. "We were playing poker. We'd all had a few beers. I thought I could take him. I was wrong."

She gave him a sly look. "Do you think your arm is hurt too badly for you to be able to participate in the Great Chefs' Showdown?"

"Don't sound so hopeful." His eyes held a devilish twinkle. "I intend to compete and I intend to win."

"Brave words," she taunted. The truth was, he might win. Her need to prove to him that she was a great baker had pushed her into trying to perfect a chocolate dessert, but it still wasn't quite right. The only good thing about having her shop closed was that she could devote time to her contest entry.

Gabe seemed to have thought of that, too, because he said, "My insurance company is ready to roll on your repairs."

She nodded. "Week after next. I plan to have a grand reopening when it's finished. Should attract lots of business."

"Why? What are you giving away?"

"Wait and see." Darned if she knew, but she wouldn't tell him that. Let him stew. "What about your car? Can it be fixed?"

"Yup, brakes and all."

"Keep it away from my shop, will you?"

"Now, I thought you might want to go for a ride with me someday."

"I don't think so. I've seen you drive."

"Chicken," he taunted.

Ready for a lively argument, Lainey opened her mouth to respond, but was interrupted by Bull Fina, who came up behind her, took her arm and said, "Come on, Lainey. The dancing is starting."

Before she could catch a breath, he'd pulled her into the dancing right behind Julius and Martha, who had finished the traditional first dance of the bride and groom. Other people were crowding onto the floor, as well. Cedric, wearing a tuxedo that looked like a charming relic of the nineteen fifties, and Charlotte in a lavender taffeta gown, swept into a fox-trot.

Starina glided by with a partner and Lainey stared. Starina's hair stood up around her head in a shiny, white crest. She had forsaken her usual mechanic's overalls for a hot little red dress that showed off her legs. It was amazing what could be hidden under a pair of overalls, Lainey thought.

It took her a few seconds to get over her surprise at Starina's appearance and give her attention to Bull. He was looking down at their feet, laboriously counting steps.

"One, two, three, four," he said under his breath as if counting cadence in a military march. He caught her looking at him and said, "My mom taught all three of us boys to dance, but I'm not good at the slow ones."

Since the band was playing a fast tune, and everyone else was dancing to it, Lainey said, "I think we could pick up the pace a little."

He gave her a grateful look. "You think so?" He grasped her around the waist with both hands and bounced her into the air.

"Wait, Bull, I—" She gulped as he set her back on

the dance floor with a thud that reverberated from the soles of her feet to the top of her head. Bull swung her around, spinning her away from him and then back. With a delighted chuckle, he dipped her into a swoop that had the hair she'd piled so artfully on top of her head brushing the floor. The hem of her long, lime-green slip dress whipped above her knees.

"Now this is dancing!" he crowed as he spun her again.

"Bull, I'm... Wait... Could we just...?" She wanted to stop, catch her breath, throw up, anything to stop the dizzying ride she was on, but Bull had a manic light in his eyes as he swirled and twirled her around the floor. Alarmed that he might pick her up and swing her over his shoulders, she held on for dear life. Other dancers scattered away from them like chaff before the wind and still they danced, galloping across the floor in wild abandon to the music.

It seemed to go on forever—trotting, galloping, turning, spinning. It was like being caught in a washing machine gone mad. They moved so fast, Lainey could feel her cheeks getting windburned. She prayed for the dance to end.

Finally, the song ended just as black spots were beginning to form before Lainey's eyes. She gasped and looked for a place to pass out. She managed to remain upright as Bull said, "Lainey, you're a great little dancer. Wanna go again?"

"N-n-no," she stammered, trying to hold onto her stomach and smooth her hair at the same time. "Maybe later," she added, when she saw his hopeful expression fall. "Your mom did a great job of teaching you to dance. No doubt about that."

He beamed. "She's a great little lady. Raised us all

by herself and supported us with her job at a theme park.''

"Theme park?" Lainey wheezed. Centrifugal force seemed to have sucked all of the air out of her lungs and she was fighting to get it back.

"Yeah, she operated some of the rides," he said proudly, hitching up his pants. "Roller coaster, Tilt-A-Whirl carousel, Death Doom. You know, the more exciting ones."

"How lovely." No doubt, that was where she'd learned the dancing techniques she'd taught her son. She turned away from him to see Bison and Bruiser coming toward her as if thrown from a rocket launcher, the same reckless light in their eyes that Bull had shown.

With a squawk of alarm, she looked for a place to hide. She was saved when an arm slid around her waist and Gabe pulled her to him. "Camden Damsel Rescue Service," he whispered into her ear, and slipped her into the crowd of dancers. She peeked over his shoulder to see the disappointed expression on Bison and Bruiser's faces. She gave them a smile that said, "Maybe later," even as she made plans to find an escape route if either of them asked her to dance.

Finally, she glanced at Gabe, who tilted his head and grinned at her. "That was quite a performance."

"Purely involuntary on my part," she admitted, grateful that the world seemed to be righting itself. "I was just hanging on for dear life and praying for it to end."

He chuckled and Lainey felt a delicious shiver run up her spine and into the roots of her hair. Gabe scooped her closer.

Lainey's heart, which had just settled back to its normal rhythm, picked up again. Confusion overtook her because she didn't know what to make of this man. Gabe had seemed determined to run her out of business, he'd practically destroyed her shop, he'd warned her away from his nephew, he challenged her at every turn, and now he'd rescued her and was dancing as if he actually enjoyed it. No, she didn't know what to make of this man.

"What's the matter?" he asked, his dark blue eyes studying the confusion on her face.

"I'm not sure I should be dancing with the competition."

"Oh, quit analyzing things and just enjoy it," he advised.

So she gave up trying to think it through and did as he suggested, moving with him in a smooth rhythm that matched their steps, and even, she discovered to her further surprise, their heartbeats.

The dance lasted for several seconds in silence. As he'd suggested, Lainey felt herself relaxing and actually enjoying the dance. "Bull said his mother taught him to dance," she finally said.

Gabe craned his neck to see Bull lift his new partner, a girl who worked at the bank, into the air, twirl her around a couple of times and thump her back onto her feet before taking off with her at a thundering gallop. "Really? I thought he'd learned that technique from a Mixmaster blender."

Lainey giggled as he took her through a smooth turn. "Where did you learn?"

"My mom did it the easy way, made me take dancing lessons when I was ten. I ask you, what mother makes their kid do that these days?"

"Did Cody take lessons?" Lainey asked, spying the

young man standing alone near the bar, sipping some punch.

Gabe turned his head and followed her gaze. ''No. Maybe I should have made him take them.''

''He looks lonely,'' Lainey said, and felt Gabe stiffen. ''Hasn't he made any friends since moving here? He always seems to be alone.''

''He'll be all right. He's a tough kid.'' His tone had a harsh edge to it that warned her away from saying anything more and the dance ended at that moment.

Uncomfortable with the sudden change in Gabe, she gave him a swift smile. ''Thanks for the dance, and for rescuing me from the Finas. I think I'll go get something to drink.''

That must have been the wrong thing to say because he simply took her arm and said, ''I'm thirsty, too.''

Looking ahead, she realized the mistake she'd made. Cody was still standing by the bar and it must have looked to Gabe like she was heading straight for his vulnerable young nephew. She pulled her arm from his grasp and said, ''I've changed my mind. It looks like Grandpa and Martha are ready to cut the cake. I want to watch.'' She whirled away from him.

She didn't glance back, but could almost feel his annoyance directed right between her shoulder blades because she had that disturbing tingle there again.

As she was positioning herself in the crowd to get a good view of the cake cutting, she heard a familiar voice say, ''There you are.'' She glanced around and with a glad cry, turned to hug her best friend, Jo Quillan Houston and her husband, Case.

''I didn't think you two were going to make it,'' she said.

Jo patted her rounded tummy, five months pregnant

with her first baby. "I'm sorry we missed the ceremony. Junior here was sitting on my bladder the whole drive from Phoenix. I've seen the inside of every gas station bathroom along Interstate 10. The one in that new truck stop east of Tucson is quite nice in case you're interested."

Lainey laughed and hugged her again, then asked how they were. Jo, a reporter for several years at her uncle's newspaper, the Calamity Falls *Ingot,* was now working at a major paper in Phoenix. Case was an investigator with the attorney general's office. They had met the previous fall when Case had been in town investigating a case of fraud and Jo had dogged his every step until he had let her help him and given her an exclusive on the story. They'd fallen in love during that time and after they had married, Jo had left Calamity Falls. Lainey was thrilled for their happiness, but she missed her best friend.

Case brought them glasses of punch though Jo warned him he might regret it later. Then he was drawn away by Starina who'd gotten to know him on his first visit. In fact, he'd been in her workshop when her yet-to-be perfected perpetual motion machine had blown sky-high, taking the roof, their eyebrows and some of Starina's hair. No doubt, she was telling him of the improvements she'd made to the machine. Lainey only hoped Starina would give the fire department a little warning before she tested the "improvements" this time. Her test runs usually happened around noon, interrupting everyone's lunch when the fire whistle went off.

Jo and Lainey found a couple of chairs against the wall, away from the merriment and sat down.

After they'd caught up on the local news, Jo said,

"Uncle Don called and told me about your shop being wrecked."

Lainey winced at the memory. "I should have called you, but I was pretty busy." She nodded toward Gabe, who was leading Martha onto the dance floor.

"That's the guy who lost his brakes."

Jo straightened and craned her neck. "And he's here?"

Lainey told the story of the cake, the way he'd charmed Martha and befriended Julius. "All of which I wouldn't mind if he wasn't trying to take my livelihood away from me."

"Oh, don't you think you're exaggerating just a little?"

"Well, maybe," Lainey admitted. "But there's this...other thing."

"What other thing?"

Lainey looked around, embarrassed to have anyone else hear what she was about to say. "He makes me itch."

Jo looked concerned. "Itch? You mean like an allergy?"

"I guess. No. It's more like a tingle."

Jo stared at her. "A tingle?"

"Yeah, and it never hits in the same place twice."

"I don't believe you," Jo said, shaking her head.

"Why would I lie?"

"No, I mean I can't believe you've forgotten about the tingle."

Lainey rolled her eyes. "Oh, please, this isn't like what you used to get. Yours always preceded disaster."

"Not always."

"Remember when you used to get the tingle and

you'd set me up with a blind date which would turn out to be a disaster?''

''You're exaggerating.''

''Oh, yeah? Remember Maxie?''

Jo looked away. ''He was recommended by a sheriff's deputy I met on a story.''

''Maxie was a bounty hunter. He had more weapons than the Marine Corps. He carried them in the trunk of his car—which was a nineteen sixty-three Dodge, by the way.''

''You must have felt very safe on your date.''

''I was scared to death. When he tried to kiss me good-night, the handle of his gun nearly broke my rib.''

''Well, okay, sometimes when I got the tingle, things didn't work out exactly like I thought they would, but something exciting usually happened. What's happened since you met Gabe and you got the tingle?''

''He drove his car through the front of my shop.''

''See there?'' Jo said triumphantly. ''That was exciting.''

''Let's change the subject,'' Lainey said. ''I don't want to hear anymore about this tingle.''

''You're closing your eyes to reality. Gabe Camden is the most interesting man to land in this town since...well, since Case did last fall.''

''So, what's your point?''

Jo winked. ''Eligible man, beautiful single woman. Don't waste time.''

Lainey looked across to where Gabe was talking to a group of people. He excused himself and walked over to where Cody stood alone. He spoke to Cody, who shrugged. ''It's not like that,'' she said.

Jo turned to see where Lainey was looking. ''You could make it like that,'' she responded with a sly grin.

5

"DON'T YOU WORRY about a thing, Julius," Bison Fina said, nodding his closely-shaven head. "We'll look after Lainey for you."

"That isn't necessary," she tried to protest, but Julius enfolded her in a bear hug, then passed her over to Martha for a bone-cracker that rendered her speechless. By the time she regained her breath, the newlyweds were dodging birdseed and racing for their car. They would be gone for more than a month, first visiting Italy for two weeks, then going on a cruise.

Lainey felt a tremendous letdown after the wedding and reception. She stood with the rest of the well-wishers and watched her grandfather and his new bride drive away.

A huge change had just taken place in her life. She had been expecting and anticipating this for a long time, but she should have realized what an impact it would have on her. She was no stranger to changes like this. Her parents had divorced when she was fifteen and rather than choose to live with either of them in Phoenix, she had moved to Calamity Falls with Julius when he'd retired from his job as a university chemistry professor. She had finished high school in Calamity Falls and taken community college classes before deciding that a career in retail was for her. Throughout it all, Julius had always been there. A widower for twenty years, he'd shown no interest in re-marrying until Martha had come along. Somehow Lainey had thought things would remain the same forever. She knew better now. Julius and Martha would create a life together.

Lainey had to do the same thing. Something about that thought made her feel melancholy, though she couldn't pinpoint exactly why. She pondered it as she said goodbye to the rest of the guests, made a promise to visit Jo in Phoenix before the baby came, and helped clean up the community center.

The Finas left to open up the gym for the evening workout crowd and she started home to the little house she rented. She hadn't lived in it very long. Jo had once lived there before she married Chase, and though tiny, it was still larger than Lainey's previous apartment. After Jo left, Lainey had rented the little house and settled in happily.

Walking easily through the early spring evening, Lainey was glad for the welcome sight of her home. As she passed Mrs. Rios's house, she was careful to call out a cheerful hello to her neighbor who peeked through her living room curtains whenever anyone appeared outside. The old lady kept a bucket of rocks by the front door and let fly at anything that looked or sounded vaguely threatening. She'd nearly brained the Fed-Ex man a couple of weeks ago and it had taken some fast talking on Lainey's part to keep him from calling the sheriff.

Deep in thought about the changes in her life, about what Jo had said and mostly about Gabe Camden, Lainey was brought up short when she saw someone waiting for her on her front steps. Startled, she stopped, but then realized it was Cody.

He rose self-consciously when he saw her coming up the walk.

"Hi, uh, hi, Lainey," he said, hitching up one shoulder in an awkward greeting. "I just wondered if you'd gotten home okay."

Even in the uncertain glow from the porch light, Lainey could see that he looked unhappy. Immediately concerned, she said, "Oh, yes, made it just fine. Would you like to come in for a..." She stopped to think about what kinds of things he liked to drink. She could hardly offer him a glass of wine as she would an adult. "Soda?"

"Sure," he said, breaking into a smile. "That'd be great." He gave Mrs. Rios's house a wary glance. "Boy am I glad to see you. Your neighbor was threatening to call the police."

"She's a little nervous," Lainey admitted, secretly breathing a prayer of thanksgiving that the old lady hadn't defended the neighborhood with rocks.

She unlocked the door and he followed her inside, stopping to look around at her tiny home. "Nice place," he said. "Gabe is still fixing up our house. He wants to do some remodeling."

He said it as if he didn't really care what Gabe did with the place and Lainey's heart sank at his tone of indifference. The house Gabe had bought for himself and his nephew was actually one of the largest and most imposing of the Victorian structures in town. It had been built by executives of the eastern copper-mining companies who had moved in to make Calamity Falls profitable more than one hundred years ago. It was on a street which was up two more flights of stairs that connected those streets carved into the mountainside, so it wasn't visible from Lainey's home.

"It could be a beautiful house once it's fixed up," Lainey said as she found a couple of glasses, filled them with ice and cola and handed one to Cody. She sat in her favorite chair by the window and he settled himself on her small sofa.

"Yeah, I guess."

Conversation lagged. Obviously Gabe was a touchy subject with Cody, so she changed it and asked about school, then winced at the triteness of the question.

"It's all right." Cody drank his soda as he studied some watercolors on her wall.

Another touchy subject. Lainey looked at him, puzzled because she couldn't figure out what was wrong and what she should say. They never had difficulty talking when they were together at Perk Avenue.

"It's hard making the change to a new school in the middle of high school, and past the middle of the school year," she said. "I know because I moved here when I was fifteen. My parents had just divorced, my mom was moving to California and I didn't want to go, so I came here with Julius. It was culture shock."

Cody turned his attention to her and she saw some of the bleakness leave his eyes. "Yeah, it's hard," he said.

"Gabe says you haven't made any friends yet."

"My friends are all in Tucson," he responded.

With a mental sigh, Lainey sipped the soda she didn't want and tried to think of where this conversation might be going.

After a long, awkward silence, Cody said, "I was wondering if you'd like to meet some of them."

"Are they coming to see you?"

"Uh, no. I'm going to see them at a concert next

weekend. I thought maybe you'd like to go.'' Suddenly, his face flamed bright scarlet. "As my date.''

"Excuse me?'' Lainey stared at the blushing teenager.

"It's Roadkill,'' he said by way of explanation. His voice held the kind of hushed reverence an archaeologist's would have for evidence of a newly discovered civilization.

"Oh?'' Lainey's lips stretched into a stiff smile as she floundered frantically for something to say. ''Is that right?''

"They're the bomb.''

"Really?'' She had heard of them, and "the bomb'' certainly described the group. A heavy metal band with enough crashing guitars and drums to make it sound as if they truly were setting off a bomb.

"Have you heard 'Deathgrip'? That's their biggest hit.''

"Can't say that I have.''

"Great lyrics,'' Cody said, bouncing slightly as he quoted some of the lyrics. "'You don't know me, I don't know you, but death's got us in its grip, so sad, so true.' Really makes you think.''

About clinical depression, no doubt, Lainey thought, but she offered an understanding smile. "I'm sure it does.''

"So? Will you go with me?'' Cody's smile slipped and his eyes took on a worried look.

Praying that she could say the right thing and not damage his fragile teenage ego, Lainey sat forward in her chair. "I don't think that would be a very good idea, Cody. I'm quite a bit older than you are.''

"That's okay. You still look really young.''

She nearly choked. "Um, thank you, but…''

"The lighting's never good at those concerts. No one would know." He leaned forward and gave her a searching look. "You don't have any wrinkles to speak of."

"Thank you, I think. But that's not what I meant. It really wouldn't look good for us to go out. People would think…" What? She couldn't come up with anything except "…that I'm a dirty old woman."

Cody snorted with skepticism. "Nuh-uh. What are you talking about? Nobody's gonna think anything about it. In this town everyone's a little bit crazy. Who's gonna care if you go out with someone younger than you? And it's just a concert. Not like we're going to be together for life or anything." He blushed again and closed his mouth as if trying to think of another line of argument.

"Oh, Cody," she floundered, distressed. "I don't know what to say. I just don't think it would be a good idea. Besides, you're my employee. It might…might ruin our working relationship."

"That is so lame." Cody surged to his feet. The soda in his glass sloshed over the rim and onto his hand. Awkwardly, he set the glass down on the antique steamer trunk she used for a coffee table. "Ah, never mind." He lurched around it and hurried toward the door. "Good night."

Lainey jumped to her feet. "Cody, wait," she called after him, but he was gone, closing the door firmly behind himself.

She threw her hands in the air. Great. She'd offended and hurt him and she certainly hadn't meant to. She knew he was having a hard time since he'd arrived in this town where he didn't want to live. She had thought he viewed her as a friend and she'd hoped he liked her, but she hadn't realized he had other feelings. The boy had a crush on her or he never would have risked the embarrassment he'd just experienced. Oh great. She didn't know what to do.

This was going to change their pleasant working relationship, and not for the better.

Lainey walked to the door, opened it and stared out into the darkness, though he was long gone. Saddened, she closed and locked the door, then cleared their glasses off the table, and headed for her bedroom. It had been a long, eventful day and she was tired. She planned to take a long, relaxing bath and think over the changes that had taken place in her life in the past week. If she thought hard enough, she might even come to like some of them.

As promised, she lounged in the bath for nearly an hour, not thinking over the changes in her life, but stewing over Cody and his invitation. Even though she knew she'd done the right thing, she also knew she'd hurt him.

When she got out of the tub, she put on her favorite nightshirt, a hot pink one with Mickey Mouse on the front and was heading for bed when she heard a commotion out front.

"Hey, lady," she heard a man shout. "Watch out!"

A loud thunk against one of her porch posts had her scurrying through her house, flipping on lights as she went.

"Hey, ma'am! Ouch!" the man yelled. "You almost hit me with that."

"I know. I'm trying to hit you, you Peeping Tom, whoever you are." Mrs. Rios, voice quavery with fear, yelled back.

"I wasn't peeping. I'm a…a friend of Lainey's. I was going to visit her."

"That's a damned lie. Lainey doesn't have any friends who visit her this time of night, and certainly not any men!" A shower of rocks hit the side of the house.

Mrs. Rios must be throwing them with both hands, Lainey thought frantically as she unlocked the door and threw it open to find Gabe cowering on her front porch. "Stop, Mrs. Rios. You'll break my windows."

The barrage of rocks stopped.

"It's okay. He just came to visit. He's not going to hurt you."

"Hell, girl," the old lady called out. "It's not me I'm worried about. If the light was better, I could knock him in the eye at fifty paces. It's you I'm worried about. What kind of man would go sneaking around your house at this time of night? He's up to no good."

"It's okay." Lainey grabbed his arm and hauled him to his feet. Eyes wide, he stared at her as if she'd saved his life. "He really is a friend. A…friend of Julius's."

"All right, then." Bucket of rocks in hand, Mrs. Rios turned to go back into her house. "But if he gives you any trouble, just sing out. I can take care of him for you."

Lainey pulled Gabe inside. He gulped and collapsed into one of her chairs, then ran a hand over his face.

"Is she crazy?" he asked, after a second. "I thought she was going to kill me."

"Nah, if she'd wanted to, she probably could have. About sixty years ago, she was the star pitcher for the Phoenix Orange Blossoms, a women's professional baseball team. She still has a heck of a curve ball. She thought you were a prowler. Just wanted to scare you."

Gabe sat up straight and tried to regain his dignity by smoothing his hair and tugging at the collar of his dark green shirt. "She succeeded. Why doesn't she just call the cops if she's scared of a prowler?"

"She likes to take care of things for herself. She's very independent." Worried, Lainey watched him carefully until some color started returning to his face. "Were you...out for a walk or something, Gabe?"

"No. I came to see you."

A little spurt of happiness darted through her. "Oh really? Why?"

"I want to ask you to go out with my nephew."

Lainey's mouth fell open.

DAMN, GABE THOUGHT. Even when she was doing an imitation of a fish, she was beautiful. Her skin was flushed, damp hair sagged from a loose topknot and tendrils of it curved along the length of her neck, one even making the tricky little curve into the base of her throat in a seductive curl. She—and her entire tiny house—smelled of lavender.

This was the pits. Being at a loss about what to do with Cody was the pits. Sitting in her living room while she hovered over him wearing a knee-length nightshirt with Mickey's big ears resting gently over her breasts was the very pit of hell. He figured Mickey's happy smile was just about where her belly button would be. Strange, but he'd never before had the urge to kiss Mickey smack on the lips.

"...crazy?"

Oops, she was saying something. He'd better get his mind off of what was under her nightshirt and pay attention.

He forced himself to focus. "What?"

"I asked if you'd gone crazy," she said, clamping her hands onto her hips.

Uh-oh, this wasn't going quite the way he'd expected it to. "No. I want you to go out with Cody."

"I can't imagine why. Ever since he started working for me, you've been suspicious, though you had no reason to be."

"Well," he shifted uncomfortably in his chair. Damn, he wished she'd go put on a robe. He couldn't concentrate. He was here to talk about Cody, not drool over Lainey. His eyes drifted to an intriguing scar on the outside of her right knee and he wondered how it had come to be there. "He came home pretty upset, said he'd been to see you."

"And…?"

And Gabe had been jealous for about ten seconds until he'd realized how truly distraught his nephew was. On the one hand, he'd been thrilled that the boy had broken down and was willing to talk. On the other hand, Gabe could hardly believe what Cody had said.

"And he was pretty upset when you turned him down. Why did you do that?"

She gaped at him. "I should think that would be obvious. He's sixteen. I'm twenty-eight."

"It's just an age thing, then?"

"No!"

"Then you can change your mind." He stood up suddenly and began pacing. He always thought better when he paced. Her living room was so small, though, he could zip from one side of it to the other in about five strides, passing within inches of her as he did so. Each time, he caught a mighty lungful of her lavender scent. He sure wished she'd go put on a neck-to-toe robe—made of iron.

As if she'd read his mind, though he sincerely hoped she hadn't fully probed its murky depths or she'd be borrowing her neighbor's bucket of rocks, Lainey turned suddenly and disappeared down a short hallway. She came back wearing a white chenille robe and fuzzy, white bunny slippers. The robe was knee-length and didn't do much to keep his mind off her legs. What was it with this woman, anyway? She always wore long dresses or skirts, but a short robe at home. He would ask her about it sometime when he was sure she wouldn't hit him with something.

"Listen, Gabe. I don't know why you're here, but I can't believe it's to talk me into going to a heavy metal rock concert with Cody."

"You're wrong. That's exactly why I'm here. He was pretty broken up when you turned him down."

She threw her hands into the air. "I can't go out with him. He's a kid."

"He thinks he's in love with you."

"No." She rolled her eyes. "It's just a little crush. Everyone has them. He'll get over it. You said yourself he's a tough kid."

Gabe shook his head and started his pacing once again. "This is different, believe me." He paused, turned, paced some more. "He's the most intense person you'll ever meet."

"Except for you," Lainey answered. "Could you please quit pacing? I just bought that rug you're wearing out."

"Oh." He looked down at the pretty, Persian-style rug. "Sorry." He sat down again. "Let me tell you some things about Cody and you'll understand why I'm asking you to do this."

She gave him a wary look, but she perched on the

edge of the sofa opposite him and said, "Okay, go ahead."

"Cody had a girlfriend in Tucson, someone he'd liked since the seventh grade. Last fall he got up the nerve to ask her out and pretty soon they were dating. He was nuts about her. She was all he could talk about or think about. His grades in school started to slide. He quit the basketball team. I was afraid he would quit school, too, except that he saw her there every day so he had a reason to go. Then, right before Christmas, she broke up with him. He was beside himself, spent weeks in his room, depressed. When I tried to help him get over it, we fought. I didn't know what else to do, so I moved us here, bought the shop, thought we'd start a new life."

Lainey frowned. "You didn't think about what a huge change that would be for him, along with the breakup with his girlfriend?"

He shrugged. How could he explain his reasons? He'd only had Cody's best interests at heart, but now he doubted that he'd done the right thing. "Sure," he admitted. "But he seemed so apathetic, I thought the change would be good. Besides, I had other things to consider."

"Like what?"

Gabe paused, thinking it over. He hadn't talked about this very much to anyone. "Cody's mother, my younger sister, Shelly, went through the same thing, only with her, it didn't stop with one boy breaking her heart. She lurched from one bad relationship to another. I never knew what to do to stop her or to help her. She was married, and though her husband adopted Cody, he wasn't his father. I don't know who Cody's father is. She never said." He paused, remembering his sister.

''She was twenty-one when she died of Hepatitis C. Don't know where she picked it up, but she didn't try to fight it, not even for Cody's sake. He was two at the time.''

As he'd talked, he had watched Lainey's face undergo a change from annoyed to curious to compassionate. Her big, brown eyes were drenched with sympathy for Shelly and Cody. For him. Something about the look in her eyes made a knot in his gut seem to untie itself and smooth out.

''I'm so sorry, Gabe,'' Lainey said softly. ''It must have been horrible for you. If it's any comfort, you've done a great job with Cody. But I still don't understand how my going to this concert will help him.''

Sensing that he was about to break down her defenses, Gabe sat forward eagerly. ''It'll get him out, get him thinking about something besides himself. His Tucson friends will all be there. They'll see you, think he's quite a stud. It'll be a boost for his ego.''

She lifted an eyebrow at him. ''That's about the most chauvinistic statement I've ever heard. As much as I like Cody, I don't think I'm interested in being a boost for his ego. He needs to develop interests here in town, and—''

''*You're* what he's interested in here in town.''

Anxiously, Gabe watched her face, knowing she had no answer to that statement. It was true and they both knew it. From their past dealings, he was fully aware that she didn't think much of him, but she genuinely liked Cody. He was counting on that to tip her decision in his favor. ''I'm worried about him, Lainey. I don't want to see him going the same way Shelly did.''

Deep in thought, Lainey chewed her bottom lip. Gabe felt his attention wandering from his concern for

Cody to another inspection of his reluctant hostess. She was sitting with her arms looped loosely around her knees, staring at a small glass dolphin on the coffee table. Her dark auburn brows were drawn together in a frown. He didn't much like the treatment she was giving that lip. He could think of a number of things that he'd like to do with it, but each one of them involved him being the one nibbling on her lips.

Yeah, right before she decked him, he thought and was surprised by how that made his heart sink.

LAINEY GLANCED UP in time to see sadness fill Gabe's dark eyes. His frown drooped, wiping away the dimple in his right cheek that she found so intriguing. Seeing him like that, worried about Cody, had guilt kicking at her. Going with Cody to a concert was really a small thing. She liked him, after all, and wanted him to find happiness. True, he'd made little effort to find friends here in Calamity Falls, and while she didn't want him to be mooning around over her, she could at least be his friend and go to the concert with him.

Besides, Gabe had swallowed his pride and come to ask for her help. He'd even run the gauntlet of Mrs. Rios and her bucket of rocks. A man willing to do that deserved to get what he was asking for.

At last, she released a big sigh and said, "Oh, all right. I'll go with him, but I don't want you to turn around and say I'm chasing him or any other disgusting thing like that."

"It's a deal." Gabe shot to his feet, a big grin flashing across his face. "I'll make this up to you, I promise. I'll do anything."

This sounded intriguing. Lainey gave him a skeptical squint. "Oh? What, exactly?"

Immediately on guard, Gabe said, "I don't know. I'll think of something."

"Will you withdraw from the Showdown?"

He stared at her. "Heck, no."

She hadn't really wanted him to. She only wanted to see what he would say. "So when you say you'll do anything, you don't really mean *anything*, right?"

A slow smile tilted his lips, pocking his cheek with that dimple. Really, she thought, she needed to quit obsessing about that dimple.

"No."

His burst of honesty made them both laugh.

"Well, then," she continued, leaving her seat and stopping to lean against the doorpost. She crossed her arms at her waist. "In your method of thinking, what would 'anything' include?"

His smile was joined by a devilish light in his eyes. His gaze touched on her face, noting the color she could feel reddening her cheeks. That was one unfortunate thing about being a redhead. Her complexion gave her away so she could never hide her true feelings or even what she was thinking. Along with the color in her cheeks, she felt a sudden shimmer in her veins, then that familiar tingle, followed by a rush of heat through her body. She almost moaned aloud, but managed to swallow it back before she could completely embarrass herself.

"I'll have to let you know," he finally said, his voice low and intimate. "Unless, of course, *you've* got something in mind."

Lainey shook her head slowly from side to side. "Not a thing," she said, knowing that he could read the lie in her face.

He leaned forward until their noses were barely

inches apart. "Lainey, correct me if I'm wrong, but I think we've both got something in mind." His eyes had gone even darker, his voice was a low, husky growl that nearly turned the rush of heat she'd just felt into a lava flow. "Something that would convince that neighbor of yours to throw that entire bucket of rocks at me."

Lainey looked into his eyes, rimmed by his thick, dark lashes, then down to his lips, so close to hers. "You're...you're wrong," she said. Her voice cracked and quavered, but she went on. "You're assuming that I'm attracted to you, and that's completely untrue."

He laughed and bent ever so slightly to brush the tip of his nose against her skin, over the arch of her cheek-bone, then stopped near her ear. She could have sworn she felt his lips there. "Lainey, I have to tell you that you're not a good liar."

Quickly, she reached up and pushed him away. "Never mind," she said. "Tell me, how are Cody and I supposed to go on this date to Tucson? Do I drive?"

"What, and destroy his manly pride?"

Her eyes widened. "Don't tell me you're going to drive us?" She had this mental picture of it—Gabe in the front seat, driving and grinning while she and Cody sat in the back in stark silence.

"Nah. Cody's sixteen, you know. He's got his own car. He'll drive you. I bet he even washes it for the occasion. He's got to pick up a couple of his friends when he gets into Tucson."

"Okay." Suddenly, she felt foolish and at the same time, relieved that there would be other people along, even if they were a bunch of teenage boys—though heaven knew what they would think of the "older woman'' with Cody. "That's all settled then." She cleared her throat. "I'll say good-night now."

Gabe turned and put his hand on the knob. "When you get back, I'll stop by and see how it went. He might talk to me about it, but then again, he might not. I was surprised he talked to me about it tonight."

I wish he hadn't, Lainey thought, but then felt guilty because she knew that for some reason, this was very important to Cody, and also to Gabe. When, exactly, had she begun to care so much about what was important to Gabe? "That's not necessary," she said, uncomfortable with her ambivalent feelings.

This was new and strange to her. She always knew her own mind, knew her motivations—except since she'd met Gabe. He'd disturbed her from the moment of their first meeting.

It struck Lainey with a blinding shaft of clarity that she had been wildly attracted to him on that day. It made no sense, but when he'd undercut her prices and hired Delilah away, she had felt betrayed. It was completely ridiculous, but that's the way it was. Lainey, who thought she knew herself so well, had no explanation for it.

"I'll want to hear what you think."

She blinked at him. "What?"

"About the concert. I'll want to know what you think of Roadkill."

"I've got a pretty good idea right now what I think," she answered dryly.

He grinned again. "Don't make snap judgments," he advised as he opened the door and slipped outside. "You might actually enjoy this."

"That's about as likely as you winning the Showdown."

Gabe chuckled, then sobered when he saw that Mrs. Rios's front porch light had flickered on. With a hasty good-night, he took off at a run.

Lainey closed the door and locked it, then headed to bed thinking that the concert might be fun. She loved music, all kinds, but mostly jazz. Surely she'd find something she would like about Roadkill.

6

AFTER MIDNIGHT the next Saturday evening, Lainey waved feebly at Cody as he backed out of her driveway and drove away down the street. The brave smile she'd been propping up all evening was finally allowed to deflate as she pulled her weary body painfully up the front steps and let herself into the house. It was all she could do to bite back a moan as she turned to shut the front door.

All she wanted to do was collapse onto her bed and not move for several days, but it was not to be. Before she could even take her jacket off, there was a soft rap on the door. She peered out to see Gabe Camden gazing anxiously through the lace curtains that covered the front door panes.

"Lainey, let me in." He glanced nervously over his shoulder to Mrs. Rios's house where the front porch light had just come on.

Lainey pulled back the sheer curtains and glared out at him. "Only if I can kill you."

"Why? What's wrong?"

"You lied to me."

Genuinely surprised, he blinked at her. "What? What are you talking about?"

She glared at him. "I'm talking about the sneaky, underhanded, low-down method you used to get your own way. Not that I'm surprised by it, now that I think about it. I wouldn't put anything past you.''

Exasperated, he said, ''I swear I don't know what you're talking about. Come on, let me in. Tell me what happened. I'll see if I can make it right.'' He glanced over his shoulder again as Mrs. Rios stepped outside, her bucket of rocks swaying heavily from her hand. ''What's wrong? I just saw Cody drive off. He seemed okay.''

Although Lainey thought she might like to see her neighbor take aim at Gabe's vulnerable backside again, she was afraid Mrs. Rios might miss and take out a few windows. Besides, if there was any harm to be done to Gabe, Lainey wanted to be the one to do it. She jerked the door open. Gabe slipped inside carrying a covered bakery-style box which he set on a small table nearby.

''Cody *is* fine,'' Lainey answered. Lifting her hand, she jabbed a finger angrily into his chest. ''I'm not. You said I didn't need to drive. You said he had a car.''

Gabe blinked innocently. ''He does.''

''A nineteen seventy-three Volkswagen Beetle.''

''It's a classic. I bought him that car. We have plans to fix it up together.''

''Well, start fixing it.'' Frustrated, she flung out a hand. ''One of the doors won't even open. I had to slide through the window to get in, and in case you haven't noticed, I'm not exactly a tiny woman.''

Gabe's gaze traveled from her head to her toes, then back again, stopping at eye-catching intervals along the way. ''I've noticed.''

Lainey ignored the warm tone of his answer. She was too intent on her list of grievances. ''That car's floor is rusted out. I watched the highway rushing by beneath my feet.''

''Exciting, hmm?''

She gave him a poisonous look. ''You said he was going to pick up a couple of friends.''

''Yeah, so?''

''Five of them.''

Gabe looked delighted. ''Hey, all his best friends were able to go. That's great.''

''They were all crowded into the car with us. It's a wonder we weren't arrested.''

''Uh, well, maybe five extra people were too many to have in that car.''

''Maybe?'' She couldn't believe what she was hearing. Reaching up, Lainey tried to remove her jacket, but the snug sleeves were too much for her. She let her arms drop. ''Do you have any idea how many joints and angles six teenage boys have? Millions.''

''Uh, Lainey...?''

''I had to sit on the lap of a sixteen-year-old who was so embarrassed I thought he was going to die right there on the spot, and how would I have explained that to a police officer?'' Once again, she reached up, grasped the lapels of her jacket, and tried to tug them back so she could remove the jacket. This time, she managed to get it halfway off her shoulders, but then it stuck and she didn't have the strength to go further. Her arms dropped.

''What's the matter?'' Gabe asked, stepping up to ease it off her shoulders and down her arms. He laid it across the back of a chair.

''My back is twisted into a permanent corkscrew,'' she answered, hating the whiny tone of her voice, but unable to stop it. ''Sliding through the window and then maneuvering myself to sit down, then having to perch on that kid's lap...smashing my head up against the roof of the car...my back's twisted like a pretzel. I'm going to be forced to walk sideways for the rest of my life.''

Instantly sympathetic, Gabe said, ''Oh, honey, that's too bad. Here, come and sit down.'' He led her to the sofa and helped her sit, then scooped up her feet and placed them on the coffee table. ''I know just what you're thinking.''

Lainey eased her back against the sofa cushions. Instantly, she felt better, but she wasn't going to let him off that easily. ''Then why aren't you trying to hide all the knives in the house from me?''

He flashed a grin at her. ''You're worn out, exhausted, in fact, and probably hungry.''

''We ate pizza,'' she answered sulkily. Completely against her will, she felt herself beginning to soften toward him.

''That was probably hours ago.''

''Well, yeah.''

''I brought food.''

Interested, she straightened. ''You're kidding.'' She *had* noticed that an enticing smell had entered with him, but she'd been too miserable to pay much attention to it.

''Be right back.'' He scooped the box off the hall table and carried it into the kitchen. A few minutes later, he was back with a plate of food and a glass of wine on a tray. He placed it on her lap, returned to the kitchen for his own food, and sat down beside her.

Stunned, she stared down at what looked like chicken cooked in a chili sauce, topped with multicolored corn tortilla strips. The aroma had her drooling.

She picked up one of the tortilla strips and popped it into her mouth. "I don't know that I should be accepting food from you, Gabe."

"Why not?"

"Because I plan to kill you, remember?"

"You wouldn't want to do something like that on an empty stomach."

She nodded consideringly. "You're right. I need my strength. I'll eat first and then kill you."

With a soft laugh, he picked up her fork and handed it to her.

At the first bite, flavors exploded in her mouth, wakening the hunger she hadn't been aware of feeling. She didn't speak for several minutes while she devoured the meal. "Oh, this is fabulous. Did you make this?"

"Of course." He cut a bite for himself and chewed thoughtfully as if gauging the flavors. "Not bad. I've been working on it for a while."

It suddenly dawned on her that she was sampling his entry in the Great Chefs' Showdown. She looked down at her empty plate. Good grief, if he planned to enter this, she was sunk. "Um, well, maybe I overstated the case when I said it was fabulous."

He arched a brow at her. "What would you say now that you've eaten the whole thing and practically sucked the pattern off the china?"

With great dignity, she set the plate down on the tray and picked up her glass of wine. "I'd say it was adequate."

In truth, compared to the flavors, texture and presentation of his chicken dish, the chocolate dessert she'd been working on seemed bland and ordinary. She would never tell him that, but she made an immediate decision to add some sparkle to her dessert. "I think you might want to add just a pinch more cumin and thicken the sauce a little bit.''

''Oh, really?'' He didn't look the least bit worried by her criticism. ''So, didn't my nephew feed you this evening?''

''I told you, we had pizza.'' She sipped her wine and sighed with contentment. The kinks were easing out of her back. Things were beginning to look better than they had all evening. She gave Gabe a sideways glance from beneath her lashes. He was relaxing into the corner of her small sofa, his left ankle propped on his right knee, one arm stretched along the back, his other hand cradling the wine. He looked perfectly relaxed. Well, of course he was. He'd spent all evening puttering around in his kitchen creating that fabulous— no adequate—chicken dish.

''But that was before the concert?'' Gabe asked.

''Yes, and did you ever eat pizza with six boys? It goes pretty fast and if a person is polite enough to wait her turn, there's very little left.''

''Boys, yeah, I know, if they're awake, they're hungry.'' He grinned, then his expression grew solemn. ''But how was Cody? Did he seem okay around his friends? Glad to see them? What did he say about life here in Calamity Falls?''

''He didn't say much at all about it. They mostly discussed Roadkill.''

She couldn't repress a shudder.

''Bad, huh?''

''Have you ever been to a heavy metal concert?'' She finished her wine, set the glass on the tray and the tray on the table, and then leaned back. ''There were about two dozen huge, and I mean *huge*...'' She gestured with her hands about three feet apart to indicate the shoulder-width. "...guys down front with their faces painted black and white. They just stood there like statues throughout the concert. It was creepy."

"Yeah, those were the Stormtroopers. They're at all those concerts. You don't want to mess with them."

"I wouldn't go within fifty feet of them." She frowned. "So you have been to one before?"

"Of course, where do you think Cody got his love of that music?"

"Does Child Protective Services know about you?"

"Ah, chill out," Gabe advised. "Heavy metal is a part of life. Those concerts really rock."

"They don't rock. They crash. They groan. They shriek unintelligible lyrics into microphones and through amplifiers turned up to maximum decibels."

"You just don't appreciate good music."

"I didn't hear any tonight that was *worth* appreciating." She paused, thinking that she sounded an awful lot like the middle-aged stick in the mud who had once given her piano lessons. "Don't get me wrong. I love rock music. I like pop. I adore jazz, but heavy metal is a different story." She looked at him dryly. "A story with an unhappy ending."

Gabe set down his own glass and turned toward her. "That's the appeal to teenage boys."

"And to some of you who haven't quite outgrown your teenage years."

Unoffended by her barb, he grinned. "Here," he said. He took her by the shoulders and turned her so that he could reach her neck. His fingers began long, supple movements to smooth out the tension.

At first, she stiffened, surprised by the feel of his hands on her, but then the pleasure of what he was doing took over and she relaxed, letting her head drop forward slightly. The wine had given her a pleasant little buzz and the strong touch of his hands only increased the feeling.

"I'm sorry you didn't enjoy it."

Lainey was beginning to feel a ridiculous urge to forgive him, but she knew she shouldn't be too hasty. "Cody liked it. He not only had his friends there, he had a hot-looking babe with him. Or at least that's what his friend Sean said, though he thought I was kind of, well, elderly."

"Ouch."

"That was my reaction."

"But Cody seemed okay?"

"He had a great time. He'll probably want to tell you all about it when you get home." She turned her head. "By the way, won't he think it's strange to get home and find you gone?"

"Nah, I told him I had a date, too. I'd be out late."

Lainey, who'd been reveling in the feel of his hands on her neck, and now on her shoulders, went still. "Oh? Who with? Never mind. It's none of my business."

Gabe chuckled. "I was at the store cooking this meal, Lainey. I didn't want him to think I was hanging around all night waiting to check on him."

"So you came up here to ask me about him?" Lainey was annoyed for a fleeting second, but she couldn't maintain it. After all, his concern was for Cody.

"Yeah. I'm trying to give him more independence, within limits."

"Like letting him go to a rock concert with a woman twelve years older than he is."

Gabe sat forward, nudged her hair away from her ear with his nose, and said, "I knew I could trust you."

A shiver ran through her and she turned her head. "That's good to know. I have another date with him tomorrow night. We're going to play video games."

"Where?"

"At the Finas' gym. They're setting up a video arcade, lots of great games, or so I'm told. Grand opening is tomorrow night."

"Hmm," Gabe answered noncommittally. "Do you know much about video games?"

"Just that they've never interested me very much."

Gabe smiled. "I have a feeling it's going to be a short date, then. Cody loves the things. He may dump you and go back by himself."

"My heart wouldn't be broken." She glanced over her shoulder at him. "I'm surprised you didn't know about the arcade. You've been working out at their gym, haven't you?"

Gabe shrugged. "Now and then."

She twisted around so she could see him better. His hands fell away from massaging her neck. "You don't plan to bulk up like them, do you?"

He looked at her for a second before answering. "Why?"

Oh good grief, why had she said anything? "Because on some people those kinds of overdeveloped muscles aren't particularly...attractive."

One of his eyebrows lifted ever so slightly. "Is that right?"

"Not that it's any of my business, of course. I mean, it's not as though I have the right to say—"

"Go ahead and say it." A small grin tilted his mouth causing his dimple to flicker appealingly.

"Well...your neck isn't all that long."

He lifted a brow at her. "And your point is?"

She knew she never should have started this, but she blundered on. "If you build up your muscles too much, it will look like you have no neck at all. You don't want that."

"You like the way I look, huh?"

"Don't be vain." She started to stand up, but he pulled her back.

"You brought it up. Tell me. Do you think I look okay?"

"You're not too bad, considering..."

"Considering what?"

He was clearly enjoying this. Lainey couldn't resist the urge to deflate the ego she'd unknowingly been supporting. "Some people actually like guys with dimples."

"I only have the one," he said with a modest smirk.

"How'd that happen, by the way?"

"My mom said the doctor took the other one home for his little boy."

Lainey smiled. She never should have started this discussion of his looks, but she said, "That was probably a good idea, otherwise you really would have been unbearably vain."

He leaned forward. "I'm not vain, Lainey. You're the one who brought this up."

She nodded solemnly. "And I was just thinking what a mistake that was."

"You're right. Let's talk about your looks instead." They were sitting hip to hip on the sofa. Gabe reached up, turned her as if she was a rag doll, and pulled her across his lap so that she was cradled in his arms.

She tried to struggle away from him, but he said, "Relax, Lainey. You might actually enjoy this."

The pace of her heartbeat kicked up a notch. Wide-eyed, she stared up at him. "You said that about the Roadkill concert."

"You have the most beautiful eyes," he said. "And incredible skin." He ran his lips lightly across her cheekbone. Lainey's breath caught in her throat and then released in a tiny moan. "What say we don't talk anymore?" he whispered.

Gabe's lips touched hers lightly, teasing her. She turned her mouth to his as heat and longing built in her. Oh, he felt good against her lips. Whoever had thought up the whole concept of kissing must have had Gabe in mind. His firm lips, the faint scratch of his five o'clock shadow, the spicy scent of his aftershave were a perfect, heady combination.

She ran her hands over his arms and up to clasp at the back of his neck. He didn't need to work out at Finas' Gym. There was nothing at all wrong with the amount of muscles he had.

He tasted wonderful—hot like chilies, sweet like wine. She relaxed and enjoyed, though she knew she probably shouldn't. There was just something about Gabe Camden that qualified him in the "Guilty Pleasures" category of life.

He pulled his lips from hers and trailed kisses across her cheek to whisper, "You drive me crazy, Lainey. Ever since you first sashayed into my store to introduce yourself, you've made me think about all kinds of things I shouldn't think about."

She turned her face to trap his lips again. "Such as?"

"Making love to a woman in my storeroom. Right on the floor behind the counter, on top of the counter. Anywhere in my store."

Shivers ran through her. "You've never thought about that before?"

"Not until you walked in swinging that long skirt of yours. Why do you wear long skirts, anyway?" His lips remained on hers, but his fingers ran beneath the hem of the snug black T-shirt she wore with her jeans. Lainey felt as if streams of fire were shooting out from his fingers, across her skin, straight to the center of her where excitement began to build.

"I...like them," she stammered, fighting to remember what he'd asked her. "They're comfortable. Besides, I've got skinny ankles."

Gabe paused and pulled back. "I hadn't noticed. Let me see."

Hazily, Lainey stared at him. "What?"

"Let me see your ankles."

"But I'm wearing jeans, I'd have to take them off, and—"

"Exactly."

"Oh." She blinked, then stared at him as she realized what he was asking. "Oh," she said again.

Gabe raised an eyebrow at her. "Obviously, I've left you speechless."

"Yes," she gulped. "You have."

He grinned, sure of himself, and kissed her again. "So, whaddya think?"

"I...I think I'd better think about this some more."

"Not a good idea to sleep with the enemy?"

She pulled her hands from the grip they'd had around his neck even as she noticed that his thick, gorgeous hair was a mess, and wondered who had begun unbuttoning his shirt. "You're not the enemy."

He started to pull her close once again. "Good, I—"

"You're Cody's uncle," she finished, holding him off.

He stopped and his dark eyes grew solemn as they met hers. "Yeah," he answered with a sigh. "I am."

"And if I'd had any doubts about how he feels about me, I don't have them any longer. He really seems to think I'm the woman for him."

Gabe shifted so that she fell naturally into his arms in an embrace that was now more comforting than sexual. "To quote a trite, but true phrase, you're too much woman for him."

"I don't know." Lainey shook her head, then somehow found that it seemed quite natural to let it fall on his chest, tucked right up under his chin. She could hear his heart beating strong and steady against her ear. "I think he and I have had about the same amount of experience."

"You're kidding."

"Gabe, I moved here with Julius when I was fifteen, so I can sympathize with Cody on what it's like to spend his teenage years in this town. Julius fit in right away, made a place for himself, became the resident expert on fly-fishing and absolutely anything to do with chemistry, but it was harder for me. Many of Julius's new friends saw what was happening to me, knew I'd been through a rough time with my parents' divorce. It quickly became known around town that my parents were so bitter against each other that they couldn't take care of me. The people here in Calamity Falls looked after me like an unofficial granddaughter."

"Mrs. Rios is still doing it."

"I know, and she's not the only one."

She paused and thought about the parallel between her situation and Cody's. They weren't that different.

Gabe had certainly made a place for himself in Calamity Falls.

"Anyway," she continued. "Eventually, I made more friends, and sooner than Cody seems to be making them, but still, it's a small town, with not much to do...."

"You're saying you didn't date much?"

"No, I didn't. Things were different when I went to the community college. I had a steady boyfriend, but we broke up eventually, and then I came back here, worked for Red Franklin for a while before I opened Perk Avenue."

"And Calamity Falls doesn't have a whole lot to offer in the way of eligible men, right?"

"Oh, there are lots of eligible men, just not many normal ones." She lifted her head and rolled her eyes at him. "You should have seen some of the winners I've been out with."

Gabe grinned. "Something tells me I'm going to like the way you're going to compare me with these other guys. Tell me about them."

"Well, there haven't been that many. After college, I knew I wanted to stay in Calamity Falls. I felt stifled by urban life, though I like to visit cities. My life is here. The problem is that everyone knows me, knows my business, knows Julius. It's hard to have a successful relationship with a man with everyone watching, commenting, and besides..." She paused, not sure how to phrase the next thing she wanted to say.

"Besides, what?" Gabe prompted.

Lainey wrinkled her nose comically. "You've probably noticed that Julius is somewhat...unusual."

Gabe gave her a puzzled look. "Everyone around here is unusual."

"True, but Julius is brilliant, a truly innovative chemistry professor before he retired, but he also…"

"Jogs down the street every morning in his bathrobe and pajamas."

"Exactly." Relieved that she didn't have to go into a long explanation, Lainey nodded vigorously. "At least he wears his bathrobe now. He used to run just in his pajamas. At first, people thought he was crazy, but now they know he's just—"

"Eccentric."

She nodded.

"And some of the men you've dated didn't like that."

"Well, that, and when I still lived with him, he would get my dates into long philosophical discussions about some very deep issues that none of them could follow."

"In other words, they were shallow," he teased. He ran his hand lightly over her hair and began to stroke its length in steady, gentle movements.

It felt so welcome and natural that Lainey found herself arching into the touch of his hand. If she wasn't careful, she might start purring.

"Shallow?" she asked, trying to pick up the thread of what he'd been saying. "I'm afraid so," Lainey sighed. "And then if we went anywhere here in town, one of Julius's friends always seemed to be where we were, very casually keeping an eye on me. Most of my potential boyfriends got scared off."

"I can see why."

"So, a couple of years ago, my best friend Jo fixed me up with a guy who turned out to have escaped from the county jail. The sheriff tracked him down and arrested him right in front of the theater where we were supposed to be meeting for a movie. As the sheriff was leading him away, he said he'd never forget me, but I think that was actually a threat. I never saw him again, though.''

"Good. So what Mrs. Rios said is true, then, that you don't have guys like me sneaking around your house late at night?''

"Afraid not.''

Gabe lifted her chin and kissed her gently on the lips. "I knew I'd come off looking good. You're saying I'm the first normal man you've been with for a long time?''

"Normal is a relative term," she answered, just to make sure his ego wasn't getting too much of a boost.

He chuckled, but then sobered. "However, there's Cody to think about.''

"Yes." Although she didn't want to do it, Lainey sat up and pushed away from Gabe. Briskly, she straightened her T-shirt. "He thinks he's in love with me, remember?''

"And he'd be crushed if he thought I was making a move on you." Gabe ran his hands over his face. "Since you agreed to go to that concert with him, he started to act like the old Cody, talking to me, showing some interest in the plans I have to fix up our house, seeming to come back to life. I know that's because of you.''

With a sigh, Lainey stood up and moved away from the sofa. It was much easier for her to think if she wasn't too near Gabe. He was much too sexy and appealing, especially when he was slightly disheveled from her busy fingers in his hair. Self-consciously, she reached up and smoothed her hair, then neatened her shirt and jeans. Finally, she looked up, all business.

"So, I guess we're going back to being enemies, then, right?"

Gabe stood and approached her. "Not enemies, exactly, maybe rivals." He stopped right in front of her and rocked back on his heels. "I intend to win the Showdown, you know."

Lainey's competitive spirit immediately sparked to life. "Over my dead body," she answered cheerfully.

"I don't think we'll need to go that far." Gabe reached out, snagged a tendril of her hair, and tugged her gently to him. He gave her another lingering kiss as if he knew it was their last. Inwardly, she groaned with pleasure and sadness at the poignant moment. Finally, he set her away from him. "Let the best chef win," he said, then picked up the box he'd brought the chicken in and slipped out the door.

Lainey followed to lock the door and peeked through the lace curtain panels to see him pause at the end of her walk. He glanced over to the neighbor's house uneasily when Mrs. Rios's porch light came on once again. He looked back at Lainey as if to ask, "Doesn't this woman ever sleep?" then abandoned any dignity and took off at a dead run.

7

"TWENTY-SEVEN POINTS," Cody said with forced cheerfulness. "That's really good, Lainey."

"As compared to your two hundred and nine points," Lainey responded, surveying the screen of the video game. "Don't try to put a positive spin on it. I suck at this game." Just as she had at Road Blaster, Moto-Crash, and Ogre Quest. "I've never had good eye-hand coordination."

"Ah, that's okay, Lainey," her young date said with loyal sincerity. "You're good at all kinds of other things. Nobody makes coffee mochas better than you, not even Uncle Gabe, and that chocolate dessert you're working on is going to be great."

"It's so sweet of you to say that," she said, taking his arm and giving it a quick hug. He ducked his head and shrugged one shoulder.

"It's true," he mumbled.

Smiling, she glanced around. For a little while she'd managed to block out the electronic voices, beeps, squawks and explosions, but now she was becoming aware of the large number of kids who had come into the video arcade section of the gym. They stood in packs of four or five, clustered around the screens, offering advice, eager to have their own turn.

She would have to tell the Finas that their arcade was a great idea. Calamity Falls had needed something like this for years. They had leased the building next door and cut a doorway so that the gym and arcade were right next to each other. Parents could come to do their workouts while their kids played games in a safe environment. She was ashamed to say that the setup showed more business savvy than she would have thought Bull, Bison and Bruiser had between them.

"So, what game do you want to try next?" Cody asked, surveying the room.

God bless him, he was still fooling himself into thinking there was one of these games she could actually play well. "Um, I don't know," she hedged, trying to think of a way to suggest they quit for the evening.

"Hi, Cody," Lainey heard a quiet voice say behind them. They both turned around to see Melinda Franklin, Red's daughter, standing with a couple of friends. "Hi, Lainey." Melinda smiled shyly at Cody, then looked curiously at Lainey.

Lainey, who had baby-sat Melinda as a toddler, said hello to her and her two friends, then watched carefully to see what Cody's response would be. Like Gabe, she was worried that he'd made no friends yet in Calamity Falls. To her delight, she heard him greet the girls, displaying the manners Gabe had obviously drilled into him. Melinda asked about the game the two of them had been playing and Cody started to explain, giving advice when Melinda dropped her quarter in and reached for the controls.

Pleased, Lainey stepped back and drifted away. This was the first spark she'd seen of him having an interest in any of the local kids. She was especially glad that

Melinda had approached him since Lainey knew her to be a sweet and responsible girl.

That left Lainey with nothing to do, so she drifted through the doorway into the gym itself. In one corner, an aerobics class was being taught by Bull, dressed in shorts and a T-shirt emblazoned with the Finas' Gym logo, which looked something like a roadrunner on steroids. He galloped along to the music, exactly as he had while dancing at Julius and Martha's wedding. Recalling it, Lainey felt a surge of vertigo. He was kicking, turning and punching the air in cheerful abandon. He was so huge, and yet so graceful, that it made Lainey think of the dancing hippos in Disney's *Fantasia*. There were several women and a few men in his class who puffed and panted as they tried to keep up with the strenuous pace he set.

Her gaze swept the rest of the huge room, then riveted on one of the weight benches lined up near the far wall.

Gabe Camden was lying on his back, hands wrapped around a bar on which weights rested. Bruiser hovered nearby, carefully watching as Gabe lifted the bar loaded with weights. His face reddened as he pushed the bar up several inches and held it for a few seconds, then lowered it slowly.

Intrigued, since she'd never seen him do anything more physical than run an espresso machine, Lainey moved closer. He must have been at this for quite a while, she thought, because his upper body—and she could see all of it since he wore no shirt—was slick with sweat. She'd never been particularly attracted to sweaty men, but she liked the way he looked. In fact, watching him made her mouth go dry and her pulse accelerate in its own little spurt of aerobic activity. It was almost as good as kissing him.

With Bruiser quietly coaching him, Gabe braced himself to once again lift the bar. Lainey watched as his stomach muscles tightened and his biceps bulged. His neck strained, he gritted his teeth, he shoved the bar and weights up once again, his attention totally focused on lifting it as high as he could. He held it overhead for several seconds and Lainey found herself holding her breath as Bruiser counted off the seconds.

"One, one-thousand, two, two-thousand," he intoned.

Lainey moved, Gabe's attention flickered from his task to her. His eyes widened and he let out a yell as the bar slipped from his grasp. Bruiser made a grab for it and barely managed to get it back into its supports before it crashed down on Gabe's neck. Alarmed, Lainey whirled around and scampered back to the video room where Cody was still watching Melinda play, coaching and giving her advice. Melinda's two friends had drifted away to games of their own.

Lainey was trying to decide what to do next when a big sweaty palm wrapped itself around her wrist and Gabe reeled her around and into a corner beside a pinball machine.

"What are you doing here?" he asked, wiping his face with a towel he'd draped around his neck. "Besides ogling me, that is."

She raised her eyebrows and pinched her lips in a look that said, "As if." She *had* been ogling him, but she wouldn't admit it.

"I told you Cody was bringing me here to play video games." She tilted her head in the direction of his nephew. "I'm no good at those things, though, and someone else came along—Melinda Franklin. They know each other from high school. From what he's told me, this is the first time he's even noticed one of the Calamity Falls girls. I think this locks promising.''

He turned his head in the direction she'd indicated and Lainey happily resumed her ogling. He didn't have the kind of bunched and bulging muscles the Finas had. His were well-developed, sleek and smooth. His shoulders were wide and flat, his neck sinewy. She wished that he would...

"You're doing it again," he whispered out of the side of his mouth.

She blinked. "What?"

"Ogling me."

"Oh, please, that is *so* not true," she responded huffily, fighting the blush rising on her face.

Gabe let that one pass. "About Cody. You're right. This does look promising. Why don't we meet up later and discuss it? Okay if I come to your place?" Suddenly, he reached up and snagged a lock of her hair that trailed over her shoulder, twisting it around his fingers as if he couldn't stop himself.

Lainey went very still and her eyes widened. "I...I don't know why I should let you." She didn't know why her voice sounded so breathy except that it seemed to be clogged up somewhere in her throat. In this room full of electronic beeps, shouts, laughter, barbell clanging and music, he'd created a tiny corner of quiet intimacy.

His smile was slow, sexy and knowing. "So you can continue ogling my body, of course."

"Don't flatter yourself."

He leaned close so that his lips were almost touching her ear. "Having you look at me the way you've been doing just now is flattery enough, Lainey. Don't you know that?''

"I don't think I know—''

"Hey, Lainey,'' Cody's voice interrupted.

She stepped back and whirled around, her guilty glance taking in Cody's face, trying to swiftly read the expression there. To her relief, she saw that he seemed only surprised.

Cody looked at the two adults curiously. "Gabe,'' he said. "I didn't know you were going to be here.''

"Decided it was time for a workout,'' he answered, moving past the pinball machine. "You two on your way home?''

"Yeah.'' Cody moved up and took Lainey's arm in a possessive grip. "Let's go, Lainey.''

He tugged her away, but she glanced back over her shoulder at Gabe's thoughtful expression.

THE FAMILIAR sound of feet pounding up her front walk and onto her tiny porch had Lainey sweeping the door open so that Gabe could tumble inside. A smattering of rocks hit the porch railings as he did so.

"It's okay, Mrs. Rios,'' Lainey called out, then stepped outside to reassure her neighbor. The old lady was standing in her yard, backlit by her porch light, bucket of rocks at her feet, each hand loaded with ammunition. "You've really got to stop doing that, Mrs. Rios. You're scaring him to death.''

Behind her, she heard Gabe suck in an outraged breath.

"Why does he sneak around this time of night? That's what I'd like to know. If he was a decent, self-respecting man, he'd come courting you in the daylight so I could get a good look at him.''

"He's not courting me, Mrs. Rios," Lainey said.

Her neighbor propped her hands on her skinny hips. "Then why's he here? I guarantee you he's not coming around to check your water meter at this time of night."

"Uh, no, he's not. He's here strictly on...business."

"Hmph," Mrs. Rios said, picking up her bucket of rocks. "Monkey business." She went back into her house and closed the door firmly.

Lainey snickered and went inside her own house to face Gabe. He shook his head as he tried to catch his breath. "That old lady is sure making me nimble on my feet."

"You should try to make friends with her," Lainey advised. "Then she won't be so scared of you."

"Hey, she's the one being aggressive. Why is everyone in this town so protective of you? After I saw you at the gym tonight, Bruiser gave me the third degree about whether or not I was bothering you. The truth is, *you* were bothering *me*."

"Don't be ridiculous. I was simply...observing Bruiser's coaching methods."

"Didn't anyone ever tell you that lying like that will make your hair turn green?"

That silly question brought laughter bubbling up. "No. No one ever did because it's completely ridiculous."

"Hey," he said, lifting his hands, palm up. "You never know." His hands dropped and he grew serious. "Cody saw us tonight."

"We weren't doing anything." And she couldn't believe that defensive phrase had just come out of her mouth.

Gabe ran a hand through his hair in a jerky motion,

leaving it messy. Lainey curled her fingers into her palms to keep herself from reaching up and smoothing it.

"It was only a matter of time."

She crossed her arms at her waist and gave him a skeptical look. "Oh, really."

"Yes, really. He's smart. He would have figured out that there's something going on between us." Gabe turned and began to pace. Because her living room was so small, Lainey had to sit down and pull her feet up on the sofa or be trampled by her restless guest. She frowned at him as he made the turn near the kitchen doorway and said, "I want him to trust me, not to think I'm trying to—"

"Hustle me into bed?" she asked, suddenly annoyed with him and with the entire situation.

He stopped pacing to stare at her. His chin drew back as if she'd hit him.

"Listen, Gabe, you know I don't want to hurt Cody. He's a great kid, lots of fun, but he's a kid, he's resilient."

"He's already been through so many changes."

"And he'll go through many more. How he chooses to handle them is up to him. It's called life and he needs to learn how to handle it on his own."

"He's sixteen," Gabe protested. "Which isn't an age that's exactly famous for clear-headed thinking and decision-making."

"You mean like pulling up stakes in Tucson and moving lock, stock and barrel to this little town where he has no friends and little control over his own life?"

Gabe's eyes lifted to meet hers. Along with the annoyance she felt at his bullheadedness, she ached for him. There was something else going on, too, a feeling she couldn't identify.

Slowly, he shook his head. "I have to do what's best for him."

"Of course, but when you decided to make the move here, did you even ask him?"

"He was in no state to make that kind of decision."

"Gabe," she said gently. "Neither were you."

"What do you mean?" he asked, anger swelling in his voice.

"Did you act out of worry, or reason?"

"I had legitimate concerns. He could have done the same thing his mother did. Shelly was so messed up, irresponsible."

"He's not Shelly. He's one of the most responsible kids I've ever seen. I have no worries when I leave him in charge. I know everything will be taken care of, his cash drawer always balances out to the penny." She stood and walked over to lay her hand on Gabe's arm. Her brown eyes were deep with sincerity when she said, "Gabe, he's like that because you raised him. You made him that way."

His deep blue eyes delved into hers, but he couldn't speak.

Lainey smiled. "Deep down, he knows that you've got his best interests in mind. But you have to give him time, maybe a long time, to adjust to the changes in his life."

Lainey didn't know where her understanding of Gabe and Cody had come from except that she knew and cared deeply for them both. Otherwise, she never would have agreed to be Cody's date at the concert and at the arcade. Nor would she have been so willing to let Gabe make these late-night visits to her house.

Lainey felt the familiar tingle move from her palm and travel up her arms. With a burst of insight, she knew what it meant. Could this be what it was like to fall in love?

Shocked at the thought, she stepped back in confusion, jerking her hand away. She cared about him, but she didn't know him well enough to be in love with him. On the other hand, she had nothing to compare it to, so how could she know?

Startled, Gabe started to say something, but she held up her hand. "You just have to give him the time he needs."

"How much time did you have, Lainey?"

"What?"

"When your parents divorced and you moved here with Julius, how much time did it take you to adjust?"

Lainey clasped her hands in front of her and gave him a reluctant look. "This isn't about me."

"No, but you seem to be speaking as something of an authority on this kind of thing. How long did it take you to adjust?"

Lainey opened her hands and ran them down her thighs. Years, she wanted to say. She had desperately missed her mother, who had immediately remarried, then moved to California. As for her father, she'd seen him only a few times a year at the most.

"A long time," she finally admitted. "But I'd lost every stable thing in my life except Julius. Cody has you, the one he's always had. He'll be all right."

Gabe looked at her searchingly as if he wanted to ask more of her, but when she glanced at him and then away, he must have decided to let it go. "I suppose I'll never get over wanting to make things easier for him."

"That's because you love him. You know, Gabe, you're more than an uncle to him. You're his dad."

That pleased him. "Yeah. I guess I am. So tell me what happened tonight at the arcade. He came home and went straight to his room. I figured he didn't want to talk to me because he saw me practically pawing you."

Lainey was relieved at the shift in subject. "What happened after we saw you? Nothing much. We decided to come home. But like I said, I think it could be promising that he was playing video games with Melinda Franklin tonight. She's a nice girl, very popular at school, involved in everything. If they become friends..."

"He might begin making the adjustment to living here, and dump you."

"I can live with that," she assured him, then wondered how she would feel if Gabe no longer made these late-night forays to her house to discuss Cody. "He didn't mention any further dates with me, only said he'd see me at work tomorrow." Of course, like Gabe, she'd been afraid he'd been upset when he'd seen her and Gabe practically necking in the corner behind a pinball machine.

Gabe watched her face and tried to gauge her feelings. Something was on her mind, but he didn't know what it was. For a minute there, he'd watched disturbing emotions displayed on her face as obviously as if they were being cast on a movie screen, but she hadn't voiced them, leaving him wondering and confused. He felt cheated because he wanted to know what she was thinking. That surprised him. He'd never been good at the messy emotions involved in a relationship, which is what seemed to be developing between them.

It was obvious that she was pleased Cody had at last made a friend in Calamity Falls. However, if Gabe didn't have to sneak up here at night to see her, what excuse could he use? Even if Cody lost interest in her, Gabe had seen his nephew's expression tonight and he wasn't sure the boy would take kindly to Gabe's growing interest in her. He loved Cody, but having to pussyfoot around his feelings was becoming an inconvenience.

He wanted to have a relationship with her without having to worry about his nephew and their rival businesses. Then he thought about what she'd told him of her previous experiences with men and realized he also had to deal with her skittishness and skepticism. Yeah, well, he thought, his gaze sweeping over her, he'd figure out something. He was good at solving problems. He didn't know quite what to think of her analysis of his worries for Cody. While he was glad she had given so much thought to it, Gabe felt disconcerted that she seemed to understand him and Cody so well. How could she, when they'd known each other such a short time? And yet, she was willing to do what she had done for Cody; gamely sitting through a concert, riding in his beat-up old VW classic, going to the arcade with him. What really surprised him was that she hadn't asked for anything in return.

He was about to say that when shouts and the pummeling of rocks against the fence had both of them leaping for the door.

''Hey, lady, we're not going to hurt you. We just want to see Lainey,'' Bull Fina's high-pitched voice shouted in protest.

Mrs. Rios didn't answer, but released another barrage of rocks.

``Ow,'' Bison squawked. ``Watch out. You hit me.''

``That's what I'm trying to do, you…you Peeping Toms,'' Mrs. Rios answered in a panicked voice. ``I'm going to call the police.''

``We're not peeping, ma'am,'' Bruiser yelled. ``We're visiting Lainey. Ow! Now cut that out!''

Gabe swept the door open for Lainey who dashed outside to reassure the frightened woman. The sight of the three brawny men in front of her house had just about sent Mrs. Rios over the edge, but Lainey calmed her down, encouraged her to go back inside, then shooed the Fina brothers into her tiny living room. Gabe waited impatiently, afraid to stick his head out for fear that the sight of yet another man would cause Mrs. Rios to have heart failure right there on the spot. Finally, things quieted and he flattened himself against the wall to avoid the stampede of Finas coming in. Lainey was right behind them.

With a sigh of relief, she closed her front door.

Bull, Bison and Bruiser eyed Gabe suspiciously. He swallowed hard, wondering if he could outrun them as well as the neighbor's rocks. He decided that he could. His smaller size meant he was faster on his feet. ``Evening, boys,'' he said, pleased that his voice didn't quaver. He moved over to stand next to Lainey.

Alarmed, Lainey saw the way her friends were considering Gabe. Standing shoulder to shoulder as they were, they took up almost the entire living room. Cautiously, she asked them to sit down, even though she was afraid they might break her furniture. ``Did you want something, guys?''

Bison was the first to speak. ``Yeah, Bruiser here told us that there's something going on.'' He looked at

Gabe accusingly. "That you've been bothering Lainey. Is that true?"

Gabe's eyes shifted to her. "No, not exactly."

"Then what, *exactly,* have you been doing?" Bull asked. He formed his hands into fists and cracked his knuckles. It sounded like thunder in the small room.

Lainey stared from one to the other of her protectors, then at Gabe. To his credit, he didn't seem nervous. She wasn't sure what he was going to say, but knowing him, it would be the unvarnished truth. Instinctively, she knew the Finas would never understand about her actually going out with a sixteen-year-old. They might even blab it all over town, embarrassing her and Cody, so she blurted, "We've been…comparing recipes."

Gabe gave her a puzzled look.

"Comparing recipes?" Bull asked. "Recipes for what?"

"For the contest that's coming up, the Calamity Falls Great Chefs' Showdown," Gabe chimed in, sliding her a look that asked where she was going with this.

Darned if she knew.

"But, don't you both want to win that?" Bison asked.

"Of course."

"So why are you comparing recipes?" Bruiser scratched his head.

"Cooperation," she blurted. "May the best man win and all that."

"Cooperation," Bull said, mulling it over. "Team spirit just like you taught us when we became volunteer firefighters."

"Right," Gabe said, triumphantly.

Lainey breathed a sigh of relief and broke into a smile. ``That's right.''

All five of them beamed at each other.

``So, you see,'' she went on. ``There's no reason for you to worry about me, even though my grandfather asked you to watch out for me. I talked to him and Martha last night. They're having a great time on their trip. I told him that I don't worry about them, so he needs to quit worrying about me. I'm twenty-eight, I run my own business, I'm assistant fire chief of this town. I don't need people watching out for me.''

``Hey, that's right,'' Bruiser said. ``Julius acts like you're still a kid. He shouldn't do that.''

``No, he shouldn't,'' his brothers agreed. They all three thought about that for a few minutes. Gabe looked at Lainey, who shrugged.

``Bros, I think we have here what you might call a dilemma,'' Bull finally said, standing up. His brothers nodded sagely, though Lainey suspected they didn't have a clue what he was talking about.

``A *moral* dilemma,'' Gabe ventured. ``You want to fulfill your promise to Julius, but you don't want to treat Lainey like a kid, is that right?''

``Exactly,'' Bull said, nodding vigorously. ``But we owe Julius a big favor.'' Thoughtfully, he tucked his hands into the pocket of his shorts, then with a puzzled expression, pulled his hand out. ``Dang, look at that. That old lady hit me with one of those rocks right in the pocket, and I didn't even feel it.''

``That's because you were too busy running and ducking,'' Bruiser responded. ``Why does she throw rocks, anyway?''

``Her house was broken into several years ago. A number of items were taken and she's been frightened of prowlers ever since," Lainey explained. "It's not easy for an older lady living alone, and she tends to stew and worry over things. If she hears any noises, her policy is to throw rocks first and ask questions later." Lainey paused and looked at her three protectors. "Maybe that's how you could get out of watching over me, tell Julius that it panics Mrs. Rios when you come check on me. She got him once right in the butt, so he'd understand."

Gabe gave her a skeptical look. "That's pretty lame, Lainey."

"Nah, I think that's a good idea. We don't want to worry an old lady," Bull said. "A lady all alone, no one to watch out for her. Makes me think of Ma." His eyes suspiciously moist, he dropped the rock back into his pocket and pulled out a handkerchief. He blew his nose with a loud honk.

Bruiser and Bison nodded, their bottom lips trembling. "We wouldn't want anyone scaring Ma." As one, they turned toward the door. "We haven't talked to Ma in a week."

"Nine days," Bull corrected, a guilty look on his face. "We'd better go call her." He hurried after his brothers, but he paused to glance back over his shoulder. "When Martha and Julius get back from their honeymoon, we'll tell him we appreciate everything he's done, but we don't think it's right for us to be watching you and scaring your neighbor. You're a big girl. You can take care of yourself."

The three dashed out the door and galloped down the street, their big feet rattling windows all along the way.

Lainey closed the door and turned to face Gabe, breathing a big sigh of relief as she did so. She was amazed at how easy that had been. "Freedom," she said, and grinned. "Why didn't I do that sooner? Years ago, in fact, to get Julius to stop worrying about me?"

Gabe smiled back, then grew thoughtful. "I guess it's hard being the object of someone's worry."

"Like Cody is yours?"

"Yeah." He shrugged. "It's also hard to quit worrying. But if he's at least *talking* to another kid at the arcade, maybe he'll decide he likes it here."

"It's possible," Lainey agreed. "But he still thinks this town is pretty funky."

"It is."

They fell silent. Feeling vaguely depressed, Lainey wondered if Gabe was going to leave. "So, did you stop by to compare recipes?"

His gaze swept up to focus on her. "Do you think they bought that excuse?"

"No," she admitted.

"Bruiser noticed you ogling me," Gabe said, a teasing light in his eyes.

She lifted her chin. "I wasn't doing any such thing."

"Your hair's turning green," Gabe warned.

She rolled her eyes.

"Did you like what you saw, Lainey?"

"Maybe," she admitted. "You do have certain qualities that some women might find attractive."

"Don't be coy, Lainey. Do I have certain qualities *you* find attractive?" He stepped close and put his arms around her waist, tucking her in close to his body.

"I thought you were worried about Cody thinking there's something going on between us."

"He's not here right now. Tell me, Lainey. Did you like what you saw?"

With a smile that belied the heat that was beginning

to curl through her, Lainey slipped her hands up his arms and clasped them at the back of his neck. Leaning away slightly, she looked into his eyes. "Yes. Looking at you isn't too much of a hardship."

He winced. "It's a good thing I don't have a big ego, or you would destroy it."

"Oh, I think your ego is healthy enough." She tilted her head and looked at him. She had been battered by a million different emotions this evening, but now she only wanted to feel his arms around her, his lips on hers. "When I saw you tonight at the gym, it occurred to me that I've never particularly liked sweaty men."

"Really? I guess it's a good thing I showered."

"That's exactly what I was thinking." She pulled his head down to her and placed her lips on his, tasting him, breathing in his fresh scent. His mouth was firm, delicious. She had started the kiss, but he quickly took it over.

He pulled his mouth from hers and looked down at her, his eyes twinkling. "Are you trying to tell me something, Lainey?"

"You asked if I liked what I'd seen. The answer is, yeah, I did, and I also like the way you kiss and the way you smell right now."

His mouth tilted up at one corner, making his dimple appear. "Lainey, for a girl who claims not to have had much experience with men, you're doing a fine job."

"Of?"

"Gaining experience," he said, dipping his head to kiss her again.

With a grin, she held him off. "Oh, I've had experience with men. The problem was that they were mostly losers."

"Honey, your losing streak is over," he promised

her, lowering his mouth to hers once again. His hands moved smoothly over her back, arching her into his body so that she could feel the heat, the hardness and need that drove him. His legs nudged hers and she found herself moving backward to her tiny sofa. When she felt it against the back of her knees, she sank onto it, Gabe following her down to the cushions.

His lips held possession of hers, his arms cradled her and she kissed him back, reveling in the faint roughness of his late-evening whiskers, the scent of soap and healthy male that clung to him.

He sat and tried to pull her onto his lap, but the sofa was too narrow. He turned slightly to the side, but Lainey's long legs banged against the steamer trunk coffee table.

"Ouch," she said, breaking off the kiss to lean over and rub her ankle.

"Sorry," Gabe said, bending to see if there was any damage. When she straightened, her head banged into his chin, causing him to bite his tongue. "Umph!" His breath sucked in sharply and his eyes started to water.

"Oh, no." Alarmed, Lainey untangled herself from her precarious perch halfway on his lap, halfway on the sofa and stood up. "Gabe, I'm sorry. Can I get you some ice, or something?"

He drew in a deep breath and answered thickly. "No, I'm all right." He gave her a rueful look. "But I think this has kind of ruined the romantic atmosphere."

Chagrined, she nodded. "I think you're right."

He stood and headed for the door. "I don't like all this sneaking around, being chased by your neighbor, having my motives questioned by everyone in town," he said grumpily.

"What are your motives?"

He glanced over his shoulder and gave her that slow, sexy, dimple-inducing grin. "If you don't know, why don't you stay awake tonight and think about it? I bet you figure out that my motives are the same as yours."

With a wink, he stepped outside. Lainey caught the door just before he closed it, then stood with one hand on the jamb as she watched him stroll away down the street. When Mrs. Rios's living room drapes flicked back, he waved jauntily at her and continued on his way.

Lainey closed the door and locked it, thinking that she knew exactly what her motive was. Pure lust.

8

THE WORK STARTED on Perk Avenue that week. Lainey arrived at her store the morning after her last "date" with Cody to discover that the city had installed protective barriers in front of her shop. She was relieved to see they were gray, not attractive, but not the eyesores the orange ones were. Best of all, there were several carpenters ready to begin work.

She happily made coffee for them and then scurried out of the way as they took down the plywood, cleaned out the broken parts of the wall and window frame, then began replacing everything that had been wiped out by Gabe's car. The work took two days and when they were finished, a team of glaziers came to install the plate glass window.

The day after that, a sign painter named Rich arrived to paint the name of her shop on the huge window. He pulled out a sketch he'd done and Lainey was delighted to see that it was executed with flair. The capital *P* in Perk Avenue was drawn attached to the handle of a coffeepot and the steam escaping from the spout drifted back to spell out the rest of the name.

"This is great," she said, standing in front of her store and holding the paper up before the window so she could get the full effect of the design. She'd had some ideas of her own, but this was much better than anything she could have imagined.

Rich nodded. "Gabe suggested it."

"What?" She turned toward him.

"It was Gabe's idea. We've been friends for years," Rich said, beginning to remove his supplies from his truck. "I always paint the signs on his new stores."

Lainey blinked. "This isn't his store. It's mine."

"Oh? You his manager or his new lady?"

"Neither," she answered with growing annoyance. "And he's not my new man."

The painter gave her a swift look, seeming to realize his mistake. He held his hands out. "Sorry. Gabe said he's buying into another business here in town. I thought this was it."

"Oh. Well, it isn't."

"Does that mean you don't want to use this design?"

Lainey looked at the sketch. It was really very clever. Not using it would be foolish. "No, it's a good design. Use it." Lainey turned away. "I'll leave you to your work."

Once back inside, she shut the door and started the process of bringing out the items she had stored away after the accident. As she did so, she thought about Gabe and realized she knew less about him than she thought she did.

What business had he bought? Didn't he have enough to keep him busy with his own shop and with Cody? Why did he feel the need to buy another business? And why hadn't he said anything about it?

Well, why would he? It certainly wasn't as though they had any claim on each other. Still, she had thought he was as attracted to her as she was to him. That didn't mean he was going to tell her his business secrets, though. She didn't feel the need to share hers with him.

By midafternoon Rich had finished painting the sign on the front window and Lainey went out front to admire it. The design was eye-catching. The new window and woodwork and fresh paint made it seem like a brand-new store.

She stood looking at it with satisfaction and said, "It's time for my grand reopening. I'll make a really big deal of it."

"And maybe you can get back some of the customers who've been going to Gabe's place," Cody said, walking up beside her. He had just come from school and had his book bag over his shoulder.

Lainey grinned, linked her arm with his companionably and said, "That's exactly what I've got in mind."

Cody's eyes flicked to her, and she gave him a friendly nudge. "I'm so glad you're here. We've got lots of work to do."

"Yeah, well, I'm glad I'm here, too," he said, his cheeks taking on the fiery glow they usually wore whenever she complimented him. She worried sometimes that she wasn't handling this correctly. The affection he felt for her was something she had to respect without encouraging it. She had decided to be her normal, friendly self and treat him like a friend. She only hoped he took it that way.

Lainey pulled him inside and they set to work. She chattered cheerfully about her plans and Cody listened, making occasional suggestions. One of the plans he had thought up, to offer a reduced-cost breakfast to the high school students, was so clever, Lainey danced across the room and gave him a big hug.

He returned it in an embarrassed manner, then dodged away awkwardly to begin sweeping up the sawdust, dirt and specks of putty left by the repairmen. He finished up by mopping the floor.

Lainey watched him, reminding herself not to make him self-conscious. She was tempted to ask him if he'd seen any more of Melinda or made any other friends, but he had a distant, thoughtful expression on his face that made her decide to keep her questions to herself.

She went into the small kitchen at the back of the shop and began assembling the ingredients for her chocolate dessert. It was a variation on the one thing she could bake really well. It was a recipe she had learned from Delilah before her former employee had abandoned her for the higher wages at Coffee & Such. Lainey had added a few touches of her own and with the revised recipe, she produced a cake that was dense, moist, chocolate and undeniably delicious.

After tasting Gabe's contest entry, Lainey had begun experimenting with various toppings from raspberry to caramel to chocolate in an effort to give her dessert more pizzazz. She had finally decided to offer all three variations. The chocolate one needed to be light to off-set the richness of the cake, but heavy enough to flow smoothly over it. So far, the sauce had come out so thin it separated and ran down the sides of the cake to puddle at the bottom, or so thick it had sat on top of the slice of cake like a fudgey hat.

She had tasted it so often, she was losing her perspective, so she called out to Cody, "Hey, are you in the mood to sample this dessert again?"

He came in and put away the cleaning equipment. "Afraid not, Lainey. I've got homework, a chemistry problem I've got to solve."

"Chemistry, hmm," she said vaguely, her mind still on the separating chocolate sauce. "Too bad Julius isn't here. He could help you. Maybe you should talk to Starina Simms. She's a retired engineer, you know.''

"Starina who?''

Lainey quickly explained about the odd little lady who was convinced she'd found the key to creating a working perpetual motion machine—as soon as she could figure out how to keep it from blowing up.

Cody looked intrigued and Lainey gave him a wink. ''See? There might be some advantages to living in this strange place.''

With a small laugh, he answered, ''Yeah, maybe. I could ask...'' His voice trailed off and he glanced away.

It was cute that he was shy about asking, but that wouldn't get his problem solved. ''Sure, ask her to help you. She'd be flattered.'' She described how to find Starina's house, then waved him off and went back to work on her sauce. She flipped on the radio and cranked up the volume so she could think better.

GABE STOOD BACK to admire the restored front window of Perk Avenue. He felt flattered that she had used his idea. It made him feel as though he had a real stake in the place. Stepping forward, he cupped his hands around his eyes and squinted to see if Lainey was inside. There was a light at the back where he knew her kitchen was. When he tried the knob and found that the front door was unlocked, he strolled inside.

''Lainey?'' he called out, but she had a radio going and the sound of rock and roll was bouncing off the walls and rattling the coffee mugs.

Curious, he moved to the swinging half doors that led to the kitchen and peered over. She had pots, pans and bowls on every surface. The rich smell of chocolate permeated the air. She stood at the big, six-burner stove stirring yet another chocolate concoction in a steel pot. That wasn't all she was stirring up, though. Her hips swayed in time to the music, and her feet did a miniature two-step, tapping out a rhythm as she moved.

Beneath a big chef's apron, she wore one of her usual long skirts, this one a tie-dyed creation in shades of turquoise. It was cinched with a turquoise concho belt and she wore a snug-fitting T-shirt of the same color. Her long red hair was pulled up in a ponytail that made her look as if she was truly young enough to be Cody's girlfriend.

The skirt swayed around her ankles—which he thought were beautiful, not the least bit skinny. Her shoulders dipped and bounced, her hips twitched back and forth. She stopped her solitary dancing for a moment to sample her chocolate creation, lifting one of several clean spoons lined up on the counter and dipping it into the sauce. Her lips pursed as she blew on the spoonful, then her tongue darted out cautiously to scoop up a dollop. She held it in her mouth for a few seconds as if savoring it, then swallowed. She took a deep breath and let her head fall back as if allowing the rich taste to flow through her entire body.

Damn, Gabe thought. He'd never seen anyone do a taste test like that.

The desire he'd come to expect whenever he was around her surged through him once again. Funny, he had become attracted to the tall, willowy woman without realizing how sensual she could be. He had a sudden vision of the two of them with chocolate sauce, whipped cream, bright red cherries—the works.

He swallowed hard, stepped into the kitchen, and

said her name again. But his throat was so dry his voice croaked, startling her.

"Oh!" She whirled around with the spoon still in her hand. Sauce flew off of it and sent a splattering line across the front of his shirt. He jumped back, but she moved in and leaned forward to stare at it. "Darn, still too thin. I thought I had it right this time."

"Hey," Gabe complained, plucking his shirt away from his chest. "Is that all you can say?"

Lainey glanced up. "Oh, sorry." She made a grab for a rag laying on the countertop, but he stepped back when she tried to swipe it across the chocolate drips.

"Never mind. I'll just go back home and change."

"Okay." She shrugged, returning to the stove and picking up the wooden spoon. With careful strokes, she stirred the sauce. "What's the matter?" she asked, looking over her shoulder at him. "Got a date tonight?"

"Yes," he said and watched with satisfaction when her arm jerked slightly and went still for a moment before she resumed her stirring of the sauce.

"I see. Anyone I know?"

Intrigued, he stepped closer. He knew he wasn't the most astute man in the world when it came to women. One of his former girlfriends had complained of that very thing—along with her complaints that he spent too much time at his restaurants, and he had a nephew to raise. But Lainey hid very little. She simply wasn't the kind of woman to indulge in petty games.

"Yes, she is. In fact, it's someone very close to you."

Seeming to forget about her sauce, she turned and stared. When she did so, he saw something he hadn't noticed before—there was a small streak of chocolate at the right corner of her mouth. It moved when her lips did, mesmerizing him.

``Close to me?'' she asked.

``Very close.''

She gave him a blank look and he fought a grin. He loved teasing her. In fact, he was getting very good at it.

``I can't think who it would be. My best friend lives in Phoenix, *and* she's happily married, so I don't know who it could be unless it's someone from my high school years. Is it?''

He answered with a mysterious smile.

``Well, I don't know...'' Lainey stopped and stared at him. ``Oh, don't tell me it's Bertha June Riley over at the candle shop. We were friends years ago, high school, in fact, until she tried to steal someone else's boyfriend. I can't imagine why she would think we're close now. I haven't even seen her in ages. Trust me, Gabe, you don't want to go out with her. She's only interested in one thing.''

Fascinated, he couldn't help asking, ``What's that?''

``A free meal. She eats like a horse. This date is going to cost you a fortune.''

``It's not Bertha June, who, by the way, I've never met.''

Lainey blinked. ``Oh? Who is it, then?''

He'd been so intrigued by listening to her and watching that chocolate streak dance up and down that he'd almost forgotten what they were talking about. ``It's your neighbor, Mrs. Rios.''

He loved the way her mouth dropped open and her eyes bugged. ``Mrs. Rios? She's seventy-two.''

He dipped his head. ``I know, and I hope she doesn't

think she can make a pass at me because of my youth and inexperience.''

``Gabe, she's...I don't think...'' she floundered. ``It's your business, of course, but...Mrs. Rios?''

He grinned. ``I like older women, just like Cody does. It seems to be a family trait.'' Remembering why he was there, Gabe looked around. ``Where is he, by the way? He didn't come home after school.''

``Cody? What?'' Lainey couldn't quite twist her mind around to keep up with the change of subject, but she answered finally, ``School project. A chemistry assignment. I sent him to Starina. She should be able to help him.''

``Starina Simms? The lady up on Nugget Street who's working on some kind of crazy contraption?''

``That's her, and it's a perpetual motion machine.''

Gabe's eyes shifted. ``I don't know that I want him up there.''

``How much do you know about chemistry?''

``Only what relates to cooking.''

``Then quit worrying,'' she advised.

Gabe frowned, recalling their last talk about how much he worried over Cody. He didn't want to get into that again. Right now, he had more interesting things to discuss. ``Okay, then I guess I'll see him tonight.'' He looked around. ``So you're here all alone?''

He could tell that her mind was still on his date with Mrs. Rios, but she managed to rally her senses. ``All alone with my chocolate sauce.'' She gave him a wary look. ``Which wouldn't interest you in the least.''

Who was she kidding? He was focused on that streak by her mouth like a bloodhound on the scent of an escaped convict.

"Why not?" He moved closer. "Is it your entry in the contest?"

"Maybe."

That meant yes.

"Mind if I have a taste?"

"Of course I mind."

"I let you taste my chicken recipe."

"You forced it on me."

"Oh, yeah," he answered with a knowing grin. "I practically had to hold you down and work your jaws for you to get you to eat it."

"I was extremely hungry that night, remember?"

In spite of her words, he could see that she was softening. "One taste," he said. "And then I'll go change my shirt for my date."

"One." She held out the spoon to him.

"Nuh-uh. That's not the one I want." He took her wrist with one hand, smoothly plucked the spoon from her with the other, and placed it on the counter. He then reeled her in quickly so that she landed with a whoosh of breath against his chest. He lowered his mouth to hers. "This is the one I want."

His tongue came out, slowly and gently to lick the streak of chocolate off her mouth. "Delicious," he murmured. She stood, rigid with surprise for a moment, before he felt some of the starch go out of her spine and she relaxed against him, but then he said, "If I didn't know I was going to win, I might think you would." She pushed away from him and he could see the fire of challenge in her eyes.

"You should be so lucky." Her dark red brows raised in a dismissive look. "Hadn't you better go? Your date might be getting worried about you. Don't keep her out too late, okay? When she's not out throwing rocks at prowlers, she likes to go to sleep early.''

Her spurt of instructions had him chuckling. ``I'll keep that in mind. Maybe I'll see you later?''

``I don't think so. Wouldn't that be a little crude? Going from one woman to the other in the same evening?''

He pretended to consider that by rubbing his chin thoughtfully. Actually, he was hiding a wide grin. ``I suppose you're right. Jealousy is such an ugly thing. It causes warts, you know.''

``Then I guess it would go nicely with the green hair I get from lying,'' she said snippily.

``Are you saying you're jealous, Lainey?''

He loved the way her eyes flashed when he tossed one of her comments back at her. ``I repeat, you should be so lucky. Why don't you go now so I can finish?''

He headed for the door, but she called him back. ``Oh, and Gabe? Watch out for flying rocks.''

``Hey, I figure if I take her out, she won't be so intent on braining me with one.''

Lainey picked up the spoon. ``I didn't say the rocks would be coming from her.''

He left, chuckling, then thought that he'd gotten more than he bargained for on this trip to Perk Avenue.

THOUGH SHE had tried to maintain a blasé attitude, Lainey was eaten up with curiosity about Gabe taking Mrs. Rios out to dinner. If it was to keep her from being frightened when he went by on his way to Lainey's house, he needn't bother. After Cody settled in a little more and got over his crush on Lainey, there would be no reason for Gabe to come see her—a thought that made Lainey feel heartsick.

She stirred her sauce, tasted it, and thought about how totally unfair it was for him to come waltzing into her store, kiss the chocolate from her face, then waltz out again to go on a date with another woman—even if that woman was seventy-two.

She wondered how long it would take for them to go have dinner, and where they would go. Probably to the Lotus Blossom. Mrs. Rios loved May Ling Schultz's barbecued spareribs.

Mrs. Rios also loved chocolate cake. Lainey looked down at her sauce, now perfectly smooth and glossy, exactly the way she wanted it. With a smug smile and a sigh of satisfaction, she poured it carefully into a covered container, set aside a piece of the cake, cleaned up the kitchen and closed the shop for the night. While she'd been cooking, she had been planning the grand reopening which would take place in two days' time. She would keep her dessert under wraps until the contest, but it wouldn't hurt to take one piece to Mrs. Rios. She certainly wouldn't be interested in duplicating Lainey's recipe.

It was fully dark by the time Lainey left Perk Avenue, locking the door behind her. She headed for her street and strolled along humming to herself. Since her shop had been repaired, things were definitely looking up. If she could find out what Gabe was up to, she would be perfectly happy.

As she approached Mrs. Rios's house, she could see Gabe's repaired Porsche sitting in front of her house. Lainey wondered how her arthritic neighbor had managed to get into the little sports car. She hesitated uncertainly for a second, but when she heard a burst of masculine laughter, she was drawn to the front door.

Standing on tiptoe, she peeked through the glass

panes at the top of the door, then stared in amazement. Not only was Gabe in there with Mrs. Rios, but so were the Fina brothers. Lainey stared at the surreal scene which seemed to be something out of a fairy tale.

All four men were sitting on delicate Queen Anne furniture, sipping tea from tiny cups. The Finas looked like the three bears at a tea party for Goldilocks and the self-satisfied smile on Gabe's face made him look like the big bad wolf.

Lainey thumped back onto her heels and stared at the door panels while she clutched the cake and sauce containers. She didn't know what was going on, and very possibly it was none of her business, but Lainey intended to find out. She rapped on the door.

Within a few seconds, it was swung open by Mrs. Rios, who greeted Lainey with a big smile and a fluttery wave of her hand. She was wearing her best dress, a pastel chiffon print, and her cheeks were pink with happiness and excitement.

"Come in, dear. Look at all the company I've got. You're welcome to join us. We're having quite a party."

"So I see," Lainey answered, slipping inside. "I brought you a new dessert I'm working on," she said, her gaze resting on Gabe, who winked at her, then going to the Fina brothers who greeted her with huge smiles. What was going on here?

"Oh, thank you, Lainey," Mrs. Rios said, relieving Lainey of the two containers. "I'm afraid I'll have to save these for later. I think we're all quite full of tea and cookies just now."

For the first time, Lainey noticed the plate of delicate cookies that sat on the coffee table before the Finas. Bull picked one up and it looked to be the size of a postage stamp in his massive paw. He took a teeny bite, nibbling with his front teeth.

Suddenly, she knew how Alice felt when she'd tumbled down the rabbit hole.

"Why don't you sit down, Lainey?" Mrs. Rios asked and Gabe moved over to offer her a place. Feeling slightly dazed, Lainey sat.

Mrs. Rios resumed her seat, folded her hands in her lap, then opened them and placed them on her knees as she scooted forward excitely. "I'll bet you're wondering why these boys are here."

"Um, well, yes, I am."

"Your young man here," Mrs. Rios gave him a sweet smile, "took me out to eat some of May Ling's ribs. Then he gave me this." She reached down beside her chair and picked up a box containing a new cordless phone.

Lainey stared at it. "But you've got a phone."

Her neighbor nodded happily. "Yes, but I can keep this one with me all the time around the house. If I hear something suspicious, I can call the police."

"Instead of throwing rocks," Lainey broke in, smiling. "Why didn't we think of that before?"

"Because you've never had such a smart young man around before."

Lainey looked at Gabe's smug grin. "He's not my young man," she said, just to burst his bubble, but her neighbor wasn't listening.

"We're going into business together," Mrs. Rios said excitedly, clapping her hands.

Flabbergasted, Lainey stared from one to the other of them. "What? Business? Mrs. Rios, you're a retired dressmaker, what kind of business...?"

"Digging for gold," Bison said, breaking into a big,

happy grin. "We've found our great uncle Rudolph's lost mine."

"Not yet we haven't," Gabe said. "But it's only a matter of time."

"Lost mine? The one that he and Lord Battlehaven found that got covered by the earthquake that created the falls?"

"That's right," Bull said as if she'd uttered something brilliant. "That's exactly right."

"But what's that got to do with Mrs. Rios?"

Bruiser beamed. "She's the one who found it, or at least one nugget." He picked up a rock from the coffee table. "She threw this at me the other night and it landed in my pocket."

"I remember."

"Well, when I got home, I started looking at it because it felt awful heavy, scratched off some of the surface clay, and found gold. Not much, but there it is. She found it down in that dry wash that cuts off below the falls. She's going to show us where."

He handed it to Lainey who held it up to the lamplight and squinted. "I can't see anything."

"You need a stronger light," Gabe told her.

"Or a better imagination," she whispered back. "They're not serious about this, are they?"

"They are and now she is. I'm going to be their backer."

She stared. This must be the new business his friend Rich had said he was going to start. "Why?"

"Because they came and told her all about it, got her excited thinking she's going to be rich." Gabe shrugged. "I can't stand to see her taken for a ride, though these three wouldn't do it intentionally."

"Oh, no," Lainey said, looking at him in dismay.

"When this gets out we'll have gold fever all over town. All over the state."

"I know, that's why we're going to keep this strictly between ourselves."

Lainey looked at the beefy prospectors who were talking excitedly with their new partner. They were nice boys but not really bright. She didn't see much chance of this being kept quiet.

She had the same feeling she'd had when Gabe's car had been careening toward the front of her shop.

She wanted to stand up and yell for everyone to stop. Things were moving so fast, changing so quickly, she didn't know if she could keep up.

Gabe touched her hand. "What's the matter, Lainey?"

She looked at him and gave her head a small shake. Nothing was wrong, and yet, everything was and it had all started when Gabe had come to town.

They stayed at Mrs. Rios's house until she began to droop with exhaustion from the effects of the evening's excitement. Lainey, Gabe and the Fina brothers said good-night and left.

When they stepped onto the street, Lainey turned toward her house, but looked back over her shoulder at Gabe. When she lifted her eyebrows in invitation, he gave her that slow, sexy smile of his and moved to take her hand. Before he reached her, though, Bull looped a beefy arm over his shoulders from one side, and Bison did the same from the other. They fell into step, heading for Lainey's house. Left behind, she stared at them. Gabe, trapped on either side, craned his neck around and gave her a helpless look.

"We owe you a lot, Gabe," Bull said. "We're gonna repay you just as soon as we strike it rich."

"We're all gonna be rich," Bison said. "People will finally know that Great Uncle Rudy was telling the truth about the gold in these mountains."

"Hey, you two headed over to Lainey's?" Bruiser wanted to know as he brought up the rear of the parade.

"Yeah," Bull answered. "We need to talk about how we're going to work this."

"Not tonight. We've got plenty of time for that," Gabe said, but the brothers ignored him as they compelled him up her front walk. Bruiser plodded along behind them.

Helplessly, Lainey threw her hands in the air and followed, squeezing past the crowd to unlock her front door and let everyone inside. The Finas convinced Gabe to sit in a chair while they told him about their plans and peppered him with questions.

Ducking, he looked past them and gave Lainey a regretful look, which she returned. It appeared as though it was going to be a long night. "Anyone want some coffee?" she asked.

9

LAINEY HELD the grand reopening of Perk Avenue three days later. Many of her former customers came, though she suspected it was because she was offering half-price drinks. The three people she employed were happy to come back from their unintentional vacation to begin working once again. She had updated some of her stock, changed a few things around and stocked those vitamin packets Gabe had at his place. She planned to add them to fruit smoothies.

Cody showed up after school, slipped in behind the counter, tied on an apron and gave Lainey his slow smile.

"It looks great in here, Lainey," he said, admiring the bright red and yellow streamers the two of them had hung the day before and the red balloons massed in the corners of the ceiling. The decorations added to the party atmosphere that Lainey had been promoting all day.

"Thanks to you. I couldn't have been ready without your help." She reached out and gave him a quick, one-armed hug. They'd been working until almost ten o'clock the night before. Gabe had even come and helped out, which Cody had thought was pretty funny since Lainey and Gabe were rivals.

Cody gave one of his shy shrugs. "That's what you pay me for."

He looked up right then at a group of people coming in the door and gave Lainey a quick, almost guilty look. Curious, she glanced toward the front of the shop and saw Melinda Franklin entering with a group of girls. They surged up to the counter and ordered iced drinks and cookies, chattering among themselves, giving each other nudges. Melinda waved to Lainey and smiled broadly at Cody, who tried to appear nonchalant. A few minutes later, several boys came in and began talking to Cody about their favorite heavy metal bands as he made smoothies for them.

Lainey smiled to herself, pleased that he was making friends at last, maybe even a girlfriend, and her heart grew lighter with each beep of the cash register. That morning, a fair number of students had stopped by on their way to high school for her half-price breakfast, another reason she was grateful for Cody.

The girls sat down at the tables and pulled out their homework. The boys perched nearby and pestered the girls. Three o'clock in the afternoon was normally a slow time at Perk Avenue, but now the place was crowded with paying customers.

"God bless teenagers and their disposable income," she murmured as she watched Cody take a peach smoothie to the table where Melinda sat. He lingered to talk until he glanced over and saw Lainey watching him. Turning, he hurried away. Lainey watched him in puzzlement. She would have to talk to him. Surely, he didn't think she minded if he visited with the customers. He must know how thrilled she was that he was making friends in town. Well, maybe not. She'd never actually told him.

She picked up a tray of dirty cups and carried them into the kitchen. As she pulled clean cups from the dishwasher and stacked them, then placed the dirty ones inside, she thought about the odd signals she'd been getting from Cody lately. When they had some time alone, she would ask him what was bothering him.

She closed at five o'clock. During the late spring and summer months, Perk Avenue stayed open later and she hired extra help. For the first few days of her grand reopening, though, she would be staying at the store the whole time to make sure things ran smoothly. As far as she was concerned, this eleven hour day had lasted long enough.

"Gabe has it made," she murmured, stifling a yawn as she helped Cody stack chairs on tables in preparation for sweeping and mopping the floors.

"Huh?" he asked, looking around.

"I was just thinking what a long day this has been. Gabe works from six until two, then goes back to close up at eight."

"Yeah, he's always done that. He used to get off at two so he could take me to soccer and little league practices."

Another example of how conscientious Gabe had been as Cody's parent, Lainey thought. Dreamily, she went about her chore of cleaning the espresso machine, thinking all the while about Gabe. The two of them had started out on bad terms, the accident hadn't helped matters, but things had gradually improved. She respected him and his concern for Cody, though she thought he worried too much. Now he'd taken on Mrs. Rios's concerns and figured out a way to calm her fears about prowlers. He'd even joined the Finas in business.

She wondered where that was going to lead. The Finas obviously knew a great deal about bodybuilding. They had even shown astute business sense by opening the video arcade. But prospecting? They thought the blood of Rudolph Shipper that flowed in their veins would automatically turn them into successful prospectors. She hoped they were right.

"I'm all done, Lainey," Cody called out.

She turned and blinked at him as he walked toward her from the kitchen. She'd been so deep in thought, she hadn't even noticed that he had done all the mopping and put away his equipment while she had been polishing the chrome of the espresso machine over and over. She spread the towel she'd been using over the edge of the small sink and reached under the counter for her purse.

"Everything looks great, Cody. I guess I'll see you tomorrow, then. And thanks again for your suggestion to offer a half-price breakfast. We had quite a crowd this morning."

Cody nodded. "You're welcome." He paused, started to turn toward the door, then whipped back around and said in a rush, "I need to talk to you, Lainey."

"Sure." Surprised at the seriousness of his tone, she at first thought something was wrong with Gabe, but realized Cody would have mentioned that much earlier. Really, she needed to quit obsessing about Gabe. "What is it?"

"Why don't we sit down?"

She blinked as he took down two chairs and set them on the freshly mopped floor beside a table. Solemnly, he gestured for her to take a seat, which she did.

He sat down opposite her and placed his hands on his knees, cleared his throat, shifted his feet, then cleared his throat again.

Lainey offered an encouraging smile and reached

over to give his shoulder an encouraging pat. ``What is it, Cody? What's wrong?''

He took a deep breath and looked up, his blue eyes serious. ``Lainey, I've met someone.''

Confused, she waited for him to go on. ``Met someone?''

``I think it might lead to something.''

Nodding slowly as she tried to figure out what he meant, she repeated, ``Lead to something.''

Cody's young face twisted with regret. ``I'm sorry to have to break it to you like this, but it's best that you know.''

She might be sure it was best too, if she could understand what on earth he was talking about. He was so somber, she didn't want to blurt out that she didn't know what he meant and risk hurting his feelings.

``I see,'' she said noncommittally in hopes that he would keep talking and give her more clues.

``I want you to know that I really enjoyed our dates, and…and I'm glad you went with me. My friends thought you were really nice,'' he assured her, leaning forward earnestly. ``But, well, like I said, I've met someone.''

Finally, the light dawned, and Lainey fell back against her chair. ``Oh, you mean a girlfriend.''

Misreading her reaction, Cody raised his hands, his young face creased with concern. ``Now, Lainey, don't be upset. That's just the way these things happen. You meet someone, go out for a while, then things change and you meet someone else.''

Lainey stared as the truth sank in. *I'm being dumped by a sixteen-year-old,* she realized with a sense of shock. She almost laughed, but he was so serious, she knew it would crush him. And really, he was trying to be such a gentleman about it that she couldn't hurt his feelings.

"Cody," she began, but the effort of holding back her laughter made her voice choke and her eyes tear up. "I...I don't know what to say."

He shook his head from side to side, his face as grave as a judge's, his eyes stricken with regret as he saw the moisture in her eyes. "Gee, Lainey," he said, his voice breaking. "I...I didn't think you'd cry."

Blinking quickly, she answered, "I'm...I'm not, really."

His shoulders slumped and his head fell forward. "I've broken your heart. Oh, I knew this would happen. There's no easy way to do this, but..."

Her hand shot out to squeeze his shoulder. "No, Cody, really it's all right."

He didn't seem to hear her. "I know what it's like to be dumped, so I was trying not to hurt you. Last December, right before Christmas, my old girlfriend, Cara, dumped me."

"I'm so sorry. That must have really hurt."

He shrugged as if he knew he needed to appear brave, but couldn't quite do it. "Yeah, it did, but I'm over her now."

"That's good, Cody. You've moved on with your life."

His face sincere, he said, "And you'll move on with yours, too, Lainey. We have a good working relationship. Let's not ruin that."

"O-okay." She swallowed hard and cleared her throat. "I appreciate your honesty."

"It's the only way," he assured her.

"This someone you've met. Is it Melinda?"

This time, he lost his attempt at maturity. He broke into a grin. ``Yeah, Melinda. She's cool.''

``The bomb.''

``Oh, yeah,'' he responded fervently.

``I'm happy for you, Cody, I really am. We had fun, but you and Melinda obviously have more in common.''

``Yeah, yeah, we do.'' He all but bounced in his chair. ``Did you know she's a science brain? We've been going up to Starina's together, watching her work on her machine. She even let us help a little. She's going to try it again in a couple of weeks.''

``You'll want to stand well away from it when she does. It's been known to blow up.''

``Probably too much friction.''

``Probably.''

Cody stood to go. ``Thanks, Lainey,'' he said, his face full of relief and happiness. ``And don't you worry. Someday your Mr. Right will come along. I'm just sorry it wasn't me.''

She pinched her lips together. ``That's good of you, Cody. I appreciate it.''

``I've got to go,'' he said, shifting his feet toward the door. ``We're going up to Starina's, then I've been invited to Melinda's house for dinner. See ya tomorrow.''

Lainey waved him off and finally gave in to the need to chuckle. What a huge relief. She couldn't wait to tell Gabe. She would call him. No, she decided, she would go by his house. After all, he'd visited hers enough times. She should visit his. Eagerly, she locked Perk Avenue and hurried up the sidewalk, taking the stairs up the hillside two at a time to reach Frost Boulevard, where the nicest homes in Calamity Falls were located.

Gabe's house was a Victorian that had been painted bright turquoise when he'd bought the place. He'd had it repainted a soft beige and the trim was done in deep blue. Lainey smiled as she approached it, wondering if he realized the trim was the same color as his eyes.

There was an old-fashioned crank-type bell in the middle of the door. Lainey gave it a mighty turn and heard it clang in the foyer.

A couple of minutes later, Gabe answered the door. With a welcoming grin, he invited her in and she burst out with her news. ``I've been dumped by your nephew.''

``Well, it's about time,'' he answered, and drew her into his arms. ``It was hell being in competition with him.''

``Afraid you couldn't measure up?'' she teased.

``Younger men are always a threat,'' he said. Arm around her waist, he drew her into the living room, a large, airy place with coved ceilings and an archway leading to a formal dining room. The area seemed especially large since it held very little furniture, only a sofa and a couple of lamps and chairs.

Gabe gave her an apologetic look. ``We haven't decided what direction the décor is going to take. We can't have too many tables and knickknacks around because Cody's feet seem to get hung up on everything.'' He cleared a stack of newspapers off the sofa, dropped them on the floor and indicated that she should sit down. Then he took a hard look at the exhaustion rimming her eyes and brought her a glass of wine before sitting down beside her and demanding, ``Now tell me what he said.''

Lainey recounted the entire conversation and was finally able to chuckle over it with Gabe. "So, I think your worries with Cody are over," she concluded, scooting into the corner of the sofa and making herself comfortable as she sipped her wine. Immediately, she began to relax.

"Don't kid yourself. Worries with teenagers are never over. I discovered that when Cody was about thirteen and decided he wanted to drive my car."

"The Porsche?"

"Yes. He's always been fascinated by mechanical things, so he decided to take a closer look at the Porsche one day and drove it through the back fence of our house in Tucson."

Lainey grinned. "Have you ever considered the possibility that that car attracts trouble?"

Gabe's chin drew back and his eyebrows snapped together. "No way. It's a classic. It's worth a lot of money."

"When it's not in the repair shop."

He shrugged. "Well, yeah." He finished his own glass of wine and set the glass on the floor by the sofa. "Any idea where my nephew is now? He was supposed to be home after you closed up."

"He went to Starina's, and then to dinner at his new girlfriend's house. Don't worry, Red and Julia will make sure he's on his best behavior."

Gabe frowned. "It's not dinner at the Franklin's I'm worried about. Why is he spending so much time at this Starina's place? I thought he was getting help on a chemistry problem, but he turned that in—or at least he told me he did."

"It's her machine. Her perpetual motion machine. I

guess it's that interest of his in mechanical things. He's fascinated by it.''

``Isn't that the one that's blown up three different times? I don't want him hanging around that.''

``Starina swears she's getting the bugs worked out, but just in case, she's doing her testing on a smaller scale model of the machine.'' Lainey's lips quirked. ``So any explosion would be smaller.''

``That's not much comfort.''

``She's got her smaller version housed in an old motor home. When she's ready to test, she'll drive it out into the desert and start it up.'' Lainey finished her wine and set down her own glass. ``As assistant fire chief, I'm supposed to accompany her to the test—with a few dozen fire extinguishers, no doubt.''

``Just so Cody's not around when she tests it.''

``You might not be able to keep him away.''

Gabe sat forward and gave her a fierce look. ``He's sixteen, still a minor. I guarantee you, I can make sure he doesn't get into something dangerous like that.''

``You're being unreasonable. He's got to have a certain amount of choice and freedom, otherwise you'll be right back where you were, with him sulking around or closed up in his room. That's not what you want,'' Lainey insisted, and knew immediately that she'd said the wrong thing.

His breath drew in sharply. ``It's a family problem, Lainey.''

Hurt shafted through her and her spine stiffened. ``I see. It's all right for you to ask for my help with him, for me to go to a rock concert and a video arcade with him, to listen to your concerns about him, but I shouldn't offer any advice. Is that right?''

Gabe's jaw was set. ``I appreciated your help. I've

told you that, but this is different. This is about his safety.''

No, Lainey thought. It was about Gabe's unwillingness to let her into his life. Funny, because since they had arrived, he'd grabbed her life by the scruff of the neck and shaken it up. Hurt and dismayed, she stood up. ''It's been a long day. I'm going home.''

Gabe climbed awkwardly to his feet. ''Lainey, I...''

''I'll see myself out,'' she called over her shoulder. ''Thanks for the wine. I'll see you at the Showdown on Saturday. May the best chef win.''

Before he could stop her, Lainey was out the door and down the front steps. He didn't try to get her to stay, to listen to what she had to say. And why should he, she asked herself furiously as she hurried along in the gathering dusk. He had only asked her to help him, be there for his nephew, not to fall in love with him. She was the one who had been foolish enough to do that.

Her hand on the smooth iron handrail of the first set of steps leading to her street, Lainey stopped. Foolish, that's exactly what she was. She had known she was falling in love with Gabe and hadn't done anything to prevent it. There ought to be a way to safeguard a person's heart from letting such a thing happen, she thought miserably, as she continued on her way home.

Men like Gabe, stubborn know-it-alls who also happened to be successful, funny and sexy should be required to carry some kind of immunization. They could hand it out to women as foolish as she was.

She felt discouraged, but waved to Mrs. Rios, who waved back with the cordless phone Gabe had given her.

If he didn't do so many nice things for people, she could really dislike him—if she didn't love him so much.

HER ANNOYANCE with Gabe made Lainey that much more determined to win the Great Chefs' Showdown. She had baked her rich chocolate cake so many times, she could do it in her sleep. She had perfected the three toppings to within an inch of their lives. There was no way anyone was going to beat her at this contest— even Gabe's chicken dish paled in comparison to her dessert. She'd show him.

On Friday afternoon, she placed Cody and one of her other workers in charge of the store and closed herself in the kitchen to prepare her contest entry.

With supreme confidence, she mixed, beat and poured the ingredients into the four large pans, enough for all the contest judges, and plenty of extra, just in case.

She picked up the first cake pan and, stepping as carefully as if she carried the crown jewels, walked to the stove. She set the pan down and bent to open the oven door. When a blast of heat didn't roll out to hit her in the face, she checked quickly to see if the oven was on. It was.

"What in the world?" She straightened and looked around, trying to think what could be wrong. Then it hit her. "The propane tank." She dashed outside to look. Because of the danger of landslides when Calamity Falls had first been built, no gas lines had been installed in town. Most residents had all electric appliances or used propane tanks.

Lainey stared dumbly at the gauge that registered zero on her tank. With everything that had been going on—the situation with Cody and Gabe, the grand re-opening, she had forgotten to order propane.

Turning, blindly, she walked back inside and tried to think what to do. She grabbed the phone and ordered propane but it wouldn't be delivered until tomorrow morning. That would be too late. Disappointed, she hung up.

She couldn't believe she had done this. The most important day of her retail career was going to be ruined because of her forgetfulness.

She would have to use another oven, but she needed a big one, one that exactly duplicated the conditions of her own oven so that all her cakes would bake uniformly.

There was only one other in town exactly like hers.

Snatching up the telephone, she dialed a number and when it was answered, she said, "Gabe, you owe me and I'm going to collect. You're going to let me use the oven at Coffee & Such tonight."

"Why would you want to use my oven?"

"Obviously, because mine isn't working. You've got one exactly like mine. I'm assuming it's in proper working order?"

"Of course it is."

"Fine, then I'll be right over."

"But why mine?"

For some reason, the question, asked in a calm reasonable voice had tears spurting to her eyes. Her answer came out in emotional fits and starts. "Because it's the same model as mine and I'm not as—as good a—a baker as some people so I don't want to change anything. It's been hard to get it right, and..." She couldn't think of anything else to say, so she turned and gave her dependable stove a baleful glance as she swiped tears off her cheeks. She didn't know why this was such an emotional issue for her. It was just chocolate cake, a baking contest. And it bothered her to ask him for this when he had made it so clear he didn't want her interference with Cody.

"Lainey, calm down, and…"

She barely heard him as she nudged his memory testily. "When I agreed to go to that concert with Cody, you said you'd do anything to make it up to me. This is the anything."

"So it would seem," he answered slowly. "Sure, come on over. What temperature do you need?"

She told him and hung up, then stood staring at the phone for a minute as her emotions calmed down and her reason took over.

Something was fishy here. He'd agreed too readily.

GABE STOOD by the front door of Coffee & Such and watched Lainey march to the door with brisk, competent strides, a covered cake pan in each hand. She had driven to his store in a small Ford truck. Funny, as much as he liked cars, he'd never given much thought to what kind she drove, or if she even owned one.

It didn't take a fortune teller with a crystal ball to tell him that he was in hot water with her. He'd known that since last night. Now as she came up the sidewalk, her face was set, high color rode in her cheeks, her rope of shiny red hair twitched across her back and she walked with the long-legged stride of an old west sheriff heading for a showdown with the bad guys.

Time to do some fence-mending. He held the door for her and said, "How many more do you have? I'll get them."

She gave him a look that would have flash-frozen

hot lava. "No thank you. I prefer to do this myself. I'm sure you understand that I never would have asked for your help if not for the extreme circumstances."

He winced and wondered if he should check himself for frostbite. "Uh, yes, right," he said, but realized he was talking to air because she had whipped right past him and headed straight for the kitchen. A few customers looked up curiously and greeted Lainey.

One guy, obviously a tourist, let his eyes follow Lainey, his gaze lingering on her backside. Gabe tried out that frosty look of Lainey's, but it must not have come off, because the guy caught Gabe's eye and winked. Gabe wished he'd charged the guy double for his iced mocha.

By the time he reached the kitchen, she was charging past him to return to her truck for the rest of the cake pans.

"Can I...?"

"No," she answered curtly.

He ducked out of the way of the closing swinging door before it clipped him, then waited around while she finished bringing the pans in. As she started to uncover them in preparation for the oven, he stepped up and said, "I'll help with—"

"No." She backed him off with another glare. "This is my contest entry. I'll do it. Shouldn't you be working on your own?"

He leaned against the counter and watched her work. "Everything's ready. I just have to finish up tomorrow."

Of course, there was more to it than that, but there was no point in talking about it. She wouldn't listen to him.

Or would she? One thing he'd learned in the restaurant business was that a man who cooked loved it when someone cooked for him. "I've made a few variations since you tasted it. I took your suggestions."

"My suggestions?" She placed the cakes carefully inside the oven and closed the door.

"About adding more cumin and thickening the sauce."

She blinked at him, having clearly forgotten she'd ever said that. He hid a smile. "Would you like to try it out again?"

"No thank you."

"Are you sure? You've worked a very long day. Did you even stop for lunch today?"

"Well..."

"You're probably pretty hungry. Why not relax for a minute?" He watched her face soften, but reluctance still seemed to drag at her. "You could eat it right here while your cakes are baking," he pointed out.

"Okay, then," she said, seating herself at the small table that stood near the window.

Gabe turned toward the refrigerator before she could change her mind. He opened the big, commercial appliance and pulled out one of the carefully wrapped containers. He had more than enough ready for tomorrow so he didn't have to worry.

Quickly, he turned on the grill and as soon as it was hot, he tossed the marinated chicken on and began heating the sauce. He watched Lainey out of the corner of his eye as he did so. She was trying to act uninterested in what he was doing, but her attention kept straying to the stove. He decided that she was either very hungry or was indulging in a little industrial espionage. Let her look, but if she asked, he would be happy to tell her every ingredient in the dish.

"Gabe, I'm curious about something."

Here it comes, he thought.

"Why are you making a chicken dish? Do you plan to offer it here in your coffee bar?"

"No."

"Then why are you doing it?"

He brought the food to the table, found her some silverware and watched her dig in. "I plan to open a restaurant."

"In addition to this place?"

"Sure. I've run two restaurants before."

"You'll be really busy. Who'll look out for Cody?"

"Same person who always has. Me. I'll hire managers for this place and for the new restaurant."

Lainey finished her food, stood up and walked over to check on her cakes. From what he could smell, they were coming along perfectly. The scent of chocolate made his mouth water. Or maybe it was the sight of Lainey wandering around his kitchen, looking over his stock, no doubt comparing his to what she knew she had on hand at Perk Avenue. He wondered if she knew that she was a born storekeeper.

He moved quietly across the room and when she turned around, he said, "Lainey, I know I worry about Cody too much, and I've told you why."

She stepped back, giving him a wary look. He couldn't blame her. After all, he'd acted like a jerk the last time they were together.

"Yes, you have. But he's a great kid, you've done a great job with him and you're not going to keep him safe by watching over him like a mother hen. If you're worried about him hanging around Starina's machine, why don't you go take a look at it? See exactly what the dangers are. You could go up there tonight. Starina loves showing it off."

Gabe knew an opportunity when he saw one. "Only if you'll come with me."

She frowned. "You don't need me."

If she only knew. But, then, how would she if he never told her? He felt generations of Camden men standing behind him, their hands on his shoulders, pushing him to his knees so he could grovel. "Please, Lainey," he said earnestly, and was relieved to see her waver.

"I suppose I should see the improvements she's made. As assistant fire chief, I should keep an eye on possible hazards, anyway."

"As soon as we finish those cakes, we'll go."

"Sounds good."

Gabe looked at her for a moment. "Part of my problem is that I've never been the dad of a sixteen-year-old before. This is new territory for me. What I said the other night, well, I'm sorry. You've been a big help, you did everything I asked of you when you certainly didn't have to."

"I wanted to. I like Cody."

This is the moment he'd been waiting for. Gabe slipped his arms around her waist and pulled her close. "I'm glad, but what about me, Lainey? How do you feel about a man who moved in on your business, wrecked your shop—though that totally was a mechanical failure and not my fault—asked you to help out with a family problem, and then practically slammed the door in your face?"

She leaned back against his arms so that their hips were together, giving him a pleasant jolt. He watched those beautiful lips of hers curve into a smile as she said, "For some reason, I can't seem to stay mad at you, no matter what boneheaded thing you do."

He drew her close. "That's what I was hoping to hear."

He settled his lips on hers, tasting and inhaling. She was delicious, sexy, wonderful. Whenever he had kissed her, he'd felt himself being drawn into her as if she was wrapping him, ever so gently, in some kind of web he couldn't escape. It had panicked him at first, but now, he felt as if he didn't want to escape. At last, something had snapped into place, that he was where he was supposed to be.

THERE WAS SOMETHING different about this, Lainey thought. There was something about his kiss that was more possessive, had more longing, was even more exciting than usual. Hazily, she thought that he'd changed somehow, but she didn't know what was behind it.

He drew her away from him and said, "Lainey, why don't we go to your place? I'd suggest mine, but I've got this teenager, who—"

"Hey, Gabe," that very teenager said, as he burst through the door. He rocked to a halt, then stood looking from one to the other of them. "Oops," he breathed.

Lainey immediately thought that he was going to be terribly hurt. She cast a quick glance at Gabe who reached down and took her hand.

Cody seemed to catch his breath, then he broke into that California surfer boy grin of his and said, "Hey, cool. See, Lainey, I told you someone else would come along. Gabe, I've got four guys with me. You got anything we can eat?"

"Sure, help yourself to anything that's in the refrigerator except the containers with red lids. That's for tomorrow.''

''Great, thanks.'' Cody headed straight for the refrigerator, scooped up armfuls of food and galloped out again.

''Do you think we're ever going to get some time alone, away from my nephew, your neighbor, the Fina boys…?''

''Only if we move somewhere and change our names,'' Lainey answered, stepping away from him. She became aware of the scent in the room. ''Oh, my cakes!'' Quickly, she grabbed pot holders and snatched the oven door open. She pulled the cakes out and placed them on the counter to cool, then looked at Gabe over her shoulder. With a teasing grin, she said, ''You weren't trying to distract me so those would burn, were you?''

He took the potholders and tossed them away. ''Honey, those aren't the only things burning, but it doesn't look like my fire's going to be put out.''

She groaned at his corniness as he wiggled his eyebrows at her, then swept her into his arms once again. This evening was turning out better than she had hoped, but not as well as she would have liked. Gabe nuzzled her neck.

Their time would come. Soon.

10

"I'VE NEVER SEEN anything like this in my life," Gabe said, staring, awestruck at the contraption that Starina Simms was so proudly displaying. There were huge tanks of liquid along one wall. Clear plastic tubing filled with a variety of colored liquids ran from those tanks to a huge vat.

``She's a beaut, isn't she?'' Starina chirped.

Gabe turned to look at her. He'd seen her around Calamity Falls, but he had never realized this skinny little woman with white hair that stood up in a crazed halo could be a scientist who had studied at MIT. Right now, she was wearing mechanic's overalls with pockets filled with tools, tape, a notepad and pencil. She clanked when she walked.

``Amazing,'' Gabe agreed, exchanging a glance with Lainey, who grinned at him.

``Starina, Gabe's nephew is Cody Jeffers.''

``Oh, yeah, the boy who comes up here with Melinda. Nice kid, make a great mechanical engineer someday.'' She pulled a rag out of her pocket and used it to polish up a couple of the spotless tanks.

``That's good to hear, but that's not what I'm worried about.'' He surveyed the stunning array of tanks, tubing, gears, pulleys and wheels that made up the machine. ``No offense, Ms. Simms, but I don't want him to be in danger.''

The petite dynamo turned and gave him a fierce look. "You mean because my machine blew up a couple of times."

"Three times," Lainey reminded her.

"Girl's got a memory like an elephant," Starina muttered, glancing away. "Don't you worry. I've got all the problems worked out. And besides that, I've made a scale model inside that old motor home."

"I heard about that."

"Well, come on out and look at it," she invited eagerly. The three of them trooped outside and she proudly pointed to the motor home parked on the lot next door. "There was an old house here," she said. "A shack, really, that one of the silver mining companies erected a hundred years ago. It was made into a house, but it was dangerous. When the landlord tore it down, I bought the property. It backs up against a worked-out mine. There are no other houses around, so it'll be all right if any...uh...." She broke off and glanced at Lainey. "...minor incidents occur. But I plan to take the motor home out into the desert or up on Rattlesnake Mesa when it comes time for the real test. And I'll go alone. I always test my machine alone."

Gabe saw Lainey give Starina a solemn look.

"Well," Starina said. "At least since the last time when that detective from Phoenix was here. He and I both got a little scorched on that trial. But I've got all those problems fixed," she assured them eagerly.

"Please let Grandpa or me know the next time you plan to test it. It would be nice if the fire department could be alerted beforehand instead of arriving after the explosion," Lainey said.

"There's not going to *be* an explosion, missy," Starina insisted, her little pixie face taking on a stubborn look.

Deciding to avoid a conflict, Gabe took Lainey's arm and turned her toward the direction that led back to her store. ``Well, thank you Ms. Simms, for letting us see your invention. I appreciate the fact that you've taken such precautions, especially if my nephew is going to be around.''

``Anytime, anytime,'' she said happily and waved them off.

``Well, what do you think?'' Lainey asked.

``I think I'd appreciate it if you'd give my nephew more hours to work at your store. On the other hand, he's got a new girlfriend now so he can concentrate on...wait, maybe I don't want to go there, either.''

Lainey laughed and Gabe put his arm around her shoulders. She looked up with a smile and slipped her arm around his waist.

He thought how perfectly she fit next to him, their strides matching almost exactly. There were many advantages to being with a tall woman, he thought, glancing over as they passed beneath a streetlight. The glow fell across her shining hair and cast her profile in shadow. The greatest advantage to being with this woman was that she was smart, spunky, beautiful and ambitious.

``So, whaddya say?'' he asked suddenly, stopping at the top of the street and swinging her around and into his arms. He dropped his head to nuzzle her ear, reveling in the quick intake of her breath. ``Your place or mine?''

``Do you mean store or home?'' She pulled away and grinned at him. ``Either way, there's a teenage boy who'll expect you home at some point.''

``Yeah, I know, worse luck.'' Gabe complained, but he didn't really mind. He had a good feeling about this, about being with her, and especially about the new friends Cody had finally begun to make. ``And I'm supposed to be setting a good example for him, blah, blah, blah.''

``Yes, you are.''

``But that doesn't mean I can't kiss you right here and now.''

``Lainey!'' Starina's voice boomed down the street.

``Wanna make a bet?'' Lainey sighed.

``Is that man bothering you?''

``No, Starina. *I'm* bothering *him*.''

``Atta girl,'' the scientist called back on a bark of laughter.

``Maybe we should just go,'' Lainey suggested. ``Tomorrow's going to be a big day.''

``All right,'' he said with a sigh. ``But I've noticed a dark corner up ahead and I plan to kiss you there.''

With a laugh, Lainey increased her pace. ``You have to catch me first.''

He did.

TWO OF THE CAKES were gone.

Lainey stood by the open refrigerator and stared dumbly into its spotless interior. They must be at the back somewhere. She removed the two she could find and set them on the counter, then whirled back to look again. Nowhere. They were nowhere to be found.

Slapping the door closed, she stood in the middle of the kitchen and mentally retraced her steps. She had finished baking them at Gabe's, cooled them, and then carried two of them out to her truck. Gabe had followed with the other two, then they'd gone up to Starina's.

And those were the two that were missing. Had he done something with them? No, that was impossible. But where were they?

Casting about, trying to come up with an answer, she turned to see Cody standing in the doorway. He had an odd look on his face, but she barely noticed it as she said, "Oh, good, you're here. Something's happened to two of the cakes. I'm not going to have enough for the judges if I don't bake two more right away." She rushed to the big table that ran along one wall and began assembling ingredients. "I don't know how this could have happened. I know I brought all four back here last night and put them in the refrigerator. I just hope I have time to make two more and cool them before the competition. Thank goodness, the propane company made a delivery this morning. They filled the tank so the oven will work."

"Lainey..."

"I'm wondering if someone is trying to sabotage me," she said, managing to keep her suspicions about Gabe to herself.

"Lainey, no one's trying to sabotage you."

She gave him a swift look as she measured chocolate. "I wish I had your faith in human nature, Cody, but..."

"It was me."

The strain in his voice finally got through to her. She turned and stared at him. "What?"

From his pocket, he pulled the front door key she had given him. "It was me and the other guys."

"The other...? You mean the ones you were with last night?" She walked toward him slowly.

"Yeah, when you and Gabe walked by with the

cakes, they looked good, so we came down here and ate two of them.''

Lainey stared, open-mouthed. ``I can't believe it.''

``I'm sorry.''

She stared at him and couldn't move. ``But why?''

He held his hands out in front of him. ``I've had a hard time making friends here. These guys seemed cool....'' He shrugged miserably. ``I guess I just wanted to impress them that I could walk in and help myself.''

Lainey shook her head slowly from side to side. ``But you'd eaten at Gabe's. I trusted you...I feel like I don't know you at all.''

``I'm sorry,'' he repeated, his young face spasming with regret.

``Sorry doesn't cover it, Cody. What you did was completely irresponsible.''

He lifted a shoulder in a defensive shrug. ``I know, but...''

``But, what?''

``But I'll help you make more.''

Angry and hurt, she shook her head. ``No, I don't want your help. I'll do this myself. You'd better go.''

``Am...am I fired?''

Too angry to be reasonable, Lainey said, ``Yes, Cody, you are.''

He tried to speak again, but she cut him off. ``You'd better go,'' she repeated.

He held out his hands and his young face was twisted with regret. ``But if you'd just listen....''

``Not now,'' she said.

``What's going on?'' Gabe asked, appearing in the doorway behind Cody. ``What's wrong?'' He looked from Cody's miserable face to Lainey's angry one.

"Ah, nothing," Cody said, pushing past his uncle and hurrying out of the store.

"What did you say to him?" Gabe asked, coming to stand beside her.

"I told him he was fired."

Gabe's eyes widened. "Why? What did he do?"

"Find him and ask him. I don't have time to discuss it right now because I've got to bake two more cakes and have everything ready in…" she glanced at the clock. "An hour and a half."

"I'll help," he said, taking off the light jacket he wore and rolling up his sleeves.

"No." She could feel time pressing on her. "This is my dish. The rules for the contest say we have to prepare our own entries and that's what I'm going to do. And besides, I've had enough 'help' from the two of you, first you wreck my store, then Cody wrecks my dessert."

Gabe threw his hands in the air. "*How* did he wreck it? If you don't tell me, I can't fix it."

"You don't have to fix it," she shot back. "Just go and let me do it."

"Fine." He grabbed his jacket and headed for the door. "You're a stubborn woman, Lainey Pangburn, and it's a sorry day when you won't let a person make amends for a mistake. Maybe you should ask yourself exactly how important it is to you to win this contest."

Lainey whirled around to answer, but he was gone. Sick at heart, she returned to her task. He didn't understand, and she didn't have time to explain it to him.

IT TOOK HER every minute of the time, but she got the desserts prepared and over to the community center before the contest started. It seemed that everyone in town was crowded into the big room. Many people spoke to her, wished her luck or gave her thumbs-up signals. She answered with smiles, but she was searching the room for one person. She finally spotted Gabe standing against a side wall. He was leaning against it, arms crossed over his chest, a brooding expression on his face.

At the front of the room, the judges were lined up, seated behind a long table. They were mostly the city council members. Red Franklin, the mayor, seemed to be the spokesperson.

As soon as the last entry was put in place, he called for quiet. "It is with great pleasure that we open these proceedings. The dishes that have been prepared by our famous local chefs look wonderful. It'll be a tough decision, but may the best chef win."

The next hour was a tense one for Lainey. She watched each judge's face whenever they took a bite of a new dish. She had served her dessert on three small dishes, each one with a different topping so that the judges could get the full effect. Knowing that presentation was at least as important as the dish itself, she had swirled the toppings on the plate, then over the top of the cake. She wished she'd been able to think of a really clever name for it, something catchy. She should have talked to Jo. Her best friend was good at thinking up clever slogans.

Lainey sighed inwardly. And maybe she'd simply better quit obsessing about it. She had done her best. Now it was in the hands of the judges. Her attention continually strayed to Gabe, who looked as cool as a December morning as he waited for the decision. Lainey had been as anxious when the judges were tasting his chicken dish as she had been when they'd tried her dessert.

She wanted to tell him that. She wanted to say she was sorry she had snapped at him and Cody. She was intensely disappointed in Cody, but she loved him, and more than anything else, she loved Gabe.

In the middle of the laughter, noise and fun of the Great Chefs' Showdown, Lainey took a deep breath and put her hands to her cheeks. She loved Gabe. She had been trying to avoid the truth of that for days now, but it had done no good. She was in love with him and probably had been since the day she had walked into Coffee & Such to introduce herself and had been assaulted by his great looks and that killer dimple.

Why had it taken her so long to figure this out? Because love meant risk. It meant possibly ending up like her parents had. It meant having someone watching over her like the people of Calamity Falls had done since she had moved here with Julius. It meant sharing and compromising, things she wasn't good at—unless she admitted she loved Gabe Camden enough to consider his needs above her own.

What were his needs? Security for his nephew and himself, self-respect, hard work, life in a community where he could feel like he was making a real contribution.

Those were all identical to her needs.

Stricken, she stared across the room at Gabe, who looked up at that moment and met her gaze. When he saw her face, he straightened away from the wall and started forward. Someone stepped in front of him, though and began pumping his hand.

Lainey felt herself grabbed in a bear hug.

"Congratulations, Lainey," Bruiser Fina bellowed. "You won."

"What?" She stared around in confusion at the people facing her with beaming smiles and hearty handshakes. "I won?" She had been so involved in thoughts of Gabe that she hadn't even heard the announcement of the winner.

"You sure did." Cedric and Charlotte gave her hugs, as well. "Wait 'til Julius and Martha hear. They'll be so proud."

She looked around in confusion, unable to believe she had missed the announcement. "Why, yes, I guess..."

"And the council's idea of two winners was inspired," Charlotte said.

Lainey blinked. "Two winners? I'm sorry, I..."

"Hey, are you in shock, or something?" Bruiser Fina asked. "You're not gonna faint, are you?" he asked. "It's okay if you are, though. I've been wanting to try out those smelling salts in the medical kit and the fire truck's right down the street."

She waved him away. "No, I'm okay."

"Gabe won, too," Bull said. "The council picked a main dish and a dessert. People will love it." He looked at his brothers. "Maybe we should open a restaurant, too."

"Nah." Bison shook his head. "We've got enough going on right now."

"Lainey," Red Franklin called out. "We need you up here to accept your ribbon."

A way was made for her and Lainey was escorted by the Finas, who then stepped back and pushed Gabe to the front.

She looked at him with a thousand thoughts crowding into her mind, but she couldn't say anything because Red Franklin was standing before them. He made a speech about how proud he and the city council members and all of the people in Calamity Falls were to present the ribbon along with the city seal to Lainey and Gabe. The mayor then proclaimed their dishes the official foods of Calamity Falls.

In a burst of happiness, Lainey accepted her award and watched as Gabe accepted his.

"Let's get a picture of the two winners," Don Quillan, editor of the Calamity Falls *Ingot* insisted, pushing his way through the crowd.

As if it was the most natural thing in the world, Gabe put his arm around Lainey and smiled for the camera.

"Congratulations," Gabe said, as Don got the camera into position.

Lainey looked up at him and said, "Congratulations to you, too. Your chicken deserved to win." Then she said in a rush, "Gabe, I need to talk to you. I—"

"Smile!" Don insisted, and took several pictures. He let the camera swing from the strap around his neck and whipped out his notebook. "Lainey, what do you call your dessert? How did you come up with the idea?"

She tried to focus on the *Ingot's* editor. "Um, well, everyone likes chocolate, and…"

"And it's the only thing she can bake really well," Gabe said.

She looked up quickly and saw the flash of humor in his eyes. He had forgiven her and she hadn't even had to say anything, or make any explanations yet. She slipped her hand into his and the familiar electric thrill ran up her arm from their joined palms and intertwined fingers.

"Chocolate Tingle," she told Don. "I call it Chocolate Tingle."

"And you, Gabe, where did you come up with your idea?"

"I thought something hot and spicy would be appropriate for this town," he said. "After all, we thrive on the unusual here. I call the dish Gold Fever because that's been a big part of this town's past."

Don asked more questions and scribbled notes. As he did so, more people congratulated them and then began drifting away. Pretty soon, the room began to empty.

When Gabe and Lainey were left to themselves, she turned to him. Her face was full of anxiety. "Gabe, I'm so sorry for what I said. I was way too hard on Cody and on you. I didn't know what I was thinking except that..."

"You had so much invested emotionally in this contest, you couldn't stand to lose," he said, his lips quirking into a smile.

"I'm afraid so."

"You're an intense person, Lainey. That's one of the things I love about you."

Her mouth fell open. "What?"

"You have to prove yourself all the time so people won't see you only as Julius's granddaughter, someone who needs to be watched over. You want to be able to live in Calamity Falls without people thinking of you as a kid. You want them to see you as a capable businesswoman."

"Yes," she breathed. "How did you know that?"

"I've spent a lot of time thinking about you." Gabe slipped his arms around her waist and gathered her close. "And I've spent a lot of time thinking about us. Why don't we go somewhere by ourselves?"

"My place," she said, standing on tiptoe to place her lips on his.

Gabe returned her kiss, but before he could answer, a loud boom shattered the air and a shock rocked the room.

They sprang apart. "What in the world was that?" Gabe asked.

Lainey had heard it before. "That was Starina's machine blowing up! I've got to go."

Within seconds the fire alarm sounded throughout Calamity Falls. Lainey raced from the community center with Gabe right behind her. Fortunately, they were only two doors from the fire station, so she arrived quickly to begin organizing the volunteer firefighters.

The Finas were wiggling into their fireman's gear. Lainey gave them a scan to make sure they had everything on correctly and were in possession of all their equipment before she donned her own. The other firefighters rushed in and were ready to go just as quickly.

"Let's move it," she yelled, jumping onto the truck.

Gabe grabbed her arm just before she climbed on the back, where she usually rode. "I'm coming with you."

"No." For an instant she thought he was being overprotective, but she saw the fright in his eyes.

"Cody could be up there. He wasn't at the Showdown just now."

She hesitated only a second. "Ride up front," she said. "But when we get there, you'll have to stay out of the way."

"Okay, chief," he said, his worry lifting for a second. Lainey realized that the fact that he hadn't argued with her or tried to get in her way meant he respected her position as assistant fire chief. He vaulted into the front seat beside Bull Fina and they roared out of the station.

They whipped through the winding, back-switching, hairpin-turning streets of Calamity Falls and arrived at Starina's workshop.

Bull practically stood the truck on its nose as they came to a stop. The firefighters swarmed out and Lainey began shouting directions. It took her a few seconds to realize that unlike all the other times, it wasn't Starina's workshop that had blown up. Where the old motor home had once stood was a giant, gaping hole. Starina, Cody and Melinda stood gazing, open-mouthed down into it.

The firefighters and Gabe dashed over to them.

''Starina, what happened?'' Lainey asked, when she reached them. When she saw the gigantic hole, she grabbed Starina with one hand and Melinda with the other and said, ''Get back. This could cave in.'' Gabe pulled Cody back, but the awestruck teens crowded in close once again.

''I don't know what happened this time,'' Starina insisted, looking up at Lainey. ''We were inside the workshop making a few adjustments when we heard the motor home explode. By the time we got out here, it had gone down.''

Gabe and the firefighters were clustered as close as they could get to the edge of the hole.

''It's an old mine shaft, Lainey,'' Gabe called out.

''I knew there was one there,'' Starina said. ''The headquarters for one of the mining companies was built there a hundred years ago and then the building was turned into a house.''

"Amazing that you weren't hurt," Lainey said. She examined the three of them closely, but they seemed to be fine.

Bull Fina had removed his helmet and stretched out on his stomach to peer into the hole. "What is that?" he asked.

His brothers got on their knees beside him and stared in cautiously. Gabe joined them.

"It's a destroyed motor home," Gabe said. He sat back on his heels, but the Finas continued to peer inside.

"No, I mean that shiny stuff," Bull answered, his voice growing excited.

"Glass?" one of the other firefighters suggested, walking up cautiously to stand behind them. Leaning from the waist, he tried to look past the massive brothers.

"Maybe." Bull got to his feet. "I'm going down in there."

"You most certainly are not," Lainey said, hurrying over to him.

"Ah, come on, Lainey, it could be..." He looked at his brothers and clamped his mouth shut.

"Be what?" she asked suspiciously.

Gabe stepped up beside her. "Gold?" he suggested.

"No. That's impossible." She shook her head emphatically. "That whole story about Rudolph Shipper finding gold was probably a myth."

"Hey, he wasn't a liar," Bruiser said, bristling.

Realizing she'd insulted his distant relative, Lainey tried to smooth things over but maintain her authority. "Okay, maybe it was true, but how could they have dropped a mine shaft right here all those years ago and not have seen it?"

"They probably just missed it," Bison said. "Come on, Lainey, at least let us look."

"It's too dangerous."

"I'm a trained firefighter," Bull insisted. "I know how to do this safely."

She doubted that with all her heart. Helplessly, she looked at Gabe, who gave her a sympathetic shrug, but said, "They won't stop until they see for themselves." He nodded toward the fire truck. "We could use the fire hose to rappel Bull down."

Everyone thought that was a great idea, but Lainey fought on. "That's not the purpose of a fire hose. Besides, if it is gold, it's waited more than a hundred years. Couldn't it wait a little longer?"

"No!" the men shouted in unison.

The decision was taken out of her hands when one of the men raced for the truck and backed it closer to the chasm. The others began unwinding the hose. Bull looped it around his waist, but Lainey put her hand on his arm and said, "Wait. You're too big, and so are your brothers. A smaller person needs to go down."

Everyone stopped and looked at her, but she threw her hands out to hold them off. "Not me!"

"I'll go," Gabe said quietly. "I've had rappelling experience."

She whirled on him. "No, I don't want you to get hurt."

He shot her a grin, leaned forward and kissed her lightly. "Then hold the other end of the hose." He took it from Bull, looped it around himself, and backed over the edge of what had once been a concrete floor. The firemen held onto the hose and played it out as he went.

Lainey watched his face, then his eyes, then the top

of his head disappear and her heart bounced up to nearly choke her.

The crowd waited anxiously, exchanging glances, holding the hose, standing on one foot, then the other. Several minutes passed, and then there was a shout from below. ``Pull me up!''

Hand over hand, they tugged Gabe out of the hole. When he was beside them once again, he grinned and held out his hand. In it were several shiny rocks, each about the size of a pea. ``I'm no expert, but I suspect that's probably gold.'' He glanced up. ``Starina, I think you're going to be rich and not because of your invention.''

A shout went up from all of them while a stunned Starina reached out for one of the nuggets. Bull, Bison, and Bruiser crowded around to see for themselves, then thumped each other on the back in congratulations.

``It was true. Old Rudolph really did find gold. Wait'll we tell ma. She'll want to come see for herself,'' Bruiser said, wiping away tears that had sprung to his eyes.

``We'll mine it out of there for you, Starina,'' Bull said immediately and both his brothers nodded.

``We're going to have to figure out a way to safeguard this,'' Lainey said. ``We'll have to call Sheriff Watson and get this cordoned off, maybe build a fence around it.''

``Ever the assistant fire chief,'' Gabe said, putting his arm around her and drawing her back. ``Let them enjoy the moment, will you?''

She looked up, grinned, and relaxed. ``You're right. But you know what this means, don't you?''

``Gold Fever. It ought to be great publicity for the town, not to mention my dish…and new restaurant. In fact, I think I'll call it that. This find might even change the usual perception of this place as a haven for odd-balls and losers.''

''Don't count on it,'' she said as she watched the Finas doing some kind of football end zone victory dance that involved a lot of hip bumping and palm slapping. Cody and Melinda looked dazed and excited. Starina stood staring down into the hole. She'd grabbed a notebook from one of her many pockets and was taking notes. No doubt there was a great deal to learn from this explosion.

''Now where were we before all this excitement?'' Gabe asked, then snapped his fingers. ''Oh, yeah, we were about to create some excitement of our own.''

She tried to loop her arms around his neck, but it was awkward because she was wearing her fireman's protective gear. She settled for placing them around his waist while he scooped her close to him and kissed her.

''I love you, Lainey,'' he said. ''I think I've been in love with you since you sashayed into my store weeks ago. It took me a while to figure it out, but I love you. Any chance you'd consider marrying me? We could run the restaurant together or you can keep Perk Avenue open. I don't care, just so you marry me.''

''Oh, yes. I love you, too. I'd consider marrying you, and I'd actually do it, too, except…''

''What?'' he asked in alarm.

''You realize of course, that the people around here won't change? They'll always be looking out for me, and now you, and Cody, and any kids we have.''

Relieved, he said, ''That's okay. That's what makes this town unique.''

People were arriving from everywhere in town, first

in response to the explosion, and now as the news of the gold spread. They crowded around the gaping hole while the firemen tried to keep them back. Even the Finas stopped their celebrating long enough to join in the crowd control. The fact that tears of joy were streaming down their faces didn't seem to detract from their authority at all.

Cody and Melinda came to join them. Lainey reached over to squeeze Cody's hand in apology for the way she'd snapped at him and he gave her a smile.

``It's only one of the things that makes this town unique,'' she responded.

Gabe held her close as their friends and neighbors joined them, filling the street with talk and laughter which echoed off the foothills. Listening carefully, she thought she could hear old Rudolph Shipper and ``Lord'' Albert Battlehaven laughing, too.

The Harlequin Reader Service® — Here's how it works:

If offer card is missing write to: Harlequin Reader Service, 3010 Walden Ave., P.O. Box 1867, Buffalo NY 14240-1867

NO POSTAGE
NECESSARY
IF MAILED
IN THE
UNITED STATES

BUSINESS REPLY MAIL
FIRST-CLASS MAIL   PERMIT NO. 717-003   BUFFALO, NY

POSTAGE WILL BE PAID BY ADDRESSEE

HARLEQUIN READER SERVICE
3010 WALDEN AVE
PO BOX 1867
BUFFALO NY 14240-9952

Play The Lucky Hearts Game

and get...
FREE BOOKS & a FREE GIFT...
YOURS to KEEP!

Scratch Here!
then look below to see
what your cards get you...

Yes! I have scratched off the silver card. Please send me my **2 FREE BOOKS** and **FREE GIFT**. I understand that I am under no obligation to purchase any books as explained on the back of this card.

To Catch a Latte

Jennifer
McKinlay

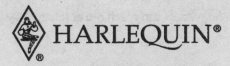

HARLEQUIN®

TORONTO • NEW YORK • LONDON
AMSTERDAM • PARIS • SYDNEY • HAMBURG
STOCKHOLM • ATHENS • TOKYO • MILAN • MADRID
PRAGUE • WARSAW • BUDAPEST • AUCKLAND

Dear Reader,

When I did my fifth tour of duty as a bridesmaid, I swore to myself never again! I mean, why is it the bride always says, "I picked a gown you can wear again"? When the only time you will ever wear the dress again is on Halloween, and that's only after you've drenched it in fake blood and lodged a phony ax on your head.

I was inspired to write *To Catch a Latte* shortly after that last experience. Now, don't get me wrong. I love weddings. Who doesn't? Even my commitment-phobic heroine, Annie Talbot, loves a good wedding. She just doesn't want to have one of her own—ever. But that's before she falls bustle over bouquet for my hero, Fisher McCoy, who not only enjoys weddings, but also wants a big one—with Annie!

As for me, I married the love of my life two year ago (small wedding party and the dress could be worn again—really!) and just recently gave birth to my son. Rounding out my little family are my dog, Lucy, and my cat, Chubby. Suffice to say, there's never a dull moment at my house!

Keep laughing,

Jennifer McKinlay

P.S. Online readers can reach me at jennmck@yahoo.com.

For my husband, Chris,
for teaching me the meaning of true love.

For my son, Beckett,
for showing me how beautiful the world can be.

For my mom,
for being a genuine heroine.

And for their constant love and support,
I thank Pop, Jed, Natalia, Phoenix, Austin,
Annette and everyone at PPL and DBG.

1

"SHE'S MAKING ME wear purple," Annie Talbot confided to her sister. They sat at a small table, beside a window at the back of Annie's shop called The Coffee Break.

"Purple? With your red hair?" Mary cringed. "Street-length or tea-length?"

"Full-length," Annie said. "With a hooped skirt and a parasol. She has a Scarlett O'Hara complex. Who knew?"

"Tara Plantation in Phoenix, Arizona?" Mary snorted. "You're going to look like Barney after a sex-change operation."

"It's not funny." Annie glared at her older sister.

"Oh, yes, it is." Mary chortled. "Just think you can twirl your parasol as you stroll down the aisle to 'I…'"

"I get the idea," Annie interrupted her sister before she could massacre the infamous children's song. She loved Mary dearly, but the woman couldn't carry a tune in a bag, and Annie wasn't up to listening to all of the dogs in the neighborhood bay in accompaniment.

"You could always say no," Mary reminded her.

"Too late. The wedding is this weekend." Annie sighed. "Eve would kill me."

"Better that than be seen in that dress," Mary said. She picked up her coffee cup and studied Annie over the rim. "Tell her you're afraid of that old wives' tale. What is it? Three times a bridesmaid never a bride?"

"Given that this is my ninth tour of duty as a bridal attendant, I don't think she'd buy it. Besides everyone knows how I feel about marriage."

"Yes, I know. 'It's an unnatural state leading to inevitable heartbreak and disappointment,'" Mary repeated Annie's well-known sentiments like a mantra. "Good grief, it's hard to believe I've been happily married for ten years."

"You and Ken are an aberration," Annie said.

"Gee, Sis, that's the nicest thing you've ever said to me."

"You know what I mean," Annie said. "Marriage, a lifetime commitment, is just not natural for human beings."

"Neither is celibacy," Mary retorted, shaking her head. Her sleek auburn bob brushed across her cheeks in a becoming sweep and Annie felt the familiar pang of envy. No matter what she tried, her mass of Bozo tangles never looked that good.

"Look at Mom and Dad," Annie said.

"They're an aberration."

"Dad's on his third marriage and Mom's on her fourth."

"See? They still haven't given up on finding the right mate," Mary said.

"Please." Annie wiped the table with her napkin. "They're professionals."

"Hmm," Mary hummed noncommittally. "You have a bigger dilemma than a purple hooped skirt."

"I do?"

"Yes." Mary plunked her cup onto the table. "I saw Stewart. He's bringing his new girlfriend to the wedding."

"Oh, good for him," Annie said and meant it. She had broken off her relationship with Stewart months ago. He was a nice guy, but he wanted to get married and that just didn't factor into Annie's plans. She had decided long ago that she wasn't the marrying kind.

"It's not fine," Mary said. "He has some ridiculous idea that seeing him with someone else will make you jealous enough to take him up on his proposal."

"He told you that?"

"Yes."

"Subtlety never was one of his strengths," Annie observed. "I guess I'll just have to dredge up a date and hammer it home to him that we're finished."

"Are you?"

"Yes," she said with little regret. "After I broke up with him, I realized I never really loved him. Not as much as I should have."

"So, where are you going to dig up a date in three days?" Mary asked.

"I don't know. The cemetery?" Annie joked with a shrug.

"I wouldn't. Corpses make terrible dates—they're dead bores," Mary quipped.

"Ugh! That was terrible." Annie grimaced with a chuckle. Glancing over her sister's shoulder, she checked to see that her staff had the shop under control. Annie wasn't one to take a break in the middle of the day, but it wasn't often that Mary escaped her domestic bliss, and she was loathe to pass up any time with her sister.

"How about Paul Lester from Dad's firm?" Mary suggested.

"He has hair growing out of his ears," Annie said. "Lots of it."

"Billy Winchester?"

"Still lives with his mother."

"Chuck Newton?"

"In jail."

"What for?" Mary blinked.

"Grand theft auto."

"What?"

"Apparently, his wife got the car in the divorce, but he didn't agree."

"Oh. Well, Ken has a friend at work…"

A crash from outside interrupted whatever Mary had been about to say. Both women whipped their heads in the direction of the staircase that ran outside the window up to the second floor. Simultaneously, their jaws dropped open.

Framed in the window was a perfect male torso. Suntanned skin glistened with sweat that dripped off defined pectorals and a taut stomach.

"Oh my," Mary gasped.

The torso bent at the waist, and they watched as a shock of dark brown hair and a square jaw filled the open window.

"Hi, Annie," the possessor of the perfect torso greeted them. His gaze held hers as if he were studying her.

"Hi, Fisher," Annie responded, but it was little more than a squeak.

"Sorry about the noise." He grunted as he hefted a box onto his shoulders and disappeared from sight with a glimpse of bunched forearms and muscle-knotted calves.

Mary turned to her sister with a raised eyebrow and a wicked grin. "Fisher? Your new tenant?"

"Uh-huh," Annie said, clearing her throat.

"My, my, my."

"It's not what you think."

"What do I think?"

"That I rented the apartment to him just because he's gorgeous," Annie said.

"And you didn't?"

"No, he actually has a job, which means he can pay

the rent," she said. "And besides, the day he came to see the apartment he was wearing a suit."

"Oh yeah, he'd look like Quasimodo in a suit," her sister teased.

"I really had no idea he was so good-looking without his clothes on," Annie protested, feeling her face grow hot.

"Well, now you know," Mary observed dryly. "He did pay his first month's rent in advance, I hope?"

"He wrote me a check."

"Wait and see if it bounces."

"Spoilsport."

"He would be perfect, you know," Mary mused.

"Perfect for what?"

"The wedding," she answered.

"No, I don't think..."

"He'd be a loud and clear message to Stewart that you've moved on."

"You think?"

"He's gorgeous and employed?" Mary asked and Annie nodded. "That's pretty much perfect."

"I don't think I could..."

"I dare you," Mary interrupted her.

"Dare me?" Annie repeated.

"Double-dare you," Mary said.

"Double-dare? Are you nuts? We're not kids anymore. I don't have to accept a double-dare."

"Bock...bo-bo-bo-bock," Mary clucked. Tucking her thumbs under her armpits, she began to flap her elbows.

Annie could feel the stares of nearby customers and felt her already warm face grow hot with embarrassment. "Mary, you're making a scene."

"Bock...bo-bock," Mary squawked louder and began to bob her head.

Annie started laughing. She couldn't help it. Her sophisticated sister looked ridiculous.

"All right. All right. I give," she said, raising her hands in surrender.

Mary picked up her coffee cup and took a delicate sip. "Good for you. After all, what's the worst that could happen? He says no? Big deal."

"Yeah, big deal." Annie rolled her eyes.

FISHER HEARD the footsteps on the stairs long before they reached the landing. Judging from the pace—quick but light—it had to be his landlord Annie. He'd noticed when he leased the apartment that she moved with a speed that made him dizzy. She never walked. She ran.

Sure enough, her mane of fiery red hair peeked around his doorway accompanied by a cursory knock. "Fisher?"

"In here," he invited her into his living room.

She took a hurried step forward, but then leapt back with a shriek. Fisher felt the hair on his neck stand on end, but then he relaxed. Harpy, his pet cockatiel, had swung down from her perch on top of the door frame and was hanging upside down in Annie's face.

"Hello," Harpy said. "Hello."

Fisher glanced out the door to see Annie leaning against the rail her hand pressed against her rib cage as if trying to keep her heart where it belonged. One long, curling strand of hair fell across her face. She pursed her lips and blew it aside. She looked thoroughly exasperated. Fisher swallowed a laugh.

"Sorry about that," he said. "Harpy's just getting used to her new digs."

"Harpy, huh?" She lifted an eyebrow.

"Come here, Harpy." Fisher held out his finger, and

Harpy gripped it with her beak and swung down to perch on his hand. "Meet our new landlady."

"Hello," Harpy said.

"Hello, Harpy," Annie said. "Can I pet her?"

"Sure. She loves to have her pinfeathers scratched."

"Hi, Harpy." Annie's voice dropped an octave as she rubbed the back of Harpy's head between her index finger and her thumb. Harpy sagged forward, her head bent, giving Annie full access. "Oh, who's a pretty bird?" Annie cooed and Fisher felt her voice skitter over his skin like sandpaper on wood.

When he'd signed the lease, he'd been struck by her resemblance to Orphan Annie. With her red hair and freckles, the similarity was close enough to warrant the name. He was pretty sure, however, that Orphan Annie didn't have a voice that could bring a grown man to his knees.

A waft of scent, faintly floral and very sexy, drifted by his nose. She sure didn't smell like a cartoon, either. He looked away and tried to envision a curly-topped kid in a red dress with a white collar, standing next to a dog. What was the dog's name? It had shaggy hair and it was sort of brown...

"Fisher, are you all right?"

He glanced back, hoping that the image in his mind would be standing before him. No such luck. Dark sapphire-blue eyes met his, and he felt himself swallow. Damn. With those eyes, that voice and that scent, she bore no resemblance to the fictional character in his mind.

"Are you okay?" she asked again.

"Just fine," he lied. So she was attractive. So what? There were plenty of attractive women in the world. He was a professional. He never let his personal feelings get in the way of a job. And this was a job, nothing more. "What can I do for you?"

"Well, I..." she stammered. "I...was just wondering how you were settling in?"

He narrowed his eyes. A hint of red crept into her face, covering the spray of freckles on her cheeks. She looked like a sticky-fingered, three-year-old caught raiding the candy dish. Cute.

He turned away from her, hoping to give her a chance to build up the nerve to say what she really wanted. He carried Harpy to her cage in the corner of the living room. He opened the door and lifted her to her perch. Harpy immediately assumed her favorite position; she hung upside down and began to squawk for food.

"I'm settling in just fine," he said. "And Harpy certainly seems at home."

"Does she always hang upside down?" Annie asked with a laugh as if relieved by the change of subject.

"Always," he confirmed, ignoring the way her laugh made him want to laugh in return. It was deep and throaty and thoroughly provoking. "Was there anything else?"

"Actually." She paused, and Fisher glanced over his shoulder to see her face bloom a deeper shade of red. "There was one thing."

"Yes?" he prompted.

"I was wondering if you'd consider being my date."

"Date?" he repeated, feeling as if she'd belted him in the solar plexus.

"You see, the thing is, I have to be in a wedding." She paused.

"And?"

"And I need a date," she rushed to explain. "Now I know you just moved in, and you don't even know me, but this might be a good way for you to meet some new people. And it won't be a date in the technical sense. It would be more like two friends going to a wedding together.''

''Why do you need a date so badly?'' he asked. The fiery color had receded from her cheeks, but her gaze was firmly fastened on the floor as if she were hoping a hole would open up and give her a swift getaway. She was obviously embarrassed, but he had to give her credit for nerve. She didn't seem the kind to ask out a total stranger…unless she had a very good reason.

''Well, there's this ex-boyfriend,'' she began.

''Ah.'' He nodded.

''He's a nice guy, but he doesn't seem to understand that I've moved on,'' she explained.

''And he'll be at the wedding,'' Fisher deduced aloud, ''and you think if you bring a date, he'll realize it's over.''

''That's the idea,'' she admitted.

''I only have one question,'' he said. ''Why me? Don't you know someone else who could escort you?''

''Honestly?'' She wrinkled her nose before answering. ''No. Running the shop doesn't give me much of a chance to socialize.''

''Really? I'd have thought you'd have to beat 'em off with the coffeepot.''

She snorted a surprised laugh through her nose, and Fisher blinked. The woman was a snorter! Why he found this charming he had no idea. As her laughter faded she watched him with wide eyes as if awaiting a sentence. He didn't have the heart to torture her and besides she was handing him the very thing he needed. An in.

''I'd be happy to go,'' he said.

''Really?'' Her eyebrows hit her hairline and then she grinned. ''I don't suppose you'd be available for the rehearsal dinner, too?''

''Uh, well, I don't see why not,'' he said.

"Okay. I'll meet you Friday evening at six-thirty," she said.

"Sounds fine."

"Great." She beamed at him as she walked backward toward the door. "Friday then."

She stumbled over the doorframe, and Fisher leapt forward, catching her by the arm to keep her from falling.

"Oh!" She shook her head and laughed at herself. "That's me, grace in motion."

Fisher couldn't help but smile. She was a charmer. Her skin felt soft and warm beneath his fingers. He squeezed her arm before letting her go.

"Thank you, Fisher," she said.

"My pleasure," he said and meant it.

"So, how does she look?"

Fisher squinted across the desk at his partner. Look? She looked great. A spray of freckles, a mane of wild red hair and a contagious laugh… Oh yeah, she looked just fine.

"Fish?" Brian Phillips, Fisher's partner, waved his hand in front of his face. "You in there?"

He shook his head, trying to dislodge Annie's image. "Yeah, I'm here."

"So." Brian leaned back in his chair. "How does she look?"

"She's a redhead," he said.

"Uh-oh," Brian said. "You don't mix well with redheads. Remember the one in Tucson who we nabbed for check fraud. She kicked you in the…"

"I remember," Fisher interrupted with a wince. "Annie's not like that."

"Annie is it?" Brian asked. "Better watch it, Special Agent McCoy, you know you're not supposed to become personally involved with your suspects."

"We're not sure she's a suspect," he protested.

Brian sat up straight all humor wiped from his face. "Yes, she is. Someone at The Coffee Break is laundering huge amounts of dirty money through a secondary account. She's the owner, so she's the chief suspect. The criminals using her services are some very nasty thugs. Don't underestimate her."

"Come on," Fisher snapped, annoyed. "I've been with the Bureau for more than ten years. I'm not about to let some dizzy redhead bring me down."

"Be sure you don't," Brian warned and then teased, "Unless, of course, it's part of your cover."

"Shut up," Fisher chided him. "Or I'll tell Susan about the Cayman Islands."

"What? I went to bed at nine o'clock every night...alone."

"Yeah, well, that might not be the way I tell it," Fisher said.

"Go ahead. My wife knows better than to believe you," Brian dared him.

"She always was too smart for her own good," Fisher acknowledged. "That's why I just don't get it."

"Get what?"

"Why she married you."

"Love," Brian sighed and put a hand over his heart. "Well, that and my big..."

"McCoy. Phillips. I need an update on Operation Coffee Break. What have you uncovered so far?" Paul Van Buren strode toward their desks

"Well, I almost had Brian to his shorts," Fisher answered dryly.

"What?" Van Buren frowned. He was a no-nonsense guy who wore responsibility like a well-cut suit. He'd been with the FBI for over thirty years. He was tough but fair and despite his lack of humor, there wasn't a man in his service who didn't respect him.

"Nothing," Brian interrupted, eyeballing Fisher from behind his wire rims.

"Have you established yourself on the premises, McCoy?" Van Buren asked.

"Moved in yesterday," he confirmed.

"Any point of contact yet?"

"Well…" Fisher paused.

"Spit it out, Special Agent McCoy," Van Buren said.

"Yeah." Brian echoed. "Spit it out."

"I'm going to a wedding with her on Saturday and a rehearsal dinner on Friday," Fisher said.

"Ha!" Brian hooted. "Way to move, you dog."

Van Buren's eyebrows lifted, but he said nothing, waiting for Fisher's explanation.

"It's not like it sounds," he said. "She needed a date because of an ex-boyfriend who's going to the wedding. She asked me to help her out. I thought it would be a good opportunity to observe her and the people in her life, to see exactly who has access to the accounts of the shop, etc."

"Sounds good," Van Buren agreed. He left, calling over his shoulder, "Don't screw it up."

"Or her," Brian added.

Fisher threw a pencil at him but he ducked just in time. Too bad.

ANNIE HEFTED the last chair up onto a table and grabbed her broom. She swept up the crumbs that littered the wooden floor. The Coffee Break had done a brisk business today, and she was grateful. She loved living hip deep in coffee beans and crème brulée.

She left the counter light on while she dumped the refuse into the garbage bin and shoved the broom in the closet. She was about to take off her apron and head upstairs when the front door clanged open with a rattle of bells.

A scream was halfway up her throat before she recognized the man standing in the shadows before her.

"Fisher! You scared me," she said, feeling her heart knock on her ribs.

"Was there a reason you didn't lock the door?" He stepped into the shop, scowling.

He moved with a predatory grace that Annie couldn't help but admire. Shoulders back, square jaw jutting forward, he walked into the room as if he owned it. Every silly, feminine nerve in her body responded with a nervous flutter. Oh dear.

"Uh...I forgot," she stammered, forcing herself to concentrate on the conversation.

"Forgot?" he echoed in disbelief. "We're in central Phoenix and you forgot to lock your front door?"

"I would have remembered eventually," she protested, stepping around him to lock the door.

"After you were robbed or raped or worse?"

"You're just a ray of sunshine this evening, aren't you?" she asked, trying to lighten the serious cast to his features. When she'd first met him, he'd struck her as an overly serious sort. Someone who needed to smile more. It was an impossible challenge to refuse.

"Just promise me that you'll be more careful," he said, his features softening a fraction. Annie was encouraged.

"Scout's honor," she said, raising her right hand.

"That's no good." He shook his head. "How do I know you were a Scout?"

"Are you doubting me?" she asked, plunking her hands on her hips with mock offense.

"Prove it," he said. "What's the Scout's credo?"

"Thou shalt not nag?" she asked pointedly.

"Try, 'always be prepared,'" he said.

"That was my second guess."

"Guess? Aha!" He pointed at her. "You weren't a Scout."

"No, I was, but I didn't make it out of Brownies," she confessed. He crossed his arms over his chest, awaiting her explanation. Annie mumbled, "I failed comp-fur-coo-gig."

"Excuse me," he said with a twinkle in his eye. He was teasing her! "I couldn't make that out."

She hung her head to hide her laughter and said, "I failed campfire cooking. Okay? Are you happy now?"

"You failed cooking?" he repeated. Annie glanced up at him through her lashes and saw his lips twitch.

"No, I failed campfire cooking. They wanted us to roast hot dogs on sticks. Do you know what's in those things? Yuck! I just couldn't do it."

"So you failed out of Scouts because you're a food snob," he concluded with a laugh.

"Um...basically...yeah." She smiled. She'd never thought of her shop as huge, but with Fisher standing in the middle of it, it seemed dwarfed by his presence. Just looking up at him made her dizzy. "How about some Death by Chocolate?"

"What by what?"

"You've never had Death by Chocolate?"

He shook his head.

"Let me tell you, it beats the heck out of 'Smores.' Sit." She gestured him toward a seat at the counter while she circled it. She slid open the back door to the refrigerated display case and pulled out the decadent torte. She could feel his eyes upon her as she cut him a man-size wedge. Filling a glass of ice-cold milk to go with it, she pushed the plate in front of him.

He eyed the plate as if it were lethal. It was to her hips, but he didn't need to know that. Handing him a fork, she said, "Try it."

Fisher tucked into the torte as if it were as innocuous as apple pie. He paused in midchew, and his eyes bugged at Annie in awed delight. He mumbled something that sounded like a benediction, but then shut his eyes as a look of bliss crept across his face.

Wow! Annie felt her pulse skitter somewhere south. She had hoped to coax a smile out of him but this... She wasn't prepared for this. She watched as he took a drink of milk from the glass. She watched it slide down his throat and felt her own mouth go dry. As he set the glass back down, one corner of his mouth tipped up in a devil's grin, parting just enough for her to see a glimpse of teeth. His brown eyes twinkled at her, and Annie was pretty sure there wasn't going to be enough left of her to mop up with a sponge.

She watched him eat. She knew she was staring, but she couldn't help it. If he looked that sexy eating Death by Chocolate, then what would he look like... She shook her head, glanced away and then back.

She watched him suck the last of the chocolate off of his fork, and she felt the back of her neck grow hot. Horrified, she jerked upright, yanking his plate away from him as she went. This was way more than she had bargained for.

Dumping the plate in the sink, she flipped on the tap and drowned the plate as if it held her desire and not just chocolate crumbs. She couldn't have those sort of feelings for her tenant. He lived across the hall from her for Pete's sake! If she let him get under her skin, she'd never sleep again.

"You forgot these."

"What?" She spun to find him just behind her, holding a fork and an empty glass.

He reached around her to deposit them in the sink and she felt his arm press against hers. The contact sizzled. She glanced at his face. He showed no sign of awareness. Instead, his dark brown eyes seemed to be studying her, as if looking for something. Annie couldn't comprehend what and she couldn't look away.

He was the first to straighten. "Thanks for the dessert."

"You're welcome," she forced the words out.

"Do you want me to walk you up?" he asked.

"No," she said swiftly, too swiftly. "I mean, that is, I have some bookkeeping to do before I turn in."

"All right." He stepped back toward the door. "I'll say good-night then."

"Good night," she croaked.

"Sweet dreams, Annie-girl," he said and disappeared up the back stairs to the apartments above.

Annie wilted against the sink like a cake falling after a loud bang. The man was intoxicating and she didn't have to try to touch her finger to her nose to know that she was drunk.

FISHER SLAPPED a hand down on his snooze button.

An old song about a widow who would only marry guys named Henry continued to play.

Fisher slapped the button again. The song kept playing. Fisher opened one eye and glanced at his alarm clock. The red digits glowed five-thirty. He'd set his alarm for seven. The singing started again and he groaned.

He forced both of his eyes open and then it hit him. The smell of cinnamon filled his nostrils like salt on a sea breeze. He glanced at his unfamiliar surroundings. Oh yeah, he was living above The Coffee Break. That explained the cinnamon but not the singing.

He pushed his covers aside and pulled on a pair of jeans. Harpy had started to squawk in accompaniment to whoever was belting out the tune in the alley. There was no way he would be getting any more sleep this morning. He took his key and wandered out into the hallway.

The singing grew louder toward the back of the house so he let himself out the back door and onto the deck at the top of the stairs. The rich baritone was deafening now. Fisher glanced over the rail and saw an older man, perhaps in his fifties, standing outside the kitchen door.

Just as he started the third verse, the back door flew open and out marched Annie. Although she was fully dressed, her red hair stuck out in all directions as if she hadn't had time to comb it. In her hands, she held a plate with three huge muffins and a glass of milk.

"Here you go, Henry," she said. "You can stop singing now."

Henry took the plate and glass of milk and gave her a broad grin. "I was only on the third verse."

"I have a new tenant. I hope you didn't wake him," she said.

"Early bird catches the worm," Henry declared.

"Yeah, well, I need the rent so let's hope the early bird is a deep sleeper," she said with a worried glance up. Just then, she caught sight of Fisher leaning over the rail. "Oh, good morning."

"Tweet, tweet," he said. "This early bird is not a deep sleeper."

"Oh." She winced and twisted her fingers together. "I'm so sorry. This is Henry."

As if that explained anything, he thought with a shake of his head.

"Henry, this is Fisher," she said.

Henry didn't even glance up. Instead he took his muffins to the picnic table at the side of the house and sat down to enjoy his breakfast in peace. Fisher tried to ignore the irony.

Annie sighed and tripped up the stairs to his side.

Even on the dark side of dawn, she moved with a speed that made him woozy.

"Henry?" he asked.

"I don't know if that's his real name," she said. "That's just what I call him, because of the song."

"The song?"

"You must have heard it." She began to sing the same song Fisher never wanted to hear again.

"I heard it," he interrupted. "But how does that explain him?"

"Well, a few months after I opened The Coffee Break, Henry just showed up. I kept finding him picking through our garbage every morning and he was always singing that song. I told him not to…go through the trash that is. I mean it's just not sanitary, but he said we had the best dumpster in town."

"And?" he prompted her.

"And he kept raiding the dumpster, so I gave up. I told him to knock on the backdoor and I would bring him some fresh muffins. Well, Henry never got the knack of knocking."

"So he sings for his breakfast?"

"Yeah. I'm so sorry he woke you up," she said. "I'll make sure it doesn't happen again."

"How will you do that?"

"I'll just get up earlier and make sure I meet Henry at the door."

Fisher glanced over the rail at the man seated below them devouring his breakfast. His skin was leathery from years on the streets, his clothes were ragged and his hair was uncombed and filthy. Breakfast from Annie every day was probably the one certainty in his life.

"Don't worry about it. I usually get up at five-thirty anyway," he lied.

"Really?" she asked. "That's great. Then you don't mind?"

"No, I don't mind," he said and meant it.

Annie glanced at her watch and jumped. "Oh, I had better get moving or I won't get all of my baking done. I'm so glad you're an early riser. I knew this would work out. I just knew it."

Fisher watched as she disappeared into the house at a run. One more piece in the puzzle that was Annie, and it didn't help one little bit.

2

THE SMELL OF fresh-brewed coffee drew Fisher downstairs like an invitation. Breakfast in the shop would give him a good chance to observe Annie. He could watch who came and went and get a feel for her regulars.

He found her standing in the center of the shop with one hand on her hip and the other clutching a coffeepot like a weapon.

"Why don't you just sell?" a short man wearing khaki's and a blue denim shirt asked.

"I told you before you bought Mucho Latte, Martin, that I wasn't going to sell," she said.

"But you'll never be able to compete with me," he argued. "Annie, I'm just thinking of you."

A long curly strand of red hair fell over Annie's face and she blew it aside before answering, "I really appreciate that, Martin, but as you can see I'm fine."

The man glanced around the room. It was just after seven and the shop was packed with morning customers. His head snapped from side to side, giving Fisher a good look at his face. He had small pinched features and a thin black mustache that hung over his upper lip like a chocolate milk stain.

"Oh sure, you're fine now," he sneered. "But you can't compete with a chain like the Mucho Latte. One by one, your customers will leave, coming to my shop instead. Do you really want to watch the slow demise and eventual death of everything you've worked for?"

Annie took a deep breath, and Fisher marveled at her patience. He'd have punched the little jerk in the nose by now.

"Martin, the fact that you're here, trying to buy out my shop tells me one thing. You're the one who's worried about losing your business. Not me. Now, for the last time, I am not selling The Coffee Break. Not to you. Not to anyone. Have I made myself clear?"

"Crystal," he snapped. "You'll regret this."

"I don't think so," she said. "Have a good day, Martin."

Martin stalked toward the front door. Fisher reached out and pulled it open, not allowing the little man to slam it in a fit of temper.

"Thank you for visiting The Coffee Break," he said. "Be sure to come again and have a nice day."

Martin growled at him before stomping through the door and across the patio toward the street.

Fisher shut the door and turned to Annie. "Who was that?"

"My rival," she said, putting the coffeepot on a warming plate on the counter. "Martin Delgado."

"Rival?"

"He just opened a coffee house, Mucho Latte, up the street. He's been trying to buy me out ever since he bought his franchise, but I won't sell."

"How very uncooperative of you," he said.

"Martin seems to think so," she said with a shrug. "I hope you know that just because you live upstairs doesn't mean you have to eat here."

Fisher took a seat at the counter. "Are you kidding?" he asked. "The smell of cinnamon dragged me out from under the covers this morning. Henry was lucky I didn't steal one of his muffins."

"Then you'll have to have one of my apple spice muffins on the house," she said. "That'll start your day right."

"Annie-girl, you have found my weakness." He winked at her.

"Sweet tooth?" she guessed, glancing away from him, but not before he saw the color creep into her cheeks. She was a blusher.

"I think sweet teeth would be more accurate," he said.

"I kind of figured," she said. "Judging by the way you devoured your dessert last night."

"Don't remind me," he groaned. "If you keep feeding me like that, I'll have to start working out."

"Aw, poor baby," she said. "Maybe you should only have half of a bran muffin instead."

"Don't be a tease," he said with a mock frown.

"Annie!" A cry sounded from the back of the shop.

"I'm being paged." She put a muffin on a plate before him and stepped away from the counter. "I'll see you later?"

"Count on it," he promised.

"Oh." She blinked in surprise. "All right."

"We have the rehearsal dinner tomorrow night, right?" he asked.

"Oh, oh yeah." She shook her head. "How could I forget?"

"You're busy," he suggested.

"That must be it." She latched on to the excuse like a life preserver. Fisher frowned. Something was up with Annie-girl and he was going to figure out what.

"Annie!" Another cry sounded.

"Bye," she said and hurried off.

"Bye," he returned, but she was long gone. The woman moved faster than a jaywalker in oncoming traffic.

Fisher spent an hour watching her work the room. Pretending to read the newspaper, he studied her over the edge as she chatted with two businessmen at a nearby table. The October morning was cool, and she wore a snug pair of jeans and a dark green thermal top. Fisher frowned when she bent over to refill their cups. Was the fabric gaping a bit? Why wasn't she wearing that big flouncy apron she'd had on the day he'd met her? It kept her covered from neck to knee and besides he liked it.

One of the men said something, and Annie tipped her head back and laughed. Fisher felt his mouth start to curve up. He couldn't help it. Her laughter struck him like a mallet on a chime. He bit the inside of his cheek and winced. He would not be charmed by a suspect.

"Can I get you anything else?" a surly voice asked. Fisher glanced at the woman standing across from him. She was tapping her pencil on her pad and looking as if she'd just bitten a lemon.

"A refill on the coffee, please," he said.

"Is that all?" she asked, looking put out.

"For now," he answered, wondering at her hostility.

"Fine," she snapped and stomped away.

She marched away like a storm trooper charging the enemy. She was short with a boxy frame, reminding him of an angry Rotweiler. Interesting. She wasn't the sort he would have thought Annie would hire, but then again, he supposed good help was hard to find.

Try as he might, Fisher couldn't see Annie as part of a money laundering scheme. He'd met hundreds of felons during his time with the Bureau and while some had been the least likely suspects, none had ever seemed as genuine as Annie Talbot. She couldn't be involved he told himself, hoping he was right.

"Here." His waitress plunked down his mug with a splash.

"Thanks," he said, wondering if he should check the coffee for rat poison.

Settling back in his chair, he resumed watching Annie flit around the shop, refilling mugs with a smile and a laugh. She was as light and airy as the breeze, hardly the hardened criminal he was used to observing. She'd wound her thick hair into a braid that hung down her back and was tied with a bright blue scarf. When she passed by, he had to curb the urge to tug the scarf free and watch her hair unravel in a sensuous spin. His fingers tightened around his mug and he forced his eyes away from his very tempting suspect.

Instead Fisher took a moment to study the clientele. Two students with backpacks were seated outside, chomping on muffins while they quizzed each other from their textbooks. A woman in a suit shared a *Wall Street Journal* and a cell phone with a man in similar attire. Two house painters in coveralls stood by the chalkboard trying to choose their morning coffee. Fisher couldn't see the rest of the room, but he knew it was a varied mix of people. Situated on a busy corner in the historic district of downtown Phoenix, The Coffee Break was in a great location.

Annie had done a terrific job of making the shop feel like home. A rack by the door offered customers their choice of several local newspapers as well as the *New York Times* and *Los Angeles Times*. Board games filled a shelf along one wall; two older gentlemen had already started a game of chess. Handcrafted coffee and tea mugs were for sale in one bookcase and beside that was a wall full of coffee beans and teas to be sold by the pound. A photo album sat on the dessert counter and when Fisher thumbed through it, he discovered pictures of wedding cakes that Annie baked by special order.

Lifting his mug, he took a long sip of the hot brew. He could feel a pair of shrewd brown eyes examining him from behind the counter. His waitress. He'd heard one of the other waitresses call her Denise. Observing her from the corner of his eye, he feigned interest in his newspaper. He was going to have to find out more about her. She could very well have access to the books and he wouldn't mind pinching her for laundering money.

He heard Annie's laugh from across the room and he couldn't help but glance up. She was lovely when her full lips parted in a smile. He forced his attention back to the paper. Oh, yeah, given a choice between the two women, he would much rather arrest the surly Denise. But as for pinching, Annie was a definite temptation.

"SO, WHO'S TALL, dark and sullen?"

"What?" Annie asked, glancing up from her mixing bowl.

"Who's tall, dark and sullen?" Denise repeated her question.

"Oh, he's my new tenant," Annie answered, not bothering to pretend she didn't know who Denise was talking about.

"He looks dangerous," she said, leaning on the counter beside Annie.

"He's harmless," she assured her.

"I don't know." Denise pilfered a raisin from Annie's supply of ingredients and popped it into her mouth before continuing. "He was watching you all morning. I didn't like the look in his eye."

"What look in his eye?" Annie scoffed, feeling her body go still as she waited for the answer.

"He looked at you like you were a chicken and he was a chicken hawk," Denise said.

Annie laughed. Denise hadn't teased her in a long time. Even though it made her blush, it was good to see a glimmer of the old Denise.

"You can't come up with a better analogy than that? I'm a chicken?"

"He was staring at you."

"He's probably just curious about his landlord," Annie said, trying to sound reasonable.

"Yeah. Curious about seeing you in an apron and nothing else, I'll bet."

"Denise!"

"It's true," she said with a sigh. "Men are pigs."

"Except for Edmund," Annie said, watching her friend's expression.

"Yeah, Edmund," she agreed without smiling.

Annie felt her heart ache for her friend. That Denise was unhappy in her marriage to Edmund was obvious, but no matter what opening Anne gave her, Denise said nothing and Annie felt helpless.

"Well, at least tall, dark and sullen is a good tipper." Denise said, returning to the front of the shop. "Not to mention cute."

"Cute?" Annie asked.

"I'm married not dead," Denise said with a faint smile.

"Same thing," Annie muttered as she watched the door swing closed behind her friend.

Marriage. What a ridiculous institution. Everyone she knew who was married wanted out and everyone she knew who wasn't married wanted in. Except herself of course. She knew better. Her sister's marriage aside, she didn't know one happily married couple.

Why put yourself through all of the heartache and angst? If she wanted that much permanent pain and anguish in her life, she'd get a tattoo. A big one. Better yet, if she wanted a long-term relationship, she'd get a desert tortoise. They lived for sixty years and they hibernated for six months of the year. A perfect relationship.

Her thoughts strayed to Stewart. Maybe if he'd hibernated for six months of the year, she'd have been able to marry him. But his constant presence had soon become an irritant. His incessant nagging about the shop had made her crazy. He'd wanted to turn her quiet little haven into a booming franchise like Mucho Latte with chains all over the city. Ugh! He didn't understand at all.

She'd done her time as a pastry chef at the posh Lemon Grove Resort in Scottsdale. She'd won numerous awards and been written up in *Bon Appetit* and *Gourmet*. It had been a glamorous and arduous existence and she had hated it. She wanted a slower pace of life. She wanted to cook for people who didn't need a gold card to eat.

But Stewart couldn't understand that. He was an entrepreneur always looking for a quick buck. When they'd first met, he'd been fun and supportive. But as their relationship had grown closer, he'd begun to press her about her business interests. Annie didn't think of The Coffee Break as a business. It was more than that. It was her baby.

A picture of Fisher sitting at the counter flashed through her mind. He had looked right sitting there as if he belonged. His hair had been wet from his recent shower and when she'd refilled his coffee cup, she could smell the damp scent of his shampoo mingling with his aftershave. It was spicy and very masculine.

She'd felt him watching her but had convinced herself that it was all in her mind. But Denise's observation made her pause. Did Fisher find her attractive? It was laughable. That man could have any woman in Maricopa County. Why would he be interested in a redhaired, freckled baker? Still, she couldn't forget the way he'd winked at her and said her name in that deep growl of his. Feeling a grin part her lips, she resumed beating her muffin dough into submission.

"Look at this," Brian greeted Fisher as soon as he walked into the office. "Solid evidence, my friend.

Your little coffee perker is definitely guilty of laundering.''

''What?'' Fisher frowned, throwing his jacket over the back of his chair and reaching for the papers Brian was examining.

''The question is who is she laundering for? And why would they use her shop as a front? She can't have that much money going in and out the door. Not to cover the kind of laundering we're looking at.''

Fisher scanned the paperwork in his hand. Had someone spiked his coffee? Because suddenly the room was spinning. The bank statements in front of him didn't lie. The discrepancy between her income and her net worth was too large to ignore. The difference in what she reported to the IRS and what she was actually earning was the equivalent to a mansion on Camelback Mountain. There was no doubt about it. It was so blatant, almost defiant.

Fisher sank into his seat with a shake of his head. Despite the stereotypical red hair, Annie hadn't seemed like that much of a wild card to him and certainly not a felon.

Could she have gotten in over her head when trying to open her business? It had happened to more than one restauranteur. He'd seen it a dozen times. Restaurants came and went unless they had a loyal following or a lot of backing. That's why they were so perfect for money laundering. They were a cash-based operation and it was difficult to match the costs of providing food with the revenues they pulled in.

But these records screamed fraud. With a sick feeling, Fisher dropped the papers onto his desk. ''Where did you get these?''

''I searched FinCEN. You know, the Financial Crimes Enforcement Network, to track any reports filed under the Bank Secrecy Act. The BSA requires disclosure of any large currency transactions. She has several in and out of a secondary account for The Coffee Break. We can nail her with this.''

"I want to wait," Fisher said.

"What? Why?" Brian pushed his glasses back up his nose and ran a hand over his thinning hairline. "We have all the evidence we need."

"No, there's something more going on here," Fisher said. "I want to watch for a while and see what I can uncover."

"Oh, no." Brian dropped his head into his hands.

"Oh, no, what?"

"You've got a thing for the cappuccino pusher, don't you?"

Fisher leveled his partner with a glare. "I do not have a 'thing' for her. And even if I did, have I ever let my libido do my thinking for me?"

"No," Brian agreed. "But there's always a first time."

"Don't you find it the least bit odd that she's depositing several thousand dollars more than she's declaring, and yet she operates that place on a nickel and a prayer?" Fisher asked. "She does all the cooking, all the cleaning, she even waitresses. If she's being paid off, why isn't she using the money to pump up her business?"

"Maybe she's hoarding it for an early retirement," Brian suggested.

"No, there's something not right here," Fisher said. "I want one more week to figure out what's going on. I want to trace every single deposit and see where they are coming from."

"A week?" Brian ripped off his glasses and shoved a hand through his hair, making it stand up in exasperated tufts. "She could be on Grand Cayman sucking down a daiquiri and laughing at us in a week. Are you willing to risk that?"

"Yes, I am," he said.

Brian studied him, looking as frustrated as a cat stalking a caged canary. "All right, we'll play it your way. But if you blow it, I'm going to let Van Buren rip you a new…"

"I get the idea," Fisher interrupted his partner, not wanting to think about what Van Buren would do to him if he was wrong. But he had a hunch. There was something more to this than Annie and her business. He had to figure out what and soon.

WHEN ANNIE answered his knock, she was wearing a bright yellow sundress with matching sandals. She looked as capable of deceit as a daisy and Fisher wondered, not for the first time, if he was being a class-A idiot. She was either as innocent as she looked or she was the most deceptive felon he'd ever encountered.

"Are you ready to go?" he asked, feeling surly.

"Sure, but don't you want to change?" she asked, gesturing to his suit. "We're meeting at the church to rehearse, but dinner is just a barbecue at the groom's parents' house."

"Jeans okay?" he asked.

"Just fine," she agreed.

"I'll be back in two minutes," he said and turned to enter his own apartment.

"I'll time you," she called after him.

Despite himself, Fisher felt a smile part his lips. She was nothing if not amusing.

Rushing into his apartment, he paused to scratch Harpy's pinfeathers and tell her what a good girl she was. When Harpy's eyes rolled back in ecstasy, he gave her a quick peck on her head and hurried to his closet. He flung his tie over the doorknob, kicked off his shoes and shrugged out of his suit. He pulled on a faded pair of Levi's jeans and his favorite Henley and rushed out the door not wanting to make them late.

She was waiting outside on the deck, leaning against

the rail and watching a hummingbird hover over a pot of purple petunias in the yard below.

"How did I do?" he asked.

She glanced at her watch. "Ten seconds to spare," she said. Her gaze moved over him and she frowned. "Then again…"

"What? Am I too casual?"

"No, but you might want shoes."

Fisher glanced down at his feet. A pair of brown socks stared back up at him. He wiggled his toes to be certain they were his. Yep, they were. Shoes? How could he have forgotten his shoes? When he glanced back up, she was laughing. She was trying not to but failing miserably. Her muffled snorts gave her away.

"Ten seconds," he promised with a grin and raced back into the house.

He'd never forgotten his shoes before. It had to be her. He could see her wide lips parted with laughter, her voluminous red hair tied back at the nape of her neck. It had to be her. She affected him in ways he didn't understand. She distracted him, made him smile, made him want to loosen her hair and bury his face in it.

Grabbing his shoes from the closet floor, Fisher knotted the laces and raced back outside. Brian's exasperated face appeared in his mind's eye. *The little cappuccino pusher has gotten to you, hasn't she?* No! She wasn't getting to him. He couldn't let her affect his judgment. Not if he wanted to keep his career alive.

He was going tonight strictly to observe the people she interacted with. To see who she associated with and get a list of names to check out. She was a suspect. The chief suspect. And he'd best not forget it.

They arrived at the church just in time. The minister was talking the bride and groom through the ceremony and Annie joined the other bridesmaids to receive her instructions for tomorrow's ceremony.

Fisher took a seat at the back of the church and watched as the wedding party was put through their paces. The girls practiced walking down the aisle while the men stood beside the groom. Fisher wondered if their job was to keep the groom from bolting if he had second thoughts or to help him escape. Having never been in a wedding, he had no idea.

He did know that he didn't like the groomsman Annie was paired with. He was only a few inches taller than Annie, he had white blonde hair, an even tan and a silly cleft in his chin. He looked like Dudley Do-Right. He held her too close and too tight, and he kept whispering in her ear as they practiced walking down the aisle in the wake of the bride and groom. Judging by the wrinkle in Annie's nose, the guy either smelled bad or she was less than thrilled with his attention. Fisher was betting on the latter.

As if she felt his gaze upon her, she glanced up and her deep blue gaze met his. Fisher winked at her and she tripped, stumbling over her feet and causing her escort to loosen his grip upon her. Fisher grinned. So she wasn't immune to him, either. Good.

Her partner paused in midstep and glanced at Fisher as if noticing him for the first time. His light blue gaze was bewildered and he glanced at Annie in confusion. She picked up her pace, practically pulling the poor sap behind her as she hurried down the aisle.

Not wanting to laugh in a house of worship, Fisher tucked his mirth into his cheek and waited for Annie to join him.

''Who's the chatterbox?'' he asked when she sat beside him in the pew.

''Stewart Anderson,'' she answered.

''The ex?'' he guessed.

''Yes,'' she confirmed.

''So, why did you break up with him?'' he asked. ''Did he talk you to death?''

"He does love the sound of his own voice, but no, that wasn't it," she said.

"Well?"

"We just wanted different things," she said.

Fisher admired her diplomacy, but he was more than a little curious as to the real reason for their breakup. "Does he know I'm your date?"

"He does now." Annie nodded and forced a smile at someone over Fisher's shoulder.

He glanced around to see Dudley Do-Right making his way toward them with a blond bombshell on his arm.

"Anne," he said, almost shouting, as if he feared they'd get away from him. "I'd like you to meet Tiffany."

"Tiffany, this is Anne and her...guest," Stewart said, glaring at Fisher.

"Date," Fisher corrected him as he rose from his seat. "My name is Fisher. Nice to meet you."

"Fisher?" Tiffany repeated, her voice was high with a trace of a lisp. "I dated a man named Fisher once, but he was nothing like you. You're gorgeous." Her vacant brown eyes blinked at him, and she giggled as she tossed her hair. Fisher suspected it was a move she'd spent hours perfecting in front of a mirror. He felt Annie stand beside him.

"It's a pleasure to meet you, Tiffany," Annie said. Fisher glanced at her. She looked as if she meant it. "If you two will excuse us, I want to get to the house and help with the barbecue."

As she took his arm and led him away, Fisher leaned down to whisper in her ear, "Nice getaway. Very smooth."

"Was it?" she asked. "I didn't want to look like I was running, but *puleeze*."

"You don't like the new girlfriend?" he asked.

"Oh, no. She's not the sharpest pencil in the box, but she's fine," Annie said. "It's him. Ugh!"

"Hmm," Fisher hummed in total agreement.

THEY ARRIVED at the groom's parents' house just behind the bride and groom. At the end of a cul-de-sac, the house boasted a large yard and an unrestricted view of Camelback Mountain. The house was decorated with luminaries and ristras, and a huge barbecue pit had been dug in the backyard.

Fisher stood back from the group, observing the people around him. The bride and groom, Eve and Tony, rarely left one another's side. When they gazed at each other, they beamed a wattage matched only by the sun.

Fisher wondered if he would ever know that kind of joy. He'd always planned to get married, but he hadn't found Ms. Right...yet.

"Something wrong with your spare ribs?" Annie asked, appearing beside him.

"No, why?"

"You're frowning," she said.

"Am I?" He drew in a breath and let it out. "I didn't realize."

"What were you thinking about?" she asked.

"Marriage," he answered.

"Ah." She nodded. "It makes me frown, too. Actually, just the thought of it gives me hives."

"Why? Afraid you'll be an old maid?" he asked.

She laughed. "Actually, no. I'm more afraid I'll end up as someone's missus. No thank you!"

"You don't want to get married?" he asked in surprise.

"No, I don't believe in it."

"Oh no." He shook his head in disbelief.

"What?"

"You sound just like my mother," he said.

"She doesn't believe in marriage?" she asked in astonishment.

"No, she and my father don't believe in the institution of marriage," he said.

"Wow, that's remarkable."

"No, it's ridiculous," he corrected her. "They've been together for thirty-five years. It's just asinine."

"But they're happy?"

"Very."

"Maybe they just know what works for them," she offered.

"No, they're just nuts," he said, unable to mask the affection in his voice.

"Oh, please," she said. "I'll tell you nuts. My parents have seven marriages between them. Mom's plunged four times. Dad's jumped three."

"You win." Fisher raised his hands. "That's nuts. Is that why you don't believe in marriage?"

"I'm sure it's a part of it," she said. "But, honestly, I've never..."

"Anne, here you are," Stewart called as he came striding across the lawn toward them. "Eve is looking for you."

"Oh, I'll be right there. Excuse me," she said, turning to Fisher.

"Sure," he said and watched her dash across the lawn. He watched her yellow skirt swirl around her long legs as her hair swung across her back. His fingers tightened around his beer.

"Don't lose your heart to that one."

"What?" He turned to find Stewart standing beside him.

"Don't lose your heart to her. She belongs to someone else."

"You?" Fisher asked.

Stewart nodded. "She doesn't know it yet, but we belong together."

"Then you brought Tiffany because...?"

"To make Anne realize what she was going to lose," Stewart explained. "I knew that once she saw me with another woman, she'd come around."

"She did," he said.

"Really? What did she say?" Stewart asked, his pale blue eyes glittering with triumph.

"She said she felt sorry for Tiffany." Fisher swallowed the last of his beer and left Stewart gaping like an open-mouthed bass. He crossed the yard, following the bright yellow dress. She was flitting from group to group, fetching and carrying like a perfect hostess. For reasons Fisher couldn't understand, he wanted to get her away from here. He found her refilling a coffee cup for an older woman.

"Are you sure that's decaf, honey?" the old woman asked.

"Yes, Mrs. Hampton," Annie said.

"Well, that's good otherwise I'll be up all night. It's bad enough I'm getting up three and four times a night to trek to the facility." The old woman sighed. "Don't ever get old, sugar."

"I'll try not to," Annie promised. Turning, she caught sight of Fisher and smiled.

Fisher put his hand around her elbow and pulled her away from the crowd. Her hair was coming undone and a flush of exertion filled her cheeks. As the evening breeze sent a long curl drifting across her cheek, Fisher couldn't help but push it away with a fingertip. He heard Annie's quick hitch of breath and his eyes met hers.

There it was, that indefinable spark that ignited between them every time their eyes met. Fisher felt his insides tighten, clenching like a fist. His gaze lowered to her lips. They were slightly parted as if she'd been caught by surprise.

Before he could think it over, debate the pros and

cons, or remember that she was a suspect, Fisher felt his head lower to hers. He could feel her breath against his lips; it was erratic and warm and lured him like a promised caress.

"Annie!" An ear-splitting cry jerked Fisher back as if he were on a leash.

Annie blinked at him, but then turned to find the person who had yelled for her.

Eve was making her way toward them. "I'm going to go home now. A bride needs her beauty rest."

"Not you, Eve. You're going to be gorgeous," Annie assured her friend. "Is there anything I can do?"

"No, thanks," the bride said. "I want you to get some rest, too. Now remember, we're meeting at the hairdresser's at two."

"I'll be there as soon as I drop off the cake at the reception hall," Annie promised, giving her friend a quick hug and kiss good-night.

Fisher and Annie followed the bride and her parents to their car. As Eve climbed into the car behind her parents, Tony gave her a passionate kiss causing the assembled guests to whoop and cheer.

"You'd better be there tomorrow," he chided his bride with a grin.

"Don't you worry. A blizzard in Phoenix wouldn't stop me," she promised.

"Isn't that sweet?" Annie asked Fisher as he helped her into his Jeep.

"You're a sucker for love, aren't you?" he asked, climbing into the driver's seat.

"I'm a sap for sure," she agreed. "I cry at the drop of a hankie."

"Are you having second thoughts about your breakup with Stew? He sounds as if he'd marry you in a heartbeat."

"I'm sure he would," she agreed while buckling her seat belt. "But only because he thinks he can turn The

Coffee Break into a national chain. Even if I were in love with him, which I'm not, I'd never marry him.''

''Yes, you would,'' Fisher said, starting the engine.

''No, I wouldn't,'' she argued.

''You think that now, but when you fall in love it'll be different,'' he said.

''No,'' she repeated more firmly. ''I like the arrangement your parents have. I mean look at them. They've been together for thirty-five years. I bet if they'd gotten married they would've divorced a long time ago.''

''No, they wouldn't,'' he said, as he paused at a red light. ''They're both crazy. No one else could put up with them.''

''What makes them crazy? Just because they don't want to get married…''

''They're still living in the sixties,'' he interrupted with a sigh. ''They've never owned a home. I grew up in a converted school bus, driving all over the country, while my parents cataloged rare and new species of birds for the Audubon Society. They're ornithologists.''

''Really? That's amazing,'' she said. ''You must have felt like a gypsy all your life.''

''Pretty close,'' he agreed. ''I never knew when I woke up in the morning, where we'd be. Sometimes it was exciting, but most of the time it was awful. It was no way to raise three kids.''

''You have siblings?''

''Two sisters, Piper and Wren.''

''Unusual names,'' she said.

''My father named us after whatever bird they happened to be studying at the time.''

''Fisher? I don't know any bird by that name,'' she said.

''It's shortened,'' he said, cursing himself for having gotten into this conversation. He hated talking about his family. They were so unexplainable. He hated to see people's reactions to his unconventional upbringing. But Annie was so easy to talk to, it had just slipped out.

"Shortened for what?" she asked.

Fisher turned onto the exit for their road. He stopped at the end of the exit ramp and turned to face her. "It's short for Kingfisher," he said and held his breath, waiting for the usual laughter that accompanied this disclosure.

She smiled at him. "I like it," she said. "It suits you."

Taken aback, he gaped at her. The light turned green and they just sat there.

"You don't like your name?" she guessed.

A honk behind them prompted Fisher to start driving again as he tried to think of how to explain.

"It's not that I dislike it, it's just that I've spent my entire life explaining it. It's embarrassing."

"Well, it could be worse," she said. "Your father could have been studying woodpeckers. Then what would your nickname be? Woody or Pecker? Now that name would have been embarrassing."

Fisher pulled up in front of The Coffee Break just as Annie finished her speech. He couldn't believe what he was hearing. Had she just...? He switched off the engine and turned to look at her. She winked at him and he felt himself grin. Annie understood. Without his having to explain it, she understood what it had been like. The years of being constantly uprooted, always an outsider looking in. And in true Annie fashion, she refused to let him take himself too seriously. In a world where most people saw the glass as half empty or half full, Fisher marveled that Annie's glass was always full.

With a laugh, he cupped her chin and pulled her face close. "Woody or Pecker? You're a riot, Annie-girl."

Her gaze met his for just the briefest moment, before

she turned away. It was as if she were afraid he would see too much in her glance, as if she were trying to avoid revealing herself, her feelings, to him. Fisher felt the sharp point of curiosity poke him.

He wanted to know what she thought and how she felt. His thumb was pressing against the soft flesh of her chin, and he saw her lips quiver just a half inch above his finger. If he slid his thumb up, he could stroke that full lower lip.

Leaning back, he released her. She was a suspect! She was adorable and charming, but she was still a suspect. He had no right to be thinking of her lips and how they would feel beneath his.

"Come on," he said, clearing the gravel out of his throat. "I'll walk you up."

She leaped from the car and Fisher found cold comfort in the fact that she was just as edgy as he was.

3

"FISHER?" SHE SAID as they made their way up the back stairs to the apartments above.

"Yeah?"

"You really believe in marriage, don't you?"

"You bet," he said, unlocking the door. "If you love someone, you should be able to commit your life to them. Only them. When I find the right woman, there'll be none of that wishy-washy living together stuff for me."

"How can you be sure?" she asked. "People change. One day you could be perfectly content with someone and the next you want to strangle them because they left the seat up."

"Then you tell them if they leave the seat up one more time you're going to glue it down permanently," he said.

Annie felt her breath halt in her lungs. He was serious. His dark gaze was as steadfast as a promise. It was also cocky, arrogant and completely mesmerizing. Oh dear.

"I…I guess, that's an option," she stammered, feeling numb from the neck up. She just couldn't look away from his mouth. The dim light in the hallway accentuated his straight white teeth, and she saw them flash with his smile.

"There are always options, Annie," he said.

"Not for you." She glanced away from him. "You

are the quintessential good or bad, right or wrong, no maybes kind of guy.''

''You think so?''

''I know so,'' she affirmed.

''How do you know?''

''Marriage only. No living together,'' she said. ''And I've seen your apartment. A place for everything and everything in its place. No mess. No piles of stuff straightened to look neat. You're probably one of those people who actually cares which way the toilet paper is unrolling, against the wall or out.''

''Always out, never against the wall. Hey, are you calling me uptight?'' he asked, leaning toward her.

''Uptight? No, I was thinking more along the lines of anal retentive,'' she teased. It was easier this way. The tension that had been building between them was defused by their banter. She inhaled, relieved. It would be a bad idea to have feelings for her tenant. Very bad.

''Anal retentive?'' he repeated, his offended stance belied by the amused gleam in his eyes. ''Just for that I'm going to booby-trap your door tomorrow. Then you'll be sorry.''

''See? You don't tell someone you're going to booby-trap their door. You just do it. I'm telling you, you are Mr. By-The-Book.'' Annie shook her head in mock despair.

''Oh, I am, am I?'' he asked, leaning closer.

Annie felt the wall against her back and stilled. Fisher placed a hand on either side of her shoulders, until she was boxed between him and the wall. She felt the smile slide from her face. His dark brown gaze narrowed, and she felt him studying her with an intensity that left her shaking from the inside out.

''Would a by-the-book man make the mistake of kissing his landlord senseless?'' he asked, his voice just a rasp against her ear.

Annie gasped as her insides clenched at the rub of his breath against her skin. Oh dear. His face was just inches from hers and she watched as he moved closer, until they were only a sigh apart. Then his lips met hers and she went completely still.

The feel of his mouth upon hers was warm and firm and blocked out everything else around her. Her entire world narrowed to the feel of his lips on hers. Slowly he opened his mouth, taking her lips with his. The rough, wet rub of his tongue against hers sent Annie fluttering into a hot flame of desire. Wow!

Crash!

One moment he was there and the next he was gone. Annie leaned against the wall and hugged herself. She heard Fisher's shout to wait right there over his disappearing footsteps. Yeah, like she could move if she tried.

Her entire body had gone limp from the impact of his kiss. It was a moment before the sound of The Coffee Break's front door slamming registered in her brain. Her first thought was to run down there, but Fisher had said to wait and she trusted him. That realization was more devastating than his kiss. She trusted him.

Annie pushed off of the wall, surprised to find that her legs, which felt like noodles, could support her. The jittery feeling inside of her was a bad omen she knew. It was the start of a completely ridiculous, juvenile infatuation. Fisher's grin flashed through her mind and she started to pace.

It was just a kiss. It didn't mean anything. So what if it was spectacular? It would be completely irresponsible of her to develop a crush on her tenant. Irresponsible? It would be downright dumb.

She reached the end of the hall, spun on her heel and paced back toward her door. Okay, it was a kiss, a great kiss, but that didn't mean anything. It could have been a fluke. A moment in time. Nothing else. Yeah, right.

She reached her door and spun on her heel again. The man had lived here less than a week. She was not going to have a crush on him. She wouldn't. She couldn't. Okay, she could, but that didn't mean he had to know. She'd just put the kiss out of her mind. She'd treat him just like she always did. As for the kiss, she'd think of it as a gift. A spontaneous surprise that she could relive any time she wanted.

When she was old and gray, sitting on her rocker at the old folks home, she'd think about his kiss and smile. Annie stopped pacing and leaned against the wall. She slid down the wall, heedless of her yellow sundress as it bunched up beneath her.

What had happened? One minute the Earth was spinning just fine and the next it spun out of control, sending her into orbit. She sighed and wrapped her arms around her knees. Where was Fisher? What was taking him so long?

She was so shocked by his kiss, she didn't think much about the crash. Something in the shop must have toppled over. Lord knew, she had enough stuff down there. But the front door had slammed. Had she been robbed? Her skin prickled on her arms, and she shivered. Where was he?

"Annie!" Fisher came racing up the stairs. "Annie?"

"I'm here," she said, rising to her feet.

"Are you all right?" he asked, grabbing her by the elbows and helping her up.

"I'm fine," she lied. "What about you? Are you all right?"

"Yeah," he said. Tipping his head, he studied her. "You waited."

"Of course," she said. "I've seen enough horror flicks to know when someone says stay put, you do it."

Fisher cupped the back of her head and pulled her close. Leaning against him, she could feel the heat and sweat radiating off his body and she sighed.

"Oh, Annie, you're a wonder," he chuckled, but then sobered. "I've got some bad news. It looks like you were robbed."

"Robbed?" she echoed. Breaking away from him, she dashed for the stairs.

"Wait!" Fisher grabbed her hand, stopping her. "Let's call the police first. We don't want to mess up any evidence."

"But…" she started to protest but stopped, knowing he was right. She felt as if someone were squeezing her heart tight with their fist. Her shop. Her store. Who would rob her? Sure, she had some antiques, but it was mostly quirky old stuff, nothing of any real value. And the cash was always locked up at night so there was no money around. Who would do this? And why?

"It'll be all right," he promised, leading her into his apartment. "Come on, let's check on Harpy and call the police."

"All right," she agreed, feeling cold all the way down to her bones.

"Are you sure that's all you saw?" The officer questioning Fisher was young, fresh out of police school and damp enough behind the ears to grow potatoes. He studied Fisher as if he doubted him. Fisher felt like pulling out his badge and hitting the kid over the head with it, but he couldn't reveal his identity, not yet.

"Yes, the guy was shorter than me, maybe five-ten," he repeated his story one more time. "He had a stocking over his face, but his hair was gray. He was big, around one hundred and ninety pounds. He had on a sweatshirt, could have been blue or black and jeans. He took off down the street the minute he saw me coming. I lost him about a block and a half away. There was a car waiting for him. A big, green Impala with no plates.''

''You're pretty observant.'' The officer tapped his pad against his chin and narrowed his gaze at Fisher. ''How long have you been living here?''

''Less than a week,'' he said, feeling his teeth clench.

''Interesting,'' the officer drawled and turned to Annie. ''Ms. Talbot, have you ever had any kind of trouble before?''

''None,'' she said. Her voice was just above a whisper. Freckles Fisher had never noticed before stood out on her pale skin. She looked as if she were trying very hard not to cry.

''Interesting,'' the officer said again.

Fisher resisted the urge to smack him. The kid was just doing his job, but Fisher couldn't wait to have Van Buren sit on this prepubescent's superior tomorrow. The first rule to any investigation was never jump to any conclusions, otherwise you spent all of your time trying to fit the crime to the easiest suspect, instead of gathering actual facts and finding the real culprit.

''Can I go into my shop now?'' Annie asked.

Fisher glanced at her. In the streetlight, she looked about a strong as a buttercup. He wanted to hug her. He didn't.

''Sure. We're done in there.'' The officer stepped away. ''If either of you think of anything that might help us with this investigation, here's my card. Just give me a call.''

Fisher didn't bother to tell him that he wouldn't be on this investigation very long.

"Sure," he said and slid the card into his pocket.

Following Annie into the shop, he winced. The place looked as if it had been hit by a tornado with an attitude. Tables and chairs were overturned. Pottery smashed. Even the baked goods in the display case had been mangled.

"Oh no!" Annie whispered in a strangled gasp. "Eve's cake!"

She raced through the store, vaulting over the wreckage in her path, to the kitchen in back. She slid to a stop in front of the walk-in cooler and yanked its massive steel door open. She sagged against the doorjamb. Fisher looped a supportive arm about her shoulders and glanced over her head. Eve's cake stood in all of its five-tiered, ivory glory in the center of the cooler.

"Thank Heavens," she sighed. She turned and glanced around the kitchen. It was a mess. Flour, sugar, bottles of extract, all of her spices, even her cooking utensils were strewn across the floor. It was like being on the inside of a mixing bowl peering out. "Who would have…?"

Fisher couldn't stand it any longer. Opening his arms, he let her walk into them. Holding her close he breathed in the sweet scent of her hair while he ran a hand up and down her back, trying to give her comfort. He could feel her shaking and he knew—there was no way Annie Talbot was a criminal. She was a victim and whoever was using her business to launder money was more vicious than he and Brian had imagined.

"It's going to be all right," he said, promising himself that it would be. "I'll help you clean up."

"No, it's all right," she said, stepping out of his arms. "I can't thank you enough for what you've already done."

"It's no…"

"No, it could have been dangerous. You could have

been hurt or worse...." Her voice broke and she took a long steadying breath. She walked back out to the main room as she spoke. "You didn't sign on for this when you signed the lease. If you want to move out, I'll understand."

"No!" Fisher snapped more forcefully than he intended. She frowned at him, and he stammered, "What I mean is...I...I'm glad I was here. The thought of you here alone and what could have happened... Why the hell don't you have an alarm system?"

She blinked. "I never thought I needed one."

"Well think again."

"But this is just a coffee shop."

"Yes, in a city where crimes occur," Fisher argued, feeling belligerent. "It's not like you live in East Podunk, Nowhere. You have to be more careful. I'll call tomorrow and see what I can arrange."

"No!" she said. "This was a random incident. It will probably never happen again. I'm not going to bar the windows and buy attack dogs to patrol the grounds."

"Annie, what do you think would have happened if I hadn't been here?"

"I'd have called the police," she said.

"No, you wouldn't," he shouted. "You'd have come down here to investigate and probably gotten yourself raped or killed or both."

"You don't know that," she said, shoving her curly hair out of her face. Her eyes snapped blue fire and Fisher took a moment to appreciate how pretty she was when she was mad. The realization only made him crankier. "Do you even own a personal protection device?"

"A what?"

"Pepper spray? Mace? A gun?" he asked.

"Never!" She shook her head and turned away from

him. Lifting a chair from the floor, she said, "I don't believe in them."

"Oh, for crying out lo..." Fisher cut himself off knowing the angry outburst would gain him nothing. "What do you mean you don't believe in them?"

He strode over to where she struggled to right a table and helped her lift it up.

Setting the table down, she turned to him and said, "I don't believe in them."

"You're joking?" he asked hopefully.

"No," she said and moved on to fix other furniture. Fisher moved along beside her, helping her. "I don't believe in guns. I don't believe people should carry weapons of any kind."

"But what about protection?"

"I don't want to live in a world where I feel I need to carry a weapon if I'm by myself," she said. "I won't do it."

"What if some scumbag broke in here or came in because you forgot to lock the door and attacked you?"

"So, I shoot him?" she asked. "Doesn't that reduce me to his level? Doesn't that make me just as much of an animal as he is?"

"No, you'd be protecting yourself," he said.

"No, I'd be murdering someone," she argued.

"And you call me the 'good or bad, right or wrong, no maybes type of guy'?" he asked. "Annie, this is serious. This guy could come back. You have to take some precautions."

She met his gaze and the fear in her eyes was as tangible as the destruction they stood in. She was wrestling with her beliefs and her fears. He hated to be the one to force her to choose, but he would if he had to.

"I'll think about it," she said.

"That's all I ask," he lied. "In the meantime, I'm

just across the hall. If you need anything or if you hear anything come get me.''

''All right,'' she agreed, but he knew she was fibbing. Cupping her chin, he frowned at her. ''I mean it. Promise me you'll come to me if you're frightened.''

''What if it's just a mouse?'' she asked and then smiled. ''Not that I have any in the shop.''

''Of course not,'' he agreed. ''But if you did, then I'd get one of those humanitarian traps and haul it away for you.''

''Really?''

''Really,'' he said.

''Thank you,'' she said, her voice as soft as a whisper.

''You're welcome,'' he said, hugging her close.

She felt right in his arms and he knew he could have held her like this for hours. How had this happened? How had she charmed him so thoroughly in such a short span of time? She nestled closer to him and Fisher felt his body tighten. Just the scent of her stirred him. He let his hand stroke down her back. She'd stopped shaking and he told himself it was just a hug of comfort, but he knew it was something more.

He'd protect her. He'd catch the bad guys. And then he'd tell her who and what he was. He could only hope that she didn't kick him in the teeth—or lower—when he did.

''Come on, you've got a wedding tomorrow,'' he said and led her from the shop.

''You're right,'' she sighed. ''I'll have to close the shop tomorrow. There's just not enough time to set it right before we open. I hope my staff is happy about having the unexpected holiday.''

''I'm sure they'll understand,'' he said, leading her towards her apartment.

"I hope so." She stopped in front of her door. "Fisher?"

"Yeah?"

"Thanks for everything."

"Any time," he said and meant it. He waited while she let herself into her apartment. When she didn't reappear, he let himself into his own place.

Crossing to Harpy's cage, he opened the door. "Well, Harpy, what do we do now?"

The sleepy cockatiel bent over and Fisher scratched her neck while she cooed. Why weren't all women as easy to understand as his bird?

ANNIE SLID between the cool bed sheets and reached over to switch off the lamp on her nightstand. Lying in the dark, she knew she should be thinking about the loss of business tomorrow and why someone would have broken into her shop.

But she wasn't thinking of those things. Instead, her thoughts were consumed with the man across the hall. The feel of his mouth upon hers. Maybe it was just more pleasant to think about that than the robbery or maybe she just hadn't been kissed with that much passion in…okay, forever.

She felt her body grow warm. A smile parted her lips. She couldn't help it. His kiss had been amazing. It would be wrong to get involved with her tenant. She knew that. It would be incredibly complicated. What if it didn't work out and then they had to share living space and watch each other's comings and goings. No, that would be bad.

Even though his kiss had been incredible, it would be foolish of her to become attached to him. She would take him to the wedding tomorrow and that would be that. No more kisses in the dark. No longing for things that shouldn't be.

Rolling onto her side, Annie hugged her pillow close while she tried to wipe the image of him from her mind. But when she fell asleep, she was still thinking of him.

"WHAT HAPPENED? Did you throw a party and forget to invite me?"

Annie turned from hanging the Closed sign in the window to see Denise standing behind her.

"We were robbed last night," she said.

"You're kidding!"

"I wish." Annie shook her head.

"What did they take?"

"Well, fortunately, Fisher chased the person away before they made off with anything," she said. "They trashed the place though."

"I can't believe this." Denise gaped at the mess surrounding them. "When I closed last night everything was locked up nice and tight. I was out of here by eight-fifteen."

"We got home from the rehearsal dinner just after ten. That gave the burglar more than an hour to do this," Annie said. "The police will probably want to ask you if there were any suspicious characters hanging around at closing. Would you mind talking to them?"

"Not a bit," she said.

"Thanks. Consider today a bonus day off," Annie said. "I left a message on your machine, but you must not have gotten it. Sorry you came all the way down here for nothing."

"Not for nothing." Denise shook her head. "I'll help you clean up."

"Oh, you don't have to," Annie said.

"Yes, I do," Denise argued. "You have the wedding today. You'll never be able to clean this and get there on time."

"Well, if you want to help." Annie shrugged. "I'd be an idiot to refuse you."

"Humph," Denise grunted and went to put on an apron.

"Morning."

Annie glanced up to see Fisher standing in the doorway. He was freshly showered, his dark brown hair was still damp. In jeans and a T-shirt, he looked every bit the Saturday man at play. Annie felt her entire body grow warm. Afraid she was staring, she glanced away.

"Good morning," she said. "Want some coffee?"

"No, thanks," he said.

She could feel his gaze upon her and felt her fingers begin to shake.

"How are you feeling this morning?" he asked.

"How do you think she feels?" Denise said as she returned from the kitchen. "The place is a mess. How would you feel?"

"I'm fine," she said, glancing at Fisher and seeing his jaw set. "Really, I'm fine."

"Can I help with the cleanup?" he asked.

"That's why I'm here." Denise hefted a broom and began to sweep around Fisher. "If you don't mind."

Fisher stepped away from her vicious whacks with the broom. Honestly, if Annie didn't know better, she'd think Denise was trying to hit him.

Hopping over Denise's maniacal broom wielding, Fisher grabbed Annie by the elbow and led her toward the door.

"What's up with Stormy Weather over there?" he asked.

Annie winced. "She's probably upset about the break-in."

"I'd say it seems to be a chronic condition," he said. "Are we still on for the wedding tonight?"

"If you're willing," she said, not wanting him to feel obligated.

"Of course I'm willing," he said. "What time should I pick you up?"

"I have to meet Eve at the hairdresser's this afternoon, and then we're all getting dressed at her house. If you could just meet me at the church about five o'clock…?"

"Sounds good," he said. "I'll just buzz into my office for a bit. Are you sure you don't want my help with cleanup?"

Annie glanced at Denise and back at Fisher. "I'm sure, but thanks for the offer. I really appreciate it, especially after last night."

"Last night?" he asked. Annie felt her heart thunk in her chest. He was staring at her lips and she knew what he was thinking about. The kiss.

"Chasing away the burglar…and all," she said, clearing her throat. "That was very brave."

"'And all' didn't require much bravery," he said, still staring at her mouth. Annie felt her face grow warm and she cursed her pale skin. Dignity was lost when she knew she must resemble a tomato.

"Yes, well, thank you," she said again, staring at the collar of his shirt. "I owe you."

"No worries. You'll pay me back," he said.

Her gaze flew up to his and she was caught by his slow, devilish smile. The man could melt ice with a slow burner grin like that.

"With some Death by Chocolate?" he suggested.

She blinked. He was asking for dessert? She might have known!

"Sure. Anytime," she said and stepped away from him. What did she think he was going to ask for? A kiss? Yes, a kiss! Leave it to her to find a man who valued her baking skills more than her body. Ugh!

"See you at the church," he promised and disappeared out the door.

She watched it close behind him.

"Don't tell me you've fallen for him," Denise said from behind her.

"No, I haven't," she said, trying to convince herself. "He's just helping me out by playing escort for Eve's wedding."

"Uh-huh."

"It's true."

"Right. And the sparks flying between you are just static electricity."

"Sparks?" Annie asked.

"Yes, sparks. The way you two are staring at each other, I'm surprised you didn't torch the place."

Why this made Annie grin, she had no idea. Picking up another broom, she set to work beside her friend, whistling a happy tune.

4

———————

"WHO DO YOU THINK IT WAS?" Brian asked Fisher as they munched tacos from a vendor just outside Encanto Park.

"I have no idea," Fisher answered. "But he managed to lose me."

"He had a car waiting," Brian said. "Which means he's not working alone."

"It could be a question of who is he working for?"

"Have you managed to get a look at her books yet?" Brian asked.

"No, I'm not sure they'd tell me much," Fisher said. "Annie doesn't strike me as someone with a real head for business. Doing all she does at the shop. That can't leave her much time to crunch numbers."

"So find out who's crunching for her. I got a line on a few of her larger deposits. They were cashier's checks from a casino in Vegas."

Fisher stopped in his tracks. "Get the dates of the deposits."

"Why?"

"So I can verify Annie's whereabouts at the time."

"You're not on this case to prove her innocence," Brian said.

"I know," Fisher snapped. "But we have the wedding tonight. I plan to canvas the entire guest list until I find out some hard and useful facts about who has access to The Coffee Break's accounts."

"Just so long as you're using your skill to find out about her business and not her personal life."

Fisher wadded up his taco wrapper and tossed it into a nearby garbage can. "What do you mean?"

"I mean that you get a peculiar gleam in your eye every time you say her name," Brian said. "I know you know better than to fall for a suspect."

The softly spoken censure made Fisher's teeth clench. "I don't think she's a suspect."

"What you think and what's reality are two different things. Until we find some hard evidence that she's not involved with the laundering, she's a suspect. Don't you forget it."

"Shove your lecture, Bri," he said. "I've been in this business just as long as you have. I know what I'm doing."

"Don't get cocky, Fish," Brian snapped. They were walking the path along the canal when he stopped and grabbed Fisher's arm. "Remember Mulrooney."

Fisher shrugged Brian's hand off of his arm. Mulrooney. Good guy, but ultimately a schmuck. He'd gotten involved with a mobster's girlfriend and the next thing they knew they were fishing him out of this very canal...headless.

"Is that why we're meeting here? So, you can remind me what happens to guys who get caught in the spider's web?"

"I figured you could use the reminder," his partner confessed.

"Don't worry about me," he said. "I have no intention of ending up decapitated in a canal."

"Good." Brian breathed a sigh of relief. "I don't think you'd be half as good looking without your head."

"You're a pal, Bri. A real pal."

ANNIE STEPPED into the eight layer, purple taffeta dress feeling like a Tijuana hooker. Glancing at the other bridesmaids, she was relieved to see that she wasn't the only one who looked like one of Cinderella's ugly stepsisters. Of course, she was the only one with fire-red hair, but that couldn't be helped.

Eve had them looking like seven Cupie dolls. They all wore the same dress, shoes, hairdo, jewelry, even makeup. Annie felt as if she were going to a costume party. No such luck, at least then she'd get to wear a mask.

As for Eve, she looked beautiful. Despite the frequent tears, cold hands and chain smoking—a habit she'd given up years ago—she was still a radiant bride.

"Eve, it's time for you to get dressed." Eve's mother strode into the room, looking the epitome of the Scottsdale lady. As usual, she had not a hair out of place and her dress was suitably chic for a wedding of which she didn't approve.

"All right." Eve took one last drag of her cigarette before rising.

"You don't have to go through with this if you don't want to, dear," her mother said.

"I love him, Mother," Eve said. "I'm going to marry him."

"Fine." Eve's mother let loose a long-suffering sigh.

"Eve," Annie interrupted, holding back the urge to kick Eve's mother. "Let me help you into your gown."

"Thanks, Annie." Eve smiled, her eyes moist. "You understand, don't you?"

"That you love him?" Annie asked as she helped Eve step into her voluminous gown. "That he's made you happier than I've ever seen you? Yes, I understand that."

"Love?" Eve's mother rolled her eyes in disapproval. "You could have married Geoffrey from Grosse Point. But no. Who did you choose? An olive oil salesman from New Jersey. I just don't understand it."

"He imports olive oil, Mother," Eve said. "And he makes a fortune at it."

"But he's so...so...Italian," her mother wailed.

"Yes, he's Italian, Mother, and I'm going to marry him. Do you want to know why?" Eve straightened her spine while Annie fastened the hundreds of buttons that led up the back of her gown.

"Why?" her mother asked.

"Because on our very first date, he looked at me and said, 'Eve doll, you know what you are? You're the salt in my stew.' He's the first man who has ever loved me for me and not my pedigree. And I have fallen more in love with him every day ever since. I'm marrying Tony Iannocci. Get over it!"

"Good girl," Annie whispered in her friend's ear.

"Humph," Eve's mother sniffed in Annie's direction and strode out of the room.

THE NEXT TWO HOURS passed in a haze of photographs and a cramped limo ride to the church. The wedding was to start at five o'clock and the eager bride arrived at the stroke of five. In a parade of purple, the bridesmaids led the way into Trinity Cathedral. Eve's father stood waiting for them at the front door and they all filed into an antechamber while they waited for their cue to begin the march down the aisle.

Clutching her bouquet of white lilies, Eve stood beside her father, looking pale and shaken. Annie tried to cheer her up with small talk, but Eve just gazed through her. She was the ninth bride Annie had watched get green around the gills before the ceremony. She was beginning to think that bouquets should come with emergency barf bags built into them.

A knock at the antechamber door sounded and they all hushed. Taking their positions, they waited for the signal to start walking. But instead of the wedding hostess, it was Fisher who appeared.

"Annie?" His eyes popped wide, leaving her no doubt about his opinion of her dress. She felt her lip curl. It wasn't as if she'd picked it out!

"Fisher?" She approached the door. "What's wrong? Why aren't you sitting down?"

"There's a little problem," he whispered, but the six bridesmaids straining to hear him all began to whisper and a shriek sounded from the back of the room.

"Problem? What problem?" Eve pushed her way through a sea of purple hoops.

"Tony's been delayed," he said.

"Delayed?" Her voice was shrill. "How?"

"Well." Fisher glanced at Annie as if for support. "We're not sure, but he's not here."

"You're not sure? He's not here?" Eve echoed. Letting loose a wail, she threw herself into her father's arms and began to bawl.

"Eve!" Annie grabbed her friend by the shoulders and shook her. "Eve, get a grip! Tony will be here. Something must have come up, but he'll be here. You know that man would walk through fire for you."

"You think?" Eve hiccuped, looking desperate.

"I know so. Now pull yourself together," Annie ordered. "Someone help fix her makeup."

"Uh," Fisher cleared his throat. "We could use some crowd control out here. You've got three hundred people getting mighty restless."

"Oh no!" Eve sobbed. "They're going to think I've been dumped at the altar. Oh, I'm just going to die."

"You'll do no such thing!" Annie ordered. "Fisher

and I will keep them entertained until Tony gets here. Come on, Fisher.''

IT WASN'T AS IF she gave him a choice, Fisher reasoned as he found himself being dragged down the aisle in her bouncing purple wake. Not even pausing for breath, she strode up to the altar and picked up the microphone that would be used to magnify the couple's vows.

A murmur that grew to a dull roar swept the crowd. ''Is this on?'' Annie asked a nearby photographer and blasted the assembly with her question. The answer was obvious.

''Okay then,'' she said and it echoed through the cathedral. The crowd gaped at her and Fisher shifted on his feet, unaccustomed to the scrutiny of so many. Annie wasn't phased in the least. ''Good evening, everyone. On behalf of the bride and groom, I want to welcome you to their wedding. Now, we were talking in the antechamber about weddings and receptions and how people never have much fun at the wedding, but they always have a great time at the reception. Weren't we, Fisher?''

Annie thrust the microphone in his face and Fisher grunted in agreement. What was she up to? Apparently, he wasn't the only one concerned. Eve's mother was doubled over in her pew, whispering Annie's name. Annie paid her no mind.

''So, we decided to get everyone warmed up for the reception in advance. If I could just have some assistance from the organist?''

A bespectacled man blinked at Annie from the balcony. Annie began to hum into the microphone. ''Could you just play this beat?'' she asked.

The organist began to work the pedals, mimicking Annie. The low beat from the massive pipe organ filled the room.

"Good. Now if everyone would stand up, Fisher and I are going to teach you the macarena."

"Annie!" he growled through gritted teeth. "I'm not doing this."

"Shh," she hushed him. "Just follow me and you'll be fine. Don't worry it's easy."

"Annie," he hissed, but she ignored him.

Turning back toward the crowd, she motioned for everyone to stand up. Most appeared reluctant so she hopped off of the dais and began to grab people's hands and pull them to their feet.

"Come on, everyone, follow me," she ordered. Bouncing her hips, she began to sing into the mike.

Her enormous purple skirt began to bob up and down, showing off her legs and when she lifted her arms over her head, she looked as if she'd pop right out of her gown. Fisher sighed. He had no choice but to protect Annie from herself. Moving to stand in front of her, he began to mimic her moves.

"That's right," she encouraged him with a saucy smile. "But swing your hips a little more."

Fisher glared at her, but as her hands went from her elbows to her head, he stepped closer, trying to keep the entire assemblage from catching the glimpse of her right nipple he was getting. He could feel the sweat bead up on his forehead. Was it hot in here or was it just him? How had he gotten himself into this mess? If his mother could see him now she'd be pleased.

"What the hell?" A roar sounded from the back door of the church and the organist stumbled to a halt, as did the entire roomful of dancers.

"Tony?" Annie dropped the mike and dashed up the aisle with Fisher hot on her heels. "What happened to you?"

"Stupid car broke down," Tony growled. His cheek was streaked with grease and his tux looked as if it had walked to the church under its own power. His best man stood beside him, looking equally grubby. "Where's Eve? What's going on?"

"Fisher and I were just keeping everyone entertained until you got here," Annie said. "Go get cleaned up. I'll tell Eve that you're here. She'll be so relieved."

"Come on." Fisher led the bewildered groom and best man away. "You've got a wedding to get ready for."

"What were you and Annie doing?" Tony asked.

"I believe she called it the macarena," Fisher answered.

"No kidding?" Tony laughed. "That Annie. She's a card."

"Yes, she is," Fisher answered, unable to hold back his grin. "Yes, she certainly is."

"NICE CEREMONY. Don't you think?" Fisher asked.

"Lovely," Annie sighed, scraping the remnants of her mascara off of her chin with her handkerchief.

"Are you going to be all right?" Fisher asked.

"Oh, yeah." She waved her hankie at him. "I'll be fine. I always cry at weddings."

"I thought you didn't like weddings," he said.

"Oh no, I love weddings. It's marriage I don't trust," she said. "But weddings are wonderful. They're so…optimistic."

"Annie." Fisher shook his head at her. "So Stew was a jerk. That doesn't mean you won't find someone worth marrying."

"Oh, no," she said. "I've been in nine weddings most of which have already ended in divorce. You're not going to see me walking down the aisle any day soon."

"Nine?" He gaped.

"Three for Mom. Two for Dad. One sister. Three

friends.'' Annie ticked off the list on her fingers. ''Nine. I have the hideous gown collection to prove it. I keep thinking I should put a rack in The Coffee Break and sell some of these gems.''

Lifting her skirt, she twirled in front on him. ''What do you think?''

''Unless Little Bo Peep stops by for a caffeine fix, you'll never unload it,'' he said. ''Come on, let's see if we can stuff you into the Jeep.''

''Too bad you don't have a pickup truck,'' she joked as she took his arm and let him lead her to the car. ''I could sit in the bed.''

''Tie you to the gun rack?'' he joked.

''Oh, wouldn't that be a pretty picture?'' She laughed. ''Me at your mercy?''

Fisher studied at her with a considered gaze. His eyes grew dark and his voice low. ''Actually, yeah, that'd be a hell of a pretty picture.''

Annie felt as if he'd drawn the breath out of her lungs with that look. How did he do that? She'd never known a man who could bowl her over with just the tilt of an eyebrow. As Fisher opened the door, she studied his hands. They were large and square and utterly masculine. Oh dear.

He turned and placed his hands on her hips. Lifting her with a groan—okay, she did weigh a ton in this concrete getup—he placed her on the passenger seat. Rattled by the feel of his hands upon her waist, Annie didn't think to adjust her hoops before she sat. As her bottom touched the seat, her skirt shot up into the air, catching Fisher on the chin and knocking him sideways.

''Oh! Fisher? Are you all right?'' she cried, batting at the skirt that blocked her view. ''Fisher?''

When she succeeded in mashing down the purple

monstrosity, she saw him holding his chin and laughing.

"Are you all right?" she asked again.

"Nice legs," he said between chuckles.

She felt her face grow hot and she straightened her back, striving for dignity. "Thank you," she said stiffly.

"No, thank you," he roared.

Annie reached out and grabbed the door, slamming it in his face. Men! Couldn't live with 'em, couldn't shoot 'em.

"This is absolutely my last wedding," she grumbled as Fisher got beside her.

"Until you get married yourself," he said, starting the car and heading toward the Desert Country Club where the reception was to be held.

"Ha!" She snorted. "No way. Not me."

"Don't you plan to have kids?" he asked.

"You don't have to be married to have kids," she argued. "People do it all the time."

"It's not right," he said, turning into the resort's drive.

"Why?" she asked, forgetting her annoyance. She sensed this issue went deep with Fisher and she couldn't deny her curiosity.

"It just isn't." He shrugged.

"But..." she began to protest.

"Look, we're here," he interrupted as he parked.

Annie frowned. The man was dodging the issue like a bullet and it was becoming a very annoying habit of his. Perhaps some champagne would loosen his tongue, she hoped.

Annie and Fisher found themselves seated at the head table beside another bridesmaid and her husband. When the new Mr. and Mrs. Anthony Iannocci were announced to the crowd, they all stood up and cheered.

The newlyweds looked radiant. Halfway across the room, Tony swept his bride into his arms and began to waltz around the room with her.

"Oh, aren't they perfect together?" another bridesmaid asked at Annie.

"Yeah, perfect." Annie sniffed and Fisher handed her his handkerchief. "Don't laugh at me."

"I wouldn't think of it," he whispered in her ear and she felt the hair at the nape of her neck prickle. She glanced at him and saw the twitch of his lips that belied his words, but she didn't call him on it.

"Softy," he teased.

"I've been called worse," she retorted, pulling her gaze away from his. Those chocolate-brown eyes of his were as lethal to her presence of mind as Godiva chocolates were to her thighs.

"I doubt it," he said, leaning close. "You're too nice to inspire any derogatory comments."

"You don't know me very well," she said.

"I know you better than you think," he returned.

Something in his tone caused Annie to turn away from the waltzing couple and study him. When he turned to meet her glance he wasn't smiling. Annie felt her heart skip a beat. It was as if he were looking into her very soul. He did know her.

"No, you don't," she argued, refusing to believe. To prove her point, she said, "After all, you think I want to marry and I'm telling you I don't."

"No, I think you should marry," he argued. "I also think you will marry when you meet the right guy."

"If I were to judge by my parents, it would be right guys," she said.

"Your parents are idiots," he said and added, "But don't worry so are mine."

"Why are you so adamant about marriage?" she

asked. ''If your parents are happy then what's wrong with never marrying?''

Fisher opened his mouth to speak, but the first waltz ended and the crowd broke into applause. Tony and Eve smiled at their guests and started to make their way around the room.

''Well?'' Annie prodded, but the band broke into ''In the Mood'' by Benny Goodman.

''Come on. Let's jitterbug,'' Fisher said and grabbed her hand to lead her toward the floor.

''I don't know how,'' she protested.

''How can you have been in nine weddings and not know how to jitterbug?''

''I don't dance much,'' she said.

''Oh, no, just the macarena.'' He rolled his eyes. ''This is *real* dancing, honey.''

She shrieked as he twirled her across the floor.

Several older couples were already cutting up, and Annie dodged one matron who was flashing her knee-high stockings as she kicked in time with her partner.

''Don't look at your feet, just follow me,'' Fisher ordered. ''Step toe to heel, toe to heel, step back, step forward.''

Annie mirrored his steps and when they completed the routine a couple of times, she laughed.

''See? You're getting it. Now keep those basics in mind and you'll be fine.''

''Basics?'' she asked.

''Oh yeah, 'cause now we're going to get fancy,'' he said and reeled her in like a yo-yo until her back was pressed to his front. ''Same steps,'' he said, but Annie's brain shut off. She couldn't think with his warm body pressed against hers and she stumbled.

''I've got you,'' he whispered. ''Follow me.''

''All right,'' she agreed, forcing herself to breathe.

''Good girl,'' he said and spun her back out.

She shrieked again as he hauled her across the floor in a pattern of spins and dips that left her dizzy and breathless. Her hoops banged against his shins, but he didn't seem to mind. It certainly didn't slow him down any.

"Big finish now," he said. "This is called the pretzel."

In a flurry of twists and turns, Annie found herself spun into him, around him and under him. How they didn't end up in a knot of limbs she would never know, but she was laughing with sheer exhilaration. And when he dipped her, it was all she could do not to wrap her arms around his neck and kiss him within an inch of his life.

Applause erupted about them and Annie glanced up from her reclined position in his arms to see that the entire crowd of three hundred guests was cheering them on. As he helped her up, she felt her already warm skin burn hot with embarrassment.

"Curtsey," Fisher coaxed her with a grin. Mortified past reason, Annie obeyed. Why performing the macarena in a church was less embarrassing than being seen lying in a man's arms while thinking about kissing him, she didn't know. But it was and it was all his fault!

Striving for nonchalance, she slunk off the floor, fanning herself with one hand. "It's warm in here, isn't it?"

"Want some champagne?" he asked.

"That'd be lovely."

"Why don't I meet you on the terrace?" he said. "It should be cooler out there now that the sun has set."

"Good idea. I swear this dress is as heavy as an ape suit."

Fisher blinked at her and burst into laughter. It rumbled up from his chest and burst forth in a contagious bark of sound. His mouth split into a wide grin and several heads, mostly female, spun to watch him. Annie felt ridiculously pleased to have made him laugh.

Grateful to escape the scrutiny of the crowd, she made for the door. A cool breeze stirred the orange trees surrounding the balcony. Annie strolled to the far end and gazed out at the gardens.

The only sound to be heard was the muted thump of a bass drum beating in time with the rustle of leaves in the breeze. Glancing up, she saw the few stars bright enough to shine over the blaze of city lights.

An image of warm brown eyes and a captivating grin filled her mind. What was it about Fisher McCoy that took her breath away? It was as if they had some connection. It wasn't just sexual tension, although there was a healthy dose of that. No, he managed to touch her in a much more intimate place. Her soul perhaps? Oh brother, she was beginning to sound like a sap. She bit her lip. Was she in over her head already?

FISHER SAW her ridiculous skirt first. It wafted in the breeze like a hot air balloon on the rise. She was right. That dress was an ape suit, he thought with a grin. But she was still stunning. Then he noticed the joker standing beside her. Her ex, Dudley Do-Right.

The night air carried the sound of their voices in his direction.

"But Anne, you and I belong together. You know we do."

"No, Stewart, I don't. That's why I broke up with you," she said, sounding exasperated. Then she softened her tone, "I'm sorry, Stewart."

"Well, you can't be serious about *him*," Stewart protested. "I saw you two dancing. It was a most undignified display, not to mention that bit at the church. What possessed you?''

''It was fun,'' she said. ''And that bit at the church was necessary.''

''You need someone with a calming influence on you, Anne,'' Stewart lectured. ''Not someone who indulges your silly, little whims.''

''Silly, little whims?'' she repeated, obviously clinging to her temper by a fine, red hair. ''I don't suppose you consider The Coffee Break one of my silly, little whims?''

''No,'' he said, looking nervous. ''But you have to admit, you don't have a strong head for business.''

''No, but I have a mighty strong fist,'' she retorted, looking ready to punch Dudley Do-Right in the nose.

''Here you are, Annie.'' Fisher stepped forward and handed Annie her glass. Although, what possessed him to save Stew's neck he didn't know. He should have let Annie clean his clock, but he knew she would never forgive herself. And he couldn't stand to watch that.

''Do you mind? Anne and I were having a very important discussion.'' Stew glared at him.

''I don't mind at all,'' Fisher said. ''I only came out to give Annie her champagne.'' He turned as if to leave, but then turned back to Annie. ''Oh, and this.''

With his free hand, he cupped her face and stepped toward her. He heard the breath puff out from between her lips as she was caught by surprise. He would have smiled, but the moment his mouth touched hers, he was no longer amused.

Her lips were cold and tart from the champagne and he wondered if he could get drunk from them. Lord knew, the sweet scent of her made his head spin.

It was supposed to be a kiss designed to humiliate Stew, to let him know that Annie was no longer available, but it turned into a quest to know Annie. To know the taste of her, the feel of her mouth against his and the warmth of her body as it melted into his.

The spark that had surprised him last night was still there, but today it was even more intense, shocking him with the force of his own desire. He buried his hand in her hair, mussing her elaborate hairdo. He angled her mouth to give himself better access. It wasn't enough. He wanted more. It stunned him, this primal need to possess her.

The sound of running water caught his attention and he reluctantly released her. He glanced down. Her glass was dangling limply from her fingers. She seemed completely unaware that she'd spilled her champagne all over his shoes.

She slumped against the balcony rail as if her legs had given out. She pushed the curls from her face while she fought for breath. She looked rumpled, disheveled and thoroughly nonplussed. Fisher decided she was the sexiest woman he'd ever laid eyes on.

He retrieved the glass from her hand and glanced about. There was no sign of good old Stew. He grinned. "I guess we lost our audience."

"Audience?" she asked between pants.

"Stew."

"Who?" she asked.

"Your ex," he reminded her. "Remember? The reason you invited me?"

"Oh, Stewart." She nodded. "I forgot…I mean… uh…should we go back in?"

"Sure," he agreed. Because she was irresistible in her confusion, he tipped her chin up and placed his lips on hers. Just a brief kiss to let her know that he wasn't just kissing her because of Stew.

He pulled her hand into the crook of his elbow and led her toward the door. "It certainly is a fine evening for a wedding," he said.

"Annie? Fisher?" One of the bridesmaids ducked her head through the balcony doors. "Come on. They're about to cut the cake."

"Your shining moment," he said.

"I have to admit this cake is one of my best," she said. Five tiers of rich, ivory butter-cream frosting in a basket-weave pattern, decorated with hundreds of edible purple and yellow Johnny Jump-ups, this was by far one of Annie's most inspired creations. She'd spent an hour photographing it that afternoon for her album at the shop. "It's going to be painful to watch them cut it up."

"Yes, but they probably need you for the singing," he said. "A bridesmaid's work is never done."

"Don't I know it," she agreed. "I don't know why they just don't give bridesmaids pom-poms. I mean we're really just cheerleaders in fancy dresses."

"Purple pom-poms?" He laughed. "It couldn't be any worse than that parasol she had you carrying."

"I know, a parasol at an evening wedding. What was she thinking?" Annie shook her head. "Too bad I didn't have it with me when Stewart was here. I could have hit him over the head with it."

"That's one option," he agreed as he led her back into the banquet hall.

"Oh, you are bad," she said, trying to ignore the feel of his fingers around her elbow.

"Good bad or bad bad?" he asked. Annie glanced at his face and the intensity in his regard left her no doubt that he was referring to their kiss. She felt her insides clench in response. Oh dear!

They entered the reception hall to hear the wedding guests cheering as Eve cut a slice of cake and fed it to Tony.

Tony took the cake from Eve's fingers, licking the frosting from her fingertips as he went. One glance at

Eve's mother, and Annie could see the lines of disapproval etched in her face.

"Wow! Do all couples feed each other like that?" Fisher asked, a surprised look on his face.

Annie watched as Eve ate the cake from Tony's fingers. These two were positively hungry for one another. A surge of heat warmed Annie from the inside out. She felt like a voyeur watching the obvious passion between Tony and Eve. Was it like that between herself and Fisher?

She glanced at him out of the corner of her eye. He clapped with the rest of the crowd when the bride and groom kissed. She studied his profile. His brown hair hung over his forehead, defying any attempt at order. His prominent nose looked as if it had been broken once or twice, and his lips were wide and full, as if they were made for kissing.

Annie felt a trickle of perspiration run down her back and she jerked her gaze away. She would not fall for her tenant. She would not fall for her tenant. She would not...

"What are you thinking?" he whispered in her ear.

Stepping away from him, she said, "Nothing."

He smiled and his teeth were a slash of white against those lips. "Liar," he accused.

Annie met his dark brown gaze and felt suddenly legless. His glance held humor with a glint of understanding. As if he knew very well what she'd been thinking and that she was fighting to deny it.

"Will all of the single ladies in the crowd please come to the center of the dance floor?" The DJ's voice boomed through the hall and a squeal went up among several of the women. "That's right. It's time for the bride to toss the bouquet."

"Well, that's my cue to go hide in the ladies'

room,'' Annie said and stepped away from Fisher with a grimace.

''Coward,'' he teased.

''You betcha,'' she said.

''Annie, there you are,'' Eve cried as she rushed through the crush of guests to grab her arm.

''Help me,'' Annie whispered to Fisher through clenched teeth.

''Oh, you don't need me,'' he said and nudged her forward. ''I'm sure you'll be able to catch that bouquet all by yourself.''

''Rat fink,'' she hissed as Eve dragged her toward the dance floor.

He winked at her and Annie felt herself go weak in the knees.

5

TWENTY-FIVE TIPSY WOMEN crowded the floor jostling for the best position. Eve shoved Annie front and center and ordered her not to move.

"I'm aiming for you," she said. "You're long overdue to get married."

Marriage must be a disease, Annie thought. Once a person suffered the disorder, they weren't happy until everyone else had it, too. Well, it wasn't going to happen to her.

Lifting her skirts, Annie waited until Eve turned her back to the group before she began to sidle off the floor. The women beside her were more than happy to let her move. This was true Darwinism and only the fittest would survive, or in this case, wrestle her fellow women to the floor for a fistful of flowers.

The crowd was chanting, "One...two..." Annie was almost in the clear. Just another couple of feet and she could slip out the back toward the rest room. "Three!"

Eve let the bouquet fly and Annie dodged toward the door. One moment it was in her line of sight. The next it was obscured by a forest of white lilies. The bouquet bounced off of her forehead and rolled down her face, getting stuck in the bodice of her dress.

"It's mine!" shrieked one of the bridesmaids and she dove at Annie as if she would tackle her and tear the dress from her body in order to get the bouquet. Annie felt her jaw open and she would have screamed but an arm looped around her waist, scooping her off of her feet even as it halted the breath in her lungs. The would-be bouquet snatcher was left to skid across the floor, her arms floundering as they grasped nothing but air.

"Well, it appears you're the big winner." Fisher chuckled, carrying Annie across the floor.

Annie felt the handle of the bouquet dig into her left breast and she fought to untangle it from her bra. The urge to hit him on the head with it was almost too much to resist.

"Quit pouting," he teased. "You caught it fair and square. I saw you diving for it. If you didn't want it, you shouldn't have caught it."

"I did not dive…" Belatedly, she noticed the gleam in his eye. He was teasing her. "Argh!"

Fisher laughed, adjusting her in his arms as he did so. "Relax. So you caught the bouquet. It doesn't mean you have to marry next."

"No," she agreed. "But it means some dork is going to get to feel up my leg when he puts the garter on me."

"What?" His gaze snapped to hers.

"That's how this little ritual goes. Whoever catches the garter puts it on the person who catches the bouquet." She sighed. "With my luck, Stewart will catch the garter and I'll be back at square one."

"Oh, no," he said. "Not while I'm here he won't."

Annie watched his square jaw lock into place. He looked more forceful than she would have thought possible. Why it made her heart pound, she didn't want to know.

"You don't have to do this," she said.

"Oh, yes I do," he said. His tone didn't allow for discussion.

"You can put me down now," she said, feeling the stares of the crowd upon them.

Fisher glanced at her. His dark brown eyes were inscrutable. She felt trapped within his gaze. He released his arm from beneath her knees, but retained his grip about her waist, keeping her close as she slid down his body to stand on her own two feet. She couldn't tell what he was thinking, but the intensity of his look was disturbing. Had it been anyone but him, she would have run.

"All right, ladies and gents, now it's time for the garter," the DJ's voice boomed through the room.

Annie turned to watch Tony take the garter off of Eve. To his credit, he did it with a lot of humor. Throwing up the hem of Eve's skirt with a wicked wink, he made his bride blush and laugh and she playfully swatted his shoulder. Once Tony had the garter, he stood and waved it over his head like a trophy. The crowd cheered.

"Now if we could have all of the single men come forward," the DJ instructed.

"Wish me luck," Fisher said. Releasing Annie with a quick squeeze of her waist, he strode forward.

Annie felt her palms grow damp around the bouquet. She was actually nervous. Oh, how ridiculous, she thought. It was just a silly wedding ritual. It didn't mean anything, yet she couldn't look away.

"Annie," Eve said as she raced to her side. "I'm so glad you caught the bouquet. You know what that means?"

"Yes, Eve, I know," Annie said, not looking at her friend.

"It means you're next," Eve chimed as if this was the greatest news on Earth.

"Don't bet on it," Annie said. If Eve heard the sarcasm in Annie's voice, she ignored it.

"So, who do you think will catch the garter?" Eve asked. "Stewart? Or your new beau?"

"He's not..." Annie's voice trailed off in the midst of her denial. Fisher wasn't her new beau, but he wasn't just her tenant, either. How had life become so complicated so fast?

She watched the men form a jovial group in the center of the dance floor. Most were laughing, nudging each other in the ribs. Two were not. Stewart and Fisher. They stood in the center of the melee, elbow to elbow. Neither of them was smiling.

Tony sashayed around the group, taunting them a bit. He made to toss the garter and half of the group stumbled in that direction. Only Fisher stood still, motionless, watching Tony with a single-minded concentration that might have been unnerving had Tony been aware of it. Annie knew it unnerved her.

What would it be like to be on the receiving end of that attention when there was no one else around? When it was just the two of them? Her stomach fluttered. Oh my, she thought and forced some air into her lungs.

Tony twirled the garter on his finger and grinned. Turning his back to the men, he flung the garter over his shoulder. The garter didn't weigh enough to propel it very far. It fell short of the group, heading for the floor at their feet. Annie saw Stewart elbow Fisher hard in the side. Fisher took the blow and somehow used it to push himself forward. Hands outstretched, he dove onto the floor like a runner heading for home plate. He curled his fingers around the garter.

"Yes!" Annie shouted with a raised fist.

Fisher met her eyes from his sprawled position on the floor and laughed. Annie looked at her fist and then pretended that she was in midstretch, twisting as if she'd just been relieving a backache. Fisher laughed harder. She felt the heat of embarrassment rush into her face and she jerked her gaze down to her bouquet, pretending a sudden interest in its arrangement.

"Hey, he pushed me," Stewart protested, his voice high and whiny like a child tasting defeat.

Annie's head snapped up. "Was that before or after you elbowed him, Stewart?"

"You know what they say, Stew, all's fair in love and war," Fisher declared as he rose from the floor and dusted off his suit front.

"Ain't that a fact?" Tony laughed and looped his arm about Eve's waist.

"Humph!" Stewart sniffed and stalked away.

"Now for the fun part," the DJ's voice boomed. "Will our lovely couple please step forward so that the gentleman may bestow the garter upon the lady?"

"We don't have to do this, do we?" Annie asked Eve.

"Of course you do," Eve declared. "It's tradition."

"But..." Annie began, but Fisher interrupted her.

"Come on, honey, it'll be fun."

The look in his eyes promised much more than fun. Annie gulped. The ribbon wrapped handle of the bouquet dug into her palm and she realized she was holding it much too tightly. How could he make her so nervous with just a look?

Fisher led her to the lone chair in the middle of the dance floor. Annie had been in nine weddings and had attended more than double that many. She knew the shtick. She had always managed to avoid participating in this particular event. It was more than a little unnerving to be under the scrutiny of three hundred guests and the wolfish look Fisher was giving her was not helping.

"All rightee then," the DJ boomed into his microphone and Annie jumped. "How about a little mood music?"

The bass beat of a stripper's number thumped through the room. Annie felt her face flush hot. Laughter erupted throughout the room and she tried to smile through gritted teeth. It was one thing to place one's self in the spotlight for a good cause, it was quite another to be thrust there for no good purpose.

"Hurry up," she growled at Fisher as he knelt before her.

"Oh, I don't think so." He grinned and then he winked. It was a wicked wink. He was lucky there were three hundred witnesses around them, or she would have kicked him. "What's the matter, Annie? Nervous?"

The fact that he guessed so accurately was perturbing. Annie refused to give him the satisfaction of knowing her so well. Parting her lips into a facsimile of a smile, she lied, "No, I'm not."

"Really?" He leaned close. "I am."

Annie felt all of the blood in her body rush south.

She had no time to react. Fisher tossed the hem of her skirt up and lifted her foot onto his thigh. He made to slide the garter over the gaudy purple shoe, but then appeared to think better of it. Lifting her foot with one hand, he slid her shoe off then tossed it over his shoulder. The crowd went wild.

Replacing her foot on his thigh, Fisher began to work the garter over her toes. Her heel rested against his thigh, and Annie was stunned by the heat and hardness of him she could feel through his slacks. She'd never met a man with thighs like rocks before. She was speechless.

He cradled her foot again, his thumb digging into the arch for an impromptu massage. Annie had to bite her lip to keep from moaning and sagging in the chair. How did he know her feet were killing her?

His hands moved over her ankle and slid slowly up her calf. She glanced at him. His gaze was intent upon her face as if seeking her every reaction to his touch. As his fingers rubbed against the silk of her stockings, Annie thought she might faint from the sheer delicious torture. He smiled. Somehow, he knew. He knew what she was thinking.

"You do have great legs," he said.

"The other one is wood," she joked, trying to diffuse the tension. He laughed, but his gaze still bespoke desire.

"Really? When you flashed me in the parking lot, I could have sworn they were both flesh and bone. But I'm happy to check out the other one to be sure."

"Oh no," she protested, batting her skirt down. "That's not necessary."

"Darn," he said with regret. His fingers had stilled halfway up her calf.

"Are you done?" she asked, trying to rise.

"Not quite." He held her in her seat. "I think it's supposed to go up around your thigh."

"The knee will do," she said breathlessly.

His fingers began to move again, slowly, steadily. Annie felt all of the heat in her body pool low in her belly and she squirmed in her chair. He lifted the garter up over her knee. His fingers traced the satin band, making it lie flat against her skin. His gaze met hers and locked. The desire thumping between them was like an aching physical presence.

The crowd burst into rowdy cheers and the moment was broken.

"Kiss her," one heckler yelled from the sidelines and soon others joined in, making it a chant.

"We can't disappoint our public," Fisher said extending his hand to help her out of the chair.

"Yes, we can," she said as she brushed at the skirt of her dress.

"Why so shy all of the sudden, Annie-girl?" He caught her chin in the palm of his hand forcing her to meet his gaze.

"I wasn't looking for this," she said.

"Neither was I," he sighed just before his mouth claimed hers.

The kiss was brief. The mere brushing of lips, but it shook Annie all the way down to her shoeless toes.

THE DJ TURNED OFF the bump and grind, replacing it with Nat King Cole singing "Unforgettable." Fisher gazed at the woman before him and thought how appropriate it was. Annie Talbot was like no one he had ever known…unforgettable.

Even in that horrible purple dress she was striking. Her long fiery hair framed a delicate face lightly brushed with freckles. She was a rare combination of seductive innocence and compassionate toughness. She would do anything for a loved one, giving of herself so freely that he was moved to worry about her.

Without thinking about it, he pulled her into his arms and they began to sway to the music. Her eyes were still shut from their kiss and she flowed into him.

He could feel her heat against him, her softness pressing into him. He felt as if he were being pulled over and under by a tide. She was bewitching him. With her easy smile and enchanting laughter, her quick wit and sympathetic soul, she had him completely under her spell.

She couldn't be a criminal. He couldn't be that wrong about her. His hand tightened about her waist and his fingers brushed the abrupt flare of her hip. Oh hell! The woman was built like an hourglass. He moved his hand back up.

He wasn't going to touch her. But she leaned her head against his shoulder and the scent of her hair taunted him. Fisher inhaled, feeling both soothed and stirred by her. How was that possible?

He'd worked for the Bureau for ten years. Never had he gotten personally involved with a suspect and he'd been much deeper undercover than this. He had to be more careful or Annie Talbot would have the power to destroy him and everything he'd worked for.

The song ended. Fisher stepped away from her, avoiding her seductive blue gaze. He had to keep her at a distance. Stepping back, he asked, "Do you want something to drink?"

"Water would be great," she said, her voice was low and sexy. He took another step back.

"I'll be back," he said and felt himself all but run from her. The big, bad FBI guy was afraid of a little, red-haired baker. If he wasn't so appalled he would have laughed.

"HOW WAS THE WEDDING?" Brian asked as soon as Fisher stepped into the office Monday morning.

"Fine," Fisher said, feeling unaccountably defensive.

"Fine?" Brian repeated, pushing his round spectacles up on his nose. His tie was askew and he looked rumpled, as if he'd slept in his clothes.

"Yeah, fine," he repeated. "What's wrong? Baby keep you up?"

"Yeah. Bri Jr.'s got colic." Brian shook his head. "Who knew that could rip your heart out?"

"How's Susan?"

"Managing," Brian said with a smile. "She's a wonder with the little guy."

"You picked a good one."

"Sure did," Brian sighed. "But you still haven't answered my question. Fine is a good description for the weather, but it tells me diddly-squat about the wedding. So, what happened? Any suspects?"

"There are a couple of background checks I want to run," Fisher said. "Her ex-boyfriend, Stewart Anderson, her rival in business, Martin Delgado and one of her employees, Denise Barrows. We can start with Stew."

"The ex?" Brian asked with raised eyebrows.

"Yeah, if he's had so much as a parking ticket, I want to know."

"Why him?"

"He's too intent on Annie. He won't let go of her, and I don't think it's because he's in love with her," Fisher said.

"Why do you suppose then?"

"I don't know, but it has something to do with the business."

"He's an entrepreneur, isn't he?"

"Yeah, maybe we need to check out some of his business dealings a bit more closely."

"Good idea."

"McCoy, Phillips, how's Operation Coffee Break going?" Paul Van Buren strode into the office, clutching a can of soda. He looked surly this morning, more surly than usual.

"Good," Fisher lied. "We've got a lead on her ex."

"What about the girl?" Van Buren asked.

"She's innocent," Fisher said automatically.

"How do you know?" Van Buren snapped.

"I was there when the shop was robbed," he said. "She loves that place. She was devastated when it was vandalized. This is not someone who would risk her own shop."

"Maybe she's mixed up with some heavy hitters," Brian offered.

"What are you saying? She's a bimbo?" Van Buren asked.

"No!" Fisher denied more adamantly than he'd intended. Both Brian and Van Buren looked at him with raised eyebrows. "No," he said more softly, "I would say she is naive and a bit too trusting."

"Should we bring her into the loop?" Van Buren asked. "Can she be trusted?"

"I'd stake my job on it," Fisher said.

"You will be," Van Buren said. "Sit her down and have a talk with her. See if she knows anything that might tell us who is using The Coffee Break to launder money in and out of Phoenix."

"All right," Fisher agreed. "I'll talk to her tonight."

"Oh, and McCoy." Van Buren paused before he left. "You'd better be right about her."

"I am," Fisher said.

FISHER LEFT HIS Jeep parked on the curb. He could see the lights on inside The Coffee Break and suspected that Annie was still cleaning up the mess left from the burglary. She'd been hoping to reopen today, but with the wedding all day Saturday, Sunday hadn't given them enough time to clean up and restock the supplies. He'd spent all day yesterday fixing broken furniture, sorting coffee beans and chasing around Phoenix trying to replace the food goods.

She'd thrown out all of her baked goods. It made him furious to think of someone trashing all of her hard work. Who had done this and why?

He jogged up the three steps to the front door. He could see her placing fresh muffins in the display counter at the front of the store. Her hair was pulled back in a thick braid that swung over her shoulder as she bent. He felt his fingers flex with the desire to touch it.

The urge to protect her hit him low and hard. He didn't want to bring her into the loop. He didn't want to see her hurt. And she would be hurt. He knew that as surely as he knew he desired her. She would think he'd been using her all along. Perhaps he had been in the beginning, but things had changed between them.

He had no choice, however. They needed her help. He only hoped she'd still be willing to help after he told her the truth.

As if sensing his gaze upon her, Annie glanced up. A smile parted her lips as soon as she recognized him. It made his gut twist. He grasped the door handle and pulled. He couldn't budge it. The door was locked. He frowned. Why did she lock it? Surely, she couldn't already know...

"Hi, Fisher," she said as she unlocked the door. "See? I remembered to lock it."

Fisher felt a sigh of relief escape him. She hadn't been locking him out.

"Why are you coming in the front door? Did you lose your key?"

"No." He followed her into the shop, turning the door's dead bolt behind him. "I thought you might be here."

"Oh?" she asked, glancing down as if avoiding his gaze. "Did you want to see me?"

"Yes," he replied. "I need to talk to you about something."

She glanced up at him. She looked fearful, cautious, as if expecting a blow. But in a blink the look was gone. She stiffened her back and marched back to the display case.

"Okay. How about a slice of hazelnut torte while we talk?" She didn't wait for him to answer but began dishing out the decadent dessert. She disappeared into the kitchen, returning a moment later with a glass of milk. Placing the food on a nearby table, she gestured for Fisher to sit down.

"Go ahead," she said. "Talk."

"I'm glad you locked the door," he said, stalling for time.

She lifted her eyebrows and then wrinkled her nose at him. "I'm still not buying a personal assault system."

"Personal protection device," he corrected her. He would have continued his lecture, but he took a bite of the torte and was rendered speechless. How could anyone create such perfection? It was the perfect blend of flavors, sweet chocolate and crunchy nuts. If there was a heaven, this was it.

"Fisher?" She watched him with a small smile tipping her lips. "Fisher? Was there something you wanted to tell me?"

He dropped his fork. "Yeah."

At his somber tone, the spark in her eyes dimmed and she plopped onto the seat across from him with a thump.

"I wish I could have told you sooner, but..." he paused. Was there a tactful way to tell a woman you'd been lying to her for days? Did Hallmark greetings make a card for this?

"You're married, aren't you?" she interrupted his thoughts.

"Married? No." He shook his head. "Nothing like that."

"Gay?"

"No."

"Emotionally unavailable?"

"What? No."

"Commitment phobic?"

"Hell no!"

"Then what?" she asked, sounding exasperated.

He paused unable to think of a delicate way to put it.

"Oh, I get it. You don't like me *that* way," she said, rising from her seat. She began to swipe nonexistent crumbs from the tabletop. "Don't wrack your brain trying to find a nice way to tell me, just say it. You don't like me that way. You think of me as a sister, and you don't want to ruin our friendship. There. Now was that so hard?"

She began to walk away, but Fisher caught her by the wrist. He tugged her toward him. She dug in her heels. He tugged harder. Her chin was tipped up at a proud angle, but he could see the hurt in her face. It was as if every muscle had gone lax, giving her whole face a sad, wilted appearance. It broke his heart.

"Annie, sit down," he whispered. When she didn't appear inclined to follow his orders, he pulled her onto the chair beside him. "What I have to tell you has almost nothing to do with us."

"Oh...Oh?" she asked. Her face flamed a vibrant shade of scarlet and she glanced at the fingers she held clenched into fists. He watched her take a deep breath and slowly release her fingers.

"You know that I work for the government," he began, watching her face. "But do you know exactly what I do?"

"I thought you were a paper jockey for some bureaucratic office," she said.

"Close." He sent her a wry smile.

Now that the moment of truth had arrived, he found himself painfully reluctant to tell her. He didn't want to hurt her. But she needed to know what was happening. Even if it meant losing her.

"I do write reports," he said. "Some days it seems

I'm wading hip-deep in paper, but my title isn't paper jockey, it's special agent.''

"Special agent?" She blinked at him. "That sounds ominous…like Secret Service or CIA."

"Actually, it's FBI," he said. "I'm a special agent with the FBI."

"FBI?" Her mouth popped open and her eyes grew wide. "You're an FBI agent?"

"Yes." He watched the emotions pass over her face like storm clouds rolling over a blue sky. He held his breath waiting for the rumble of thunder.

It never came. She sat watching him, studying him. Her gaze scrutinized him, as if trying to figure out how this new information fit in with everything she knew about him. Fisher shifted under her watchful gaze. He'd feel better if she'd just yell at him and get it over with. No such luck.

"Well?" he prompted her.

"Well what?" she asked.

"Don't you have anything to say?"

"Not really." She shrugged. "Thank you for telling me."

Fisher frowned. He was going to have to be more blunt.

"Although," she spoke, halting his chance. "I should have known you'd have a law-and-order type of career. It suits your rigidity."

"Rigid? I am not rigid," he protested.

"Yes, you are," she argued.

"I like order, but I'm not rigid."

"Uh-huh," she grunted.

"Look, we're getting off track here." He ran a hand through his hair. "The fact is, I'm not just here because I need a place to live. I'm here to stake out The Coffee Break."

"What? Stake out?" Her eyebrows snapped up, as if at attention. "What do you mean?"

"I mean that someone has been laundering money through your shop and I was placed here to try and figure out who is doing it."

"Laundering money? My shop?" She looked at him, looked away and then back. She burst out laughing. "Oh, you almost had me. I can't believe I almost fell for it."

Her laugh was light and airy, and for the first time since he'd heard it, Fisher wasn't moved to laugh in return.

"Annie..." he said.

"You would have had me if it weren't so ridiculous," she chuckled.

"Annie, it's true."

Her sparkling blue eyes met his and the smile seeped out of them as if someone dimmed a light. Her face paled, leaving her freckles looking dark against her skin. "That's not...how could...oh my God!"

Fisher reached out to steady her on her chair. She looked as if he'd yanked the floor right out from under her.

"Annie, are you all right?"

"No! I'm not. Not by a long shot," she said, her voice clipped with anger. "Explain this to me. All of it. From the beginning. What makes you think someone is laundering money through my shop? Who and how?"

"I don't know who, but I have a pretty good idea how," he said.

"Tell me," she demanded.

"Do you remember being audited a few months ago?" he asked.

"Are you kidding? It was worse than an enema." She snorted. "I've only been in business for three years. I'm just getting a handle on things. What a nightmare.''

"Yes, well, the tax auditors found major discrepancies in your records.''

"But they said I was fine,'' she protested.

"They lied,'' he said. "The truth is your shop was discovered to have signs of serious laundering. The tax auditors informed the Bureau, and we began to investigate.''

"So you're here to investigate me?''

"Yes.''

"I see.'' She sat back in her chair. Her face was tight, pensive. Fisher couldn't hazard a guess as to what she was thinking.

"No, I don't think you do,'' he said. "The reason that I'm telling you all of this, Annie, is because I need your help. I need access to your books and financial information.''

"Why?''

"Because significant amounts of cash are being laundered through The Coffee Break.''

"But...by who?''

"That's what I want you to help me find out,'' he said.

"Why should I?'' she snapped.

The storm clouds finally rolled in and Fisher welcomed them. He'd rather deal with a furious Annie than a defeated one.

"You lied to me,'' she said, her voice increasing in volume with her temper.

"I never lied,'' he argued. "I just didn't tell you everything.''

"Lies of omission,'' she said, standing up. "It's the same thing.''

"I was doing my job,'' he argued, standing, too.

"Oh, sure. You kissed me! You...you...argh!'' She

jabbed him in the chest with a pointy finger. "I guess that's all in a day's work for an FBI guy."

"Hey, you asked me to the wedding," he reminded her. "And yes, it was a good opportunity to observe the people in your life. As for kissing you, that had nothing to do with the investigation."

"Sure," she said. "How do you know you can trust me? How do you know I'm not a criminal?"

"Honestly?" he asked and she nodded. "I don't, but I'm willing to stake my career on it."

They stood toe to toe, staring at one another like two boxers squared off in opposite corners.

He went for a jab. "Annie, I need you," he said.

He watched her temper seep out of her like air out of a balloon. She looked bewildered and deflated. Fisher wanted to pull her into his arms and comfort her, but he resisted the urge. He had to give her time to adjust to the news he'd just dumped on her. Her entire world was upside down and he couldn't take advantage of her distress just to make himself feel better.

"I'm sorry, Annie-girl," he said.

"Thank you for that," she said and sighed. "I just can't believe it. Are you sure there's no mistake?"

"I'm sure," he said.

"I just don't understand how or why," she said. "I know I'm not the most savvy businesswoman, but how could this be happening without my knowing? And who could be doing it?"

"That's what I need your help to find out," he said. "We've gone over all of the bank records for your shop. Someone from the outside is manipulating your accounts. I need to know who exactly has access to your records."

"Just about everyone," she said. "I trust all of my employees. I never even lock the safe, except at night."

"Well, things are going to have to change," he said. "I'm going to spend more time in the shop, observing who comes and goes. While I'm doing that, you can give me a rundown on everyone."

"Don't you think someone will notice if you skulk around the shop all day?"

"Put me to work then," he suggested. "We'll say you're shorthanded and I'm helping out."

"I don't like the idea of you spying on my customers and employees," she said.

"Can you think of a better idea?"

"No." She heaved a disgusted sigh.

"Just think, you get to boss me around all day," he said.

"You're right. I will enjoy that." Her smile almost met her eyes.

"Then it's settled. I'll report for work in the morning."

6

IT WAS STILL DARK when Annie pushed aside her covers and climbed out of bed. Henry always said that the early bird caught the worm. Annie wondered if anyone had ever asked the worm how he felt about it? She grimaced at her reflection in the bathroom mirror and thought she had a pretty good idea how he felt.

The three days she'd been closed had put a dent in her business and she needed to recoup her losses. No pressure there. She could only hope her regulars returned with renewed appetites.

The fact that she hadn't gotten any quality time with the insides of her eyelids the night before was not helping. She'd spent the night chewing on Fisher's news until her teeth hurt. Her business was being watched by the FBI! By him! He thought someone was laundering money through her shop. Could it be possible? The whole thing seemed surreal.

She thought of everyone who had helped her begin her business and everyone who was involved with the business now. How could one of these people be a criminal? She felt as if she'd been stabbed. Who would have betrayed her trust?

Anger replaced hurt. She was going to help Fisher catch whoever was doing this. She wasn't about to let her business, her dream, be destroyed.

Her emotions for Fisher weren't as clear. What to do about him? Could she trust him? He'd lied to her.

He hadn't told her he was with the FBI, until he was sure she was innocent. Logically, she understood his reasons, but it still smarted. He had conned her, made her believe that there was something special between them, when he'd really only been spying on her.

She supposed she should be relieved that he believed in her innocence, but somehow it wasn't enough. When he kissed her, she felt magic, a sense of rightness and belonging. Now she realized he was just very good at his job. He was very good at going undercover. Thankfully, she hadn't let him under her covers.

That he'd fooled her so completely made her feel like an idiot. She was embarrassed and ashamed. What must he think of her? Not only was someone destroying her business right under her nose, but she was falling for the man sent to spy on her as well. He must think she was the biggest chump alive. The realization made Annie cranky. She didn't like to be anyone's fool.

The kitchen was dark when she arrived downstairs. Flipping on the light switch, she set to work mixing her first batch of muffins for the day. Cooking had always been therapeutic for her. It kept her hands and her mind busy, not allowing her to dwell on big, stupid FBI men with gorgeous brown eyes and great smiles.

She'd just shoved the first batch of muffins into the oven when Fisher's head poked around the doorway.

"Good morning," he said, looking as though he were checking to see if she had any sharp implements in the vicinity. Smart man.

Annie refused to let her inner turmoil show. "Good morning," she answered, showing some teeth.

"It's not a very good one for you, is it?" he asked. His voice was full of sympathy and Annie had to look away, afraid she might burst into tears.

"No," she admitted.

"Don't worry, Annie-girl, we'll catch whoever's doing this," he said.

"I know," she said. "It just hurts."

"I'm sorry," he said.

"Why? It's not your fault."

"I know, but I hate to see you so sad," he said.

"I'll get over it," she declared, trying to be more stoic than she felt.

He sent her a dubious look but didn't argue with her.

"So, what can I do to help around here?" he asked.

"I…I'm not sure." She shrugged. "I don't suppose you cook?"

"I can't even boil water without melting the pot," he said. "Besides I'll need to work out in the shop if I'm to see everyone who comes and goes."

"Denise works the counter and I have two waitresses already," she paused. "I don't want them to have to divide up their tips anymore than they already do. I could use a busboy however."

"Busboy?" He looked offended.

"Yes, that's perfect!" She clapped her hands. "During the rush, it's a struggle clearing the tables. This would be a tremendous help. I'll go get you an apron."

"Apron?" he asked. "You've got to be kidding."

"What's the matter?" she teased. "Afraid you can't bus a few tables?"

"You're enjoying this aren't you?"

"You bet I am," she admitted with a grin. Seeing Fisher clear tables was going to be a hoot. Was it wrong to savor a small bite of revenge at his expense? Nah.

Pulling a pink, ruffled apron out of the cupboard at the back of the kitchen, she threw it at him. "I think the domestic look will work for you."

"Annie," he growled, catching the apron before it hit him in the face.

"Do you have a better idea?" she asked.

"No," he admitted with a frown.

"Here's your bin," she said and handed him a big, plastic basin to haul dishes with. "We open in fifteen minutes. Come on, I'll introduce you to my waitresses."

"Sonia, Beatrice, meet Fisher," Annie called as she entered the main room of the coffee shop. "He's going to be helping us out by busing tables."

The two women glanced up from where they were filling sugar bowls. They didn't looked surprised. Annie knew they were thinking she'd found another stray to take in. She was tempted to tell them the truth. But knowing it would jeopardize Fisher's investigation, she bit her tongue.

"Nice to meet you," Beatrice said, her gray eyes narrowed behind her round glasses. Beatrice was what Annie's grandmother would call a hippie. She had ten earring holes in each ear, she wore an eclectic selection of clothing from the local thrift store and the scent of sandalwood flowed around her as if it permeated her skin. She was a hard worker and had a great rapport with the customers. Annie knew she could depend upon Beatrice, and she genuinely liked her company.

Sonia was as opposite from Beatrice as incense from a Glade plug-in. Shy and quiet, she was a sophomore in college but still lived at home with her parents. She wore Peter Pan collared blouses under pastel cardigans. She was fluent in Spanish and devoted to her church.

"Hello," Sonia said and a blush bloomed across her cheeks.

"Nice to meet you both." Fisher inclined his head.

Annie glanced at him. Dressed in a T-shirt and jeans, he appeared casual, but there was no disregarding the lean strength of his frame or the subtle bunch of muscles beneath his shirt. Annie noticed Beatrice ogling

Fisher's forearms, and she frowned. He did have powerful-looking arms, not the kind one gets by hefting barbells, but by performing actual physical labor. But he was an FBI guy, didn't they just push paper around all day while staking out bad guys? She gave him a considering look. How much did she know about him anyway?

"It looks like we're going to need the extra help," Beatrice observed. "Denise hasn't shown up yet."

"She hasn't?" Annie frowned at the empty counter. Denise should have had it ready by now. "Sonia, will you set up the counter? I'll give Denise a call and see if everything is all right."

Annie darted back to her office, leaving her staff to fend for themselves. She knew they'd be fine. She wasn't so certain about Denise. Things hadn't been right with Denise for several weeks now. Something had to be done. With the FBI investigating, she needed everyone to keep themselves above suspicion.

She'd known Denise since cooking school. Denise had dropped out to get married, a move Annie had thought she might regret. But Denise had never said anything and for years she'd been very happy with her husband Edmund. It wasn't until last year when she came and asked for a job, that Annie suspected there might be trouble in paradise.

Annie punched in her friend's number on the phone in her office. The phone rang six times, but there was no answer, not even an answering machine. Annie hung up. She'd called Denise last night to tell her they were reopening and Denise had sounded eager to come back to work. Perhaps she was just running late. But that wasn't like her. Denise was Miss On-Time-All-The-Time even if she had to drive through fire.

"Everything all right, boss?" Fisher asked from the doorway.

"Huh? Oh, fine. Everything is fine," she lied, not knowing why she did it. Somehow she didn't want Fisher to be aware of Denise's behavior. Annie was sure it was nothing, at least nothing for the FBI to be concerned about.

"Good," he said, watching her as if trying to decide whether to believe her or not.

Annie turned her smile up in wattage. If Fisher was looking to investigate the people in her life, she was going to have to guard her reactions around him. The thought depressed her. She'd enjoyed their closeness over the past week. Like it or not, she'd been falling for the big lunk. But no more. He was Special Agent McCoy now. And until she knew who was using her business for no good, she would have to be cautious around him. She didn't want any innocent bystanders to get in trouble.

"What's got you looking so fierce?" he asked.

"Nothing," she lied. "I was just thinking."

"Happy thoughts obviously," he said.

She scowled at him. "Was there something you needed?"

"Actually, yes." He smiled in the face of her annoyance. "We're about to open, did you want me to work the counter for Denise?"

"Could you?" she asked dubiously.

"Blindfolded and with one hand tied behind my back."

She snorted.

"Trust me," he said. "You wouldn't believe some of the undercover jobs I've had."

"Like what?" she asked as she rose from her desk and led the way back into the coffee shop, locking her office behind her. If Fisher noticed, he didn't say anything.

"I was a bouncer at a strip club once," he said.

"Oh, that must have been brutal," she said. "It's a wonder you didn't get eye strain."

"And then I was the nighttime operator of the icey machine at a Circle K," he said.

"That's a chilling thought," she quipped.

"Very funny," he said, following her into the main room. "Speaking of funny, there was the time I had to pose as a clown at a kid's birthday party."

"You're joking?" she asked as she unlocked the front door to the shop and propped it open with a rock.

"Not at the moment, but I have to say I was a very good clown," he said.

"Why would you...?"

"Mobster's kid," he said.

"Oh." She gaped at him. "I don't believe it."

"I still have my big red shoes." He wiggled his eyebrows at her. "I could model them for you sometime."

"Thanks but no," she said. "Are you sure you can handle the counter? The espresso machine can be very temperamental."

"Don't worry, chief. You just shmooze your clientele. I'll be fine."

"All right but don't interrogate anyone without checking with me first," she warned.

He looked hurt. Annie was about to retract her statement, but the timer in the kitchen went off, interrupting her good intentions.

"Your muffins are cooked." He winked at her and she felt her skin tingle. The timer went off again.

"Stop that!" she snapped, not sure if she meant him or the timer or both.

THE MORNING passed in a blur. The rush didn't die down until after ten and by then Annie was too preoccupied with prepping lunch to stop and take a breath.

Denise had never appeared or called, but Fisher had done remarkably well in her stead. She needn't have feared that he would interrogate any of her customers. Instead, he charmed them silly.

Her Tuesday morning regulars included five librarians from the large public library down the street. A jovial group, they drank their double lattes while they discussed unwanted-hair removal, good dates, bad dates and where to get a smoking deal on shoes. Annie had always looked forward to their visits, primarily because she could always con one of them into taking her books back to the library for her. But today, what had they been discussing? The shape of Fisher's backside, that's what!

And they were in unanimous approval of it, from what Annie had managed to overhear. Not that she ever eavesdropped on her customers, but when she heard his name mentioned, well naturally, she was curious. He was absolutely no help at all. Refilling their cups while showcasing his slow-burning grin, the man was an incorrigible flirt! And her customers, her female customers, loved it. She sold more coffee and muffins during the morning rush than she had in weeks.

She didn't want to know why this didn't make her feel any better. Or why the thought of strangling him with his apron strings brought her so much pleasure. Using the largest knife in her kitchen, Annie chopped the head of lettuce before her as if it were Fisher's head.

Why did he have to come into her life anyway? She wasn't looking for this. She'd been quite content with her solitary existence. Now she couldn't get the man out of her mind. It was like he was sitting on her shoulder all of the time, and she couldn't get away from him or the feelings he stirred inside of her.

"Gee, what did that lettuce do to offend you?" A

low whistle brought her attention to the kitchen door. Fisher stood there holding a glass of raspberry iced tea out to her. "I thought you could use this."

Annie looked at the mangled lettuce before her and back at Fisher and said, "I meant to do that."

"Sure," he murmured.

"I did." She sniffed. "Not everyone likes big hunks of lettuce in their salad you know."

"Yeah, but I don't know many who prefer it in liquid form, either."

Annie dropped the knife and reached for the iced tea. "Thank you."

"You're welcome," he said. "Want to talk about it?"

"About what?"

"Whatever is making you mutilate defenseless vegetables?"

"No," she said with a shake of her head. *What am I supposed to say? That I want you, but you only want me to help you catch your bad guy? No thanks.*

"You're sure?" he asked.

"Yeah," she said. "We'd better get back at it. The lunch crowd starts a little after eleven."

"Whatever you say, boss." He saluted her and exited back through the kitchen door.

Boss. That was the second time today, he'd called her boss. And she'd gotten one chief. Great. He'd gone from thinking of her as a would-be criminal to a boss. Wasn't that just dandy?

"SO, YOU'VE DECIDED to hire a young stud to work the counter? And I thought you had no business sense."

Annie looked up from her desk to find her father standing in the doorway grinning at her. In a three piece suit, shiny shoes and not a hair of his full white mane out of place, he was the epitome of the suave businessman. Annie felt her lips part in a smile.

"Daddy, what brings you here?" she asked.

"I just came by to see how my baby is doing with her business," he said, enfolding her in a huge hug.

"How's Muffy?" she asked.

"Missy."

"Oh, yeah. Muffy was number two." Annie resumed her seat.

"Buffy," he corrected her.

"Oops. Sorry."

"That's all right. I know you resent my marriages." He took one of the two seats across from her desk.

"Aw, Dad," she sighed. "I don't resent your marriages. I just don't see why you had to marry someone my age."

"She's a year older than you. Now your mother..." he said, but Annie cut him off.

"I know Mom is married to that Swiss ski bum. What's his name? Hans? Hansel? Something like that."

"And he's younger than you," her father said, looking miffed. "What was she thinking?"

"Probably the same thing you were thinking when you married Bussy."

"That's Mussy...ah...Missy," he said.

"Oh, fine. You don't have time to shop with your mother, but you have plenty of time to have a tête-à-tête with your father."

Annie glanced up and saw her mother stride into the office. Her hair was a lovely shade of auburn—albeit from a bottle—which was set off by her snappy Donna Karan suit in a stunning shade of teal. She looked like a woman who always got her way, which was probably why she always did.

"Dad just popped in," Annie said and motioned for

her mother to take the vacant chair beside her father. Without looking down, she opened the middle drawer of her desk and ran her fingers over the contents, trying to find her antacid. Whenever her parents were in the same room for more then five minutes, she ended up with a monster case of indigestion.

"Olivia," her father rose to greet her mother.

"Charles," she returned.

Together they took their seats and faced Annie. It was more than a little disconcerting.

"So, what brings you here, Mom?" Annie asked.

"Your sister Mary told me about your new tenant," her mother said. "I wanted to be sure you were all right."

"What did she tell you?"

"That you asked him to Eve's wedding," her father answered.

"She told you, too? Did she tell you she dared me to do it?" Her parents exchanged a look. "So, that's why you're both here? To check up on me."

Annie popped an antacid tablet.

"Not checking up," her mother said, casting a quick glance at her father.

"No, not checking up," he agreed and then cleared his throat. "More like checking in."

"Huh-hunh," Annie grunted.

"Hey, boss, things have quieted down out front," Fisher said from the doorway. "I'm going to stop by the office and see if they've turned up any information on the burglary."

"Burglary? What burglary?" Annie's parents turned simultaneously to Fisher.

"Uh…" Fisher stalled while Annie made frantic slashing motions across her throat with her finger. He gave her an imperceptible nod.

"My Aunt Josephine's house was broken into so I'm going to check on the insurance," he lied.

"Oh, heavens. I thought you meant Annie had been robbed." Annie's mother put her hand over her heart and slumped back in her chair.

Her father patted her mother's arm in reassurance and they clutched fingers. For a second, Annie felt as if they'd never divorced.

"Fisher, I'd like you to meet my parents. Charles and Olivia Talbot. Oh, I'm sorry. It's Charles Talbot and Olivia Blickensderfer."

Annie's father shot her a look and she shrugged. It wasn't her fault that Blickensderfer was easier to remember than Bissy. Or was it Sissy?

"It's a pleasure to meet you," Fisher said as they shook hands.

"Mom, Dad, this is my tenant, Fisher McCoy."

"Tenant?" they asked in unison.

"And he works here," Annie said, beginning to enjoy herself.

"He works here?" Olivia asked. "I was under the impression that he had a job."

"He..." Annie began, but Fisher cut her off.

"I am employed. I'm just helping Annie out because one of her employees didn't show."

"Good help is hard to find," her mother commiserated. "So what do you do?"

"I work for the government."

"You can't beat that," her father chimed in. "I started my business on government contracts. Good pay, good benefits and a solid retirement. Not to mention an opportunity to buy up savings bonds."

Fisher beamed over their heads at Annie.

"A great job for a family man," her mother continued.

"I couldn't agree more, Mrs. Blickensderfer," he said without laughing.

"Call me Olivia," she said and rose to take his arm. "Now do you plan to settle in the Phoenix area?"

Annie watched as her parents walked with Fisher to the shop. She'd never seen her parents take to anyone so quickly. It was like an impromptu meeting of the Mutual Admiration Society. And her parents hadn't argued once. She shook her head as she followed them out.

Another half hour passed before her parents finally left. Fisher and her father bonded over an in-depth discussion of the stock market which left her eyelids sagging at half mast. Her mother had been won over when he correctly identified her Fendi handbag with a compliment.

"A man with good taste is very hard to find," she whispered to Annie. Annie didn't have the heart to point out that he'd probably read the label on the zipper tab.

As soon as her parents departed, she disappeared into her office. This day was becoming too much.

"Annie, I'm taking off. If that's all right?" Fisher asked from the doorway. He had changed into a gray suit and looked every inch the FBI guy that he was.

"Hmm?" She frowned at him. "Oh, yeah, sure. Go ahead."

Fisher crossed the room with a frown. "You all right?"

His steady brown gaze was penetrating and Annie glanced down at the top of her desk. Picking up a pen, she clicked the top of it again and again as if she was about to write something of great importance.

A large brown hand reached across the desk and pulled the pen from her fingers. "Annie?"

"I'm fine," she lied, trying not to be distracted by the warmth of his palm around her knuckles.

"This doesn't have anything to do with your parents, does it?"

"No," she said.

"I like them," he said. "You favor your mother."

"She has better taste than I do." Annie smiled.

"Does their divorce still bother you?"

"Not as much as it used to. Sometimes, when they're together and behaving themselves, I forget."

"It must be hard," he said. His thumb ran over her knuckles and she pulled her hand away.

"Well," she said. "I'd better call Denise again."

As soon as she said it, she winced. She didn't want Fisher to get any ideas. It was too late.

"You don't think Denise would be involved in anything illegal, do you?"

"No! No, I don't." Her eyes darted to Fisher's, but she couldn't hold his gaze.

"If you say so," he said, but his voice was heavy with doubt. "You know you can trust me, don't you?"

"Trust you?" she snapped, angry at herself for suspecting a friend and angry at Fisher for putting stupid suspicions in her head.

"Yes, trust me," he said. "I know you're hurt that I lied to you, but I'm risking my career by trusting you. That should tell you something."

"It tells me that you're desperate for a lead and you're willing to use me to get it," she snarled, feeling guilty and frustrated.

Fisher stepped back from the desk. His back was as rigid as an ironing board. "If that's what you think then there's nothing more to be said."

"No, there isn't," she agreed.

They gazed at one another across the expanse of the tiny office. It felt as if the few feet that separated them were miles. It might as well have been. A muscle twitched in Fisher's jaw. It was the only sign of his distress.

Annie opened her mouth to apologize, but then snapped it shut. She'd spoken the truth and there was no taking it back or apologizing for it. Anything that had happened between them before had been based upon a lie. There was no getting around it and they both knew it.

"Fine," he said and then he was gone.

Annie slumped back against her chair. With a grunt of disgust, she propped her feet on the corner of the desk. Had it been just days ago that they were jitterbugging in each other's arms, when she thought he was a regular government employee? A pencil pusher with a pension? Ha! He was an FBI agent, and he'd believed she was a criminal! When he'd kissed her, she'd been so sure that there was something there. A spark? Chemistry? Desire? Passion?

How could she have been so wrong? Watching him working in her shop with his gaggle of female admirers just confirmed it. He'd charmed her just like he charmed every other woman. Even her sister Mary had checked him out, and she was happily married. Annie wondered if they taught charm at FBI headquarters. What were the classes called? How to make a woman melt in your arms 101 or How to woo a confession 202.

She'd fallen for it like a house of cards under a heavy hand. She had to let go of her feelings for him. It just wasn't meant to be. She'd help him find out who was using her business as a cover and then he'd be out of her life. It was the only solution. Why then, did it leave her so depressed?

She dialed Denise's house, but there was no answer. This was so unlike her. Annie couldn't believe that

Denise was being this irresponsible. Fear hit her low and deep. Only something truly terrible would keep her friend from showing up for work. Annie feared the worst. Could Denise or her husband be the ones laundering money? The thought made Annie ill.

FISHER PAUSED OUTSIDE Annie's door. He could hear the muted hum of her television. He raised his hand to knock, but then paused. What could he say to make up for hurting her? Not a thing. Not a damn thing.

He'd been doing his job, cozying up to a suspect and slipping into her life to spy on her and collect evidence. Then why did he feel like the world's most callused heel? He blew out a breath, turned back to his own apartment and let himself in. The apartment was dark. Flicking on the light switch, he dumped his jacket onto a nearby chair.

"Harpy?" he called. There was no answering chirp. "Harpy?"

Fisher crossed the room to the cage. It was empty. Not a terribly alarming event, given the fact that Harpy knew how to open the door. He hadn't clipped her wings in ages and she'd been flying loops around the apartment for days. He meant to get to it, but time kept eluding him.

"Harpy?" Fisher checked the bathroom. Harpy frequently amused herself by pulling the drain out of the sink. Fisher switched on the bathroom light. There was no sign of her.

Panic began to thump through him. He checked the windows. They were all shut. She couldn't have gotten out. Fisher checked behind the dresser, thinking Harpy might have gotten herself stuck.

Suddenly a shriek sounded from Annie's apartment across the hall. Fisher ran to her door. Pounding on it, he shouted, "Annie, it's Fisher! Open up!"

The door swung wide and Fisher blinked. Annie was standing there with her red hair hanging over her face and a furiously flapping Harpy sitting on her head.

Through gritted teeth, she said, "Get her off of me."

Fisher reached for the bird. Laying his finger in front of Harpy's feet, he made kissing noises until Harpy stopped flapping and stepped onto his finger.

"She didn't poop on me, did she?" Annie tipped her head forward for Fisher's inspection.

"Ah, no," he said, clamping his lips together to keep from laughing.

Annie straightened back up and combed her hair from her face with her fingers. Her red curls resisted and flopped back across her face. Grabbing her hair with a sigh, Annie twisted it into a knot at the back of her head.

"How did Harpy get in here?" he asked.

"I have no idea," she said. "I was just sitting on the sofa, watching TV when she landed on my head and started singing."

Fisher glanced at the sofa. His gaze ran up the wall to the vent near the ceiling. Walking across the room, he checked the vent. Sure enough it was loose on the bottom. Harpy could have slipped through it easily.

"You think she came through the vent?"

"I can't think of any other way she got here," he said. "What were you watching?"

"What?" she asked.

"What were you watching?" he repeated, glancing at the TV to see a commercial for panty hose.

"N.Y.P.D. Blue," she said.

"Ah." He nodded.

"Ah, what?" she asked.

"That's Harpy's favorite show. I think she has a thing for Dennis Franz."

"You're teasing me," she accused.

"Nope. Watch."

Fisher lifted his finger up and down in a quick motion and Harpy leapt off and flew straight to the TV. Landing with a thump on top of the set, she began to dance from foot to foot as the distinctive music for the popular police drama filled the room. When Dennis Franz appeared on the screen, she hung over the front of the screen and began to peck at the glass, following his character across the TV.

"I don't believe it." Annie began to chuckle. "That's just…why I've never…well, I'll be."

"She must have heard the show come on through the vent and decided to come over and watch with you," he said. "She didn't scratch you, did she?"

"I don't think so."

"Let me just check your head to make sure."

He didn't give her a chance to argue. He dug his fingers into her hair and pulled her close. The knot she'd wound it into slipped free and her hair spilled over his hands in a wave of glorious red. It was soft to the touch and for a moment he forgot his purpose. Gently he began to sift through her hair looking for scratches on her scalp. The faint floral scent of her enveloped him, and he felt his insides tighten in response.

There was no sign of any scratches, but he was reluctant to let go of her. He would have liked to pull her into his arms, hold her close and kiss away all of the troubles between them. But he knew it wasn't that easy. She had to learn to trust him again and that would take time. He couldn't push her.

Stepping back, he released her. "No damage that I can see."

The face she turned up to him was flushed and her deep blue eyes looked confused and alarmed. Fisher smiled. She was flustered. He had hope.

"I'm sorry Harpy scared you," he said.

"It's all right," she said, turning her attention back to the bird. "She's a clever little dickens, isn't she?"

"That's a nice way of putting it," he agreed.

"I'm glad you're here," she said.

"Really? Why?"

"I need to speak to you about your case," she said.

"What about it?" he asked, feeling unaccountably disappointed.

"It's just that...I think someone...I'm not sure," she hedged.

"Annie, if you know something, I need you to tell me."

She frowned. "It's not that I know something. I just think there might be something not quite right going on."

"Talk to me," he ordered.

"I can't," she said. "It's just speculation. I'm not going to say anything until I know something concrete."

"Then why bring it up?" he asked.

"Because I'm trying to trust you," she said.

"Come here." Without giving her a chance to refuse, Fisher opened his arms and pulled her close. "I know this is hard for you and I'm so sorry. If there was anything I could do..."

"You could." She shrugged out of his embrace and stepped away from him. "You could end this investigation."

7

"WHAT?" FISHER FROWNED.

"You heard me," she said. "End it."

He ran a hand through his hair. "You know I can't do that."

"No, I don't," she argued. "I know you won't do it."

"You're right. I won't!" he said. "Someone is using you, Annie. They're using you to launder money probably to sell drugs. How the hell can I walk away from that? Every time I see a kid hooked on drugs, I'm going to wonder is that one I could have saved? And you should be wondering the same damn thing."

Her vibrant blue eyes went dim and her face crumpled. "Drugs? I just can't believe that someone I know would do that," she whispered. "And would use me to make it happen. I just can't believe it."

"Believe it, honey," he said. "The world is full of scumbags, and the ones who get away with it are usually the ones you'd least suspect."

"Is that why you suspected me?" she asked.

"Yeah," he said, unwilling to lie to her again.

She turned away from him and wiped at her face with a balled up fist. She was crying. Fisher felt as if a vice were squeezing his chest. He'd do anything he could to spare her this pain, but he knew he couldn't and the unusual feeling of helplessness left him frustrated and angry.

"There has to be a reason," she said, taking a seat on the sofa. "I know people do terrible things, but there's always a reason."

"Greed comes to mind," he said, taking the seat beside her.

"No, there has to be something more," she argued.

Fisher sighed. She was going to cling to her rose-colored glasses until he pried them off. Damn it. He didn't want to do that to her, but she left him no choice. For her own safety he had to be brutally honest with her.

"No, there isn't always a reason," he said. "Some people are just mean and vicious and cruel. And it's not because they were abused as children and it's not because they're mentally ill. They're just rotten to the core and there is no explaining it."

"What makes you like that?" she asked, studying him from behind a hank of red hair. Her blue eyes were narrowed as if he were something she'd found stuck on the bottom of her shoe.

"Like what?" he asked.

"Cold. Hard. Cynical," she spat each word. "You see everything in terms of black and white or right and wrong. There's no gray in your world. Why is that?"

"Am I really that rigid?" he asked, surprised by the vehemence in her tone.

"Yes."

"I don't know why I'm like that," he said. "It's just who I am."

"Baloney," she retorted. "What makes you view the world the way you do? There must be a reason or do you just have a big old stick shoved up your—"

"Now wait just a minute," he snapped, feeling his temper begin to give. "Just because I believe in right and wrong, does not mean I'm a tight ass. I spent my life tagging along behind parents whose idea of personal responsibility was seeing how many times they could get arrested. In between scientific expeditions, they practiced politics with rallies and protests. If they weren't fighting something, they weren't happy. God forbid, they should use conventional means to dispute legislation they didn't like. Oh no, that wasn't for Swift and Lark. If they weren't going limp and being shoved in a paddy wagon, well hell, they hadn't done a good day's work.''

"Swift and Lark?'' she asked.

"They named themselves after birds. I don't even know their given names. We didn't even call them Mom and Dad while we were growing up. My father is Swift and my mother is Lark.''

Annie pushed the hair away from her face and her eyes widened as she listened. Fisher was oblivious. Long denied frustration with his parents and his childhood bubbled to the surface and he began to rant.

"Do you know what I remember? I remember putting my sisters to bed and sitting up waiting for the squad car from the local police, from wherever we happened to be that week, to bring the folks home. If I was really lucky, the car came for *me,* so I could go down and pay their bail.''

"Sounds rough,'' she observed.

"It was and it wasn't.'' He sighed. "My parents loved us very much, but they were committed to their causes. I hated our life. I hated going to school, knowing that every kid with a scanner knew that my parents had been arrested again. So yeah, I suppose I do crave order and discipline and the simple truth of right and wrong.''

"But life isn't that simple,'' she said.

Their eyes met, and it was all Fisher could do not to look away. Her eyes were as clear and honest as any he'd ever seen. She made him doubt his harsher view of the world. It was a doubt he couldn't afford to have in his line of work.

"You're wrong," he said. "It is that simple, but most people don't want to accept that."

A phone ringing across the hall interrupted whatever Annie would have said. Fisher excused himself, and Annie sank back on her sofa, mulling over what he had just told her.

They were as opposite as hot and cold, night and day, or peanut butter and jelly. They would never agree, but wasn't it funny how opposites seemed to complement one another?

Fisher returned looking like the dark side of the moon. Annie knew it was bad news.

"What is it?" she asked.

"There's been more activity in those accounts," he said.

"What?"

"That was Brian," he said, sitting next to her. "Apparently, a large deposit—about ten thousand dollars—was made into the account held by The Coffee Break at the Arizona Savings and Loan."

"But that's impossible," she said. "I don't even have an account with that bank."

"What?!"

"All of my banking, both personal and business, is done at First Arizona Credit Union."

"I need to see your books, Annie," he said.

"You don't believe me," she said, feeling her stomach turn. Someone was trying to destroy her. But who?

"Oh, I believe you," he said. "But I need all of your records to see what exactly is going on."

"It's all on the computer in my office," she said.

"Let's go," he said.

The Coffee Break was eerily quiet when they went downstairs. Streetlights shined through the front window, illuminating their path. Annie led the way to her office. She flicked on the light switch and went to her desk. She booted up her computer and waited for it to run through all of its antivirus software.

Fisher took a seat at her computer and began to sift through her accounts.

Annie paced around the office, straightening her collection of cookbooks and thumbing through the photos of the more extraordinary pastries she had concocted. She paused at a snapshot of a huge cream filled swan. It had been her swan song, appropriately enough, as a pastry chef at the Lemon Grove Resort. She'd thought owning her own business would be a simple, happy venture. Now she was beginning to wonder.

"What's in the Wedding file?" he asked from the computer.

"The accounts for the catering side of the business," she explained. "Most of my commissions are for wedding cakes."

"Like Eve's?" he asked.

"Yes," she said.

"That was a spectacular cake," he said. "Did I ever tell you how much I enjoyed that wedding?"

"Did you really?" she asked.

"Very much," he said. His chocolate-brown eyes darkened to black, and Annie felt her face grow hot under his scrutiny. "Come here."

Fearing that he'd found something, Annie stepped toward him with her eyes on the computer's monitor. A spreadsheet of her deposits was on the screen. That was all she saw before Fisher pulled her into his lap, taking her completely by surprise.

Before she could even open her mouth to question him, he planted a kiss on her that singed her all the way to the bottom of her feet. The kiss was long and slow and deep and left Annie as wilted as a punch-soaked paper doily.

"What was that for?" she gasped.

"Your pacing was making me nervous," he said, pushing the hair out of her eyes.

"That's how you react to pacing?"

"Well, that and the fact that I've wanted to kiss you all day," he said. "I couldn't take it anymore."

"I thought you found something," she said, half-heartedly slugging him on the shoulder.

"I did," he said.

"You did?" She sat up straight and tried to scramble off of his lap. Fisher wouldn't let her go.

"What I found is a perfectly meticulous set of accounts," he explained. "Whoever is using your shop as a cover has a whole other set of books at work. I suspect someone has made off with your corporate identity."

Annie relaxed against him. She was feeling like the unpopular kid on the playground and she couldn't resist the comfort of Fisher's embrace. "I don't understand. How is this possible?"

"What do you know about laundering money?" he asked.

"Whenever I hear that term, I think of a huge washing machine full of dollar bills."

"I'm guessing not much?" he asked with a smile.

She tipped her head and said, "I don't even balance my personal checkbook."

"So who does the accounts here?" he asked.

"Me with help from Denise and her husband Edmund. He's a CPA," she said. "And Sonia, the quiet waitress, is an accounting major so she always double-checks everything."

"Anyone else?"

"Well, my father has been known to poke around,

but he's not an accountant. He hasn't touched my computer since he crashed it during my audit.''

"Does anyone else have access?"

"Well, I don't generally keep the office locked. So anyone could wander in whenever they felt like it."

"And get your account information?"

"What do you mean?"

"Here's a quick lesson on laundering money," he said. "The whole purpose behind laundering money is to hide vast sums of cash from the federal government. Now why would you want to do this?"

"Because you don't want to pay taxes on it," she said.

"True, but also, because it was probably gotten illegally."

"Now what you need to hide the money is a cash-based operation, like a restaurant, a casino, any business that operates mostly in cash."

"But how do they hide it?"

"They declare it incorrectly," he said. "They claim to have spent more on a service or supply than they actually have. They even create ghost employees. They also underreport, they claim the money came from a nonexistent source."

"But in my case they've made a whole new account," she said.

"Allowing them to launder a lot more," he said.

"How can we stop them?"

"We're going to catch them in the act," he promised.

He sounded so sure, so positive. Annie wished she felt the same. What if they didn't catch the bad guy and she was forced to close up her business? What if the bad guy ruined her reputation and she could never open up another business? She fretted her lower lip. Good thing she was a mature, reasonable businesswoman or she might have thrown a screaming temper tantrum on the floor. As it was, she just wanted to cry.

"It's going to be all right," he said.

Annie turned to find Fisher watching her. One of his hands stroked up and down her back, offering comfort. She didn't feel comforted, however. She felt angry and hurt. Someone she trusted was out to get her and she didn't like it one damn bit.

"How do you know?" she asked. Her fingers strayed to his tie and she began to loosen the knot.

Fisher sucked in a breath and his hand stilled on her back. Annie pulled his tie free and tossed it onto the desk. Then she began to unbutton his shirt. He'd wanted to kiss her? Well, she wanted more than that from him. She felt used and abused and she wanted to be comforted. And not with kisses on the forehead or pats on the back. This man had been wreaking havoc with her sanity from the moment he'd moved in. Annie placed her lips on the pulse at the base of his throat.

"I just know," he ground out from between his teeth. "Annie? What are you thinking, Annie?"

She pulled back and gazed at him. They'd known each other such a short time, but she felt safe with him. When everyone else in her life was suspect, she trusted him. He would make things right.

"I'm not thinking," she whispered and kissed him.

Annie did no more than place her mouth against his. That was all she needed to do. With a heartfelt groan, he buried one hand in her hair and held her head still while he kissed her until they were both gasping for breath.

"Are you sure about this?" he asked.

She thought about it for a second and nodded. She'd never been more sure of anything.

"Okay, but we're not doing this here," he said, pushing her off of his lap. "I'll race you up the stairs."

It wasn't much of a race. Annie got as far as the door when he made a grab for her. With his hands on her hips, he backed her up against the wall. She giggled when he ran his lips down her neck. He wouldn't let her leave the room, until she left behind her shoes.

Annie had her revenge when she stopped him at the bottom of the stairs. She unbuttoned his shirt and traced his chest with butterfly kisses that left him sagging against the rail. She thought his shirt looked just right hanging on the banister.

Annie hadn't cleared the stairs when Fisher grabbed her by the back of her jeans. He held her still as he kissed the back of her neck, unzipped her pants and drew them down her legs. Annie doubted they'd make it to her apartment at this rate.

At the door to her place, she stepped on the back of his heel. He looked at her in surprise, but obligingly kicked off his shoes. Any other demand she might have made was halted when he scooped her up into his arms and shut her up with a kiss.

The trail of clothing continued on the way to her bedroom. Harpy sat perched on the TV, hanging over the screen and watching the nightly news, oblivious to the clothing flying around her.

The October evening was chilly and Annie hurried under the covers, pulling the comforter up to her chin.

"Oh, no," he said, tugging the blanket out of her grasp. "I've been thinking about this too much to let you hide now."

Annie gasped when he tossed the blanket aside and moved to lie on top of her. His weight pressed her deep into the mattress, and his mouth locked on to hers with a hunger that left her shaking from the inside out.

His kiss was long and slow and wet, a deliberate possession of her senses. Annie arched up to press against him. She was restless, wanting to feel all of him. He pressed her more firmly into the mattress, running his hands along her body and kissing her until she was dizzy with desire.

She wrapped her legs around his waist and buried her fingers in his hair, longing to have him closer. She felt his skin sizzle against hers and still it wasn't enough. She felt an insatiable, vacuous need so deep inside of her that it left her writhing beneath him.

Fisher pulled away and Annie heard the sound of a foil package ripping open. Leave it to her Boy Scout to always be prepared. She felt her heart swell. Fisher was everything she'd ever looked for in a man. He was honest, kind, dependable, smart, funny and sexy. Heavens, was he sexy! And right now, in this moment, he was hers.

Fisher reached for her and Annie slid into his arms. The need to be one was all consuming. Fisher must have felt it, too. With just a shift of his hips, he joined them.

Annie gasped at the feel of him. He felt so good, so right. She watched him move his mouth over her skin. His tan face and hands moving against the fair skin of her breasts and belly was a remarkable contrast that left her awed. She felt pure joy wash through her.

Fisher gritted his teeth when he felt her tighten around him. He didn't want this intimacy to end. He wanted to feel this close to Annie always. She made him feel happy in a way he had never felt before. Like an unexpected gift, he cherished her. He tried to hold back, but it was no use. When she whispered his name and clung to him, he felt a thundering rush of pleasure course through him, leaving him weak and dazed. He collapsed on top of her and kissed her hair.

Their heartbeats thumped together as they were pressed chest to breast. Fisher rolled onto his back and hauled Annie with him, not yet ready to break their connection. She sighed against his chest and he watched her eyelids droop. She was innocence personified. Fisher felt his heart turn over. Annie. His Annie.

He pressed a kiss against her springy, red curls and whispered, "I love you, Annie-girl."

A snore was her only response.

ANNIE BLINKED AWAKE. The red glow of the alarm clock read 5:15 a.m. Henry would be appearing in fifteen minutes. She supposed she might as well get up. She tried to push out of the bed, but the weight of an arm and a leg held her down.

Fisher! A flash of heat hit her low in the belly. He was curled up around her, spooning her against his chest. She took a moment to appreciate how truly safe and secure she felt. A woman could get used to feeling cherished like this. She barely remembered falling asleep in his arms last night. He'd whispered something to her. What had he said? *I love you, Annie-girl.*

Annie went rigid. No, she must have imagined that. He wouldn't…he couldn't… She turned in his arms. His thick brown hair had fallen over his forehead. His long dark lashes rested against his cheeks. His face was slack with sleep, softening his features. He was gorgeous. Annie resisted the urge to trace his mouth with her forefinger. She didn't want to wake him.

His arms tightened about her, pulling her into his chest. She went willingly, resting her cheek against his warm bare skin. She couldn't resist being this close to him for just a moment. She would treasure the feel of him, the scent of him, the warmth of him always.

"What are you thinking, Annie-girl?" his voice was gravel deep and sleepy. Annie was glad it was still dark, this way she didn't have to meet his gaze when she lied.

"That Henry is going to start singing any moment," she said.

"Better him than Harpy," he said.

"Harpy?" She tried to sit up but he held her still. "Where is Harpy?"

"Look over my shoulder," he said.

Harpy was sitting on the corner of Fisher's pillow. Her head drooped as if in sleep.

"Does she do that often?" she asked.

"When we're in a strange place, she likes to sleep on my pillow," he said.

"I've never slept with a bird before," she said.

"What do you think?"

"Not too fowl," she joked. "Of course I've never slept with an FBI guy before, either."

"And what do you think of that?"

"I can see why they call you 'special' agents," she teased.

He growled and kissed her.

"I've never slept with a chef," he said.

"What do you think?"

"That I'm ready for a second course," he whispered against her ear.

Her toes curled into the blanket. How did he do that? How did this man reduce her to mush with a few words?

He started to kiss the side of her neck and she felt her body arch against his, craving the feel of him. She felt as if she could never get enough of this man.

Their intimacy was broken by a loud voice singing outside.

She rolled away from him with a groan. "Henry. Duty calls."

"Let duty feed himself today," he said, reaching for her.

"I can't," she said, dodging his hands while planting a swift kiss on his lips. "He might disturb the neighbors."

"Who cares?" he asked, cupping the back of her head and holding her still while he kissed her so thoroughly he left her breathless.

"Behave and I'll save you a muffin," she teased him as she rolled out of the bed.

"Apple spice?"

"Of course."

"Well, what's taking you so long? Get down there and start baking," he ordered.

"I might have known," she said, shrugging into her bathrobe. "You've been after my muffins all along."

He tugged the belt of her robe loose. His hands ran the length of her body, pausing to cup her breasts. "Best muffins in town," he said, his words muffled against her skin.

She laughed and jumped away from him. Knotting the belt on her robe, she tried to frown at him, but couldn't stop the smile that parted her lips. He looked wonderfully unshaven and sleepy amidst the pillows with Harpy still snoozing beside him.

It hit her like a flash. A glaring moment of rightness. Fisher belonged here with her. She knew it as surely as she knew that she loved him. Oh dear!

Henry's voice broke through the quiet morning air and Annie jumped.

"I have to go," she said grabbing her clothes before running from the room.

Downstairs she dumped three of yesterday's muffins on a plate and filled a glass with milk. Henry's singing was loud enough to drown out a flock of birds. She opened the door and shoved the plate into Henry's hands without so much as a good morning.

She slammed the back door and hurried to the front of the shop. They'd be opening in just an hour and she had a million things to do. She raced around the shop firing up the coffee machine and then went back to the kitchen to preheat the oven. She dumped ingredients into a bowl, turned on the mixer and then rushed to get the morning's newspapers from the front stoop. Then she raced back to the kitchen to get the muffins in the oven. She spooned the dough into the muffin pan with a scoop, listening to the splat as the dough landed in each cup.

"I am not in love with him," she muttered to herself. "I can't be. I haven't known him that long. And we're total opposites. We could never live together. I'd drive him crazy in a week. What was I thinking? I knew I shouldn't get involved with my tenant. I knew it, and what did I do? I went right ahead and did it anyway. Stupid. Stupid. Stupid."

"Do you always insult your baked goods before you put them in the oven?"

Annie yelped and dropped her scoop. Wearing jeans and a T-shirt, Fisher stood in the doorway watching her.

"How long have you been there?"

"Long enough," he said. "Isn't it bad karma to insult your food? I mean I know muffins aren't the smartest of food groups, but should you really call them stupid to their faces?"

"They have faces?" she asked. This conversation was absurd, but it beat the alternative. She watched as he walked toward her. He picked the scoop up out of the bowl and plopped some dough into an empty muffin cup.

"I thought you could use some help," he said and turned to face her. When she didn't say anything, he pulled her close with one arm and lightly kissed the end of her nose. "It's going to be all right."

She let herself lean against him. Oh boy, in the love

department, she wasn't a muffin—she was toast. Burnt toast.

SHE TRIED to be professional and maintain her distance. Really, she did. But every time she turned around there he was, working the counter, clearing tables, chatting it up with her customers. She couldn't get away from him.

Three times she caught herself staring at him and the third time he turned and winked at her, letting her know that he knew she was watching him. Annie was mortified.

She knew she was being paranoid, but she felt as if everyone knew that she had spent the night with him last night. When she saw the waitresses talking, she was sure they were gossiping about her. If a customer studied her too closely, she feared they were speculating about her and Fisher. She was giddy and embarrassed and couldn't concentrate worth a damn. It was completely irrational.

She dumped a glass of ice water on a businessman's lap, put salt in someone's coffee and managed to ring up a three dollar tab as three hundred dollars. By midmorning she was ready to call it quits for the day. She opted to go hide in her office instead.

The fact that Denise hadn't shown up for work again was not helping her nerves. Annie didn't know what to do. There was no answer at her house and Annie didn't know her husband's work number. She was going to have to go over there before Fisher became too suspicious.

She sat in her high-backed desk chair and put her feet up on the corner of her desk. This was her contemplative position. It was how she usually sat when pondering a new recipe. Today she pondered her love life. The fact that it involved Fisher left her stunned.

"Annie." There was knock on the door just before it opened. Fisher poked his head around. "I need to talk to you."

"Right now?" she asked, feeling unprepared to discuss last night.

"I'm afraid so," he said and strode into the room. A shorter man with round glasses and a receding hairline followed him. "Annie, this is my partner Brian Phillips. Brian, this is Annie."

Annie dropped her feet to the floor and rose. "It's nice to meet you."

"You, too." Brian shook her hand and grinned at her.

What? Did he know, too? Annie gave herself a mental shake. She really was being paranoid.

"Annie, Brian's been monitoring the bogus account," Fisher said. "There's been an awful lot of activity lately."

"What kind of activity?" she asked.

"The kind we see just before they flee the country," Brian said. "Here's the problem, we need you to sell your business."

"But—" Annie protested.

Brian interrupted her, "Now, it wouldn't be for real. We just need you to sign over ownership to someone else—an agent—so that they could go to the Arizona Savings and Loan and put their name on the bogus account, thus forcing our bad guy to make a move to reclaim it. Then we nail him."

"I can't do that," she said.

"Now, Ms. Talbot, you don't understand," Brian said. "We need to make the perp think you're undergoing a power change that might reveal him. It will force him out of hiding."

"No, you don't understand," she said. "Anyone who has been watching the business closely has seen me fight with Martin Delgado over this very issue. Everyone knows I would never, ever sell.''

"She's right," Fisher said. "If our perp is as tied in as we think, he would never believe that she would sell. He'll know it's a setup."

"Damn," Brian said. "We need to do something to shake him up. Something that will make him fear losing the phoney account."

"I'm happy to help, but what can I do?" Annie asked.

"Marry me," Fisher said.

"What?!" she shouted.

"That's brilliant!" Brian exclaimed. "Then the business will become yours."

"What?!" Annie shouted again.

"And then I'll put my name on the bogus account." Fisher laughed.

"Hey?!" she snapped.

"The perp will be forced to make a move. You've still got it, partner," Brian said with a nod.

"Excuse me!" Annie hollered.

"Yeah, I do, don't I?" Fisher asked, looking proud of himself.

Exasperated Annie slammed her hands down on her desk and yelled, "Hello! Remember me?"

Both Fisher and Brian turned to gape at her.

"Something wrong, Annie?"

"You bet there's something wrong. I will not, and I do mean ever in this life, marry you," she said.

"I think I'll let you two discuss this amongst yourselves," Brian said, backing slowly toward the door.

When the door shut behind him, Fisher turned to Annie, "What's the problem?"

"What's the problem? What's the problem? I'll tell you what the problem is: I am not getting married to anyone ever!"

"Not even me?" Fisher asked, watching her from beneath his lashes.

"No, not even to you," she said, refusing to believe he could possibly be hurt by this. They'd spent one glorious night together. She wasn't even sure she could call him her boyfriend yet, never mind marry him.

"Ouch!" Fisher winced, leaning against her desk. "Talk about rejection."

"It's not rejection," she said. "It's not personal. I promised myself a long time ago that I would never marry."

"Well, it's not as if this would be a real marriage," he reasoned. "It's merely a ploy to draw the bad guy out."

"Would it be legal?" she asked.

"Well, yeah. We can't risk having him check it out and find out it's phony. Then he'd be on to us."

"If it's legal then it's real. I'm not doing it," she said. "It goes against everything I believe in."

"More accurately everything you don't believe in," he chided her. "Fine. Then the bad guy wins because without this we won't be able to catch him."

"Don't do that," she said.

"Do what?" he asked, studying her.

"Don't make me feel like I let you down," she said.

"Do you feel that way?" he asked.

"No…yes…maybe, a little," she stammered.

"Good," he said. "Because you did."

Annie watched in silence as he strode from the room, slamming the door behind him. He couldn't be angry with her. He had no right. What he was asking of her was unreasonable.

She sank back into her chair and leaned forward to rest her head on the desk. When she had leased the apartment across the hall to that man she'd had no idea that her life was to become this complicated. In two weeks, she'd been robbed, proposed to—sort of—and had fallen desperately in love.

When Fisher had uttered those two stupid words—marry me—she had actually felt an answer inside of her that she had never anticipated. The answer was yes.

IT WAS LATE afternoon when Annie pulled her minivan—used for hauling wedding cakes—onto Denise's street. Denise and her husband lived in a new housing development on the outskirts of the West Valley. Stucco houses with tile roofs, spaced exactly ten feet apart, went as far the eye could see. Living this close to your neighbors had to have some perks, but Annie was damned if she could think of any. These houses were so close together that if you asked someone to pass the salt, your neighbor's arm would probably appear in your window. No thanks.

Annie rang the bell and waited, not really expecting an answer.

Denise opened the door without bothering to ask who it was. She was wearing a ratty old sweat suit, no makeup and her hair was sporting a day-old case of bed head.

"Denise? Are you all right?" Annie gasped. "I've been so worried. Are you sick?"

"No...I...yes," Denise stuttered then burst into tears. "I...he...left...for...her..."

Annie opened her arms and Denise stepped into them. When Denise's sobs receded, they stepped into the house. Annie went straight to the kitchen and put on a pot of coffee while Denise went to wash her face. Annie made a couple of sandwiches to go with the coffee. Denise looked as if she could use some sustenance.

They curled up on the sofa in the living room. Annie

had to coax Denise to eat. Between mouthfuls, Denise confided to Annie what had happened.

"Edmund left me for a nail girl," she said.

"A who?"

"A nail girl, you know, from a beauty salon," Denise said, waving her tissue in the air. "Some girl he met at a bar during happy hour."

"Oh my...that jerk! That no good, lying, cheating jerk!" Annie cursed.

"Yeah. She has long blond hair and boobs the size of Kansas."

"How did you find out?" Annie asked.

"His secretary—who hates him—quit and sent me a letter with all of the details. I followed him the other night and found them...together."

"Oh, Denise, I am so sorry." Annie hugged her friend. "Is there anything I can do?"

"That depends. How do you feel about arson?"

"Excuse me?"

"I was thinking we could torch his precious sports car," Denise said.

"If we did, I bet his little nail girl would drop him like a swollen bunion. How about we break into his place and plant large-size lingerie in his underwear drawer? I bet the nail girl would just love to be with a cross-dresser."

Denise laughed. "I wonder what he's taking to cure his flatulence problem. I can't imagine she would enjoy his usual morning symphony."

"Maybe we could replace his vitamins with plain old beans. Wouldn't she just love a toot-toot serenade? Preferably when he's meeting her parents," Annie suggested, bursting into laughter. Denise laughed with her until they were both weak.

"How dumb am I that I didn't see the signs?" Denise asked, suddenly serious. "The sports car, going out with the guys every night, joining a gym, all of it. What was I thinking? I thought it was a phase. I'm such an idiot."

"No, you're not. You loved him," she said.

"Yeah, 'loved' being the operative word," Denise grunted. "Annie, why is it that bad people always get away with hurting others? It's not right."

"No, it isn't," Annie agreed.

"ALL RIGHT," she announced, storming into Fisher's apartment without knocking. "I'll do that wedding thing, but it's in name only and as soon as this case is over, you're out of here."

Maybe Denise's jerk of an ex-husband was going to get away with treating her badly, but whoever was using Annie's business as a front for money laundering wasn't going to get away with it. Not by a long shot.

Fisher rose from where he sat on the sofa.

"And another thing—" she began, but he interrupted her.

"Annie, I'd like you to meet my parents."

"Your...who?"

"This is Swift and Lark," Fisher gestured to the two people sitting across from him.

"Oh!" Annie clapped a hand over her mouth.

"Did I hear you right, my dear?" Lark rose from her seat. She was short and plump, her gray hair was loosely knotted at the top of her head. She wore a brightly patterned caftan that covered her from her chin to her ankles with several ropes of multi-colored beads looping her neck. "Did you say marry?"

"That's what I heard." Swift rose to stand beside her. He was tall and thin, wearing an outrageously bright tie-dyed T-shirt, jeans and sandals. His long white hair was combed back from his forehead and held in a ponytail at the nape of his neck. Harpy sat perched on his shoulder looking quite at home.

"Fisher? Marriage?" Lark sighed. "How conventional."

Fisher waved her forward, and Annie stepped cautiously into the room. Fisher hadn't exaggerated when he'd described his parents. They were vintage sixties.

"Lark, Swift, I want you to meet my landlord Annie," Fisher said.

"Landlord? I thought she was your fiancée," Lark said.

"She might be," he said. "If you'll excuse us?"

He didn't wait for an answer but led Annie out into the hall, shutting the door behind them.

"So, you've changed your mind?" he asked.

"Yes," she said.

"But you're kicking me out as soon as we catch our perp," he said.

"Not kicking you out," she corrected him. "I just think that once this case is over, it would be better if you moved."

"Better for whom?" he asked, plucking a long strand of hair from her shoulder and twirling it between his fingers.

Annie felt the breath stall in her lungs. She tried to back away from his touch, but he didn't let go of her hair.

"What's the matter, Annie?" he asked.

"Nothing," she said. "I just think we should keep it a marriage in name only."

"Why?" he asked.

"To make it easier to annul," she said.

"What if you decide you don't want to?" he asked, taking a step closer to her.

"Don't worry." She took a step back. "I will."

"Maybe you'll change your mind." He took another step toward her.

"I won't." She backed into the wall.

"What if I don't want to annul it?" he asked, closing the space between them.

"Fisher, what are you doing?" she asked. He was leaning against her, pressing her into the wall. He'd dropped her hair and his hands rested on her waist.

"Kissing you," he said just before his mouth met hers.

8

ANNIE KNEW this was foolish. She knew she should resist him and steer this, whatever it was, back to an impersonal, professional type of relationship. But she wasn't made of stone. The feel of his mouth against hers turned her resolve into the consistency of a fistful of sand.

"Sweeter than Death by Chocolate," he murmured against her lips as he gently pulled away. He hugged her close and said, "I'd better be careful or you're going to give me cavities."

"In your teeth?" she asked as she hugged him back.

"Nope. In my heart," he said and pulled away from her. Gazing into her eyes, he pushed the hair out of her face.

The sincerity of his warm brown gaze left Annie shaking. Was he...? Did he...? What he'd said the night before...was it true? Had Fisher fallen in love with her?

"Well are you two going to be conformists to the patriarchal institution of matrimony, or what?" Swift stuck his head out of the door, interrupting the moment.

"Well?" Fisher looked at Annie.

"Yes," Annie cleared her throat. "I'll...ahem...you know."

"When?" Lark asked, peeking around Swift.

"Tomorrow," Fisher said.

"Tomorrow?" Annie asked. "But I have a million things to do."

"Pencil in elope," Fisher said.

"Elope?" Lark repeated, stepping into the hallway, her caftan billowing about her. "If you have to get married, the least you can do is let your mother be there. Even your sisters did that."

"No can do, Lark," Fisher said. "We're under a time constraint."

"But I can't just leave the shop," Annie protested. "I can't leave it unattended."

"Swift and Lark will watch it. Won't you?"

"You betcha," Swift agreed.

"I do have a mean recipe for tofu burgers," Lark said.

"Oh no," Annie started to argue.

Fisher cut her off. "There. It's all settled. Go pack."

"But—"

Fisher opened her door and pushed her through it.

"We'll be gone overnight so pack your toothbrush."

"But—"

Fisher shut the door on her.

"Good night, Annie-girl," he said.

AT FIVE the next morning, Fisher knocked on her door.

"Annie, get a wiggle on," he yelled.

Annie opened the door with a frown. "Do you have any idea what time it is? Who's going to marry us this early in the morning?"

"I've got it covered," he said. "You go hit the shower and dress for a wedding. We leave in a half hour."

"What about Henry?"

"I'll tell my mother to give him some of her seven grain muffins."

"Seven grain?" Annie sighed. "I'd better have a business to come back to."

"Don't worry. You will."

They rolled out of the driveway at five forty-five. Annie saw Henry at the back door. He was frowning. Whether it was at her or the seven grain muffins she couldn't tell.

Swift and Lark stood beside their Volkswagen bus, which was covered in fluorescent pink and green flowers. Lark flashed them a peace sign as they passed. Annie waved.

When Fisher headed north out of the city, Annie began to get suspicious.

"Where are we going?" she asked.

"We're going to get married," he said.

"I know, but where?" she asked.

"Vegas."

"Vegas?!" she shrieked. "That's a five-hour drive. We don't have time to go to Vegas."

"We'll be back tomorrow," he said.

"I thought we were going to go to a local JP," she said. "My mother is going to kill me."

"No, she won't," Fisher said. "We'll be annulled before she even finds out we're married."

"You don't know my mother." She shook her head. "She loves weddings. Big ones with all of the trimmings. There's a reason she's had four of them, you know, and every one has been bigger than the last."

"Isn't that kind of—" he paused.

"Excessive?" Annie supplied. "Yes, it is. But that's my mom."

"Good for her," he said.

"What?" she blinked.

"She hasn't given up," he said. "And she celebrates every trip down the aisle as if it's her last. That's an optimist."

"I think you mean masochist."

"No, I mean optimist," he said. "I always thought I'd have a big wedding."

"Really?"

"Yup. I figured when I found the girl of my dreams, I would propose, she'd say yes, and we'd have the biggest shindig the city of Phoenix has ever seen."

"That could still happen," Annie said.

"Maybe." He shrugged.

"So you really want a big wedding?"

"Yeah. When I marry, I want everyone to know how crazy in love I am. I want to share my happiness with everyone. I suppose that sounds corny to an antimarriage person like you."

"No," she said. "It sounds…nice."

The rest of the trip was spent in relative silence. Annie tried not to think about what Fisher had said. She failed. He was going to marry someday and it was going to be a big to-do. A spurt of what felt like jealousy gnawed at her. She couldn't be jealous of a future wife who didn't even exist yet. That would be ridiculous. And yet, she did feel jealous…and, well, mad.

When they reached Vegas, they headed straight to city hall for their wedding license. Thirty-five dollars later they were on their way to the Strip, the notorious street in Vegas that was home to most of the large casinos and some infamous wedding chapels.

"There are some options," Fisher said. "We can get married by a bloated Elvis, we can get married in a drive-thru, we can get married while bungee jumping or we can just find a quiet, out-of-the-way chapel."

"A quiet, out-of-the-way chapel, please," Annie said.

Fisher consulted a list of chapels as he inched north in the clogging traffic of the Strip. The street was jammed with pedestrians, clutching cups full of change and wandering from one colossal casino to the next. A huge pyramid, a castle, an enormous emerald building with a gold lion perched out front and a replica of New York City were just a few of the buildings that caused Annie's eyes to pop. She hadn't been to Vegas in years and it looked as if it had tripled in size.

"Here we go." Fisher consulted the map and turned off of the Strip at the next light. They drove east, past the airport, until they were on the outskirts of town.

They turned onto a dirt road and the Jeep jutted over divots and bumps until Annie was sure her teeth were loose. They pulled up in front of a pretty, whitewashed adobe house with a verandah that was covered in deep magenta and golden yellow bougainvillea. A sign hung from a wrought iron post. It read: Chapel in the Garden of Eden.

The front door burst open with a blast from an organ and out danced a beaming young couple. The bride was swathed in white sequins and the groom wore a black tux jacket over blue jeans and cowboy boots. The couple laughed and ran to their car, apparently eager to begin their honeymoon.

Annie felt Fisher take her elbow and turn her toward the house. "Ready?"

"Sure," she said with a bravado she didn't feel.

When they walked through the door, an enormous pile of platinum blond hair greeted them from behind a desk.

"Good evening," a sultry voice said. "How may I help you?"

Annie blinked and looked down. The pile of hair was attached to the biggest bosom she'd ever seen. If Elvis was still alive, well then, so was Mae West.

"We're here to get married," Fisher said, handing her their license.

"How wonderful!" the woman exclaimed with a

clap. "I'm Bambie and my husband Frank is the minister. Do you know what kind of ceremony you would like?"

Fisher glanced at Annie and she shrugged. "What are our options?"

"Well," Bambie sucked in a breath, giving her bosom a life of its own. Obviously, the repetition of this speech had not diminished her enthusiasm for the task at hand.

Annie glanced around the foyer. Big scarlet roses, the size of her fist, trailed up the floral wallpaper that matched the red carpet, which matched the overstuffed velvet couch and chairs in the corner of the room. Annie wasn't sure if she was in a chapel or a bordello. Then again, this was Vegas, it could be both.

"What do you think Annie-girl?" Fisher asked her.

"Whatever you decide is fine," she said, unwilling to admit she hadn't been listening.

"We'll go with the short ceremony, with music, flowers and some photos," Fisher said.

Annie felt the room lurch to her right. She grabbed Fisher's arm to keep from falling.

"Annie, are you all right?" he asked, steadying her with his hand.

"Oh, I'm fine," she lied. This time the room lurched to the left and she stumbled into his shirtfront.

"Annie, what's wrong?" He held her by the shoulders and pushed her back so he could study her face.

"No...no...nothing," she answered. Her teeth began to chatter, and she had to clench her jaw to keep it from clacking.

"Are you sure?" he asked.

"Oh, she's just got prewedding jitters," Bambie said. Reaching around Fisher, she patted Annie's hand. "Oh, your hands are like ice. Not to worry, dear, that's perfectly normal."

Fisher glanced at Annie with a frown. She forced a smile, but it felt more like a snarl. He took her hands in his and began to chafe them.

"You look like you're about to be executed," he said.

"This might be easier with a blindfold and a cigarette," she joked.

"Annie," he whispered as he pulled her close and hugged her. "This isn't for real. It isn't a real wedding or marriage. We'll have it annulled as soon as possible."

"I know," she said, feeling her stomach constrict into a painful knot. What Fisher said was true. She wondered why it didn't make her feel any better.

While Fisher went into the chapel to meet the minister, Annie went to the ladies' room to freshen up. Freshen up was a relative term as she spent most of her time sitting on a yellow chaise lounge with her head between her knees, willing herself not to throw up while Bambie fussed with her hair. When it was time to perform the ceremony, she didn't know if she felt relieved or resigned.

Bambie played the organ while Annie, clutching a fistful of cream-colored roses, walked through the courtyard towards Fisher. Hundreds of tiny white lights illuminated the lush rose garden that surrounded them. Rose bushes bursting with flowers of every size, shape and color covered the walls, and the walkway was ankle-deep in scattered petals. The scent of the roses was so strong it made Annie dizzy.

Fisher stood beside the minister at a small stone altar at the end of the courtyard. He looked gorgeous in a dark navy suit and burgundy tie. If they were here for any other purpose, Annie would have been intoxicated just by the sight of him. But they were here to perform this bogus wedding ceremony and she was having a hard time just placing one foot in front of the other. She felt as if she were wading through quick drying cement.

Fisher watched Annie struggle with each step she took. She'd said she didn't believe in marriage, but he'd had no idea it was an absolute phobia for her. She looked so frightened and fragile, he was tempted to call the whole thing off. But then, there was a ridiculous, egoistic part of him that was hurt by her reaction to marrying him. Granted he was no great prize, but still, she could do a lot worse. But this wasn't really a marriage, he reminded himself.

Too bad. Annie made a stunning bride. Her curly red hair had been piled on top of her head and cream-colored roses were tucked carefully amidst the fiery curls—Bambie's doing, no doubt. A few strands had escaped her topknot to trail down the back of her neck and the sides of her face, softening her features into a look of striking beauty. Her cream-colored suit was cut to fit her figure and what a figure it was. Her matching high heels accentuated the shape of her legs, and it was all Fisher could do not to give her a hearty wolf whistle of approval.

When she drew near, he saw that her blue eyes were wide and her lips were compressed into a thin, tight line. She looked scared to death.

He took her hand in his and squeezed. Her eyes darted up to meet his and he winked at her. A small smile was her only response.

Bambie ended her boisterous rendition of "Here Comes The Bride" and came to stand beside her husband to witness the ceremony.

"Dearly beloved..." Minister Frank began to read the ceremony, and Annie felt her stomach flip over. She couldn't do this. She couldn't get married. It didn't matter if it was in name only. Marriage was an unnatural state leading to inevitable heartbreak and disappointment.

She'd seen her parents fail repeatedly and she was seeing one of her closest friends suffer more of the same. She didn't want to be one of the failures. She didn't want to have to get a divorce or an annulment. She didn't want to add to the depressing statistics that stated human beings were a fickle bunch and incapable of loving anyone more than themselves. She didn't want to do this.

"I do," Fisher said.

Annie snapped her gaze up to his. Oh my God, she thought, we're halfway to married. It's my turn and I can't do it! I can't do this!

"Well, Annie, do you?"

"Huh?" Annie turned to look at Frank. His gray mustache drooped over his lip in disapproval.

"Say, 'I do,'" Fisher prompted her.

"What?" Annie turned to find Fisher watching her with one eyebrow raised. He was beginning to look vexed.

"Say 'I do,'" he repeated.

Annie looked into his chocolate-brown eyes. He'd become more important to her than she wanted to acknowledge, but she had to. If they went through with this, things would change between them whether the ceremony was bogus or not. They'd start to feel shackled to one another and it would kill the love they'd shared so freely. She didn't want that to happen. She was in love with him and she didn't want to lose him. She knew that if they married, things would never be the same between them and she would lose him and what they'd shared forever.

She felt a tear spill out of the corner of her eye and she gulped back a sob.

"I do," she whispered.

"THERE, NOW that wasn't so bad, was it?" Fisher asked as they drove away from the Chapel in the Garden of Eden. Annie was plucking loose petals out of her hair and tucking them into the pocket of her jacket.

"No, I suppose not," she answered and turned to face him. Bambie had tossed rose petals at them as they'd hurried to the Jeep. A bright pink petal was stuck behind Fisher's collar and Annie reached up to brush it away. Fisher caught her hand and raised her fingers to his lips.

"I know how hard that was for you," he said. "Thank you. Let's hope our plan works and we catch our perp real soon."

"Yeah, otherwise you might be stuck with me for life," she joked.

Fisher squeezed her fingers in his and said, "I can think of worse ways to spend the rest of my life…without you comes to mind."

Annie felt her breath stall in her lungs. He couldn't mean…nah! She gently pulled her hand out of his. She didn't want to think about the ramifications of being tied to him for life. She didn't want to wonder why the thought didn't distress her more.

9

"SO, WHERE ARE WE STAYING?" she asked as they drove down the Strip.

"The Palms."

"Next to Caesar's Palace?"

"Is that okay?" he asked.

"Sure." Annie cleared her throat. "One room or two?"

"Honeymoon suite," he said.

Annie felt her stomach flip-flop. One room? One bed? With Fisher? Oh dear.

They parked and checked into the Palms. The inside was huge, full of towering palm trees under an enormous skylight and a fountain that shimmered like an oasis in the desert. Annie felt her jaw drop open in surprise. It was beautiful. The sound of bells ringing and change clanging echoed throughout the lobby and Annie felt as if she were at a fair. She walked closer to the archway that led into the casino.

It looked like a high stakes carnival. Lights flashed in all colors in all directions. People sat hunched over slot machines while more people roamed from one felt-covered table to the next. Annie could hear the shouts of the winners over the clang of bells and she was irresistibly drawn toward the commotion.

"I've got our key." Fisher appeared at her elbow. "Let's go on up."

Annie glanced at him and then at the plastic card

key in his hand. For all intents and purposes, this man was legally her husband. Yikes!

"Let's gamble first," she said and strode into the casino.

"Annie!" Fisher followed on her heels. "I don't gamble. I'm a Fed."

"Oh, well I'm not." She flashed some teeth and marched toward the roulette wheel. "I have a feeling about number twenty-seven."

"Annie…" Fisher's voice carried a note of warning. She ignored it.

She found an empty stool between an older man sporting a ten gallon Stetson hat and a tiny woman covered in purple sequins who was lighting a fresh cigarette from the burning remains of another one. They each had a pile of chips in front of them.

"Number twenty-seven." Annie plunked a dollar on the table. The dealer glanced at her with one eyebrow raised. "It's a five dollar minimum, ma'am."

"Oh." Annie dug into her purse and pulled out a five. "Here you go."

The dealer handed Annie a five dollar chip, dragged her bill across the table and using a clear plastic handle deposited the money into a slot in the table.

"You sound pretty sure about that twenty-seven," the old cowboy said.

"I just have a feeling," she said and placed the chip on twenty-seven. She heard Fisher heave a bored sigh behind her.

The dealer tossed the ball into the spinning wheel and waved his hand over the table to indicate no more bets were to be placed. Annie watched as the wheel slowed and the ball stuttered to a stop.

"Well, I'll be," the cowboy said. "Twenty-seven!"

Annie felt a rush of excitement zip through her. She'd had a feeling, but she hadn't really expected it to come up. The dealer began to count out her winnings and she turned to Fisher and hugged him.

"Can you believe it?" she asked.

"Only you," Fisher said, laughing. "Thirty-five to one odds. Only you."

A waitress, wearing a grass skirt and a coconut-shell bra, came by and Annie ordered champagne for the entire table. The chain-smoking woman grudgingly accepted hers while the cowboy thumped her on the back and slurped his down like it was a shot of Jack Daniel's whiskey.

"Are you ready to cash out?" Fisher asked.

"You can't leave now," the cowboy protested. "What else do you have a feeling about, little lady?"

"Six," Annie said decisively.

"Six it is," the cowboy declared and placed a hefty wager on the number.

Annie placed a ten dollar bet on the number and held her breath. The ball spun and bounced and landed on five.

Annie deflated in one long breath.

Fisher put his hand on her shoulder and whispered, "That's why they call it gambling."

"But I was so sure," she said. "I'm still sure. Six is going to come up."

"Let's play it again," the cowboy said. The woman on her other side patted Annie's arm while she stubbed out her cigarette. Annie watched as the cowboy and the smoker put their chips on, around and beside number six. Feeling obligated, Annie put another ten dollars down on six.

This time it came up! Cheers went up and Annie watched as the dealer pushed a huge stack of blue chips in her direction. This was fun. They ordered more champagne and took turns predicting what the next number would be.

Having won two and lost three chances at the wheel, Annie took a second to savor her surroundings. The tables were full to bursting with gamblers and the surrounding slot machines clanged and rang in a never-ending cacophony of success and failure. She felt as if she were in a James Bond flick. All she needed was a handsome, older man asking her to blow on his dice and the scene would be complete.

Feeling someone watching her, Annie glanced to her right and saw a man at a blackjack table looking at her. He was wearing a white suit over a black silk shirt that was unbuttoned to his navel. Amidst the gray chest hair on display was a huge gold medallion. Very seventies, she thought. His hair was slicked back into a stubby gray ponytail at the nape of his neck, and he wore yellow tinted glasses that covered the upper half of his face. As their gazes met, Annie was startled by a sudden sense of recognition, but she couldn't place him. Who was he? A customer? A friend of her parents? Who?

"Are you all right?" Fisher asked from behind her, and Annie turned to face him.

"Oh, fine," she said. "I just thought I saw someone I recognized."

She glanced back at the blackjack table, but the man was gone. Curious.

An hour later, Annie was woozy from the champagne and down to her original five dollars. She glanced around the casino and found Fisher leaning against a slot machine behind her.

"Well, we gave it a hell of a run," the cowboy said and the small woman nodded. They both had piles of chips in front of them so Annie didn't feel too bad about their abrupt turn of luck.

"We sure did," she said. She tipped the dealer with her last five dollar chip and wobbled over to Fisher.

"That was a hoot. What should I play next? Poker? Craps? Blackjack?"

"How about 'Now I lay me down to sleep'?" he asked.

"Oh, very funny." She snorted. "Are you telling me it's bedtime?"

"Yes, I am," he said and took her elbow to lead her out of the casino.

"Just because we're married don't think you're the boss of me," she teased.

"If I were the boss of you, we wouldn't have spent the past hour in the casino," he said.

"We wouldn't?"

"Well, let's see, given a choice between losing my shirt on games designed for just that purpose or losing my shirt in the process of making love to you, I think I would definitely choose the latter."

"Oh." Annie felt her knees wobble.

Fisher flashed their room card at the security guard and the man pressed the elevator button for them. Annie weaved into the elevator as soon as the doors opened.

She didn't know what to expect tonight. They'd become lovers the night before last, but with all that had happened were they still? To go from the role of would-be girlfriend to wife in less than two days left her floundering. Now that they were married, she wasn't sure making love to Fisher was such a good idea. It might confuse things. Confuse things? Ha!

Fisher used the card key to open their door. It was a big suite with a sitting room and a hot tub, set in a wide tiled ledge beside the windows. One mammoth king-size bed filled the main room. Wow!

Annie glanced away. The couch in the sitting room looked comfortable enough. She could sleep just fine in there.

"Are you hungry?" he asked.

"No, thank you," she lied, plopping herself down on the plush arm chair. She heard Fisher pick up the phone to order room service. Her stomach growled but her pride refused to let her change her mind and order anything. She picked up the remote control and began to flip through the TV channels. A docu-advertisement told her all about the Palms.

She heard Fisher finish his order and then place another call. Curious, she turned down the volume. Fisher was on the phone with Brian and she shamelessly eavesdropped, wanting to hear if anything had happened with their perp. Fisher hung up before she could glean any information. She surfed through a few more channels, looking for a good movie.

Fisher came to stand beside her just as she flipped to an adult entertainment channel. A long-haired, big-busted, sweaty woman wearing nothing but a hot pink thong and a smile was moaning in full Technicolor glory. Horrified, Annie pressed her thumb on the remote trying to change the channel. She inadvertently hit the volume and the woman's moans filled the small suite. Frantic, Annie hit the power button and the screen went black.

She could feel a mortified blush heat her face and she muttered, "There's nothing on TV."

"Yeah, I could see that," he said, muffling what sounded suspiciously like a laugh.

There was a knock on the door and a man wearing khaki shorts and a Hawaiian shirt wheeled in a cart loaded with food. Fisher tipped him and the man disappeared.

"Let's eat," he said. "And don't give me that 'I'm not hungry' business. I can hear your stomach growling in the next room."

Annie narrowed her eyes at him. "You're awfully pushy."

"Only because I care," he said. Annie tried to see his face, but he had his head down examining the contents of the cart.

Annie wandered over to where he stood. Steak and potatoes, salad, rolls with whipped butter and strawberries with whipped cream loaded the cart. Her stomach growled and Fisher smiled as he handed her a plate.

They sat on the tile ledge that surrounded the hot tub and gazed at the lights of Las Vegas spread out before them. Annie felt Fisher studying her, but she refused to wonder what he was thinking about. She couldn't help thinking that if they weren't married, this would be a terribly romantic trip.

They returned their empty plates to the cart and poured two cups of coffee. They placed the strawberries and whipped cream between them on the ledge and munched. Neither of them spoke and Annie was surprised to discover that it was a comfortable silence. She felt as if she'd known Fisher for years. That must be one more downside to getting married. Instant frumpdom.

"It's spectacular," Fisher said consideringly.

"The city of sin? It sure is." She turned to face him and their gazes met.

"You have some whipped cream here," he said and pointed to his upper lip. Embarrassed, she licked her lip.

"No, the other…oh, hell." He cupped the back of her neck and pulled her close. His tongue licked at the spot of cream on her lip before deepening the kiss into one of wicked, knee-wilting passion. So much for frumpdom, Annie thought as she buried her fingers in his hair.

The kiss was long and hot and sweet, tasting of

strawberries and cream. Annie felt as if she could never get enough of him. She pressed against him until they shifted, and she found herself on her back against the tile and Fisher lying on top of her.

"I've wanted to do this all day," he confessed between kisses.

They kissed and kissed and kissed some more until Annie began to feel whisker burn sting her chin. She didn't care. She wanted to feel marked by their time together.

They weren't civil about taking off their clothes. Her cream-colored top was launched across the room to tangle with his suit coat on the floor. Buttons popped and zippers were drawn until she was wearing nothing but thigh-high stockings and heels. He took about three seconds to appreciate the look and then those, too, joined the puddle of clothing on the floor.

Pressed skin to skin, there was no question of their belonging together. It was right. Absolutely. Annie loved Fisher McCoy with all her heart. She knew he was the one, the one man she would always love.

"Annie-girl," Fisher growled in her ear and Annie shivered. "Wrap your legs around my waist."

Hot and hazy with desire, Annie did as she was told. Fisher sat up and pulled her onto his lap. She gazed at him through a stray lock of red curly hair. The lines of his face looked taut with barely checked desire. He was breathing hard and Annie could feel his heart racing beneath her fingertips.

He cupped her bottom and held her in place. The feel of his fingers against her skin made her arch with need. He was so close. It was torture to be so close and not be joined. Annie rocked forward and Fisher gasped.

"My wife," Fisher said through gritted teeth. "You are my wife."

"Yes," Annie whispered. "Yes."

Wrapping her arms about him, she surrendered to the passion between them. The feel of his mouth on her skin, the feel of his hands as he pulled her hips close and pushed them away in a steady rhythm left her breathless.

Time ceased. There was nothing but the two of them and the power of their union as the passion between them exploded with harsh cries of pleasure and silent whispers of love.

THE SOUND of running water broke through her sleepy haze and Annie pushed off of Fisher to glance around the room. Fisher had turned on the tap and hot, steamy water was filling the hot tub. She glanced at him in surprise.

"I want to see you all wet and soapy," he said with a leer. "Besides I think I hurt myself on this tile."

Annie laughed and then winced. "Ouch. I think I did, too."

"In you go," he said and nudged her toward the water.

It was hot and she hissed as she sank into the bubbles. Fisher slid in beside her. He ducked under the water and came back up with a pile of suds on his head. Annie burst out laughing.

"What?" he asked.

"You have..." She pointed to the top of his head and giggled. Fisher scooped off the bubbles with one hand and blew them at her. She smacked them away with a splash. Fisher stuck his chin in the water and came up with a big beard of bubbles.

He looked ridiculous and she couldn't hold in her laughter. Had she really thought he was too rigid? It was so much fun to play with him. She felt as if she were three years old as she rediscovered the joys of bath time. She stuck her chin in the bubbles and came up with a beard of her own. Fisher howled.

"I always wanted to make love to a bearded woman," he said with a wicked wink. And then he reached for her. The steam rose and the water sloshed over the side as they kissed and splashed, enjoying the feel of one another and the powerful feelings between them.

Fisher reached for the big fluffy towels sitting beside the tub. Pulling Annie to her feet, he wrapped a towel around her and took one for himself.

"The room is freezing," she said as she shivered into her towel.

Fisher lifted her out of the tub and pulled her close. "I'll warm you up."

"How?" she purred, trying to sound seductive.

"Well," he said, stepping closer and reducing Annie to a state of breathless excitement. "I could order some hot chocolate from room service."

"Oh, you," she growled and leaned into him. She began to kiss his neck and his laughter turned into a hiss.

"Fisher?" she whispered against his ear.

"Uh-huh."

"Could you ask them to put marshmallows in it?" she asked and stepped back, leaving him dazed and bewildered.

She took three steps before he scooped her up and carried her to the bed.

"Cute, very cute," he said as he settled in beside her.

Annie wrapped her arms about his neck as he proceeded to kiss her senseless. Fisher was the most amazing man she had ever known. They were so different and yet there was a connection, an understanding of one another that neither could explain. They were like two halves of a whole. With different strengths and weaknesses, they balanced each other.

Annie felt a passion with Fisher that she had never before experienced. He was gentle and kind, but also determined and aggressive. It was a heady mix that left her weak in the knees every time he touched her.

When he kissed her like he was now, with such single-minded concentration, she was lost. Every caress of his mouth against hers left her dizzy and craving more. She wanted to feel more of him, be closer to him, and touch every bit of him. It was as if she would never get enough of him, of them, of this.

"Annie-girl," he whispered into her ear. "I want this to be—"

The phone rang.

"What?" she asked, sensing by his tone that it was important.

The phone rang again. Fisher's dark brown gaze met hers and she could see a seriousness in his eyes that made everything inside of her pause.

The phone rang for a third time, and she said, "You'd better get that."

Fisher grabbed the phone with a curse. He kept one arm wrapped about her, preventing any escape she might have made.

His side of the conversation was full of terse one word questions with a variety of colorful curses thrown in. It wasn't good news. He hung up the receiver with a bang.

"We have to go," he said.

"Perp on the move?" she guessed.

"Yeah," he grunted. He rolled over, trapping her beneath him. "I have to say this guy is really getting on my nerves."

Then he planted a long, bone wilter of a kiss on her.

Annie felt the heat of it sear her all the way down to her toes.

"Let's go," he said and hopped off of her to retrieve his clothes from the floor.

"Oh sure, fine, get me all hot and bothered and drag me home. Lucky thing we're not really married, because this would be some honeymoon," she joked as she gathered up her things.

Fisher hugged her from behind, planting hot wet kisses on her neck as he whispered, "I could always give you a real honeymoon after we catch this guy."

Annie froze. Real honeymoon? Wouldn't that follow a real marriage? Okay, technically they were really married, but only to catch a bad guy and then it was annulment city here we come. Or was it? Oh dear!

"Think about it," he whispered and squeezed her once more before he let her go and headed toward the bathroom.

Annie finished dressing with shaky fingers. Then she planted her head firmly between her knees in an attempt to dispel the light-headed feeling she had.

"Are you all right?" He came back out of the bathroom and Annie jerked to an upright position.

"Oh yeah, I thought I lost an earring, but...ha...I was wearing it the whole time."

"Hmm," he murmured. "You look a little green."

"Must be the champagne," she said.

Fisher turned on the television and using the remote control, he punched in some numbers and checked out of the room.

"You can check out using the TV? That is so cool."

"That's Vegas. Are you ready? We have a long drive."

FISHER SPED through the desert. At two in the morning, the highway was a lonely stretch of road. But the white crosses on the side of the road marking where others had driven too fast or dozed at the wheel kept him awake and alert as they left Nevada.

Annie was unconscious beside him. As soon as they'd left the lights of Las Vegas behind, she'd let out a big yawn and promptly fallen asleep. Her head was tipped back and her mouth hung slightly open as she emitted soft snores and the occasional muffled grunt. Her arm was thrown across the seat and her hand rested on his leg. He liked to think that even asleep she desired some sort of contact with him.

Too bad she didn't want to make it permanent. He wasn't an idiot. She'd hated getting married. Even when the wedding wasn't real, she'd been made physically sick by the whole idea. Who could blame her? Her parents had made matrimony into a joke, a wrenching emotional joke, with their multiple marriages.

Maybe he could prove to her…yeah, right. He couldn't change her mind. He couldn't even get her to admit how she felt about him and he knew she felt something. Okay, more than something. He suspected that she was in love with him. He saw it in her big, blue eyes everytime she looked at him.

He knew she loved him as surely as he knew he loved her. She was the calm to his storm. She kept everything in perspective with her kindness and her sense of humor. She made everything fun. She made him laugh. Fisher had no doubt that he could spend the rest of his days loving and laughing with Annie Talbot. If he could just get her to see that. But how?

Fisher puzzled and puzzled but as they drew closer to Phoenix, he had no solution.

It was just after nine when he pulled up in front of the bank. Annie was still asleep beside him. Fisher hated to wake her up.

"Hey sleepyhead," he said as he nudged her. She rolled away from him. "Come on. Rise and shine."

She tucked deeper into her seat and let out an unladylike snore. Fisher sighed. This was obviously going to require drastic measures.

He cleared his throat and launched into Henry's song. She didn't move. He increased the volume.

"Henry?" she muttered. "Henry? What are you doing in Las Vegas?"

"We're not in Las Vegas anymore," Fisher said and reached across the seat to hug her close.

"Huh?" She blinked awake.

"We're at the First Arizona Credit Union," he said.

"The bank? In Phoenix? You mean you drove all that way without a break? Why didn't you wake me?"

"You were sound asleep, besides I was fine."

She struggled to sit upright. "Well, I feel terrible. Next time you have to promise to wake me."

"I promise," he said solemnly, trying not to take too much heart in the words *next time*. "Come on. Let's get this over with."

Fisher grabbed their marriage license and together they made their way into the bank. After a couple of short forms, several signatures and a show of identification, Fisher owned the majority interest in The Coffee Break. Annie felt herself break out into a very unladylike sweat.

"Are you okay?" Fisher asked as they headed back to the Jeep.

"Oh, yeah, fine," she said, dabbing at her forehead with a tissue.

"Don't worry," he said. "This will be over in a matter of days and your business will be yours again. I promise."

"Thank you," she smiled. Even if he was just giving her lip service, it was nice to hear.

Then they went to the Arizona Savings and Loan, where after an official meeting with the bank president, Fisher signed a packet of papers changing the ownership of the bogus account from A. Talbot to Fisher and Annie McCoy. When the bank officer showed Annie the balance of the bogus account, she saw spots and everything began to turn gray.

"Five hundred thousand dollars?" she squeaked at Fisher as they walked away.

"I believe it was more like four hundred ninety-five thousand," he said. "And after my first withdrawal goes through, it will read four hundred eighty thousand."

"I've never seen that many zeros attached to my name before," she said as she climbed into the Jeep. "What do you think the perp will do when he finds out you've put your name on the account and you've begun to withdraw funds?"

"He probably won't know until the bank informs him that he needs my signature to access his account. Then the bank will seize him and call me."

"Just like that?"

"Just like that." Fisher turned to look at her. "You look tired. Let's go home. I have a feeling Brian will be waiting for us."

Brian wasn't so much waiting as he was pacing a hole in the floor. It was a little after ten and the shop was in full swing. They could hear the clang and rattle of pans in the kitchen, and Annie headed in that direction. Fisher stopped her by putting a hand on her elbow.

"Don't you want to hear what Brian has to say?" he asked.

"Oh, yeah," she said, biting her lip with a wistful glance at the kitchen.

"Hey partner," he greeted his friend with a handshake. "So what's happened since we left?"

Brian's thin hair stood on end like he'd been caught unaware by a firecracker. He motioned them to a secluded corner table. "What hasn't happened?" he asked in return. "Do you have any idea how many people have absolutely flipped out over Annie's marriage?"

Annie finally turned her head from the kitchen to the two men. "Really?" She pursed her lips as if to keep from saying, I told you so.

"Let's see…" Brian ticked off the people on his fingers. "We can start with your sister Mary. She didn't believe it and wanted to call the Phoenix police and file a missing persons report. Then there was your mother. She seemed more furious that you would elope. Apparently, that's not the Talbot way. Then there was your father. You'd think someone had kidnapped his baby. Fortunately, Fisher's mother was able to calm them down with some herbal tea and sunflower seed scones."

"That must have been interesting," Annie said. She and Fisher exchanged amused glances.

"Then there was your former beau Stewart Anderson. He almost blew a gasket when he heard the news. He stomped out of here like someone had made off with his wife! Then there was your rival Martin Delgado. When he heard the news, he just laughed. He seems to think he'll be able to talk your husband into selling. So what do you make of those reactions?"

"Sounds reasonable to me," Annie said. "Everyone knows I never planned to marry. It stands to reason that they wouldn't believe it."

"I think I'm beginning to feel offended." Fisher frowned. "Why is it so inconceivable that you would marry me? I'm not that bad of a catch."

"Maybe you're just not the stud you thought you were," Brian mocked him.

"Hardly," Annie said. "You're wonderful. It's just that I made no secret that I would never marry. People are bound to be shocked."

"Oh! Annie and Fisher. You're back." Fisher's mother came bustling out of the kitchen. "Annie, where do you keep your wheat germ?"

"Wheat germ?" she asked.

"Yes. I wanted to make a nice yogurt spread to go on my sprout and curry muffins."

"Sprout and curry?" Annie lifted a censoring eyebrow in Fisher's direction.

"Did I forget to mention that my parents are very organic?" he asked.

"Aren't we all?" Annie glared at him and followed his mother into the kitchen, greeting her regulars along the way.

"If I'm not mistaken, you are in deep doo-doo," Brian said.

"How would you know?"

"I've been on the receiving end of that look quite a few times over the past five years. Allow me to translate. It means, 'Just wait until we're alone, dear.'"

"I don't suppose they mean that in the...uh... romantic sense?"

"That's a definite no."

Fisher sighed, then changed the subject. "So, what's our perp been up to?"

"Juggling accounts like there is no tomorrow," Brain said. "I was just waiting for the last batch of electronic information to come in."

"Let's go take a look," Fisher said, happy to escape to the office. After all, who knew what else his parents had done in their absence.

"Fisher!"

Too late. A door slammed and Annie's heels clicked across the wooden floor back into the main room.

"What happened to my office?" she snapped. "I don't even recognize it."

"I think I can explain," Brian offered, raising his hand like a kid in school.

"What happened?" she asked through gritted teeth.

Brian took a step backward. Fisher couldn't blame him. Annie looked furious. She also looked pretty damn sexy. Her white suit was the worse for her long nap in the car. Deep creases crossed her lap and dented the elbows. Her hair had come loose and fell down around her shoulders in long twisting curls, which smelled like the roses she'd worn in her hair for their wedding. Desire slammed him harder than a fist.

"You see I had to commandeer the office to make it easier to keep tabs on the files and to monitor who came and went into the store. I promise it will all be restored as soon as we catch the perp."

Brian was giving her his best Boy Scout routine and Annie was falling for it. Grudgingly. The color slowly faded from her cheeks and she looked resigned to the chaotic disarray her life had become. Fisher felt bad for her.

He walked toward her intending to give her a quick hug of comfort, but her scent enveloped him as soon as he wrapped his arms about her. The mingled scent of crushed rose petals and Annie would forever be married in his mind.

Before he had time to check the impulse, he found himself planting a long, slow, deep kiss on her very soft and pliant lips. A bawdy chorus of whoops and cheers surrounded them.

"Well, it must be love," he heard his mother say. He glanced up to see his parents standing in the doorway of the kitchen with their arms around one another.

"I still don't see why they had to buy into that societal nonsense called matrimony, but if it makes them happy," his father sighed and planted a quick kiss on his mother's head.

Annie took a step back from him, looking both dazed and bewildered. "I'm going to go take a shower." Fisher wiggled his eyebrows at her and she giggled but then frowned. "A cold one."

"Oh, Fish, you've got it bad," Brian said as they made their way toward Annie's office.

"Got what bad?" he asked, trying to sound innocent.

"It."

"What is 'it'?"

"The love bug," Brian said. "You have the sorriest case I've ever seen. You're pitiful, just pitiful."

"What makes you say that?" he asked.

"I saw your face when she walked into the room," he said. "You lit up. You beam at the sight of her. You're in love with her. Deep-fried, flambéed, roasted on a spit in love."

"I am not...okay, maybe a little," he confessed. "So what?"

"You want to stay married to her, don't you?"

Fisher was silent.

"Don't you?" Brian persisted.

"I can think of worse ways to spend my life."

"Oh, boy, you've got it bad!"

"Let's just get to work," he suggested.

"Fine, but—" Brian began.

"Work!" Fisher interrupted him.

"Okay," Brian agreed and began to tap on the keyboard. "This will tell us all of the transactions made in the account over the past few hours."

Brian was silent as he read the incoming report. His face looked grim.

"Hey, Fish, where did you and Annie stay when you were in Vegas?"

"The Palms," he said. "Why?"

"Because our perp deposited a huge cashier's check made out to A. Talbot from the Palms just after midnight last night."

"What?"

"You know what that means," Brian said.

"No. I don't believe it."

"It's the only explanation."

"No, there has to be another one."

"Face it, Fish. Annie is our perp."

10

"You don't know that," he said.

"I'm sorry, Fish, but she's—"

"No, she isn't. She spent every moment with me. She was never out of my sight," he argued. "There's no way it could be Annie."

"No way what could be Annie?" she asked as she entered the office.

Both men were silent.

"Well?" she asked, hands on hips.

She was fresh from her shower. Her wet hair was twisted into a knot on the top of her head. Fisher could smell the scent of her shampoo all the way across the room. She wore dark jeans and bright white Keds canvas shoes. A powder-blue knit top that clung in all the right places completed the outfit. She wore no makeup and the spray of freckles on her nose stood out against her pale skin. She didn't look old enough to drive.

Fisher knew she wasn't criminal. Now he just had to prove it.

"Our perp deposited a cashier's check this morning for the sum of ten grand. It looks like he's getting ready to bail."

"Tell her the rest," Brian said. "Or I will."

Fisher panted out a quick breath. "The cashier's check was from the Palms."

"The Palms?" she repeated confused. "But that's where we were staying."

"I know," he said, waiting for her to think it through.

"Then that means he was there when we were there," she said. "Do you think he saw us? Do you think he knows?"

"That we're married?"

"Yes, maybe that's why he's getting ready to bail," she said.

"If it's a 'he'," Brian said.

"What do you mean?" she asked.

"Don't you find it the least bit odd that our perp was at the same casino as you?" Brian asked.

Fisher put a steadying hand on Brian's shoulder. He was using the same tone of voice he used when they badgered information out of suspects. But Annie was no suspect, she was his wife.

"What are you saying?" she asked. "Do you think that I...?"

"No," Fisher answered for them both. "We don't."

Annie's blue eyes darkened, and she looked at him as if he'd just belted her.

"You do, don't you?" she asked. "After all of this, you still think of me as a criminal."

"No, I don't," he said. He took a step toward her, but she held up a hand, warding him off.

"This whole thing has just been one big lie, hasn't it?" she asked. "You don't give half a hoot about me. I'm just a part of the game. What did you think? That if you got me to marry you, I would confess all? Isn't that above and beyond the call of duty even for you?"

Tears dampened her eyes, giving them a sad glitter. Fisher reached for her, but she side-stepped, slamming into the doorjamb.

"And I was actually beginning to believe that you care about me," she whispered to herself.

"I do care about you," he protested. "And if we ever get out of this mess, I fully intend to ask you to marry me for real. Not only that, but we're going to have a big wedding at a church. And I don't give a damn if you do the macarena in the middle of the ceremony or play roulette at the reception."

Her lips wobbled. Tears spilled over onto her cheeks. She opened her mouth, but nothing came out. And then, on a sigh, she said, "I don't believe you."

With a sob, she spun on her heel and ran. Fisher heard her footsteps pound up the stairs. A door slammed against its frame and all was quiet.

"My bad," Brian said. "I'm sorry."

"No," Fisher said. "It's my fault. Honestly? There was a part of me that wanted to see her reaction. To gauge how she feels...felt about marrying me for real. It was stupid and selfish."

"Maybe," Brian said. "But now you know."

"Know what?"

"That she loves you," he said.

"No, I'm pretty sure she despises me with heretofore unknown levels of loathing."

"Don't worry. She'll get over it," Brian said. "Then you can look forward to the make-up sex."

"There isn't going to be any sex if I don't fix this mess. So, married man, what do I do?"

"Get your butt up those stairs and do some serious groveling," Brian suggested. "I'll keep an eye on the shop and our perp."

"You don't believe it's Annie?" Fisher asked.

Brian considered him for a moment. "We've been partners since we both joined the Bureau ten years ago. I've seen you pull some dumb stunts, and I've seen you make some brilliant maneuvers, but I've never seen you make a mistake when it comes to judging a bad guy. No, I don't think it's Annie.''

''Good.'' Fisher grinned at him. ''A man's partner and his wife should get along.''

''Good luck.'' Brian turned back to the computer screen.

''Thanks. I'll need it,'' Fisher muttered as he strode up the stairs.

''Don't take any prisoners,'' Brian yelled after him. ''Unless, of course, you're into that sort of thing.''

Fisher shook his head and kept walking.

Her door was closed. He knocked. There was no answer. Not even a terse order to go away. He frowned. That was unlike Annie. He'd figured as soon as he knocked, she'd open the door and tell him precisely what she thought of him. Truth to be told, he'd kind of been looking forward to it. She was a real firecracker when she lost her temper.

He knocked again. There was no answer.

''Annie?'' he called through the door. ''Annie? We need to talk. Come on, Annie-girl. Open up.''

She didn't answer. Fisher felt the hair on the back of his neck begin to prickle. Something wasn't right. He banged the door harder. He felt the wood vibrate beneath his fist. Still there was no answer. If Annie was in there, she would have answered. If for no other reason than to give him hell for thumping her door so hard.

He glanced down the hall at the door that led out to the deck. He checked it. It was closed and locked. He looked across the hall at his own door. It, too, was closed and locked. Panic made his heart thump faster. He had to get into her apartment just to be sure. He slammed the door with his right shoulder. It flew back on its hinges.

"What in tarnation are you doing?" his father shouted from the base of the stairs in the coffee shop. "Son?"

Fisher stormed into the apartment. There was no sign of her. He strode into her bedroom. He didn't even think to draw his gun. It didn't matter. It was empty. The white eyelet curtains fluttered in the breeze and Fisher thought he might throw up.

"What's going on in here?" Brian strode into the room with Fisher's father on his heels.

"He's got her. Our perp has got her."

"NOW DON'T MAKE a sound and everything will be all right," a gruff voice ordered.

Annie spit at the wool blanket that was wrapped over her head and around her upper body. She gagged at the stale odor that permeated its scratchy texture. When she'd stormed into her apartment, she'd been knocked down, wrapped in the blanket and dragged through her bedroom window and down the porch stairs all in a matter of minutes. Her ribs hurt from where she'd hit the windowsill and they pulled every time she took a breath.

She was lying on her side in the back of a van. She knew it was a van, because she'd recognized the sound of the sliding door. They were driving fast through the city streets. The floor below her was hard and she bounced across it whenever the driver hit the brakes. She'd been trying to keep track of the driver's turns to get a sense of where they were headed.

The van took an abrupt left and Annie lost track of where they could be. Fear clamped her throat, but she refused to give in to it. If she collapsed into her terror, she was afraid she'd fall apart.

She thought about Fisher and all of the wonderful

things he'd said to her. He wanted to marry her in a church—for real. She'd said she didn't believe him, but just now, with the fear so thick around her that it left her weak and vulnerable and honest, she knew she did believe him.

Not only that, but if she ever got the chance, she would marry him. She would marry him and spend the rest of her life making up for her stupid, stubborn pride. It was pride that had sent her running from the room. She'd known in her heart that Fisher loved her, that he believed in her innocence, but she'd allowed a bruised ego and a bucketful of pride to take over. She'd thrown a tantrum. Why? Because he'd been doing his job. She was an idiot!

And now, she might never see him again. She'd probably be dragged out into the desert and shot. Her body would be left to rot in the scorching sun and Fisher would never know how she felt about him. No! That was unacceptable. She wouldn't let that happen.

She began to wriggle against the bonds that held the blanket around her. She dragged herself across the floor, hoping to catch the blanket on something and allow herself to wiggle out of it. A foot, a big one, landed on her middle stopping her. Her ribs cried out in protest, but she was afraid to move.

"Quit it. We'll let you out when we're ready and not a minute before. Understand?"

Annie nodded, but realized they couldn't see her. "Okay," she mumbled and spat more of the woolen fibers out of her mouth.

The voice was deep and gruff. She didn't recognize it, but she guessed it belonged to an older man. He sounded as tough as boot leather. He sounded like a man who meant what he said.

The van slowed and turned onto a jutted drive that

crunched like gravel. Annie strained to hear any noises that would identify where she was. But the wool covering her head muffled anything beyond the sound of the tires.

The van stopped and she rolled. The door was jerked open and Annie was pulled to her feet.

"Walk," the gruff voice ordered.

Annie didn't hesitate, cringing with each step.

She was shoved through a doorway and pushed down onto a hard chair. The bonds around her body were loosened and the blanket was pulled off of her head. She blinked against the bright light. Squinting she looked at her captors, trying to gauge their intent. She was ready to duck and roll if they took a swing at her.

She blinked and then she blinked again. It couldn't be. They were an older couple. They appeared to be in their early to mid fifties. The man wore a white suit and a black shirt. Annie gasped.

"You're the man from the blackjack table," she said. "And you, you're the woman in purple sequins who played roulette with me."

"Very good, Annie," he said. "I was afraid you recognized me. But, of course you didn't because I am a master of disguise."

"You sure are, baby," the woman said as she lit a cigarette.

"Who are you?" Annie asked. "What do you want?"

"Now, this ain't personal," the man said. "I suppose I am a bit better looking all cleaned up. Here let me give you a hint." He launched into Henry's song.

"Henry?" Annie felt the room spin. She looked closely. He had shaved. His hair was neatly combed back into a ponytail and what his clothes lacked in taste they made up for in cleanliness. It was his eyes that clinched it. This man's eyes crinkled around the corners just like Henry's and his singing voice was just as rich as Henry's had been.

She realized that she was thinking of him as an impostor who had taken over Henry when it was probably Henry who'd been fictitious all along. Still, she felt as if her old friend was dead. Her shoulders slumped.

"I don't understand," she said.

"Don't you?" the man, Henry, asked.

"You used me," she accused.

"Not on purpose," the woman said. "Me and Eric just saw an opportunity and we took it."

"Hush, Dotty," Henry, or rather, Eric said. "Annie, you're a good chef, but a terrible businesswoman. You want to save yourself some grief? Invest in a paper shredder."

"A paper shredder?"

"I was going through your trash cans when I found it," Eric said. "A way to get me and Dotty out of our hard times. It was easy really. You see, Dotty and I are entrepreneurs."

"Crooks would be more like it," Annie interrupted him.

He shrugged. "If you like. What we do is take money from our investors and hide it for them so that they don't have to report it. Your business was just small enough not to attract any notice, or so we thought."

"So you laundered money for your 'investors' by setting up a bogus account attached to my business. Your 'investors' are probably dope-dealing dirtbags. Do you even care that you're breaking the law? I trusted you. I looked out for you. How could you do this to me?"

"What? We weren't hurting you! Everything was fine until you let that man move in. When I broke in—"

"You broke in?" Annie gasped. "You're the one who trashed my shop?"

"Yeah. I thought it might scare that guy off. Once I discovered the two of you were an item, I knew the gig was up. That guy's not what he appears to be. Don't be thinking he married you because he loves you, because he doesn't. It's my money he's after. I don't know how he figured me out, but he did. I know he's taking money from my account."

"That account had the name A. Talbot on it," Annie said. "That makes it mine. Mine and my husband's."

"Ha. Your husband thinks he's so smart, cutting in on my action. But I'm smarter. I got me a partner at the bank, see? You and Dotty are going back to the bank to see my buddy Raul, and then you're going to close that account for me in unmarked hundreds and twenties. Thank you very much."

"My husband will be very upset when he hears about this," Annie said.

"Oh, will he now?" Eric laughed. "Well, we'll be sipping piña coladas on a beach somewhere near the equator by then."

"I'm not helping you," she said.

"Unless you want your husband to find your body, suffering a deadly sunburn in the desert you will."

"You wouldn't."

"Do you want to risk that?" he asked, cracking his knuckles.

"Okay. Fine. I'll do it!" she reluctantly agreed, hoping she could somehow stall for time.

"ARE YOU SURE about this?" Fisher asked Brian for the umpteenth time.

"As sure as I can be," Brian said from the driver's seat.

They were sitting in an unmarked car, watching the entrance of the main branch of the Arizona Savings and Loan. So far no one unusual had appeared.

"That's not very reassuring," he said. Annie had been missing for six hours, and Fisher felt as if his sanity were teetering. If anything happened to her...he just couldn't bear it.

"Look, we've locked the account up under your name as her husband, so the only way they can get access to it is to use her to get it for them. They have to convince her to go to the bank for them or they lose the whole shebang."

"How do we know they'll use this bank?"

"We don't," Brian said.

"I hate this," Fisher said. "My wife is in danger and there isn't a damn thing I can do about it."

"Hang in there, Fish." Brian patted him on the arm. "We'll get her out safely."

"Hand me the binoculars," Fisher said.

"Do you see her?" Brian asked, handing them over.

"No, but I do see...Henry?"

"Henry? Who's that?"

"It's the homeless guy I told you about. The one who sings outside the shop every morning."

"Well, now you know what he does with his days," Brian joked. "Pretty smart of him to panhandle for money outside of a bank. Quite a coincidence, too, his picking this bank."

"Yeah, too bad I don't believe in coincidences," Fisher said and pulled his gun from his shoulder holster. He checked the clip. He was ready.

"Fish, what are you…?"

"I think he's our perp," Fisher interrupted. Brian looked unconvinced. "Think about it. Annie said she caught him eating out of the dumpster three years ago. How long has the laundering been going on? Just under three years. What if he wasn't foraging for food? In the dumpster, he had access to every thing Annie has ever thrown away—receipts, purchase orders, voided checks, everything."

"Holy—" Brian whistled. "We never even considered him."

"He appears agitated," Fisher said. "He looks like he's waiting for someone."

"He is." Brian pointed out the window.

Two women, one with Annie's distinctive red hair, were making their way up the sidewalk towards the bank.

"So, he has a partner," Fisher said. "You follow Annie. He doesn't know you. If he sees you he won't be suspicious. I'll watch him."

"Done," Brian said and ducked out of the car.

Fisher watched Henry. He was getting more and more skittish, glancing at the building and shaking his head in frustration. If he got too spooked, he might bolt. Fisher decided to get behind him. He wrapped his gun in a newspaper and crept out of the car. He slipped into the shadow of the building and followed the sidewalk until he was ten feet from where Henry paced.

Henry looked as if he were on the verge of a breakdown. Finally, he must have suspected the game was up. Taking swift looks about him, Henry began to hurry down the sidewalk.

Fisher stepped out of the shadows and into his path. "Henry, is that you?" Fisher asked and grabbed his arm. "You shaved. I almost didn't recognize you. Almost."

Henry tried to shake him off, but Fisher dropped his paper and held up his gun.

"Henry the Eighth," Fisher began, "you have the right to remain silent..."

Henry protested right through his Miranda rights. "You've got nothing on me. It's her. She's the one."

Fisher snapped the handcuffs onto Henry's wrists and glanced over his shoulder to where Brian was leading the woman who'd been with Annie out of the building. She was covered in mud from her neck to her knees.

"What the...?" Fisher glanced at Brian.

Brian looked as if he were trying to hold back a laugh. "Go ask your wife."

Fisher took the steps up to the bank two at a time. He slammed through the front door only to have his feet shoot out from under him on the slick marble. He landed with a bone crunching thump on the ground. Around him lay three wasted potted plants.

"Oh, Fisher!" Annie wailed as she slid across the floor toward him. She crashed into his hip and threw her arms about his neck. "I'm so glad you're here. It was Henry...uh...Eric all along. Can you believe that? They dragged me out of my room. Eric and Dotty. Dotty was the smoking woman at the roulette table in Vegas. She's been his partner all along. And..."

Fisher reached up, grabbed Annie by the back of the neck and kissed her. She was safe. That was all he cared about.

Annie hummed low in the back of her throat and when Fisher released her, she looked completely bemused.

"What happened here?" he asked.

Bank officials and customers had formed a mob around them. Several people shouted questions and one woman saw Fisher's gun and fainted dead away into a security guard.

"It's all right." Fisher pulled out his badge. "I'm FBI."

"Dotty brought me in here to sign some papers that would free up the account. They have an accomplice working in the bank named Raul, but we never met him. When we entered the building, I knocked her into a plant and they all went down like dominoes. Apparently, they'd just been watered. What a mess. I knocked her flat on her rump!"

Fisher brushed some of the mud off of his pants and grinned. "Grace in motion."

"That's me." She sighed.

Fisher stood, dragging Annie with him. He hugged her close and whispered against her springy red hair, "I was so worried about you. I don't know what I'd do if..."

"Special Agent, sir," one of the bank officers interrupted. "We need to talk to Ms. Talbot. We need to debrief her."

Fisher glared at the balding little man in the bad suit. "Her name is Mrs. McCoy. You don't need to talk to her. You can talk to me."

"With all due respect..." the little man began, but Fisher interrupted him. "She said there is an accomplice named Raul working at the bank. That's all she knows. Now, I'm going to see my wife home. I'll be back to talk to you shortly."

Fisher led Annie out of the building without giving the banker a chance to draw a breath.

"Thank you. I'm not really up for explaining something I don't understand myself," she said as he stuffed her into his unmarked car. Several other special agents had arrived and Fisher told Brian to sweep the bank for Raul and he'd meet him back at the bank within the hour.

"Are you all right?" Fisher asked as he got into the driver's seat. "They didn't hurt you, did they?"

"Just my pride," Annie said. "I can't believe that it was Henry all the time and I never even suspected."

"Tell me about it," Fisher said as he headed north on Central Avenue. "I should have suspected him, but I never gave him a second thought. I'm so sorry, Annie. I made a rookie mistake. I just…I'm so sorry."

"There's no need to be. He fooled us all. Could you drop me at my sister's?" Annie asked. "I need to let her know I'm safe."

"Sure," he agreed, even though he didn't want to part with her.

They were silent as he drove toward her sister's house. Annie pointed and Fisher steered, but neither of them said a word. The air in the car crackled with tension and awareness. Fisher wondered which of them would break the silence first.

When he pulled into her sister's driveway, Annie spoke, "Fisher, did you mean what you said earlier today?"

"What did I say?"

She studied her hands. Her fingers were clenched so hard that her knuckles were white. "That you would marry me for real."

He studied her bent head with her long strawberry curls spilling forward obstructing his view of her face. He had nothing to lose by telling the truth. "Yes, I meant it."

"Oh." She snapped her head up and her eyes studied him as if not sure what to make of him.

"Annie!" Her sister banged out through the front door of the house. "Annie! We've been so worried."

Annie slid out of the car to greet her sister and Fisher watched her go. He put the car in reverse and backed out of the driveway, wondering if the next time he went home there'd be an eviction notice waiting for him.

IT'D BEEN three days of taking testimony, interviewing witnesses and writing reports. Eric and Dotty Balsowitz were going to be locked away until Eric's bad taste in clothes came back into style again. The only time Fisher saw Annie was when he and Brian were taking her statement. He missed her. He missed the way she moved at the speed of light, the sound of her voice, the sound of her laugh, the sight of her long red hair, the way she talked to herself and the feel of her body against his. He missed her more than he'd thought possible. When had she become a part of him? The other half, the better half, of him?

He arrived at The Coffee Break well after dark. All of the lights in the shop were off and the Closed sign was up. He parked in back, next to his parents' psychedelic van and trudged up the stairs to his own apartment. He wanted to knock on Annie's door, but he was afraid. He was afraid she'd remember that they needed to annul their marriage. He supposed it was crazy, but he didn't want to do it. He wanted to stay married to his delightful redhead.

He opened his apartment door to find the lights on. His father was pacing the length of the room with Harpy riding on his shoulder. He was wearing a black suit coat over his usual tie-dye.

"Where have you been? Everyone is waiting for you," his father snapped. "Put these on. We're late already."

"Late for what?" Fisher asked, catching the wad of clothes his father threw at him.

"No questions," Swift said. "You'll have to dress in the car. Come on."

Fisher followed his father and Harpy out the door. He knew better than to question his father. Swift would tell him what he wanted him to know when he wanted him to know it and not before. Fisher sat in the back seat and unfolded the clothes. It was a tux.

"Why do I have to put on this monkey suit?" he asked.

His father didn't answer. Fisher shrugged and began to change in the cramped quarters of the car. He'd just finished knotting his tie when they pulled up to the front of a church. It was a small chapel set amidst a grove of orange trees. The evening was cool, and Fisher paused to take a deep breath.

"Okay, Swift, what are we doing here?" he asked.

"No time," his father said and strode toward the church.

"No time," Harpy repeated, watching him from Swift's shoulder.

When they entered the church, his father rushed him up the aisle, hardly giving Fisher a chance to greet the people he knew that filled the pews. Brian was there with his wife Susan and their baby. A bunch of guys from the Bureau, including his boss Paul Van Buren along with their wives and girlfriends. He saw his sisters Piper and Wren with their husbands. Tony and Eve Iannocci were there. Tony sent him a thumbs-up sign and Fisher smiled. Across the way he saw a cluster of regulars from The Coffee Break. In front, sat Annie's mother with a young Nordic type who must be her current spouse, and a young woman who was probably Annie's latest stepmother.

His father stopped at the front of the church, but when Fisher would have sat down, Swift grabbed him by the elbow and propelled him next to the altar. Just then the organist in the balcony of the church began to thump out a processional, and everyone rose to face the back of the church.

Fisher felt someone fuss with his collar and he turned to see his mother. A single tear ran down her cheek. She wiped it away and smiled. He heard a sigh echo throughout the congregation and looked down the aisle to see Annie, escorted by her father, walking toward him. She was a vision in white gossamer.

He felt his heart beat once and then twice really hard. He couldn't catch his breath, and then he thought he might faint. He was at a wedding. His wedding to Annie!

She must have been watching his face, because she beamed at him from beneath a filmy veil. If the minister and one hundred of their closest friends and family hadn't been standing there watching them, Fisher would have grabbed her and kissed her within an inch of her life. Heck, he might anyway.

When she and her father reached his side, Annie tossed back her veil and looked at him from beneath her lashes. Her cheeks were pink and she whispered, "I hope you meant it."

"Meant what?" he asked, stunned by the beauty of the woman before him.

"That you wanted to marry me in a church for real," she said.

"Oh, Annie-girl." Fisher reached out and pulled her close. "I meant it and how."

Annie tossed her bouquet of yellow roses to her mother and looped her arms about his neck. Her eyes glistened with unshed tears.

Fisher swallowed around the lump in his throat. "Annie Talbot, I want to ask you, will you marry me...for real?"

"Oh, yes," she whispered. "Yes, Fisher McCoy. I'll marry you...for real."

Then he kissed her. It didn't matter that her father was standing right beside them or that the minister was clearing his throat, trying to prevent this highly unusual occurrence. He kissed her until he was satisfied that she knew how very much he loved her and then he kissed her again.

When he released her, her lips were swollen and her chin was sporting a touch of whisker burn. She looked thoroughly bemused. Fisher grinned and pressed his forehead against hers.

"I love you, Annie-girl," he said.

"I love you, too," she whispered.

Fisher took her hand in his and together they turned to face the minister.

As the minister began his sermon, Annie leaned toward Fisher and whispered, "Does this mean I never have to be a bridesmaid again?"

"Yes. Now you'll always be a bride. My bride."

Annie grinned and squeezed his hand. She had a feeling she was going to like being a bride.

Every day is
A Mother's Day
in this heartwarming anthology
celebrating motherhood and romance!

Featuring the classic story "Nobody's Child" by Emilie Richards
He had come to a child's rescue, and now Officer Farrell Riley was
suddenly sharing parenthood with beautiful Gemma Hancock.
But would their ready-made family last forever?

Plus two brand-new romances:

"Baby on the Way" by Marie Ferrarella
Single and pregnant, Madeline Reed found the perfect husband in the
handsome cop who helped bring her infant son into the world. But did his
dutiful role in the surprise delivery make J. T. Walker a daddy?

"A Daddy for Her Daughters" by Elizabeth Bevarly
When confronted with spirited Naomi Carmichael and her brood of girls,
bachelor Sloan Sullivan realized he had a lot to learn about women!
Especially if he hoped to win this sexy single mom's heart....

Available this April from Silhouette Books!

Silhouette®
Where love comes alive™

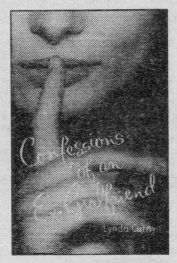

If you enjoyed what you just read,
then we've got an offer you can't resist!

Take 2 bestselling love stories FREE!

Plus get a FREE surprise gift!

Clip this page and mail it to Harlequin Reader Service®

IN U.S.A.	IN CANADA
3010 Walden Ave.	P.O. Box 609
P.O. Box 1867	Fort Erie, Ontario
Buffalo, N.Y. 14240-1867	L2A 5X3

YES! Please send me 2 free Harlequin Duets™ novels and my free surprise gift. After receiving them, if I don't wish to receive anymore, I can return the shipping statement marked cancel. If I don't cancel, I will receive 2 brand-new novels every month, before they're available in stores! In the U.S.A., bill me at the bargain price of $5.14 plus 50¢ shipping & handling per book and applicable sales tax, if any*. In Canada, bill me at the bargain price of $6.14 plus 50¢ shipping & handling per book and applicable taxes**. That's the complete price—what a great deal! I understand that accepting the 2 free books and gift places me under no obligation ever to buy any books. I can always return a shipment and cancel at any time. Even if I never buy another book from Harlequin, the 2 free books and gift are mine to keep forever.

111 HEN DC7P
311 HEN DC7Q

Name	(PLEASE PRINT)	
Address	Apt.#	
City	State/Prov.	Zip/Postal Code

* Terms and prices subject to change without notice. Sales tax applicable in N.Y.
** Canadian residents will be charged applicable provincial taxes and GST.
   All orders subject to approval. Offer limited to one per household and not valid to current Harlequin Duets™ subscribers.
® and ™ are registered trademarks of Harlequin Enterprises Limited.

DUETS01

These New York Times *bestselling authors*
have created stories to capture the hearts and minds
of women everywhere.
Here are three classic tales about the power of love—
and the wonder of discovering the place
where you belong....

FINDING HOME

DUNCAN'S BRIDE
by
LINDA HOWARD

CHAIN LIGHTNING
by
ELIZABETH LOWELL

POPCORN AND KISSES
by
KASEY MICHAELS

Available only from Silhouette
at your favorite retail outlet.